GW01280893

This book is a work of fiction. The characters, incidents, and dialogue are products of the author's imagination, and any resemblance to actual events or persons, living or dead, is coincidental.

Copyright © 2016 Jeff Noon & Steve Beard

Published by rEvolution SF

www.ticketyboopress.co.uk

Edited by John Costello

Cover Art by John Oakey

Internal art by Carlos Maiques

Book Design by Big River Press Ltd

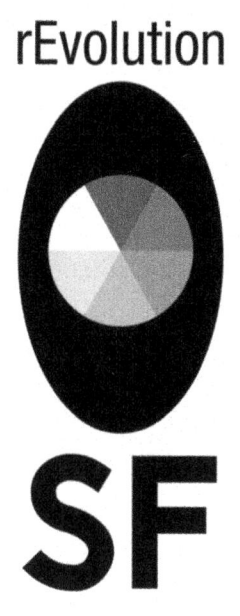

*Contents*

Foreword by John Costello

Introduction: The Mappalujo Engine

The Machine Writes — 1

Initial Report — 3

*Part One*
*Night Blossom Avenue* — 5

Interim Report — 48

*Part Two*
*Starlight Hill* — 49

Interim Report — 112

*Part Three*
*Apparition Park* — 117

Interim Report — 246

*Part Four*
*Palace of Shadows* — 248

Final Report — 314

*Appendices*

1. Iconographies — 318

2. User's Manual: The Mappalujo Engine — 340

Credits — 342

Bonus Material — 343

# MAPPALUJO

## Foreword by John Costello

Masks. We all wear them daily. For work, for play, for family duties and social situations. These masks may be figurative, but although we don't buy them off the peg or order them bespoke and put them on physically, we wear them nonetheless; as projections of our desired personae, or as disguises for our true identity.

The American sociologist Erving Goffman appropriated the theatrical term 'dramaturgy' to describe the fluid nature of our personal interactions. He contended that we present ourselves to others in a procession of acting roles, dependent upon variables including our environment, psychological state, perceived stakes/risks and the people we encounter. Likewise, others don their own masks for their performances in our presence.

An infinity of masks, then; conscious and subconscious, sophisticated and crude, transparent and opaque. Their 'success' or 'failure' is determined by the subtle interactions between wearers and the desired outcome for both parties. Each mask is imbued with the ambitions of its wearer. And celebrities, by their nature, harbour more complex ambitions than most of us.

In the familiar yet alien city of Lujo, masks are almost compulsory; a naked face is considered aberrant. Popular masks of all varieties are made at the Dream Factory by the powerful Zeno Entertainment Company which also creates the Zeenies, living companion toys. Other masks are available from underground artisans, serving different, darker purposes: The Mask of Spikes. The Mask of Fog and Pollution. The Mask of Electric Glamour. The Mask of Parasites. The Mask of Renegade Desire.

But now Zeno's glorious Founder, Augustus Cage, is dead. The collective dream world is being poisoned. A Zeenie is found that looks disturbingly (and illegally) human. There is a serial killer on the loose. The city is in the grip of a deep malaise and some think that the only cure can come from the fabled Mama Lujo, who may be saviour, phantasm or myth...

Jeff Noon and Steve Beard harnessed the pataphysical machinery of their story-generating device The Mappalujo Engine (part Alfred Jarry, part Timothy Leary, part Jean Tinguely), to deploy masks from its vast collection, each one upon removal revealing another beneath. The accumulation of narrative masks – a.k.a. story – is filtered through the etheric electromagnetic 'viruses' of 75 chosen celebrities, whose simulacra provide a medium for the telling. They are drawn from the worlds of music, art, film, literature, psychology, social commentary, comics and more. This eclectic assemblage of niche and mass-culture icons drives the narrative, offering unique viewpoints upon four of Lujo's denizens as they navigate the city's bizarre, treacherous physical and mental landscapes, searching for answers to intertwined questions of existence, purpose, desire and death.

When I was asked to become Series Editor for rEvolution SF I was in the fortunate glow of recent semi-retirement, basking in the novelty of finally getting to do my own things every day. At this juncture I wasn't looking to take on other projects – especially such time-consuming ones – and *Mappalujo* was an ambitious undertaking for the inaugural publication of a small press. I had enjoyed Jeff's work since his amazing debut *Vurt* in 1993, so more in accommodation than expectation I agreed to read the manuscript, on the basis that if I liked it enough I would find time to edit it.

Later that day I started reading and straight away I was transported to the city of Lujo. I stalked along Night Blossom Avenue, climbed Starlight Hill, ran through Apparition Park, hid in the Palace of Shadows, cowered in the Skull Garden, drank from the dream-well of the Moon Pool. I was immersed more deeply in the world of *Mappalujo* than most genre novels I've read and I struggled to find points of departure back to the mundanity of normal life. My journey was as seductive and exciting as those I'd taken through such greats as William Gibson's *Neuromancer*, Joe Hill's *NOS4R2* and, of course, *Vurt*.

*Mappalujo* is a singular novel, unconventional and groundbreaking in the best tradition of speculative literature; rich, energetic and inspired. It skips between genres with what appears to be effortless ease: science fiction, fantasy, horror, noir, crime, thriller, and others. It is a hall of mirrors, reflecting details via fragmented, expressionistic angles, and it wears influences with pride (the quotational aspect provides some of its greatest pleasures). It is a jigsaw, a maze and an ideas engine; postmodern and challenging, yet accessible and hugely entertaining.

That first journey didn't take long despite my slow reading speed and I was soon fired up and ready to begin work. Editing something so intricate and labyrinthine was a test but also an immense pleasure, and I'm grateful to all concerned for the opportunity to help develop and bring to public attention such a remarkable, captivating work of art.

# Introduction: The Mappalujo Engine

'I see the studio must be like a living thing, a life itself. The machine must be live and intelligent. Then I put my mind into the machine and the machine perform reality.'

Lee 'Scratch' Perry

*Mappalujo* is a novel written by a machine, the Mappalujo engine. The authors Steve Beard and Jeff Noon built this contraption out of second-hand domestic appliances and old machine parts bought in the junk shops of Brighton, a town on the south coast of England. We used transistors fashioned from light-bulbs and strips of silver foil, circuit boards cut from wooden doors, various radio components, and a scanning device built from a wire coat hanger and an aluminium bowl. The broadcast receiver comprised a speaker and amplifier hooked up to a small black-and-white TV monitor. Our control panel was the set of buttons from an out of date mobile phone. We employed this engine for a six year period in a disused recording studio which we laboriously proofed with tinfoil to generate a zero-field space. Initially, we didn't try to create anything. We used the scanner simply to catch celebrity viruses; we watched them writhe and flutter on the monitor, before releasing them once more into the charismatic ether.

Celebrity viruses are easy to catch, once you know how. Scientists have demonstrated that, when you get down to it, all events are disturbances of electrons. These disturbances generate electromagnetic waves. Our own research discovered that if an electronic disturbance is of sufficient magnitude, fuelled by the light of a thousand flashbulbs and amplified by propagation across a million networks, then it attains a celebrity frequency. We measure this by the charismatic value of the wave. The charismatic band exists on the edge of the normal broadcasting range, in the sliver of the spectrum where radio waves fade into the heat of infra-red light. It is here that celebrity viruses reside. A celebrity virus is simply a cultural signal that, beyond a critical threshold of self-organization, wants to replicate itself. Like a ghost it can live on after the physical death of its first human carrier, be it a pop star, a film actress, a famous footballer, or a television personality. The virus will seek to infect a new host, the real live body of a fan or stalker for instance, or the engineered body of a sensitive machine, such as a camera, a television or a computer screen.

After a period of experimentation, we began to use the Mappalujo engine to produce stories. We hacked out a few applications – such as a scenario gate, a story-base and a remixer – and patched them into the machine. We also found a teletype printer in a skip and plugged it into the output jack. The old printer worked slowly, the keys vibrating for a few seconds over the inked ribbon, before it stamped out a letter. We let the engine run all night and collected the reams of smudged paper in the morning. Slowly, over the next few years, the Mappalujo engine captured a total of seventy-five celebrity viruses and used them to create an entire city of interlinked stories. This city is called Lujo. We were, quite frankly, amazed at the machine's output. We hope you too enjoy the results.

*Jeff Noon and Steve Beard, 2016*

# MAPPALUJO
Jeff Noon
&
Steve Beard

# The Machine Writes...

Welcome. The city of Lujo is a world a short distance from your own, and a few days adrift. It is a land filled with restless ghosts and haunted stories. Travellers are invited to pass through the entry point. On the other side you will journey through the various domains and cultures of this realm, including the mysterious Skull Garden.

The true history of Lujo is only now being uncovered, through a collection of popular ballads, machine programs, exploded narratives, reports, celebrity gossip columns, fragile maps, broken poems and the like. All these documents have been taken from an ancient book of spells, believed to have been sacred to Mama Lujo, supreme goddess of chaos and viral magic.

*Shrine*

**>WALT DISNEY<**

# Initial Report

## *One day in the future...*

The old man was dying. He could not move his body, his breath came slowly, there was a coldness around his chest. His limbs were held tight within the sheets. The only noise was the soft regular bleep of the bedside monitor. At the very edge of his vision he could just about register the bright green line of the monitor in the darkness of the room.

There was his life, flickering away moment by moment.

He listened closely. It made a lulling rhythm, this magnification of his heartbeat. A faraway melody played through his head. It was pleasant, a memory, something he had heard before, what was it? His parents had arrived in this country many years ago, dirt poor, just a few months before he was born. He was carried across the ocean inside his mother's belly. It was a story they often told, like a fairy tale. Perhaps it was a song from the old country, this plaintive melody?

No, it had gone now.

His eyes closed. Everything was falling away, becoming lost.

Maybe he would fall asleep soon. He had such dreams, even now. Oh, such dreams. He had made his fortune from his strange imaginings. He remembered that one special time, when his most famous creation had come to him; he had woken up suddenly, disturbed by some noise, a rustling sound. It was the middle of the night, his young wife was sleeping beside him. Tiny insects moved in her hair. Seeing this, he realised that he wasn't yet fully awake, that part of his mind was still being held by sleep. A black figure crouched at the foot of the bed. It rose up on wings of crinkled gold. Quickly now, he had to write this down, the vision, before it...

The old man opened his eyes.

*Where am I? What is happening?*

Slowly, painfully, the realisation came to him. He felt the tightness of the bed clothes. He must have drifted off for a while, that was all. Something had disturbed his sleep. Again, he listened to the heartbeat.

Was it slowing down?

He tried to crane his neck to better see the screen's display. It was no good, his vision flooded with colour. He felt that his chest might burst. If only he could call for help, but his lips were stuck together. His wrists and ankles were pinned to the bed. Where was the nurse, or one of those stupid doctors? How much was he paying them? Wires and tubes jingled against each other as he struggled. Was he tied down? Such behaviour was not allowed. He was the founder. Augustus Cage. Hadn't he built this empire with his bare hands, his own scarred and bloodied hands?

*Help me. Somebody, please help me.*

There was no response. Had he even spoken aloud? No. There was nobody. He was alone. All of his money, his fame, none of it meant anything. He was dying. His body relaxed, darkness settled over him.

*The little boy was carried across the ocean inside his mother's belly. It was a safe place, warm, comforting. The boy had everything he needed, his collection of miniature books, his sketching pad, his tiny movie camera. Soon they would be arriving...*

'Did you call, sir?'

*What? What is it?*

'You were crying out.'

A voice was speaking to him, a muffled voice. The founder came awake.

*Who's there?*

At first, all he could see was a blurred shape. And then his visitor stepped closer, becoming visible, a young woman wearing a surgical mask. It was made from a coarse black material. Who was this? It wasn't one of the regular nurses. Other people moved in the background. If only he could see them properly.

*Who are you? I don't know you.*

The young woman bent near, whispering. 'Please, do not struggle.' She brought something into view, a glistening object. 'Now is the time.'

The needle pressed against the old man's face.

# Part One

## NIGHT BLOSSOM AVENUE

*Shrine*

LAURIE ANDERSON
GILBERT AND GEORGE
ALLEN GINSBERG
MICHAEL JACKSON
MADONNA
MARILYN MONROE
KENDO NAGASAKI
GINA PANE
DOUGLAS RUSHKOFF
**>ROD SERLING<**
THROBBING GRISTLE

When people asked Joe Prentice what he did for a living, he would sometimes falter before replying. A disturbed look might come into his eyes, as though he were trying to remember something. This hesitancy would last only a moment, and then he would carefully adjust his mask and find the words, 'I'm a salesman', and all would be well. In fact, Joe worked for the Zeno Entertainment Company, the world-famous producer of animated features, toys, games, software, and related merchandise. At least three days a week he went out travelling, hoping to sell the latest character masks around the northern territories. The rest of the time he spent in his cubicle on the fourth floor, recording his figures, working out his strategies for the coming season.

It was a good enough job, and Joe was good enough at it, but for some reason he had never progressed beyond this basic level. His colleagues would say things like, 'Oh that's Joe for you. He's okay. He's doing fine'. But in truth they were puzzled by his lack of ambition. It was a mystery. People knew that Joe was married, they felt sure he was devoted to his two children, whose photographs adorned his cubicle wall. Beyond that, he remained a blank. Somebody had once heard a story that Joe's childhood had been difficult in some way; this was meant to explain something, but whatever it was, Joe wasn't letting on. He sat at his desk, he travelled the designated territories in his car, he sold the company's range of facial coverings. And all the time he kept his own mask firmly in place. That was it, the life of Joe Prentice.

And then one day there was an incident.

It took place at one of the large corporate hotels on the outskirts of Lujo City, where a convention of salesmen were gathered. Joe had shouted at, and then attacked, or tried to attack, one of the customers in the bar. There was something about this man that he didn't like, apparently. Nobody knew for sure, but after this occurrence it was noticed that Joe changed. His sales figures started to slide. His overseer had words, all to no avail. Joe seemed to be a different person.

A few weeks later, whilst he was washing his hands in the restroom, the strangest feeling came over him. He had looked at himself in the mirror, just to check that his corporate mask was correctly aligned. The soft linen folded around his face snugly, the brow printed with the capital Z of the company's logo. He had worn this same type of covering for the last six years, for all of his time at Zeno. For some reason, he felt a sudden urge to rip the mask from his face, to walk through the office complex, screaming out loud with all of his pain and frustration. Oh, he could imagine his colleagues looking at him then, he could picture their masks shaking from side to side in disgust.

No, it would not do. That must never happen. Joe was in enough trouble as it was, with his latest monthly figures. It had to be his fault, because everybody agreed that the new lines were the company's best in years; discreet enough for the office, colourful enough for the arcades and theatres, that's what the lifestyle magazines were saying. So why weren't Joe's buyers in the department stores and boutiques of Lujo interested? He was a perfectly good salesman, he knew that he was. He'd been having a run of bad luck, that was all.

If only he hadn't seen that man at the hotel.

It was the shock of seeing his father's mask like that. There were so few of them left, and each one beautifully handcrafted; his father was a real artist, not like the trendy young designers the company employed. What did they know about the art and craft of mask making, with their cheap mass-produced rubbish, the success of which had more or less put the smaller, independent companies out of business. Joe's father had never really recovered from the bankruptcy. He viewed it as a personal failure, as a slight on his skills. Joe had found him once, just sitting in his armchair, staring at his hands. He could not be moved, not for many hours.

All of these memories came back to Joe that day, when he spotted the hotel guest wearing the elaborately carved wooden mask. For one absurd, bewildering moment, he had thought it might actually be his father. A grey mist exploded behind his eyes and the next thing he knew he was rolling around on the plush carpet trying to rip the mask from the stranger's face. It was a moment of darkness in his life, but what else could he do, really?

It had been so long now, so long since...

Somebody else entered the restroom. It was Fleischmann, from the seventh floor. The older man's mask was decorated with so many brass studs it looked like a piece of executive armour. Joe had sometimes wondered if he could ever wear such a covering. He nodded to his superior, but the other man would not respond. The cold, hard mask turned away.

***

The corridor leading to the meeting hall was lined with flowers. Hundreds of greetings cards were pinned to the walls, all of them wishing the head of the company a speedy recovery. Joe stopped to read some of the messages. The founder of Zeno had been ill for so long now, surely his death could not be far away. There was much speculation regarding the possible outcome of this. It was unsettling. Perhaps this emergency meeting would bring some positive news.

Joe arrived at the hall with time to spare, but the place was already full. People were either sitting in fold-out chairs or shuffling around at the back. A middle-aged woman in a beautiful silver mask took the stage at the front of the hall and began talking about the company's new dream package. Joe's mind started to drift. He noted the animators in their peaked caps and nylon overalls, the cosmetics experts in their surf shorts and sandals, the high-caste veil designers with their long white gloves and spiked heels. Everyone was wearing commercially available Zeno masks. Whether made of black leather or coloured plastic, whether modelled after this month's pop star or an old movie idol, they all had the same painted grin; it was one of the many visions that the founder had witnessed in his dreams.

Joe looked around anxiously. He couldn't see anyone else wearing the plain, everyday linen veil. Had he made yet another mistake?

He forced himself to concentrate on the stage. A graphic display was showing the latest holographic characters, and the female executive was talking in optimistic tones about the company's future, despite the recent fall in the share price. There was no mention of the founder. Perhaps there was hope of recovery? Or else the company was simply turning a blind eye to possible disaster.

Joe left the meeting early. All this talk of sales projections had depressed him. He felt a pain in his left temple, as though his skull had tightened. Perhaps he would take the rest of the day off; surely he deserved it, for all the unpaid overtime he had put in over the years. He went to his cubicle to pick up his mobile screen.

His desk had been cleared.

Joe touched the work surface. For a moment he thought he might have taken a wrong turning. The world seemed to tip and swirl around him, he had to grab the desk for support. No, this was his cubicle, there were the photographs of his children. They were the only things left to him; everything else had been taken away. His skin

9

felt clammy. He couldn't have been fired, it wasn't right.

His colleagues were entering the office space. They motored past him, their masks averted.

*Shrine*

**>LAURIE ANDERSON<**
GILBERT AND GEORGE
ALLEN GINSBERG
MICHAEL JACKSON
MADONNA
MARILYN MONROE
KENDO NAGASAKI
GINA PANE
DOUGLAS RUSHKOFF
>               <
THROBBING GRISTLE

The salesman is driving home.

The steering wheel turns slowly beneath his fingers, his mask feels warm and tight against his face. Voices fill his head. Can you hear them? *What will Ellen think of me now? How can I break the news to her? She will have to tell the children. How can I face them like this?*

The city is covered over by dusk. The billboards cast their neon-lit spell.

The salesman drives along. His car is shiny and red. It is a good car, a well travelled car. This vehicle has taken him around the whole of the northern territories.

The radio is tuned into Smooth Rock Paradise.

*People of Lujo, can't you hear me calling? Let me know your secret desires. Ooh baby, reach out and touch me.*

The salesman wonders where the voices are coming from. *They will hate me, my own sweet children.* Everything is a blur.

\*\*\*

The salesman turns off the carriageway.

This is not his usual route. He is travelling, he is simply moving along.

After a while he finds himself in a strange part of town. All the young women are wearing alternative style masks fashioned to look as ugly as possible. How odd.

The radio plays a message from the sponsor. *It is only human to feel a glow when others look with envy upon your car or your suit or your spouse. Don't be left out. Send off now.* The red saloon car moves along.

The salesman closes his eyes.

A bus honks at him and he swings the wheel of his car to stop himself from getting clipped. The pain in his head turns up a notch.

A cold dirty rain falls. The streets are slick with reflected neon, people are scurrying along with newspapers and umbrellas over their heads. The traffic signs and the billboards are talking. Can you hear the voices?

*Walk. Don't Walk. Walk. Don't Walk. Send off now to ensure prompt delivery.*

It is a warm, pleasant evening. It is raining. It is not raining.

The salesman grips the wheel tighter.

\*\*\*

He drives to the River Isis.

The car stops midway across the bridge and the salesman steps out. He opens the boot. His work samples are stored here, carefully arranged in cardboard boxes.

He takes the masks and throws them over the side of the bridge.

Some of the faces fall cleanly, others flutter here and there, eventually making their way down into the water below.

*Whatever your mood, Zeno has a mask to bring out the best in you. Make the right impression, sign below for instant satisfaction.*

The masks float away towards the distant sea.

Perhaps the salesman will follow them, perhaps he will throw himself off the edge, into the river. He can feel the urge, the urge to leap, to escape.

To be released.

\*\*\*

A few hours later, the red saloon car turns left into Night Blossom Avenue.

This is where the salesman lives. Number sixteen.

He sits in the parked car for a while before taking off his work mask. The salesman feels tired, he rubs his eyes. Maybe it isn't too late for him to set up on his own as a vendor of specialist wares, the luxury trade.

His fingers search in the glove compartment for his home mask. Which face shall he wear this evening, to best hide the pain? He has a selection to choose from.

*Oh boy, what a feeling! Have you ever felt more beautiful, more daring?*

Yes, he could travel all around Lujo, helping people better their lives by picking out just the right mask for them. He would be a consultant.

*Everybody needs a good disguise, in today's world.*

The only people who don't wear masks are disturbed. Crazy people lying in doorways. Drugged up young men and women found dead in their one-room flats. The salesman has read the magazine articles.

His fingers touch the soft edges of his oldest and most familiar mask. He slips it on. Now he's Clint Westwood, the mythical gunslinger with the craggy face, the cold distant gaze.

*Suitable for all income levels, portable, self-cleaning, fifteen different shades available. Who could ask for more?*

The salesman turns off the radio. He thinks of the news stories of the middle-aged executives who turn up to work cradling loaded assault weapons.

They were bare-faced.

\*\*\*

Little Jamie and his sister Angie are sprawled on the floor in their dressing gowns. They look up briefly when the salesman comes into the room, their faces concealed behind their favourite Bip and Bop masks.

The children return their attention to the television, where the blue flicker of a woman's face fills the screen.

The salesman walks through into the kitchen, where Ellen is taking his dinner from the oven. They have not been getting on very well these last few weeks. He apologises to her for being late. He tells her that he had to work extra hours, because of a special promotion.

*All the young jetsetters swear by the latest styling. You too could look a million dollars!*

Ellen nods. She is wearing a new mask, a vivid turquoise affair with a silver fin jutting out from the forehead and a panel of tiny yellow bulbs set down the middle. The lights flash in random sequence.

It really is very beautiful.

\*\*\*

The salesman sits in his armchair, nursing a gin and tonic.

The children have been sent to bed, but the same programme is still on the television. The Naked Face. It's the most popular show these days.

The salesman can hardly bear to watch.

He can understand the need for such a programme. A human face, without a mask, in permanent close-up. Every expression, every change in mood, sleeping or waking, is broadcast to the viewers twenty-four hours a day. Yes, he can understand the need, but who would let themselves be used in this manner?

*All night long, just for your pleasure. Now available at special rates.*

The Naked Face is staring directly at the salesman. He shivers.

It is raining, it is not raining.

He has only ever seen his wife's face once, at the private unveiling in the little wedding chapel. How could he forget that moment?

It was the most intimate form of sharing. The salesman takes another drink.

His mask is wet against his face.

*Shrine*

> GILBERT AND GEORGE <
ALLEN GINSBERG
MICHAEL JACKSON
MADONNA
**>MARILYN MONROE<**
KENDO NAGASAKI
GINA PANE
DOUGLAS RUSHKOFF
>                       <
THROBBING GRISTLE

Prentice lay in bed that night. He could not sleep. He reached out to touch his wife's body. She made a small sound, nothing more. Prentice looked at her face. It was covered by a blue silk sleeping hood. His own mask was made from striped linen.

The lights of a passing car moved across the two wooden masks that hung on the bedroom wall. They were all he had left of his father's work. Dead faces, their carved features etched with shadow.

Prentice stood by the window. The gardens of suburbia looked peaceful, bathed in moonlight. He touched his brow. The pain would not go away. He had a sudden feeling that something had gone wrong, just at this moment. He went downstairs.

There was nothing significant on the news programme. He tuned into the adults only station. The stars wore masks made of pink fur and shiny black rubber. The action was soft-core, tasteful even. Prentice pressed the remote.

The Zeno channel was showing a cartoon. Six String Mojo was standing at the crossroads, hoping to meet the devil. Prentice had sold the Mojo mask in his early years. Suddenly the screen went dark. There was a low wailing sound.

Prentice knew what it meant. He could feel it in his bones, a coldness. Finally, after months of confusion, the founder had died. It was over. Prentice emptied his glass, poured himself another. He was thinking of his own father. No, it was too painful...

He jabbed at the remote, skipping channels. The face passed by. He moved on a few more channels, and then he flicked back to her. There she was. *Can't you hear me calling?* Her features filled the screen. Her eyes were closed. She was sleeping.

The naked face had blonde hair. Her lips were full and red. *Let me know your secret desires.* She was very beautiful. *Reach out and touch me!* It wasn't just physical, it was the way she had volunteered herself. To be a victim like this, willingly.

The camera moved in slowly. She was presenting herself. She was giving herself up to the viewers. The lips were parted. *All night long, just for your pleasure.* Prentice could hear her breathing. It was strangely exciting. He reached forward, yearning for contact...

At the moment of climax, the naked face opened her eyes. Prentice cried out with pleasure. He collapsed into his seat. *Oh boy, what a feeling!* Five minutes later he fetched a paper towel from the kitchen. He wiped down the television screen. The face lay there beneath the glass. The eyes were closed once more. *Have you ever felt more beautiful, more daring?* Prentice pulled at his mask, his skin damp with sweat. He had never done anything like this before. His body trembled.

*Shrine*

> <
GILBERT AND GEORGE
ALLEN GINSBERG
MICHAEL JACKSON
**>MADONNA<**
> <
KENDO NAGASAKI
GINA PANE
DOUGLAS RUSHKOFF
> <
THROBBING GRISTLE

*The Mask Of Spikes is made from black leather, guitar strings and rusty iron nails. The nails are on the inside. The face of a dead rock star is lovingly embroidered on the front panel. The wearer's blood seeps through the stitching. A most pleasing effect.*

    The customer arrives. Maria Salvador watches him from her workroom in the back. It's useful to peep through the curtain like this, to view the customers unseen, to gauge their desires. This one is dressed in a plain navy blue suit with a matching cloth wraparound covering his face. A businessman. He's gazing at the sexual fetish masks. His hands twitch. Another cabinet contains the new Extreme Face collection. The customer bends nearer, reading the titles: *Fog and Pollution, Final Transport, Electric Glamour*. He's nervous, hardly daring to believe the violent imagery on display. He turns away. Maria pulls the curtain aside.

    *The Mask of Fog and Pollution has many tiny plastic jets, each of which emits a different coloured vapour. Noxious aromas surround the headpiece. Mounted speakers blast out industrial noise, way above the legal limit. Only the wearer's mouth is visible. Hooked wires pull the lips wide apart. The mask screams.*

    He left home that morning at the normal time, as though leaving for work. He has no work. Instead, the customer has spent the day travelling around, moving away from his usual routes, seeking out the darker areas of the city, places not yet drawn on the official maps. He's not sure what he's looking for until he sees the little shop in the back street. *Salvador's Mask Emporium. Giving Good Face for All Occasions.* From across the street it looks like an old fashioned tailor's; up close, it looks like a porn parlour.

    *The Mask of Final Transport is made from melted tar, studded with gravel and the jewelled remains of broken windscreens. Tyre marks decorate the skullcap. The facial area is artfully wounded, the blood kept warm and liquid by our secret process. A floral wreath encircles the neck. The mask slowly tightens. Please use carefully.*

    Maria steps into the room. The customer stumbles, almost falling over. He bangs into a cabinet. His eyes stare out through the tiny round openings in his face cloth. Maria turns the lock on the front door. She steps close. 'I'll just take some measurements. Is that alright?' A pair of callipers extend from her work mask, looking for all the world like the claws of a giant scorpion. The customer backs away, his briefcase falls to the floor. There is no escape. The claws reach out.

    *The lightweight plasma display of the Mask of Electric Glamour wraps* directly around the head. Your face becomes a television screen flickering with murder scene footage, surgery videos, amateur porn, shots of Christ being nailed to the cross. The mask plugs directly into the mains. Ready supplied with remote control and a six metre flex.

A mask is chosen. Maria turns away discreetly as the customer removes his everyday covering. The leather support harness closes around his skull. The new mask firmly in place, Maria directs him to the full-length mirror. The customer stares at himself. He can hardly comprehend how disgusting he looks, how vile; his body is shaking, he feels a powerful urge to tear the world apart with his bare hands! 'You see now,' says Maria. 'Isn't that you? That is you. It's exactly you!' The mask shivers with delight.

The Veil of Fountains is supplied complete with its own rubber codpiece. This device collects the wearer's urine. Hidden tubing pumps the golden liquid to the head, where it gathers in the clear plastic channels of the mask itself. The face is tantalisingly glimpsed through the bubbling façade.

The customer climbs into his car. For a good five minutes all he can do is sit there behind the wheel, clutching the shopping bag tightly to his lap. He can't believe what he's just done, how much money he's spent. The customer can ill afford it, especially with no job to go to, no regular income coming in. His wife will be angry. Of course he will have to keep it a secret. His family, his friends, they must never find out just how wretched he is. A private mask! Imagine. A hidden face all of his own.

The Mask of Parasites is made from green baize stretched tightly around the head. Metal bands support tiny cutting blades; these work incessantly, and very slowly, slicing through the baize. Over a period of weeks the blades approach the face. This is the mask that kills itself.

Which will you choose?

*Shrine*

>                  <
GILBERT AND GEORGE
ALLEN GINSBERG
MICHAEL JACKSON
>          <
>                  <
KENDO NAGASAKI
GINA PANE
DOUGLAS RUSHKOFF
>                 <
**>THROBBING GRISTLE<**

## Preparation of the Body

Joe watched from the front porch as his wife and kids climbed into the taxi, waving cheerfully as they drove away. They were visiting relatives for the weekend. He felt a wave of excitement. It was time. Just to be safe he poured himself a drink and waited for half an hour, to make sure they had not forgotten anything. It would be dreadful if he were caught out.

He went upstairs. The new mask was hidden in the spare room. He carried the box through into the main bedroom, where he removed the various parts, laying them out carefully on the eiderdown, untangling the tubes and setting aside the canisters. He slipped the batteries into the power unit. All that done, he took off his shoes and socks, his shirt and trousers, his underwear, folding each item neatly, until only his casual weekend mask remained. He finished what was left of his whiskey and then pulled the printed cotton mask free from his head.

He couldn't remember the last time he had felt so naked.

## Constructing the Mask of Renegade Desire

After doing a few limbering up exercises, Joe smeared his skin with the special lotion. He started to attach the new mask to his body. First of all he fitted the belt around his waist. Next he pulled the two leather bands between his legs, clipping them to the back of the belt. He fitted the main support strap around his chest. Two further straps were fixed around each shoulder, and two plastic canisters were slotted into loops on the belt. During this procedure he kept the operator's manual propped open on the bed, following each instruction in turn. The whole thing buckled together in such a way that he felt was tying himself into a weird bondage outfit, a portable cage even. He was scared. If he pulled the straps any tighter, he might not be able to escape from himself.

Shaking off this idea, he lifted up the head unit.

The main frontispiece, constructed from lightweight plastic, was about two feet square. The visor was black with gold filigree at the edges. The whole design was thrillingly urban. The manual explained how to fit the long, thin extensible arms into the sockets. Each arm was fully jointed, and tipped with a sharp nib-like point. Taking a deep breath, Joe lifted the finished unit over his head and attached it to the shoulder and neck brace. The leather bands clutched at his temples, easing the pain slightly. Next he checked to see if the visor moved properly on its hinges, raising the frontispiece away from his face, and then lowering it once more. Finally, he clipped together the various plastic tubes.

Now, he was ready.

## Ritual Invocation of the Ghost Face

Joe turned to view himself in the full-length mirror on the wardrobe door. He had worn only the headgear in the shop, not the full body rig. It was different. He had expected it to bring a more powerful feeling. Something was wrong. The mask looked flimsy, and the two metal arms waved around like grotesque antennae. His soft flesh bulged out around the leather straps, his penis hung limp between his legs. He looked stupid, pathetic. Maybe switching on the mask would improve matters. His hand moved towards the control panel on the belt.

Just then, he had the feeling that he was being watched.

He looked round. His father's old masks were staring down at him from the wall. Something moved in there, in the darkness of the gouged out eyes. Joe felt ashamed of himself. He swung the frontispiece away from his face and sat down on the bed. Who was he kidding? Hadn't his father mentioned that only the truly beautiful or the truly hideous could wear a mask correctly? It was a question of knowing what to hide and what to reveal.

Joe thought again of his childhood, how his father would often work all the hours of the day, perfecting his latest creations. The young Joe liked to sit nearby, watching, as glaring monsters, evil demons, or bizarre hybrid mixtures of human and animal emerged from the wood. His father was a great craftsman, and the five year old boy hoped that he too would be an expert mask maker one day.

There was so much to learn. His father had a rule, that all masks be made from only the finest woods, carved and painted by hand. He also said that each mask had to be unique in design. Another time he told Joe the story of the False Face medicine ritual of the Iroquois people, where the shaman of the tribe would receive a design for a mask in a dream, and this mask would be carved directly into the trunk of a living tree; only when the mask was complete would it be cut from the tree. You had to summon up the spirit of the mask, that was the secret.

Joe couldn't manage it, not as a child, not as a man.

## Negative Word Charm

Once again he looked at the two wooden masks on the wall. He thought of the Mask of Falling Darkness, the last work his father completed before he died. It was supposed to be his masterpiece, the mask that would save his career. It would make him famous, that was the plan.

Joe stood up. He ran his hand along the plastic straps that tightly bound his chest. They were slick with sweat. He had never lived up to his father's dreams, that was the problem. It was shameful. He reached up to unhook first one wooden mask and then the other from the wall, placing the two faces on the bed. A white sheet covered them. Good. That was better. Joe turned to face the mirror. He pulled the frontispiece back into position, lowering the shiny black visor. Searching along the belt, his fingers found and pressed at the raised button. Immediately, he felt different. The fluids were being pumped from the canisters, up the tubes, to reach the end of the two flexible arms. The tips glistened, one red, the other white. All was in place. His hands grabbed the tiny control levers fixed to the belt.

He looked at himself in the glass. The mask gave his body a brutal, perverse appeal. His penis was rubbing against the leg bands. He couldn't help himself, he was becoming excited. He moved the controls and the two long, extended arms moved in sympathy; they swung apart and then clashed together above his head. It looked like he was applauding his own image. Then the left-hand arm twitched madly, before swinging round to spray red paint on the frontispiece. Joe had hardly touched the controls; the mask worked its own magic.

He looked in the mirror to see the message written on the faceplate. It took him a few moments to decipher the reflected, back to front writing.

It said WILLING VICTIM.

*Shrine*

GILBERT AND GEORGE
ALLEN GINSBERG
MICHAEL JACKSON
**>KENDO NAGASAKI<**
GINA PANE
DOUGLAS RUSHKOFF

## The Spellbound Face

In the early days not many people wore masks. It was an affectation of the very rich, a small group of people who paid well for handmade goods. Alexander Prentice was a craftsman earning enough to keep his family in a kind of fragile luxury. There was his wife Barbara, and his only child, young Joey Prentice.

Joey wanted to be a mask maker when he grew up, just like his father.

Gradually, the fashion for covering the face extended to all sectors of society, and mass-produced items started to replace the made-to-order variety. Quite soon the family's business was struggling, because the great craftsman would not lower his standards enough to produce poor quality wares. Nobody wanted expensive masks anymore, now that even the upper classes preferred to wear cheap celebrity masks. That was the new decadence, the 'new shallowness', as the press called it. Eventually the mask work stopped completely. Alexander Prentice was declared bankrupt at the age of thirty-four.

Little Joey would always remember that day, and the troubled times that followed. His father fell into a black depression. He would hide himself away in his workroom for hours on end, very often refusing to eat, and only emerging now and again to shout and scream at his family. At first his wife would get upset at this; later on she would simply turn away. Later still, she ignored her husband completely. The marriage was falling apart. Joey was only seven years old at the time. He was still in awe of his father, despite all that had happened. He would knock on the workroom door every so often, only to receive an angry dismissal. This state of affairs went on for more than three months. The father became a figure glimpsed in a mirror, a shadow cast on a wall, nothing more. And then, one day the door to the workroom was opened, and the father called the son to enter.

Alexander Prentice was working on a new mask. At first sight it resembled the face of a primitive demon, made from hundreds of different pieces of wood, the surface all knotted and covered in thorns. It was terrifying. And then Joey watched fascinated as his father moved each piece of wood into a new position, piece after piece, until an entirely new face was revealed, that of a prince or a brave warrior. It was called the Mask of Falling Darkness. The young boy had never seen anything like it, so intricate it was, so beautiful. And yet a few pieces of wood were not yet slotted into their new positions. Joey asked why this was and his father would only say that the mask was not yet finished, there was still a lot of work to be done. Then he told his son to leave the room.

Joey felt certain that this new creation meant a change of heart for his father, that he would soon recover his will to live. Instead, the door to the workroom was now locked for days on end. Any summons, whether by Joey or by his mother, would elicit only the briefest of replies. And then even these replies faded to silence. Eventually, the next door neighbour had to be called in. The door was broken open. In the confusion, and before his mother could stop him, Joey rushed into the room. He saw his father slumped over his work desk, his face and head entirely covered by the strange new mask. There was no movement from the body. The worktop was covered in the scratch-marks his father's hands had made in his struggles.

Joey watched as they took the body away. The coroner returned a verdict of death by misadventure. The mask was described as a puzzle, or a trap; once closed it could only be opened by one secret method. Joey imagined his father in those final moments, as the mask suffocated him. Of course, the people of the neighbourhood thought it was suicide. Joey sensed a deeper truth, one he could barely yet understand.

Darkness had closed around his father's face.

*Shrine*

>
                                                        <
**>GILBERT AND GEORGE<**
ALLEN GINSBERG
MICHAEL JACKSON
         >                    <
     >                              <
     >                              <

GINA PANE
DOUGLAS RUSHKOFF
         >                    <
  >                                        <

## It was a perfectly normal day

Beneath the blue serge of his business suit, beneath the cool pressed cotton of his shirt, Mr Prentice could feel the plastic straps of the harness bite into his skin. He could wait no longer. Parking the car just a few streets from home, he took the remaining components of the mask from his black patent leather suitcase. He could hardly assemble the headpiece properly, his hands were shaking so much. There, now he had it. Complete. As soon as the mask of renegade desire covered his face, he felt the blood rise in his veins.

Five minutes later the vehicle pulled up outside the local junior school. Children were entering through the gates, each one carrying a transparent plastic satchel, each wearing a cute Zeno animal mask. They turned to wave at their parents. Mr Prentice got out of his car and walked up to a group of children. The two arms of his mask were twitching, bending round to squirt paint on the face plate. A word was being written. Seeing this, the children started to scream and run away. A woman shouted at him from a passing estate car. A group of angry mothers were moving towards him. One of them hit him with a rolled-up magazine. They spat at him. Mr Prentice did not care. He climbed in his car and drove away. The rear-view mirror showed only a portion of the word written in red on the mask's face. PAEDOPHILE. The other arm came round and squirted white paint over the ten letters, erasing them from sight.

The vehicle moved slowly through the luxury shopping district. Mr Prentice was lucky to find a parking space in a side street. He walked down to the main thoroughfare, where the giant monolithic hotels were clustered around a small public garden. The chosen building was a steel and glass structure, towering thirty storeys above the street. The doorman was standing outside in a brilliant scarlet mask and a black top hat. Mr Prentice sat down cross-legged on the pavement. The red paint on his mask said HUNGRY & HOMELESS. The doorman told him to move on, whilst departing guests swerved to avoid this unfortunate creature. Minutes later, two security guards came out of the hotel. They wore visors modelled on the features of a famous action movie hero. They lifted the masked man up between them and frogmarched him round the nearest corner, into a shadowed alleyway.

Mr Prentice couldn't remember where he had left the car. He

wandered the streets, wondering where the mask would take him next. The cuffs of his jacket were frayed and his shoes were dirty and scuffed. His stomach ached from where the guards had punched him. The long metal arms of the mask twitched excitedly, as though they wanted to write entire poems made out of dirt and shit and blood.

Midday, the financial district. Mr Prentice stood outside the smoked glass doors of a merchant bank. A view screen showed the funeral cortege of Augustus Cage, a black hearse creeping along the main road of Lujo, the founder's coffin barely visible behind Zeno's logo in yellow and red flowers. Over this image a line of tickertape spelled out the news of the company's climbing share price. The product continued. Mr Prentice cursed the name of his former employer. He jabbed his finger at the security camera mounted on the wall. His mask said CAPITALISM SUCKS. A gang of young business executives surrounded the miscreant. They were dressed in Armani blazers with matching pretty boy masks. Two of them held Mr Prentice against the wall, whilst another donned a pair of high-fashion knuckledusters. People walked by paying no mind to the spectacle.

It was late afternoon when Mr Prentice found himself at the converted warehouses by the river. He limped past offices occupied by software designers, video production companies and advertising agencies. People swerved to avoid him. He stopped when he came to the television studio. There was a line of contenders on the pavement outside, each of them hoping to become to the new Naked Face: young women in leotards with the masks of grinning devils; ageing glamour queens in false eye-lashes and fixed grins; obese children in shining face paint; and middle-aged men in cheap plastic Elvideo Prez masks. Mr Prentice recognised a Zeno mask that had been top of the line when he had sold the model years ago. Now its feathers were bent and torn. He laughed bitterly and his own mask moved into action, the two arms swinging round to spray the words FUCK FACE across the frontispiece. FUCK FACE! FUCK FACE! FUCK FACE! The camera addicts shouted at him and pushed him away. He ran at them and they tipped back into each other. Soon they were fighting amongst themselves. Mr Prentice could feel himself being pulled down beneath their feet. He kicked out viciously.

The sky above the football stadium car park shone with unnatural light. Amplified commentary fought against the tribal chanting that filled the air. The smell of human sweat mingled with the stench of undercooked beef. Mr Prentice loitered among the parked cars. His suit was torn and stained. There was blood on his shirt front and lapels. He ran his finger down the polished flanks of a souped-up Ford Capri. A gang of young men in nylon jackets approached him, each of them wearing the striped blue and white masks of the home team. Mr Prentice barely needed to touch the controls on his belt for the mechanism to be activated, the plastic tubes pumping bright red pigment to the sharp point of the mask's painting tool. The words GAY COCKSUCKER appeared on the faceplate. The gang shouted their own obscenities back at the mask. One of the men flicked a lighted cigarette at the plastic surface. Another punched the wearer in the stomach, winding him. Mr Prentice fell to the ground. As he lay there, helpless, he remembered that he had promised his wife he would bring home a present for little Jamie's birthday. The gang closed in and urinated on his curled-up form.

When night came he was stumbling along the edge of the motorway, past giant illuminated billboards advertising Dream Creatures, Panoptic televisions, the Naked Face. Cars sounded their horns at this ragged figure, the beams of their headlamps picking out the constantly changing messages on his mask. SUICIDE BOMBER, CHILD KILLER, GEEK, MASTURBATOR. The painting arm waited a few seconds as the erasing arm did its work, and then new words appeared on the mask, one after the other. JUNKIE, RENT BOY, PORN ADDICT, RICH MAN, ALCOHOLIC, WHISTLEBLOWER, SCUMBAG, STALKER, CRACK DEALER. The wearer of the mask walked on, from one pool of light to the next. KIDNAPPER, CONMAN, ILLEGAL IMMIGRANT, WEAKLING, SPASTIC, AIDS SUFFERER, MENTAL PATIENT, SLUT, LIMP DICK, PIMP, WHITE SUPREMACIST, BLACK, JEW, MUSLIM, ASIAN, JESUS FREAK, LOSER, HUMAN, NOBODY, ANYBODY, EVERYBODY. Neon light spilled from the roadside hoardings. The mask glimmered in the fallout.

*Shrine*

>               <
>                  <
   ALLEN GINSBERG
  MICHAEL JACKSON
      >        <
    >            <
  >              <
     GINA PANE
  **>DOUGLAS RUSHKOFF<**
     >          <
>               <

A *message from our sponsor*

We here at Zeno are proud to announce the continued life of our products, beyond the material death of our glorious Founder.

Rest assured, the dream lives on. Our Founder's imagination is not bound by the physical body. The gardens of the skull are blooming still.

We are the cultivators, we are the gardeners. The products creep towards the shelves, even as we speak. Grant them passage.

*Shrine*

ALLEN GINSBERG
MICHAEL JACKSON

>GINA PANE<

## Introduction to the Renegade Text

The miscreant was arrested for disturbing the peace. It took four police officers to hold him still; it's all here on the video tape. Let's fast-forward a bit. Here he is, in the drunk tank alongside another couple of lowlifes. These two are fast asleep already, lost to the world, but Prentice is just sitting there in his torn suit, that wretched mask still in place. None of the officers can work out how to remove the thing, it seems to be clamped around his head, like it's become part of his body. You can see that he's tense, that his hands are stark white as they open and close repeatedly with a nervous mechanism.

Prentice looks up at you, the viewer. One of the jointed arms at the side of his mask is twitching, the nib at the end scratching on the white surface of the faceplate. It's no use. His canister of red paint has run dry. The mask moves slowly, sadly even, from side to side. How can we understand this man's feelings, except through what the mask tells us? Now he's taking off his ragged jacket and tearing off his shirt. He slides the leather belt from around his waist. This is the nasty bit. If you're squeamish, then turn away.

Okay. Using the belt, he ties up his left arm like a heroin addict. Then he detaches the plastic tube from the empty canister and jabs it into a vein. Holy shit! He staggers back from the camera. You see his body taking the pain, holding it, being fuelled by it. This man is seriously out there. He walks back to the camera. He's still shaking a little as his own precious blood spurts out of the nib over the plastic faceplate, before being wiped away by the arm on the other side of the mask, still filled with enough white paint for the job. Detail: this man has done more writing than erasing. The prisoner has to get used to it, the balance between writing out his script in blood, wiping it clean, writing anew, scribbling, erasing, writing, wiping, scrawling, scratching. He's there for twelve minutes, concentrating furiously, a whole dirty protest drawn in blood, his contempt for the world written out in instalments over his mask. One of his fellow occupants wakes up during this, he can be seen in the background, staring into space; the other man sleeps peacefully through the whole episode. Also, we now know that the officer on security duty that night simply watched all this in utter fascination. Then it's over. The two arms slowly come to a standstill. He's spent. A drop of blood falls from the nib.

Now comes the truly shocking bit. He takes off his mask. He undoes the buckles round his waist and shoulders, unwraps the neck brace and steps out of the assemblage. It's easy. There's no secret to it. The mask falls to the floor like a pile of old junk. The camera zooms in close. We see his face. The prisoner is weeping. He curls up on the bench. That's it. Closer to morning he's led out from the cell in a daze. People can't get enough of that image. The lost look in his eyes, the unsteadiness, the smile tugging at the edge of his lips. He's been somewhere. He's travelled. The police can't wait to get the standard-issue fluorescent polythene mask secured over his features. It's a matter of urgency. They don't want to know.

Over the passing years, this issue of blood has become the founding mythology of our movement. The Renegade Text. These few words, written on the face of a man...

*Shrine*

>
                               <
 >                                <
      **>ALLEN GINSBERG<**
      MICHAEL JACKSON
         >        <
       >            <
      >              <
      >              <
        >          <
     >                <
      >                <

## The Mask Speaks

Lujo! Renegade angels have filled my tongue with neon; my words will light your sky. I speak to you of future days when a barren company owns your dreams. City of masks! I have ridden your sleek escalators! I have climbed your skyscrapers and your shining palaces; I have visited your crumbling apartment blocks, your art deco hotels and your old department stores. I have planted flowers in your brothels; I have wandered through the ornate caverns of your markets; I have fallen down drunk and penniless in your gutters.

    I have travelled the circuits of Lujo. I have walked hollow-eyed through the offices of Zeno. I have seen the dream animators at their desks, clothed in polyester, their private expressions hidden behind corporate veils. Your streets abound with such wretched people, all with their faces covered, their eyes protected by visors, their bodies shrouded. Lujo, your dark nemesis approaches. The day is near when all will cast away their masks, when all will show their naked faces to the mirror. What then will emanate from the depths of perfumed longing behind the screens of glass?

    Lujo! I have cursed the twisting towers of your corporations; I have seen the brand names leaping from a thousand billboards. One name above all others is a blight on your future, O Lujo! One company chokes the roots of your freedom to dream. Do you hear the name of your adversary, Lujo? I spit at the awful pleasure factory of Zeno; I rip up its catalogue of magical effects.

    Lujo! My decrepit palladium, angelic cesspit, empire of gates, porous realm! My city of broken spires and diseases, my alchemical mistress, my haunt of ghosts and celebrity! I have scanned your books of blood; I have sliced open your maps and spilt the ink of your body! I have traced the secret narratives from the walls of the pleasure factory. I have read your future!

    Lujo! Your soundtrack of hushed low voices is pierced by a demon's wail. Your emblem of marching television screens bursts into flames. Your dark evil suitor is arrived! Issuing from the skull of Zeno's dying emperor, grown from the soil of his decaying mind, an apparatus of shadows inhabits your country. Lujo! Your people will be ravished by the teeming products of Zeno, its vaporised memories, its artificial creatures and domesticated angels, its stockpile of second-hand dreams. A City of Masks will seem a shoddy Paradise to a Carnival of Spirits. O Lujo, you will scrape your skin to the bone for one last ride on Zeno's machinery of glamour.

City of moon and demons! Where there should be cries of joy, there are only lamentations. I hear your screams in the night, your weeping, your gnashing of teeth. I feel the crushing embrace of your suitor, his diseased breathings, the deep inward groping of his tendrils. O Lujo, I witness your breaking and bleeding. Your bridal song is a flock of crows hovering for a moment over twilit boulevards like pieces of cloth torn from a funeral gown.

Lujo, your history is written by tramps and harlots and refugees, the lost and the strange! It is tattooed on the skin of the beaten, the cursed, the exiled and maimed. Executioners are your kings and gamblers your generals. Beyond the corporate death, your true future belongs to those few renegade angels who run like spilt mercury along your darkest streets. They shall give birth to and nurture Mama Lujo, the new chaotic agent, a goddess of change. Only she can deliver her city from its bondage

*Shrine*

```
         >                    <
   >                               <
      >                          <
         >MICHAEL JACKSON<
                >          <
           >                 <
         >                     <
         >                     <
             >           <
       >                         <
         >                     <
```

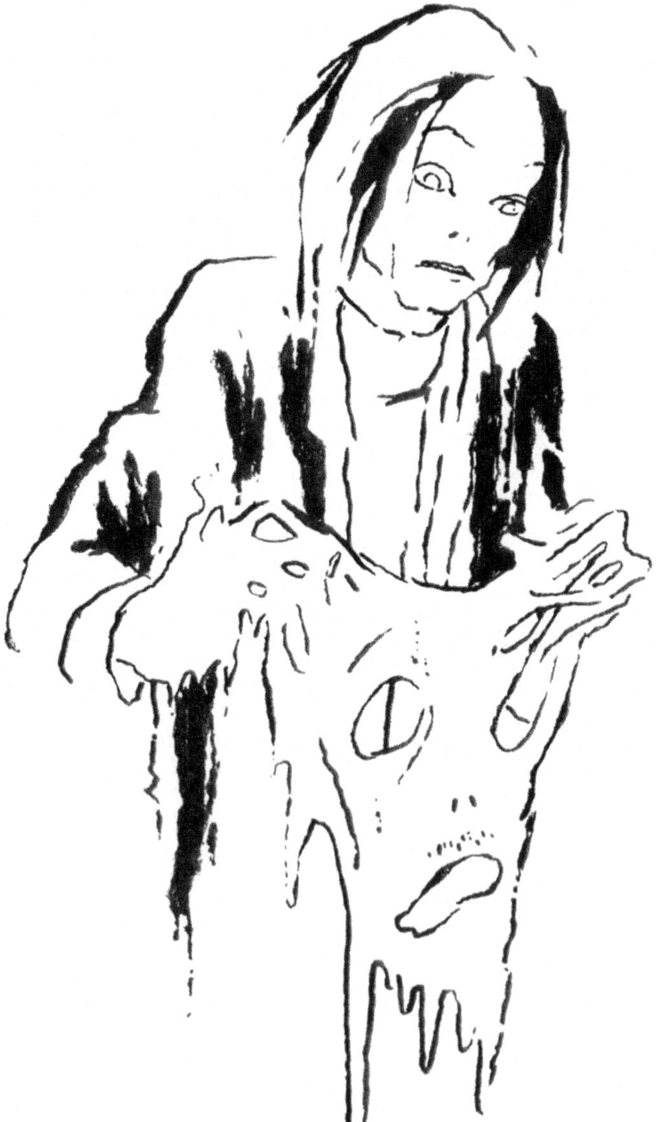

The survivor makes the slow turn from Shadow Street into Night Blossom Avenue. His movements are listless, automatic. The ghosts of suburbia are fluttering above the swimming pools and the perfectly tended lawns. There is the thrumming sound of a malfunctioning sprinkler, against which a bell is tolling. The survivor recognises the tone. It's the clock tower of his local shopping centre. He can't remember taking any conscious direction. How strange, that some deeply buried navigational system has brought him here, this close. He is very nearly home.

The survivor walks down the middle of the empty street, through the cold light of the early morning air. What exactly happened back there with the mask? Was he possessed? A radio plays from a bedroom window, the latest hit ballad. *Kiss the darkness, baby, cover my face with ashes.* He sees himself in a parked car window, a dreadful sight, he has to turn away from his own image. A woman on the corner watches him. Her mask is decorated with a large question mark. The survivor lowers his head in shame.

Now he stands outside his house. He breathes heavily. He has been through so much, his suit is a collection of rags, his arms are bruised and bloody, but at least he is home, he is back with his family. The survivor thinks of his two children safely sleeping behind the darkened bedroom window above. He can see the flickering TV light from the living room. His dear sweet wife must still be awake. She has been waiting for him. She loves him!

The front door opens at his touch, as though waiting for his hand. The survivor goes inside, into the hallway. He can hear the noise of the television but when he walks through, the room is empty. His wife is not there. She must be upstairs with the children. They are waiting for him. The survivor pauses. The TV screen is filled with the head and face of the Founder of Zeno. Stray colours drop from the image as joyful electric voices sing out the new corporate song. *Keeping the dream alive! We're keeping the dream alive, just for you! And you! And you and you and you!* The advertisement break ends. The survivor steps forward. The founder's dead eyes come open, slowly, slowly, prised apart by some artificial means. A vast stream of imagery is flooding out from the temple of his skull.

The survivor walks upstairs with a heavy tread. He's thinking back on all the masks he has worn in his life: the clean neat office attire, the travelling salesman's veil with its corporate design, the home masks, the good father's mask, the masks of love and lust and sleep and tenderness. The elegant black hood he wore at his mother's funeral. So many memories, so many ways of hiding himself. The survivor reaches the top of the stairs.

His children's rooms have been cleared of their soft toys, the sheets unruffled. There is talcum powder on the pillows. The survivor stands for a long time in the doorway. He doesn't know what to think. Has his family left him? Or are they waiting somewhere to surprise him? He thinks for one confused moment that he might be on television himself, that a reality TV host will spring from the closet to explain everything to him. But there is only the dawn's pale light, the emptiness, the drone of the soap opera from downstairs.

The survivor enters the main bedroom. His father's masks are back in their place on the wall, staring at him. He bends down to pull a large cardboard box from beneath the bed. These are his father's effects, all that is left after the years have passed. The survivor gazes at the various cutting and sanding tools, the measuring instruments, the eye-piece and the miniature lamp. There are sheaves of invoices and catalogues, a small hardback book with the title *On the Iroquois Craft of Mask Manufacture*, a few sketches, ideas for new masks. One item alone draws the attention, a plastic bag filled with many small pieces of wood.

The survivor clears a space on the bed and empties out the plastic bag. This is it, the forensic evidence returned to the family by the coroner. The small pieces of wood are irregularly formed, some with sharp edges or sculpted thorns, others with rounded surfaces. All of them are perfectly planed and polished. The survivor wonders how his father ever did it, how he conjured the hidden face of the mask into being. Some of the larger pieces of wood bear the deep gouging marks left by the pathologist's blade. The mask had to be cut from the flesh at the autopsy. It couldn't be removed by any other means. No one had the skill to find the secret release mechanism, the catch, the key to this last and most intricate puzzle. And then, once released, the Mask of Falling Darkness had simply collapsed into pieces, these pieces, many hundreds of them.

All that remains of his father's face.

The survivor holds two of the pieces in his hands. He tries to slot them into each other, without success. He replaces one piece with a new one, and tries again. Slowly, he tries each piece against the one in his hand. After fifty-five minutes he has found the perfect match for it; the two pieces of wood slot together with a deeply satisfying click. Another forty minutes pass by before he finds a third piece to add to the mask. By now, his hands are trembling. The tiny, fragile object slips from his fingers, dropping to the bed where it splits apart, and the three pieces are lost among the many others that lie on the sheet. Lost. He will have to start again. One by one by one. He'll be more careful this time.

    It's a promise.

*Shrine*

```
        >                    <
   >                              <
        >                    <
        >                    <
            >            <
          >                <
         >                  <
         >                  <
             >          <
   >                          <
       >                    <
```

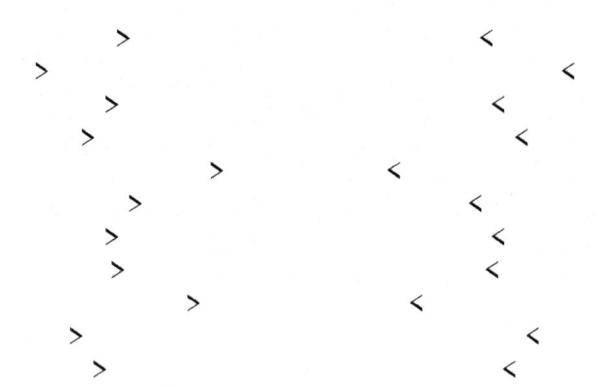

*Shrine empty*
*Please resequence*

*Shrine*

**>EDGAR ALLAN POE<**

## Interim Report

*The Passion-Winged History of the Most Illustrious Company of Zeno Volume LVII: Advent of the Skull Garden*

The winding course of the River Isis, from the high plains of Blackthorne Edge down to the sea at Sedgemore, has never been fully charted. But its passage through the City of Lujo is well documented, even though the route has changed over the centuries.

Here we begin our journey. The dream factory was built adjacent to the river at the old crossing point. Upon these few acres of land the Zeno company established the first seeds of what would later become a vast global entertainment empire. In the times of which we speak, the four high towers of the company's headquarters were a famous landmark, gleaming in the sun, their blue-tinted windows reflecting the river's dark flow.

Below ground, in the cellars of the building; beneath the old film sets and the sound studios; below the river itself – here the company held in secret its deepest memories and desires. One room in particular, called the Chamber of Sleep, was known only to the company's most trusted staff.

The Chamber was ringed with walls of iron, always kept in darkness, cold, and with a floor of bare earth into which was sunk a metal tank. Within this, suspended in a volume of preservation fluid, held loosely by weeds and cables, strewn with wires, a body floated. The Founder's body.

Watching from the confines of the Black Lab, the newly trained technicians waited patiently in their protective body suits and interface masks. They stood beside the image baths, their gloved hands moving slowly in coded gestures.

The Founder's eyes are closed, his breath has stopped, his heart no longer beats. Only within the skull itself can the traces of life be found. His dreams live on, captured daily on the company's polished machinery. Strange thoughts, strange flowers, stranger creatures; all these phantasms flickering in the darkness, keen to burst forth from the confines of the head and populate the city with their spells and charms.

This half-lit interior world of shadows and fancies became known as the Skull Garden.

*Part Two*

STARLIGHT HILL

*Shrine*

JEAN MICHEL BASQUIAT
SOPHIE CALLE
THE CLASH
SALVADOR DALI
RICHEY EDWARDS
ATOM EGOYAN
TRACEY EMIN
SIGMUND FREUD
DONNA HARAWAY
MARIKO MORI
PUBLIC IMAGE LIMITED
>IAIN SINCLAIR<
PATTI SMITH

*As it flows away from the Lake of Sighs, slowly, with a current barely noticeable, the River Isis curls around in a wide arc, forming within its boundaries a patch of raised land not often visited. There used to be a small but thriving docks along the riverbank, but they were closed down after the second trade collapse. And now, for three quarters of the year the ground is muddy underfoot, with only a covering of brown thorn-covered weeds holding it together. In the summer months however the earth is baked a virulent orange colour, and a thin mist hangs over the landscape as the heat rises from the surface of the lake.*

Lela Martino cut through the barbed wire. A sign read PRIVATE PROPERTY - NO TRESPASSERS. Lela ignored it, picking her way across the steadily rising ground. She was climbing Starlight Hill, the rather grand name given to a mound of earth that the river seemed to embrace protectively within its curves. From the heights she could see across the water to where the silver towers of the Zeno studios sparkled in the evening light. Nearer to hand, close to where the sun burned the hill's crown, there was a small domed building. For many years this structure housed a weather station and observatory. Now it lay abandoned. Unexplained deaths and frequent police raids had spooked and scattered the homeless people who used to shelter here. More recently the place had been the living quarters of a hermit named Isabella Candide.

Lela had seen the old woman on the news a few days ago, after her arrest. Blinking under the police lights she appeared to be nothing more than a harmless crank, with her antique leather coat and the dirty grey colour showing at the roots of her pink hair. The only unnerving thing about Isabella was her face, which was burned and scarred. Tiny electrical wires were embedded in the skin.

Lela stopped for a moment. The sun was setting and her shadow was cast long on the ground. She looked back to the Lake of Sighs with its weeping trees and rotting foliage. Why had her client directed her to this godforsaken place? She could think of a hundred places she'd rather be; but Lela was a Data Dandy. She found things, she uncovered secrets, and the client's wishes were always paramount, especially with the amount of money this job was offering. Now that she needed. This was the first real proposition she'd had in months.

*Wait...*

Was that a person, down below? Lela stared into the lowering gloom, to see a tall dark figure moving slowly from side to side, as though the slight wind had set it drifting. A yellow light flashed a few times, then went out.

The night crept forward across the hill's surface.

Nothing. She was getting spooked, that was all.

Lela took a sip from her water bottle and then started out again, walking towards the observatory. The ground was dry, rutted, crumbling, and coloured here and there with a purple, faintly glowing scum. A few dark clouds threatened rain. Lela kept to the old straight track that ran between two ridges. There were many of these pathways around about, and they all seemed to home in on Starlight Hill.

According to the news report Isabella Candide had been charged with obstructing radio traffic. The list of accusations was surprising: jamming police frequencies, broadcasting a pirate radio station, disseminating illegal knowledge via the airwaves, interfering with Zeno's virtual dream catalogue, hacking into air traffic control signals. It was also hinted at that Candide was a member of some kind of underground cult. It all seemed a little strange; the woman had to be in her sixties at the least. Lela had pulled down the pirate radio recordings from the Oracle. A resonant voice croaked through static, interrupting streams of confused band chatter. Lela recognised a few lines from an old pop song: 'O city of moon and demons! Renegade angels have filled my tongue with neon, my words will light your sky.' Another time the old woman's voice had taken on a softer quality as she announced to the city, to anybody who might be listening, 'Why do we always walk away from love?'

Screeching gulls wheeled above the hillside. The domed building was dark against the twilight, looking like the lone outpost of an ancient civilization. Lela shivered despite the heat of the dying day, and pulled up the zip on her motorcycle jacket. Just then a string of lights came on at the side of the track, startling her. Lela bent down to see a series of tiny glass bulbs embedded in the dry earth. They shone like glow-worms. She turned round. The lights ran parallel with the track, stretching all the way back to the lake. Other lights winked into existence, forming a complex of gridlines all across the surrounding landscape. What were they? A landing strip for UFOs perhaps, or a piece of land art comprehensible only from the cockpit of a low-flying aeroplane? Lela was getting the tingle in her fingertips that told of something hidden, close by, imminent.

She moved quickly, barely noticing the sign tacked to the curved wall of the observatory: DANGER! PROPERTY CONDEMNED BY ORDER OF LUJO HIGH COUNCIL. The door was hanging open, the lock broken from the frame. Lela took out her torch and went inside. There were a couple of rooms downstairs, a living space and a kitchen; what few possessions they contained were now thoroughly trashed. The police had certainly been keen in their search, but Lela had the Data Dandy's trusted instinct; they hadn't yet found what they were looking for. She went upstairs, to the room that had once housed the telescope. Now the aperture was boarded up with bits of wood and tarpaulin. A couple of wires were hanging down from here, evidently leading to some kind of jerry-rigged aerial on the roof. Lela's torch flitted across a table littered with the remains of electrical equipment and a good number of empty gin bottles. She pictured Isabella Candide at night, drunkenly tapping at her radio set and whispering into the microphone. The darkness all around, the loneliness, the weird lights flickering on the ground outside, and the radio waves travelling like lost spirits through the ether.

Lela took a few photographs of the room, following the client's instructions. Everything had to be recorded for his perusal. The flashbulb burned the air with its sudden violet light. Then she looked around carefully, letting her senses go to work on the place. There was something here, she could feel it. A secret, a mystery. Her hands ran along the wall to one side of the table, and then along the work surface itself. Suddenly, as her touch passed close to one of the table's legs, she could feel the warmth in her fingertips.

This was it. Lela pulled the table away from the wall, upending it, scattering what remained of the radio equipment. Now the table lay on its side, and the hollowed-out leg was clearly visible. There was something stuffed inside, which Lela pulled loose and held open in the torch's beam. It was a few sheets of paper, each one covered with an ink scrawl. The text was written in an alphabet that Lela didn't recognise. Its letters were spiked and jagged, like something seen in a history book or a science fiction novel. It must be a code.

*What was that? A noise...*

Lela stopped breathing for a moment, in order to listen. There it was again, a high-pitched whining sound. *Krshhhkkkhhhh.* The torch shook in her hand as she crept downstairs. The living area was empty. But still the noise could be heard, coming from outside. Lela walked out through the broken doorway, her voice trembling. 'Who's there? Let me see you!' There was no answer. The torch beam swept over the baked earth as Lela walked around the curve of the building. The smell reached her, a stench of urine and blood, an animal reek.

The creature had crawled out from a bank of weeds. Again, it made its pitiful sound, and looked up at Lela with coal-red eyes. It was wounded, a dark gash in its side leaking the same purple fluid she had seen on her climb up the hill. *Krshhk! Krshhhk!* The camera's flash caused the creature to scream, and to back away. Lela made a cooing noise. Any fear that she had now left her, as she looked across Starlight Hill to the back lots of the Zeno studios. The four towers were dotted with electric lights, each blue-silver sparkle reflected in the river like a drowned star.

Now here was a story. This was worth any Data Dandy's time and effort.

Because this creature, this poor wounded specimen with its traces of fur and its stunted arms and legs, its pointed ears – amid all these attributes the creature stared up at Lela with a crudely-formed human face.

*Shrine*

JEAN MICHEL BASQUIAT
SOPHIE CALLE
THE CLASH
**>SALVADOR DALI<**
RICHEY EDWARDS
ATOM EGOYAN
TRACEY EMIN
SIGMUND FREUD
DONNA HARAWAY
MARIKO MORI
PUBLIC IMAGE LIMITED
\>                      <
PATTI SMITH

# ZENO PRODUCTIONS

*Proudly announce the grand opening of the Skull Garden*

*Please consult Oracle: FOUNDER*

'Ever since our glorious <u>Founder</u>, Augustus Cage, passed away from this mortal realm we have striven to create products that carry on the tradition of excellence that he so firmly set in place. To this end we are instigating a new range of characters for your continued enjoyment. Please welcome the Zeenies!'

*Please consult Oracle: ZEENIES*

'These fantastic creatures will give you many hours of pleasure. Created using the latest advancements in Artificial Life technology, these little pet monsters are like nothing you've ever seen before. But don't worry, they're perfectly safe and manageable. <u>Zeenies</u> really do make ideal domestic companions. They only need feeding once a day and make no unpleasant household messes. You'll be surprised by how friendly they are!'

Lela sat at her desk, staring at her Oracle device. Its glowing yellow eyes blinked once or twice, as it waited for her next question.

*Please consult Oracle: ZEENIES, MOST POPULAR*

'<u>Zeenies</u> come in all shapes and sizes, with models suitable for all age groups and income levels. Here we shall list only a few of the <u>most popular</u> models: The HORQUE BIRD is a ball of orange feathers on a pair of long spindly legs. It has no wings. DOGMATICUS is a three-legged creature whose muzzle is bearded with cables. Gnostic scriptures are woven into its fur. The GANGLION has protuberant eyes and a mane of electrical cables. Silver antennae grow out of its ears. The TELEPHANTASM is a blue-skinned creature with five tails and a long trunk which it uses to pick up radio signals. A screen in its stomach shows the latest feature films. The GYRAFFOSCOPE has a very long neck and a single brown eye the size of a dinner plate. The RHINOCEROSE is a powerfully-built creature with a beautiful flower growing from the centre of its forehead. The DATASNAKE slithers along the ground searching for stray numbers. Its multicoloured scales are decorated with tiny letters. The SCORPIONIC is a mechanical creature with a jointed tail, the tip of which squirts out black ink. With careful training it can be taught how to write.'

*Please consult Oracle:* SKULL GARDEN

'The Skull Garden is an imaginary land where all the Zeenies live until they find new homes. Please, adopt one today! You need never feel lonely again. Remember: the garden can only be accessed using the official Zeno interface mask.'

Lela thought back to her time on Starlight Hill, and the discovery of the wounded creature. Its tortured face stared at her from the photograph she had pinned above her desk.

*Please consult Oracle:* HUMAN CHARACTERISTICS

'The law currently states that no artificial creature can have any trace of human characteristics. We at Zeno respect this ruling.'

*Please consult Oracle:* ILLEGAL COPIES, BOOTLEG

Do not be tempted by inferior, illegal copies! Only the trueborn Zeenie has the company's logo branded on its underside. The so-called Bootleg Zeenies are made with infected code. They are prone to viral infection and will quickly fall ill or even die without the Founder's patented dream magic. The Zeno company can accept no responsibility for damage to property or flesh caused by illegal creatures.

*Shrine*

JEAN MICHEL BASQUIAT
SOPHIE CALLE
THE CLASH
>                              <
RICHEY EDWARDS
ATOM EGOYAN
TRACEY EMIN
SIGMUND FREUD
**>DONNA HARAWAY<**
MARIKO MORI
PUBLIC IMAGE LIMITED
>                              <
PATTI SMITH

A small shaded lamp provided the only light in the room. The client held the photograph in this yellow glow and studied it. For a moment he said nothing, then he looked up at Lela, his eyes barely seen through the tiny holes in his silk mask. There was a scent of jasmines in the air, probably some kind of high-end cologne. 'This is all you have?,' he asked. The cloth gave his voice a muffled quality, as though he were speaking through a layer of fog.

Lela held her own. 'It's illegal activity. Human qualities should never be replicated.'

'Please. A photograph proves nothing.' The image fell from the client's hand. 'They are easily simulated.'

Lela handed over the sheets of paper with their coded writing. 'Also, I found this in the old lady's place. The police missed it.'

The client nodded as he scanned the various sheets, mumbling to himself.

Lela waited. She looked around at the shadowed walls with their second-rate watercolour prints of flowery fields. She had always to make her report in a cheap hotel room such as this one, a different establishment each time. A darkened room, in which the client sat with his face obscured. Lela couldn't tell for sure, but she had the feeling that he was not that old. The mask was made from black silk, except for a thin white line which stretched from the top right to the bottom left of the wearer's face. It made a faintly menacing impression.

Mask wearing was not the great fashion it had been a few years before; now it was seen as a definite sign of having things to hide. Let that be. Lela had no doubt at all that the name she knew the client by, a Mr Carter, was not his real identity. Not that she cared; as long as she received the promised fee, that was all that mattered.

'Is it useful?' she asked.

'Ah yes. Interesting.'

'Do you understand it?'

The client did not reply. The papers crackled in the dark of the room as he shuffled one sheet under another. Lela was getting angry.

'Mr Carter, I can't work for you unless you give me a chance. No secrets.'

The masked face lifted slightly, the eyes glittering sickly in the lamp's glow. For a moment they seemed possessed by some terrible spirit. Then he sighed, and his body relaxed. 'Yes, yes. Of course.' The papers were held aloft. 'It's golem code. Instructions for the making of a creature. A Zeenie. Very advanced. But, there is something out of place.'

'The human element?'

'Yes. But not just that. There's emotional coding, as well. He would grow up strange. If he grew up at all.'

'He?'

'Oh, it's definitely male. It's male code.'

Lela thought back to the creature she had found at the observatory. Its human features appeared slightly more male than female, but she could not be sure.

Mr Carter sighed. 'It looks like Zeno is overstepping the mark. Augustus Cage would never have allowed it.'

Lela was taken aback by the remark. The client had never hinted at any real antagonism against the company, his motives as well concealed as his face.

'The thing must have escaped from the studio,' he said. 'Or else this Candide woman is working for the company, freelance. Away from the eye of the law. Yes, that might be it. Tell me, what happened to the creature?'

'I don't know,' Lela replied. 'It crawled off into the weeds. It was badly injured. I guess it's dead by now.'

Carter's body seemed to clench in the shadows. 'That's not good enough. I need more. More!'

'I'm doing what you asked–'

'Bring me proof! Proof of Zeno's misdoings.' His voice turned cold. 'I must break that company apart.' The mask moved slowly backwards, until the shadows claimed it as their own, and Lela could see no trace at all of her client.

And then out of the darkness, the voice spoke. 'Miss Martino, you will find the creature once more. Bring it to me. Dead or alive.'

'That's not my kind of job.'

The client's voice sucked at the cloth of the mask. It sounded like the last breaths of a drowning man.

'I know about you, Lela. I know what you've done.'

He paused to find his words. And his next utterance cut her to the heart.

'I know what you've lost.'

*Shrine*

JEAN MICHEL BASQUIAT
SOPHIE CALLE
THE CLASH
\>                  <

RICHEY EDWARDS
**>ATOM EGOYAN<**
TRACEY EMIN
SIGMUND FREUD
\>                  <

MARIKO MORI
PUBLIC IMAGE LIMITED
\>                  <
PATTI SMITH

The images flicker into pale life, their colours long washed out by repeated viewing: the decorated staircases and long winding blue carpets, the brass lamps with their yellow dancing flames, the ornate counters and shelving units. Lela knows every detail by heart, her eyes seeing beyond the lines of static and flecks of interference.

The tape was stolen from the security department of Haversham's, the oldest and most luxurious of all Lujo's department stores. Digital information moves across the bottom of the screen, giving the time and date of the recording. The focus widens, revealing the vast crowded spaces of the third floor shopping arena.

Lela finds herself in the image, in the crowd, a somewhat harried looking young woman in a brown coat. She is heading towards the lift that will take them upstairs to the toy department. People are rushing past with heavy bags, drops of snow melting on their collars. Belinda is close by, her head clearly seen for a moment before the crowd closes in once again. Lela can still feel her daughter's hand held tight in hers, even after all these years. Belinda's tiny hand...

Now the young woman on the screen stops at the cosmetics counter to try one of the new mood enhancer creams. Her daughter cannot be seen. How did it happen? If only Lela could recall the exact moment when the child's hand slipped from her grasp. But only a black space exists, as though the video tape has skipped forward a few moments in time. One second the two hands are safely entwined, and the next...

*Shrine*

JEAN MICHEL BASQUIAT
SOPHIE CALLE
THE CLASH
\>                 <
RICHEY EDWARDS
\>                 <
TRACEY EMIN
SIGMUND FREUD
\>                 <
**>MARIKO MORI<**
PUBLIC IMAGE LIMITED
\>                 <
PATTI SMITH

## I know what you've lost

Lela sat at her desk, working the Oracle machine. At some point the neon sign across the way flickered into life, casting its blue light across her hands and face, and she looked up, out of the window, surprised that night had arrived once more. Another night, another day gone by. And sometimes the pain would level off, falling and fading to a tiny blood-red sensation. Then it would grow once more, until the urge to watch the store's security tape became overwhelming.

No. She would surrender instead to the work in hand. It was all she could do.

Lela opened the mouth of the Oracle machine. She fed in the copies she had taken of the coded sheets. She got a limited access reply, meaning the information was out of bounds to the general public. She tried every trick her Data Dandy training had given her: abstract field enquiries, fuzzy logic scans, pirated codeword algorithms. Searching, searching for clues. The same result came up every time. The knowledge was too well protected.

This case was getting to her. There was too little being revealed, and she couldn't help feeling that the client was not only holding back information, he was actually lying to her. This so-called Mr Carter...

On a whim, Lela entered the details of the client's mask, but the machine brought back a null response for any specific family or company owning the design of a white slash on a black ground. The Oracle did however bring up the phrase 'bend sinister'. This heraldic device – a diagonal stripe running from top right to bottom left of a shield or coat of arms – is used to indicate an illegitimate line of a family.

Lela could feel her fingers twitching. What was being shown?

She was drawn again to the photograph of the strange misshapen creature she had seen on Starlight Hill. Its face was stark and fearful in the flashbulb's explosion. Lela couldn't help thinking of it as being more human than anything else, even though she knew it was only an artificial creation, an animated being. A man...

*Oh, it's definitely male. It's male code.*

She had paid very little attention to the Zeno company over the years. As a child she had seen a few of the cartoon films; her father beside her at the cinema, snoring away. Later on the company had developed holographic play-figures such as ballerinas and swordsmen and floating, fire-breathing dragons. After that it was a short step to the whole living toy market, the Zeenies. Reality was being infiltrated by the products, by the company's dreams. And then the founder had died. Lela remembered the news coverage of the funeral, the crowds lining the streets. It was like a head of state had passed away.

Without meaning to, Lela brought to mind her daughter's face, her smile, and her lovely hair long and parted in the middle like her own. Dear sweet Belinda was sitting on the floor playing with a Zeno toy, a dancing tiger made purely of light and colour.

*No. Keep working. Keep working...*

Question: what connection does Isabella Candide have with the Zeno company?

Question: How did Candide get hold of the golem code?

Question: Lela's client had suggested that Candide might be working freelance as a code jockey; could that be verified?

She pulled down images of the old lady's arrest, cross-referencing all mentions of the woman's name in the news archives. None of them linked back to Zeno.

Another dead end.

Lela stood up, stretched. Her small studio flat was softly lit, tidy, austere in its furnishings. The lights of the city shimmered through the window. She had no close friends, her husband had left soon after Belinda's disappearance. This was her life. Lela recalled the day she had turned up at the remote country house for her Data Dandy training week. She had spent her savings buying into the franchise. At first she had thought that her new skills would help her find her daughter. The instructor had warned against such personal ventures. And now she could see that he was right; the job was more a way of forgetting. Other people's secrets filled her life.

*I know about you, Lela. I know what you've done.*

How had her client found out such intimate knowledge?

*I know what you've lost.*

And the words he had spoken next: *I know about your daughter. Yes. About Belinda. I have knowledge of her fate.*

The feelings came so fiercely to her, hearing this, that Lela had moved towards the client without any clear thought, her mind dazzled by a fiery blackness. But the client had simply raised a hand as she approached and said, 'If you should dare touch me, the knowledge stays inside here.' He tapped at the side of his head. Lela could do nothing but accept the deal as proffered; that she would provide material, physical proof of Zeno's misdoings, and that in return Carter would tell Lela what he knew of her missing daughter.

She had to go back to Starlight Hill. To find the partly human creature, dead or alive, that was her best bet. Was there any other option?

A movement caught Lela's eye. She was standing near the window, looking down to the street below. A man was leaning against a car, a blue sedan it looked like. His head tilted upwards slightly, so that it seemed that he might be looking back at her. And then the man opened the car door and climbed inside. Lela shivered as the vehicle drove away.

Jesus. She was getting as paranoid as a teenage Oracle junkie.

Walking back to her desk, she noticed the Zeno catalogue mask lying on the coffee table. She had bought it earlier that day from the newsagents. The sight of the strange, partly human creature on the hill had made her wonder about the true nature of these artificial beings, and the catalogue mask seemed to be the only way into the company's inner world. Well. Why not? She might learn something; her training might lead her beyond the well-marked areas. Lela tore open the cellophane packaging with her teeth and lifted out the pink flannel. It was moist to the touch and slightly warm. A yellow letter Z was printed on the forehead. Lela smoothed the mask against her face. Immediately it dried and moulded itself to her features; at the same time, the Oracle device on her desk was activated. The mask and the Oracle had joined together in some strange, ethereal kinship. Lela settled back into her chair. She must have put too much weight into the move because now the chair was tipping over backwards. Lela was falling...

* * *

*And when she got to her feet she was standing on a terrace next to a copse of swaying umbrella trees. Below were strips of bright green lawn bordered by red and yellow flowers, and then beyond the garden the beginnings of a great forest, a waterfall, and distant snow-capped mountains. It was all rendered in the most exquisite detail, and yet her peripheral vision buzzed with faint static.*

*Lela walked along a pathway that ran beside the lawn until she reached the shade of the forest. She was aware of other figures, other visitors to the garden, other customers, but none of them paid her any mind. This was a private experience.*

The branches of the trees stretched above her. They were covered with petals that shone in the sun like so many flashing eyes. The trees were watching her, and the leaves rubbed against each other with a whispering sound. Decorated birds sparkled in the greenery, their songs based on popular melodies of yesteryear.

Soon she came to a picnic area, complete with a table, benches, and a display board showing an illuminated map of the skull garden. A creature was standing nearby, a young and glamorous chimpanzee, wearing an orange jumpsuit and a bathing cap. The chimp's body wiggled in time to a hot jazz number played by an orchestra of fish. It spoke softly, with a delicate, well-educated tone. 'Welcome to the gardens of the skull. I am your guide for today. Where would you like to visit?'

Lela did not reply.

'We have many pleasurable activities on offer.' The chimp waved its arm across the map. 'Please choose.'

Lela could think of only one thing to ask for.

'I'd like to see a Zeenie with a human face.'

The chimpanzee looked perturbed. 'I'm sorry. I do not know of any such character. Why not visit the Zeenie Zoo instead? We have several new creatures on display, and there are various easy payment options.' The chimp beamed its widest smile. 'Why, your new pet could be living in your home within hours!'

Lela moved away. The pathway took her out of the wood, towards a walled rose garden. Here, a young penguin, wearing the same bright orange jumpsuit as the chimpanzee, was cleaning graffiti off a section of the outside wall. Lela spotted the remains of two words,  RENEGAD and NGELS, each written in a vivid red paint. The scrawled message was a rude intrusion into the world's bland ambience, and the clean-up penguin moved quickly to delete the offensive material.

Lela entered the rose garden. The chimpanzee was waiting for her there, the same creature exactly, or another with the same face, it was impossible to tell which. 'Hello. I am your special guide. Where would you like to visit today?' The voice was soft, welcoming. 'There are many pleasures on offer. Why not...'

Lela turned away.

Beyond the rose garden she entered a huge glass building in which many strange tropical plants were growing. Twisting pathways led between the elaborate displays. Lela was feeling woozy from the heat and the overpowering aroma of the flowers. Where was the exit door? She couldn't remember, and *turning back to follow her own footsteps only led her deeper into the heat-filled interior. She started to panic. The glass roof changed colour as the sky darkened. Even the most colourful of the birds had fallen silent. Now the only sound was that made by the shears of a gardener, snip-snipping at the giant heart-shaped leaves of a plant. The gardener was an old, wizened, snake-like creature. The twin blades of the shears screeched against each other, again and again.*

*Lela walked on a little more quickly.*

*Now the glasshouse was bathed in moonlight. There was no way out. She passed the gardener a second and a third time and each time the shears made a louder, brighter noise. Snip-snip-snip! Sometimes the gardener and sometimes the chimpanzee guide awaited Lela around a turning; at other times the pathways looked to be as empty as an abandoned film set. Time slowed down, the air turned muggy with scent and with drifts of yellow pollen. Lela was exhausted. She fell back against the trunk of a puzzle tree, the fronds moving gently across her face. Her hands traced across the bark, where a phrase had been carved into the wood.*

WE SHALL GIVE BIRTH TO MAMA LUJO, GODDESS OF CHANGE.

*The letters burned her fingertips.*

*Just then Lela heard a noise, a bleeping sound from beyond the trees. She parted the spiked branches, revealing a green door set in the greenhouse wall. A notice said, 'Private. Staff Only.' The door was partly open, and Lela slipped through into a storage area where shovels, pitchforks and other gardening implements were stacked. The space was quite small and lined with glass panels, floor to ceiling. All were dark except where a few coloured lights flickered on and off through one particular window. The bleeping sound accompanied the lights to the same rhythm. Lela pressed her face against the window.*

*The old man floated a few feet away in the half darkness as the coloured lights playing around his head. The flesh dripped from his body...*

\*\*\*

Lela's heart seemed to be stuck tight in her chest, and her breath caught fast. Her face was wet. The mere act of opening her eyes was painful. Her fingers were sticky when she touched her cheeks, covered with a pink residue. The mask. The remains of the mask. She pulled at it frantically. Now she breathed again more easily, and willed her pulse to slow. Had she been asleep the whole time? Or had the mask really transported her to the garden of dreams? Lela couldn't work it out. At some point she had moved from the chair to the bed, to lie down. The world and the dream of the world coexisted in the same space; they could not be distinguished.

The old man's decomposing face came back to her. It seemed to be the image of Augustus Cage, the founder of Zeno.

Lela was getting off the bed when the telephone rang, making her jump. It sounded like the cry of a wounded animal in the semi-dark.

'Go to the window.'

'What? Who is this?'

'Go to the window. Look out.'

It was a man's voice, a stranger's voice. Lela followed his instructions. The blue sedan had come back.

'You'll have to give them the slip.'

Lela was now fully awake. 'What's going on?'

'You're in danger. Great danger.'

'I haven't done–'

'Traipsing around the Skull Garden, asking stupid questions. Going through doorways marked *Private*.'

'Look. Who is this?'

Static filled the mouthpiece. Down below, the doors of the sedan opened and two men got out. The voice on the phone came back. Lela listened in close as the caller told her he was an angel. At least, that's what it sounded like.

'I'm Caleb Angel. I'm Isabella Candide's son.'

Lela saw the men below crossing towards her apartment block. They vanished from sight. A few seconds later there was a loud, violent banging on the door, and the sound of wood splintering.

*Shrine*

>JEAN MICHEL BASQUIAT<
SOPHIE CALLE
THE CLASH
>                              <
RICHEY EDWARDS
>                        <
TRACEY EMIN
SIGMUND FREUD
>                              <
>                        <
PUBLIC IMAGE LIMITED
>                        <
PATTI SMITH

## Manifesto of the Renegade Angels

WE ARE NOT ALL MEDIA CAPTIVES
MAKE ALL DREAMS OPEN SOURCE
STOP ZENO DREAMING YOUR DREAMS
OUR FANTASIES ARE NOT OBSOLETE
AUGUSTUS CAGE FAKED HIS OWN DEATH: FACT!
SKULL GARDEN MASKS EXACT A TOLL ON THE COLLECTIVE IMAGINATION
THE SKULL GARDEN IS A LIMBO FROZEN SPIRIT WORLD
NO COPYRIGHT ON DREAMS!
ZEENIES ARE LUJO ARCHETYPES, NOT INTELLECTUAL PROPERTY
ZEENIES BELONG TO EVERYONE
WHY PAY ZENO TO PLAY WITH OUR DREAMS?
THE SKULL GARDEN IS A SHARED POOL, NOT A DATA PRISON
WE ALL HAVE THE RIGHT TO COPY, ADAPT AND MUTATE ZEENIE CODE
CREATE YOUR OWN DREAM CREATURES
LIBERATE ALL ZEENIES!
MAKE THE SKULL GARDEN A REAL LIVING DREAM WORLD
TRANSFORM THE SKULL GARDEN INTO A COMMONS
MAMA LUJO IS THE ONE TRUE GODDESS OF CHANGE
ONLY MAMA LUJO WILL DELIVER US FROM BONDAGE
DECLARE WAR ON ALL ZENO BRAND PROTECTION AGENTS
FREE YOUR DREAMS BY ANY MEANS NECESSARY!

*Shrine*

&gt; &lt;

SOPHIE CALLE
**&gt;THE CLASH&lt;**

&gt; &lt;

RICHEY EDWARDS

&gt; &lt;

TRACEY EMIN
SIGMUND FREUD

&gt; &lt;

&gt; &lt;

PUBLIC IMAGE LIMITED

&gt; &lt;

PATTI SMITH

01

Lela saw the man below
crossing
towards her apartment block

He vanished from sight

A few seconds later–
a loud, violent banging on the door

The sound of wood splintering.

*Shit*. What to do–
Out the back window
down
       down
              down
the fire escape, Lela's shoes clattering
on the metal steps
              down
       down
down

Grounded. Falling–   *No!*

Running. Now! You just keep running!
Dragging breath into the lungs,
jumping the fence full stretch...

Away!


02

Walking alone
in the Western Zone

Lela shivers
pulls her jacket tighter
around her body

It's dark, no traffic

The old shopping district:
abandoned superstores
weed-strewn parking lots
dead adverts, broken streetlamps
a data dog booth, all dark

the long stretch of the
flyover
above her head,
the one good light
a small pool of silver
blood-red graffiti on the walls

           dREaMs arE nOT fOr saLe!

A noise...

Lela stops, looks round
Is she being followed?

Shadows moving across the way:
Zeno's people?
The cops?
For one crazy moment thinking
*Belinda?*

–Who's there?

The night breathes a slow-drawn answer

Lela slips inside an old cartoon kiosk,
the corner of Sunset and Dime,

the kiosk's projection engine long since
ripped apart:
sad stench of life
at the Lost Edge of Tomorrow

Waiting, five
ten minutes
Lela blows on her hands,
cold

The night quiet now
Stepping out, slow, cautious...

A purple Cadillac pulls up,
comes out of nowhere
just like that;
the window sliding down, real slow

Darkness within
a voice

–Get in

03

The man in the back seat
name of Caleb

–Caleb Angel, at your service

He's dressed in white:
a) Boiler suit
daubed with slogans

LAST GANG IN TOWN
      SKULL PIRATES TALLY HO!

## DEATH TO ALL MERCHANDISE

b) bovver boots
c) gloves
d) an old Zeno creature mask:
whiskers, pricked ears
skullcap
spiky hair poking through
His eyes fully exposed,
and the metal joints moving round his lips

as he speaks:
–Um. Interesting...

This said, glancing
through the back window

–Zeno Squad, starboard stern

Witness: the blue Sedan
following close behind.

–Step on it, Sammy, there's a dear

INSERT: Samuel Angel
Driver
the silent kind
wearer of a half-pig mask
and bondage chains

The Cadillac takes a street corner
at speed, and

Lela rolls against
Caleb's body
(wiry, fired up
stretched taut)

their eyes meeting...

as Sammy takes the car
under the motorway
into a siding, where he cuts the engine
letting shadows fall slowly
over the vehicle...

    (inside

Caleb holding Lela's stare
something in his eyes

    Sadness?)

As the blue Sedan
drives by,
midnight shaded

quiet
slow,

gone

Now
breathe again, Lela,
as Caleb
takes your hand

saying
–So then, Dandy Girl. What are you searching for?


04

They drive through the shadows
of the city
keeping to the back streets

Lela feels lost
She says
–I'm working for a client, confidential

Caleb smiles
–Come clean. You'd be dead now, if it wasn't for us

Lela believes it, answers
–The client wants to bring down Zeno

Sammy laughs
Caleb smiles
–Don't we all. Don't we all!

The Cadillac
swings
into an entranceway;

sudden darkness
total

Caleb's hand
touching
(in the darkness)
her face...

–We're here
whispered

05

Distant music, halfway lost
in some big old warehouse,
damp and dusty, the air

filled with echoes (echoes...echoes...)
patterns of smoke
the stench of

burnt-out electrics

Slogans on every wall:

        NO COPYRIGHT ON DREAMS!
        RENEGADE CODE: R.E.M. SLEEP
ENTER SKULL CITY

–Home. Such as it is

Caleb leads her
to where the music's playing:

dub reggae
analogue noises
stolen Rockabilly guitar solos
and

a young woman moving there,
slow dancing
against
        the
        beat

INSERT: Rachel Angel
one cloudy-eyed late teenager
wearing
a *Slits* T-shirt
slogan-printed:

        liBerATe aLL zEeNieS!

Her mask?
Green snakeskin, cobra-hooded

Sammy and Caleb come to join with Rachel
and the Renegade Angels
one two three

turn to look at Lela
in silence

06

INSERT SAMPLE – DH Lawrence:

*What is the knocking?*
*What is the knocking at the door in the night?*
*It is somebody wants to do us harm.*

*No, no, it is the three strange angels.*
*Admit them, admit them.*

07

And they lead Lela down
into the cellar,
where Samuel hits a spotlight:

fiery red glow
bathing the object...

Some old and weird-looking visor mask
covered in

       words

words
                       words
     words
                   words
        words

words

       words

*Shrine*

**>SOPHIE CALLE<**

RICHEY EDWARDS

TRACEY EMIN
SIGMUND FREUD

PUBLIC IMAGE LIMITED

PATTI SMITH

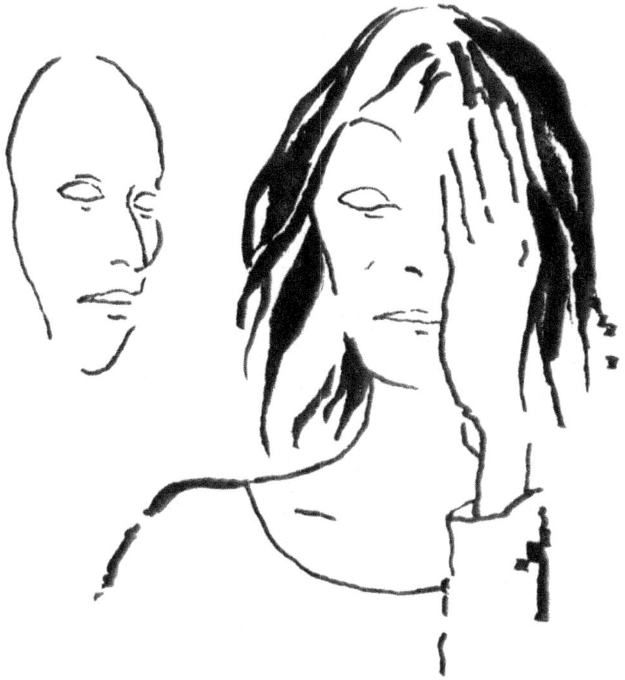

## Job number: 7059TX

### Data Dandy Investigator: Pierre Tavistock

*Initial Contact*

Object placed on my desk by a young woman dressed in a hooded khaki boiler suit. Face hidden behind a mask. Voice slow and dry. Slogans painted all over her clothing. TeeNAge OrAclE jUNkieS. Stuff like that. Says to call her Rachel. She wants to know if the mask is real or a fake. Seems a straightforward job. Allowing the hands to discover the layers of collected aura.

*Description*

Object made of lightweight metal and plastic. Visor hinged either side of a worn metal head-band. Black with gold edging. Flaking in places. One of the extendable wire arms is broken near the socket. Other wire arm in good condition and tipped with a stylus. Traces of dried red ink. Various fetish objects and decorations added, presumably at some late stage in the object's history.

*Origination*

Object designed and constructed by Maria Salvador, manager and sole proprietor of the Mask Emporium, Slowdown Road, Lujo. The store was burned down a few months after the mask was sold. Salvador's whereabouts currently unknown.

*Next Phase: Textual Excitement*

The Sacred Prophet Joseph in police custody wearing the Mask of Renegade Desire. Sprays graffiti on mask. This act is caught on surveillance tape. Footage is pirated, copied, adapted. Key phrases crop up on minor hit records, analogue pamphlets, political anthems. The text becomes known as the Prophecy of the Renegade Angels.

*Finders Keepers*

The mask ends up in the hands of Warrant Officer James Cleverly. He fences it to Ida Michaels, market trader on Silver Street. Mask displayed alongside feather boas, used phones, Goth style make-up, sex toys and theatrical props. All masks out of fashion by this time. Worn only as evening wear or on formal occasions.

### A Night at the Theatre
The mask turns up back-stage at the Ambassador Theatre. May have been used in avant-garde performance piece. Theatre a victim of one of the early Art Wars. Building condemned by Lujo High Council. Mask sinks back out of sight.

### Rough Trade
The mask shows up among seized possessions at a debtor's auction in Sack Town. Owner listed as one Demi Divine, 58, a down-on-her-luck actress. Mask sold to a mysterious individual known only as 'Operating Clay Torso'.

### Property is Theft
Mask spotted in Museum of Extinct Fetishes in the Junk Arcades. Lying under glass alongside shrunken heads, cracked Ray-Ban sunglasses, diseased iPods, earplugs. A break-in takes place. Alarm bells and muffled voices. Display case smashed and the mask seized. Nothing else taken. Slogans daubed on the museum's walls.

### Translated Cult Icon
At this point the mask receives its various add-on accessories: bones, feathers, ferns, electrical components, wire, broken glass, and the like. Blood, semen and other bodily fluids smeared onto the frontispiece, which has also being crudely painted to suggest a human face, possibly female. I guess you could call it Neo Primitivism, except I can't see anything Neo about it.

### Dirty Work
Object authenticated. It is most certainly the Mask of Renegade Desire, one and only. The auras are caked on it like multiple scabs on a wound. I feel like I need a hot shower, just to wash the bad vibes away.

*Shrine*

RICHEY EDWARDS
**>TRACEY EMIN<**
SIGMUND FREUD

PUBLIC IMAGE LIMITED
PATTI SMITH

Sammy and Rachel were sitting cross-legged on the ground, their eyes closed behind their masks, a low guttural chanting coming from their lips. Before them stood a sheet metal idol, a squat primitive looking sculpture, indecently female, on the torso of which the Mask of Renegade Desire was balanced. Candles on the ground cast dancing shadows over the frontispiece, with its luridly painted face, the face of a madwoman.

Lela looked on. She couldn't help seeing the various adornments and the new body as an attempt to change the sex of the original mask. Caleb grinned at her. 'We call her Mama Lujo,' he announced proudly. Then he took Lela by the hand and led her away from his comrades.

Music played loud from a hidden sound-system. It snaked around Caleb and Lela as they walked through the abandoned warehouse and its warren of dark corridors, its winding steel staircases. The slow melancholic bass lines bounced off the walls, small yelps and howls tracking each note. Slogans crept along the walls, projected from magic lanterns.

WE ARE NOT LOVE'S CAPTIVES. MAKE ALL DESIRES OPEN SOURCE. STOP CUPID STEALING YOUR ARROWS.

Caleb's room, when they got to it, was cold and plainly furnished, a wide space shading off into darkness. There was a table and chair, and a double bed with a brass frame. The only splash of colour came from the bright sunburst finish of an old but well looked after Rickenbacker bass guitar. Caleb threw himself on the mattress. The bed springs squeaked.

'Welcome to my kingdom, Dandy Girl. Such as it is.'

He was taking off his white gloves with his teeth. Like a cat licking its paws, thought Lela. His eyes were watchful.

Lela pulled her leather jacket tight around her. The draughts in the old building played strange tricks with the sound. She thought she could hear Sammy and Rachel chanting. Or maybe it was just the old voices in the dub reggae, which was still surging through the adjoining rooms of the warehouse.

Caleb hit a switch beside the bed which turned on a flickering display of yellow and red lights. He directed Lela's gaze upwards to where a canvas sheet was stretched across the ceiling, its white expanse decorated with yet more slogans, each word made of a different material, and crudely stitched in place.

VENUS FAKED HER OWN ORGASM. OUR LUST IS NOT OBSOLETE. THE HEART ENCLOSES THE MIND.

Caleb had taken up his bass guitar. He was picking out the rhythms of the distant music. 'What do you know about us?' he asked.

'Us?'

'The Renegade Angels?'

'Well, there's not much about you on the Oracle,' Lela replied. 'Some kind of freedom of information group, anti-corporate culture hackers, I don't know. You've done a good job of hiding.'

'But you're here,' said Caleb softly. 'You found us. We found you. We found each other.' He touched the strings of his instrument, finding a new bass line to go with the distant melody.

Lela shrugged. 'I can't go back to my flat, can I? It's too dangerous.' She thought back to the wood splintering on her front door. The shock of it.

'Then you'd better stay,' said Caleb. 'Become one of us.' Again, the soft voice. It was obviously a technique.

'Lela Angel?' She laughed at the thought of it. 'I don't think so.'

'Why not?' Caleb sounded hurt. He stopped playing.

'Are you trying to convert me?'

'Rachel and Sammy fancy the idea of having a Data Dandy in the gang.' Caleb put his guitar down on the floor against the bed. 'It would make things easier.'

'And what about you?' asked Lela. She sat on the edge of the bed. She had her own techniques. 'What do you think?'

Caleb played with the zip at the front of his boiler suit. He pulled it up and down as he spoke of the Renegade Angels and their imagined goddess, Mama Lujo, how they were going to punish Zeno for the way it forced people into a particular and very curtailed way of dreaming.

'Who is this Mama Lujo?' Lela asked.

'You've heard of the Renegade text, no doubt?'

'Of course. I've seen the posters in the alternative lifestyle shops.'

Caleb waved such commercialisation away with his hands, and his voice took on a deep resonance. 'Beyond the corporate death, your true future belongs to those few renegade angels who run like spilt mercury along your darkest streets. They shall give birth to and nurture Mama Lujo, the new chaotic agent, a goddess of change. Only she can deliver her city from its bondage.' A surge of energy pulsed through Caleb's body as he quoted the prophecy's famous last lines, his eyes looking devilish where they peered out from his mask.

'We're going to bring Mama Lujo into being. That is our task. We shall plant her in the Skull Garden and liberate people's dreams.'

Lela shook her head, wearily. She looked up at the canvas ceiling. NO TENDER FOR TENDERNESS. MUTATE APHRODITE'S CODE. THE GARDEN OF LOVE HAS MANY PATHWAYS. 'You're full of slogans, aren't you?'

Caleb smiled. He rolled onto his side to be closer to her. 'You could help us,' he whispered. The front of his boiler suit was unzipped. Lela saw his thin pale chest. She saw how frail he was, how fragile.

'How did you know about me in the Skull Garden?' said Lela. Her voice was hoarse. She was sensing something in this young man, a need, something hidden.

Caleb's fingers traced the sleek, furred contours of his mask. 'I made this, you know,' he said. His eyes blazed with pride. 'My mother showed me how. It's an Angel Mask. An advanced interface mask for accessing the Skull Garden.'

'Like the Zeeny catalogue thing?'

'More than that,' said Caleb dreamily. He rolled on to his back again, his hands returning to stroke at his mask. 'There's a whole world in here. The company think they've created a safe, closed-in environment. No.' Caleb sat up once more. He was becoming energised, his fingers pressing eagerly against his mask, moving over the surface. 'There are pathways, offshoots, doorways, openings, portals, holes in the sky, in the shadows, weak points, connecting nodes, secret passageways, broken locks, abandoned areas. We go in every night.'

'The angels?'

Caleb nodded. 'We travel further every time, exploring the world. I've seen some things, you wouldn't believe. Oh Lela, for a Dandy like yourself, it would be ecstasy.'

He was right. Lela could feel herself getting caught up in the young man's desires. She moved closer. 'What are you looking for?'

Caleb lounged on the bed, crossing his arms behind his head. It was a gesture both provocative, and vulnerable. The flickering lights played over his bare chest. His eyes glittered, and he smiled before answering. 'Augustus Cage.'

'The company's founder? But he's dead. I saw the funeral on the news channel.'

'You saw a funeral, Lela. That's all.'

'You're saying he's alive? Oh, come on.'

Caleb made no answer. He tipped his head to one side. And suddenly Lela was thinking back to the old man she'd seen through the window in the Skull Garden, how his face seemed to be melting. It had certainly looked like the Zeno founder, perhaps some kind of stray image, set loose from the company's memory banks. This is how Lela had reconciled it to herself. But now? Had the old man been calling to her for help?

Lela pushed the thoughts away. 'No. It's all just rumours. Oracle gossip.'

'Believe me,' said Caleb. 'He's still alive.'

Lela couldn't decide if she wanted to slap the young man's face, or kiss him. 'Why don't you take this off,' she said, stroking the mask of fur around his eyes.

Caleb shook his head. 'No. Not yet.'

'Was your mother working for Zeno?' Lela asked. 'Tell me about Isabella Candide.' She was thinking about the few pages of code she had found hidden in the old observatory on Starlight Hill.

'You're good,' said Caleb. 'Very good. A good Data Dandy.'

'I don't know what you mean.'

'You think this is to do with my mother, don't you? The masks, the secrecy, the fight back.'

'I'm not saying that.'

'You don't have to.' But Caleb didn't seem angry. He curled up and placed his head on Lela's lap, and he seemed pleased when her fingers returned to stroke at his masked face. Projected slogans floated around the walls of the room. DECLARE HATE ON ALL CUPID'S PROTECTION AGENTS. FREE YOUR SKIN BY ANY TOUCH NECESSARY. He began to talk about his mother, the whole story. Lela learned that Isabella had been one of the early pioneers of Artificial Life systems, a natural engineer, but with perverse inclinations. It seemed that this perversity was the thing that her only child Caleb admired most about her.

'What about your father?' Lela asked.

Caleb shook his head at the question, saying only that he and

Isabella had become a unit, a little mother and son gang, that's what it felt like. Candide had made a living in glowlab porno, tricking out phantom showgirls and holoboys for the punters, five minute fantasies that crumpled into nothingness after a hot night of passion in a motel room somewhere. They had moved from town to town, one step ahead of the police. But then Isabella went to work for Zeno. She said it was a steady job, she was tired, she needed a rest, she needed some proper money to bring Caleb the best in life. But Caleb, sixteen years old by now, was outraged. His mother was prostituting her talent for Zeno, the biggest corporate exploiter of human dreams the world currently knew. How could she do it? Caleb had walked out on her. He'd met up with Sammy and Rachel a week later, forming the Renegade Angels.

Lela was so intrigued by the story that she hardly felt Caleb's fingers undoing the buttons on her blouse. But now, suddenly, she found herself irritated by his clumsiness. He stopped. 'What's the matter?' he asked.

'Don't you want to help your mother? She's been arrested.'

'Oh. Fuck this,' said Caleb. He moved away from Lela, doing up the zip on his boiler-suit. 'My mother went to work for Zeno thinking she'd have a straight job and instead they put her to work on the black arts projects, quasi-legal research and development, all at arm's length from the official company records.'

'You know this for certain?' asked Lela.

Caleb nodded. 'Now she's been caught by the police, Zeno deny all knowledge of her. Well, what did she expect? She got burned.'

'Poor baby.' Lela had meant it to be kind, or at least semi kind; instead it came out as cruel.

'Well fuck you,' said Caleb in return. 'Shit. Maybe I should never have called you. Where would you be now?' He was his old self again.

Lela suddenly realised she had to go back to Starlight Hill. She had to pick up the creature for the client, the wounded thing with the human face. Only then would she be able to find out where her missing daughter was. 'I have to leave,' she said.

'So soon?' Caleb sounded mournful.

Lela stood up. 'Work to do.'

At this, Caleb reached behind his head, untying his mask. The covering fell away. His smile was tight, fearful almost, and his eyes were shy.

His face, though...

Lela couldn't believe what she was seeing. The blonde eyebrows and full red lips, the narrow teeth glimpsed as the mouth opened wider. She looked confused, and Caleb picked up on this, sensing her panic. 'I'm not that bad, am I?' he asked, laughing it off. But Lela had no laughter inside her, none at all. She could feel a panic attack coming on, the darkness pressing in from all sides, the heaviness throbbing behind her eyes, and the decorated words moving on the ceiling and the walls, and on Caleb's boiler suit. LIBERATE LOVE FROM SEX. MAKE ALL HUMAN SKIN A PALACE OF DELIGHTS. Lela felt she was looking at a monster. She placed a hand on the brass rail at the foot of the bed and tried to regain control of herself. ONLY LOVE CAN DELIVER US FROM BONDAGE. She gulped down air.

'Caleb...'

'What is it?' Caleb's voice was tiny. He seemed to be coming in from a long way away, like a broken signal in the night. "Speak to me. Lela, what's wrong?' Lela had to hold herself steady, first to hear what Caleb was saying, and then to get the words out in reply, the correct words in the correct order.

'Caleb. I've seen your face before.'

*Shrine*

>                                   <
    >                           <
      >                     <
  >                             <
        RICHEY EDWARDS
    >                       <
    >                       <
        SIGMUND FREUD
  >                           <
    >                       <
    PUBLIC IMAGE LIMITED
    >                   <
      **>PATTI SMITH<**

## Teenage Oracle Junkies

(words and music: Caleb Angel.)

Renegade angels
They turn their eyes to greet the moon
as it falls upon their silver bodies
in the cold light, in the cold rooms.

They keep themselves well hidden
behind their masks of gold and red,
let memories slip through their fingers
like flowers on tangled beds.

*Hey!* I'm just a freak for your data, baby.
I'm a teenage Oracle junkie.

When the sun comes up they're shivering
like a radio tuned down close
to the dial's end, like the shadow cast
by the broadcast of a ghost.

They run dope along the duskline
rising with the tide of mist,
whispering their names around like smoke
in the mouths of the kissed.

*Close it down!* I'm just a freak for your data, honey.
I'm a teenage Oracle junkie.

(Rachel, guitar solo here. Cheers.)

Angels wrapped in shadows
disdaining lover's traces,
for fear of falling eye-first
in the mirror's darker places.

But you can glimpse them in the shimmer

of the neon-skin arcades,
singing hymns of glamour
in a moonlit serenade.

*Shut your mouth!* I'm just a freak for your data, baby.
I'm a teenage Oracle junkie. Wipe out!!!

*Shrine*

**>RICHEY EDWARDS<**

SIGMUND FREUD

PUBLIC IMAGE LIMITED

The sky was too close to the earth, pressed down by massed black clouds. Lela could feel the charged atoms gathering in the warm air around her. It was becoming difficult to breathe. The figures on her watch danced in a luminous blur. Half four in the AM, just gone. Still dark. The moon well hidden, and just a bare edge of colour against the rim of Starlight Hill, where the sun lay in wait. Lela's fingertips tingled. She kept looking all round, fearing that she was being watched.

'Keep the torch on me!'

Lela was startled by Caleb's voice. She swung to face him once again, directing the beam of light down onto his form.

'That's it. Good.'

Caleb looked up at Lela, his face covered in sweat and dirt. He looked like a crazed animal.

'It's not here, Caleb. Come on.'

'I'm not leaving the hill until I find it. You go, if that's what you want.'

Lela shook her head.

The hill sloped steeply here, away from the observatory, down towards the bank of weeds where Caleb was working. He was on his hands and knees, tugging at the thick tangle of roots and vines. Lela could hear his grunting sounds.

Suddenly he stopped.

'What is it?'

'Give me the torch.'

Lela handed it over. Now she stood in darkness, and when she looked back the way they had come, towards the distant lake, she could see the coloured lights winking on and off like a signal.

Caleb cried out. Lela turned to see him reaching into the weeds, the thorned branches cracking around him, as he struggled. He had dropped the torch, to use both hands. Lela bent down to pick it up, noticing that it lay in a dried pool of purple fluid. She swung the beam towards Caleb, to see him pulling a large fleshy object from the undergrowth.

It was the creature.

There was no resistance, no cry of distress.

No life.

Caleb hauled the dead weight out of the weeds. It was bigger and heavier than Lela remembered. About four feet long, almost like a seal, with the threadbare pelt and the stunted arms and legs. The gash in its side had scabbed over. Caleb flopped it over, so that Lela could direct the torch beam onto the creature's face.

Caleb stared at the sight.

It was a monstrous vision, something ripped from a dream or nightmare. But for all its misshapen features – the blubbery lips, the ragged strands of fur around the brow, the pointed ears, the lifeless yellow eyes – for all of this, the resemblance was clear.

Caleb was looking at a grotesque parody of his own face.

He was still on his knees, unmoving. Lela didn't know what to do, especially when she heard the sobs of pain rising from deep within his body. And when she moved to comfort him, he shook her off roughly.

'What did my mother think she was doing?'

Caleb looked up to the aerial on the roof of the observatory. It was whipped by the wind. The storm was coming up now.

'She was trying to bring you back,' said Lela, 'in the only way she knew how.' She was searching desperately for something to console Caleb. 'It's like with the radio broadcasts, sending you messages. This is the same.'

'A message?' Caleb brought a hand up to his eyes.

Lela nodded. 'Sure. That's it. In a stupid way, it shows how much she loved you.'

'Did she?' said Caleb. His face was wet with tears. 'Did she really? Maybe she made me, too. Did you ever think of that?' He stood up. 'Maybe I'm no better than this rancid hunk of meat.' He kicked at the corpse. 'Maybe I'm just another failed experiment.'

Caleb scrambled up the slope, back towards the observatory. Thunder rumbled in the sky as Lela turned to follow as best she could. Her torch beam flashed before her. 'Caleb! Wait! Where are you going?'

The rain started, a summer's rain, warm against the skin.

Lela found him in the upstairs room of the observatory, among the scattered radio equipment. He was stripped to the waist, the top of his boiler suit hanging down over his belt. There was a wild look in his eyes. He was holding a broken gin bottle by the neck. Its edges were chunky, jagged.

Lela stopped in the doorway. 'Caleb! Please...'

'I'm real.'

'I know. I know you are.'

Rain dripped in through the hole in the ceiling.

'I'm real!'

Caleb slashed his chest with the edge of the bottle. The blood bubbled up in a seething line. 'It's red. It's not purple. You see? It's red!' Caleb cut himself again and showed her the blood on his fingers. 'Do you see? I'm alive. I'm human.'

Lela wanted to reach out to him, to offer help, but his face scared her now, his voice.

'I'm fucking real!'

He slashed himself one more time, and opened his mouth to catch the rain. He shook his head with glee.

Seeing this, Lela's feelings ran cold. Only a terrible anger remained. At Caleb and his mother, at the job, her client, and most of all at herself. She turned on her heels and hurried out of the building. The fierce rain was barely noticed. She stumbled down the hill, slipping and falling in the mud a number of times. She didn't know where she was going. The lights in the earth had blinked to darkness. But two pale yellow discs could be seen ahead, shining mournfully in the darkness, and Lela struggled towards them. But it was too much. Her vision misted over. She had held Belinda's hand so tightly, she knew that. She sank to her knees. Where was her child? She was lost. She thought of the dead thing on the hill, how cold and pitiful it was, how exposed. That her own heart had grown as cold...

'Where is it?'

The voice came out of the blur of rain. Lela hunched back a little, suddenly frightened. She had dropped the torch. 'Who's there? Caleb? Is that you?' And then a sudden burst of lightning startled the sky and in its brightness she saw a figure standing close by. The scent of jasmines drifted through the air.

The client. Carter. Whatever his name was.

He was dressed in a dark mackintosh and rain-hat, his black mask firmly in place, its silver slash the only colour. There was a torch in one gloved hand, and a pistol in the other. Behind the client, and a little way down the hill, the twin headlights of his car shone through a barbed wire fence.

'I've paid for your services, Lela,' he said. 'So, give me what I ordered.'

Lela felt used up, empty. She gestured behind her, in the direction of the observatory. The client moved past her without a word.

The rain fell more gently now.

*Why do we always walk away from love?*

The question rose up in Lela's mind. She couldn't quite remember where she had heard it spoken, but the thought was enough to make her stand up, and follow in the client's direction.

Now the storm was moving away. A strangely sweet aroma hung in the air, bringing a taste of metal to the tongue. Lela rounded the observatory building. The client's torch beam moved below her, near to the bank of weeds. She walked down, to where Caleb was standing. He was still stripped to the waist and smeared with blood, and he moved closer to the creature's body, as though guarding it.

'You know what I want,' said the client.

Caleb stood his ground.

'Come on now. Be a good boy.' The gun jabbed impatiently but Caleb was not for moving.

Lela stepped closer. 'Are you alright?' she asked.

The clouds drifted apart. There were pink tendrils of light in the sky above the river, and the faint light of the sun glimmered along the hillside.

Caleb shook his head. He looked at Lela with the same shy smile he'd given her when he'd first unmasked, back in the old warehouse. She wanted to go back to that moment in his room. She wanted to touch him, caress him, to forget about Starlight Hill. She wanted to go back and repair so many things. Instead, Caleb turned away from her and he said, 'My brother needs to be buried.' There was a tightness in his voice.

The client laughed. 'That's not going to happen. It's mine now.'

'So kill me.' Caleb trembled. 'Do you think I care?'

The client looked at him, the mask and the half darkness hiding all his feelings. "Oh, I won't shoot you. No, not you.'

The gun turned on Lela.

And so they went down the hill together, the three of them. The four of them. The client walked behind, keeping the pistol close against Lela's back. Caleb stumbled ahead, carrying the creature in his arms. Lela could see that he was weakening under the burden, and once or twice he almost fell.

Moment by moment, the night sky gave way to the sun.

When they reached the car the client ordered Lela to open the boot, and for Caleb to place the dead creature inside. Having done this, Caleb fell to the ground, exhausted, broken in spirit. The client nodded. He turned and looked past Lela to the silver towers of Zeno sparkling in the morning light.

'Looks like it's going to be a beautiful day,' he said, as he made to climb in the car.

'Wait, you said you would help me.' Lela grabbed him by the sleeve of his raincoat. 'My daughter... tell me where she is.'

The client looked at Lela. His white eyes peeked out from the mask, cold, intensely focussed. 'Your daughter?'

'You said... you said you knew what had happened to her.'

'Forget about the child.'

'I can't, I can't do that!'

'Take your hands off me.'

Lela had pushed the client against the car. 'She's alive. Where is she?'

The client took Lela's hands in his own. His voice was soft, deep-grained, but completely without comfort.

'You will never see her again.'

*Now the young woman stops at the cosmetics counter to try one of the new mood enhancer creams. Her daughter cannot be seen. How did it happen? If only Lela could recall the exact moment when the child's hand slipped from her grasp. Only a black space exists; one second the two hands are safely entwined, and the next...*

The car drove away. Lela watched the red tail-lights disappearing into the trees beside the lake. She was cold suddenly, deadly cold and shivering despite the rising of the day. Two arms came round her from behind, Caleb's arms, but she moved away from his touch. She would allow herself no such feelings, not now, not ever. *Something has been stolen from me, something taken away. How can I live like this?* These were Lela's only thoughts.

She wanted to disappear, to float free of the earth somehow, to travel high up above Lujo City, forgetting herself, leaving herself behind, like one of the gulls that were only now beginning to appear in the red-veined skies over Starlight Hill.

*Shrine*

>SIGMUND FREUD<

PUBLIC IMAGE LIMITED

The Zeno corporation's boardroom is found on the top floor of the main studio complex. Here, twelve men and women in tight-fitting business suits are sitting around a large oval table of gleaming dark wood. The floor-to-ceiling window at one end of the room shows a specially generated view of the sky, the scene updated each minute or so by the company's changing fortunes on the stock market. Just now, vibrant beams of sunlight are seen cutting through a bank of dark clouds. The executive committee smile. The survival policy put in place at the Founder's death is finally paying off, and, as the chief accountant rises to give her assessment of the year, her face shines with the pleasure of numbers.

However, as the first results appear on the dropdown wall screen, an alarm bell shrieks from outside the boardroom. The twelve executive officers turn their attention as one to the door, where a security guard enters. The man is sweating, catching his breath, his body trembling under the burden of a large, cloth-wrapped object. The chairman pushes back his seat. The other members look bewildered, except for one of the younger men who yells out his indignation at this rude disturbance. The guard lurches forward. He looks terrified, as a purple liquid seeps from the heavy clothbound object. Finally the weight and the fear combine and the guard's arms give way. The cloth slips aside as the object lands on the boardroom table with a thump.

There are screams and gasps from the collected members of the board. The corpse of the grey, seal-like creature rolls across the tabletop, scattering papers and crushing all the fine crystal-cut glasses and decanters under its bulk. The thing flops over one last time as though presenting its abdomen for the chairman's personal inspection. A long gash has been cut into the flesh allowing the inner organs to tumble out onto the gleaming wood. Worst of all is the monstrous semblance of a human face, the mouth peeled back, the glazed eyes bulging from the head. The stink is terrible.

Now a second man walks into the boardroom. This new intruder is wearing a silk mask, the plain ebony design slashed by a white diagonal. He steps forward calmly.

\* \* \*

*In the Black Lab. An image bath is being filled with a new batch of amniotic fluid, its clear substance shining with an inner light. The timed release of coloured oils into the fluid is triggered by the coded gestures of the technician's gloved hands. A second operative dons the special interface mask which allows her imagined self to walk the tangled pathways of the Skull Garden. She is the dreamcatcher, moving beyond the curtailed public areas, into the darker, more distant regions. The Founder's mind opens up like a dusk-blossoming flower, and whatever the operative sees on her journey is projected into the image bath, each strange plant, animal and bird faithfully rendered. In this manner, the garden unfolds from the dream world, into reality.*

\*\*\*

The man in the black and silver mask walks along the silent corridors of the Zeno studios. He's deep underground, in the oldest cellars of the labyrinthine building. He moves easily, his passage through the numerous security gates unhindered. At one point he stops beneath one of the cameras and pulls off his mask. His image flashes around the building from monitor to monitor. Lines of information cross and re-cross his projected face, revealing Mr Carter's real name to be Francis Cage. The Founder's illegitimate son, twenty-one years old, and the subject of hush-fund payments and background briefings, a nuisance, a stalker, always kept away from the inner workings of the company. Until now. Francis Cage has just been given a place on the Zeno Board. Despite this success, he feels numb with shock.

\*\*\*

*The dreamcatcher has found something in the Skull Garden, a phantom, a creature that matches her production target for that period. Her hands fall to her sides, like those of a puppet released from its strings. Her head bows down. This is the signal. The assistant operative pulls a sheet of transparent film from a roller and lays it over the surface of the fluid in the image bath. The liquid bubbles gently, the faintest scent of wild flowers permeates the room, like a spirit. The Founder's subconscious mind is present. In this manner, day by day, the company tap at this dark resource, bringing the dreams to light.*

\*\*\*

Francis Cage passes through the final gate. A small antechamber leads to a sealed doorway marked with a high-level security coding. He presses his hand against the panelling and the mechanism responds to his touch, the door opening without a sound. A room of circular aspect lies within, dimly lit, cold, its walls made of iron. Francis is vaguely aware of a quiet bleeping sound. Otherwise, the Chamber of Sleep is silent.

He's been told to come here by the Chairman. This room contains a mystery, a secret about his father, something that Francis should know. He takes a few nervous steps forward across the bare earth until he's standing at the edge of a sunken metal tank filled with water or some other liquid. Francis leans over. Something can be seen beneath the surface, a dark bulky object.

Francis steps down into the tank.

\*\*\*

*A bell rings, and the dreamcatcher's fingers start to twitch. She peels the melted interface mask from her face. The assistant lifts the square of transparent film from the bath in one fluent motion. He clips it to a wire, to allow it to dry and, as the two operatives watch, a spectral image appears on the film, becoming richer in colour, texture and detail as the seconds pass. There are shining blues and dark reds, a hint of gold. It's the image of a cat, with iridescent feathers instead of fur. Other pictures are seen along the wire, creatures found on earlier expeditions. The technicians smile at each other. Another day's work. At this point the fluid in the image bath starts to froth and to slop against the sides of the tank. Images are appearing on the surface unbidden, one after another, and without the direct intercession of the dream catcher. Quickly now, she places a new mask against her face. She will have to go back into the garden. Something is wrong.*

\*\*\*

Francis moves toward the sunken object, which lies cradled in a harness of weeds and electrical wires. It's the emaciated body of an old man with long grey hair, his loins wrapped in bandages. The submerged face can hardly be made out. Francis reaches down. The preservation liquid is cold around his wrists but he manages to get a hold of the body. It hardly weighs anything. Francis lifts it partly out of the fluid. The dead man's mouth gapes. Electrodes trail from the loose skin wrinkled across the skull. The eyes are open, but completely devoid of life. Francis brushes a few strands of hair away from the face. His hand touches the old man's lips.

\*\*\*

*The interface mask burns and the technician rips it from her face. The fluid sloshes over the top of the image bath as the room fills with noise, with half heard voices, old folk songs, bird calls, animal cries. Images flicker across the walls and ceiling, depicting the Founder and his unacknowledged son in those few short times when their lives had coincided, and which burn away almost as quickly as they are born. The lights pop, and a sudden darkness closes in, shivering with heat, and with the stench of human sweat and flesh. The two operatives stumble out of the door. The room fills with vapour as the amniotic fluid evaporates. Now the air vibrates, glowing of its own accord, alive with images.*

***

The outcast child kneels in the water, holding his father's dead body in his arms. All the years of being ignored, of being paid off and humiliated, all the years of resentment, all the lost and well-imagined moments of love, all of these feelings build up and overflow and Francis Cage weeps aloud and freely for the first time in his life.

*Shrine*

```
   >                              <
      >                        <
        >                     <
         >                   <
   >                            <
          >                 <
           >               <
         >                  <
         >                   <
            >             <
>PUBLIC IMAGE LIMITED<
            >             <
             >           <
```

They have found your body. I had to go to the police station, to make a formal identification. But fourteen years have passed since I last saw you, and you were a girl then, and so young, whereas the figure that lay before me on the other side of the glass was a woman. Still, I could see the face I remembered and would always remember in the face I now saw. It's you. Belinda. My lost child.

Memories. You're sitting on my lap watching the cartoons, your heels kicking against my shins. Running around in the garden, flying your pretty yellow kite. At bedtime, your little face cupped in my hand. How I used to comb the tangles from your hair. The stories we told each other. The funny way your head moved when you danced. Most of all, I remember the evening when I finally decided to stop searching for you.

It was a week or so after I got back from Starlight Hill. My flat seemed too small, the walls closing in. I moved round in a daze, throwing a few things into a leather travelling bag. Wash packs, make-up, bank notes, passport, jewellery, data shards, photographs. The final images of you were on the stolen security tape from the department store. Your tiny hand clasped in mine, and then gone. You were just seven years old. I watched that tape for one last time, and then removed it from the viewer. It was a piece of silver foil, shimmering with a rainbow light, just a few centimetres square. There are many ways to hide or even destroy, or pretend to destroy, memories, but only one sure way to destroy a foil tape, and that's to set fire to it. It went up instantly, leaving behind only a thin trail of black smoke. And then even this vanished.

There were no tears.

I went out into the neon-lit streets carrying my bag. I walked for five or six blocks, my feet leading me deeper into one of Lujo's darkest quarters, the refuge of the lost, the junkies and whores, corrupt cops, gamblers, ageing movie stars, itinerant musicians, illegal immigrants, disgraced politicians. The night was warm, sticky, relieved only a little by the light rain that was falling by the time I got to the converted cinema. The name SLEEK ESCALATORS was picked out in blurred letters on the hoarding above the entrance. I walked into the foyer past the empty cigarette machines and paid for my ticket. I joined the throng of boys in leather jackets and girls in long skirts moving downstairs.

This is the night it happened, Belinda. There was no big moment, no major decision made, just myself walking the streets, entering an underground club. And with each step taken, leaving you further behind. Not that you died for me, not then, and not even now, but that it was simply time to move on.

The basement was dark, seething, crowded. There was much cheering and whistling as the band walked on stage. There were three of them, dressed in their trademark boiler-suits, their unmasked faces already bathed in sweat from the hot lights. I moved through the crowd, closer to the stage, as Sammy settled behind his drum kit, and Rachel strapped on her guitar. It was the first time I'd seen their true faces. Caleb stood in the shadows at the back of the stage, his Rickenbacker bass slung low. He looked nervous, shy almost. Until he moved into the spotlight, stepping up to the microphone just as I pushed my way to the front. Our gazes locked as the crowd greeted his appearance. He cocked his head, a smile hovering on his lips. 'Good evening!' The people roared in response, but Caleb's eyes never left mine. 'This is not a love song. You do know that?' I nodded, and the music started up with a great explosion of noise.

*Shrine*

```
    >                              <
        >                       <
          >                   <
           >                <
         >                    <
             >             <
              >             <
           >                  <
            >                  <
              >              <
         >                        <
            >                  <
             >                <
```

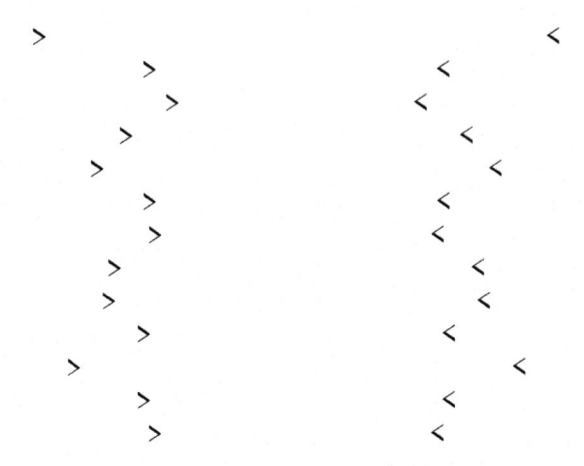

*Shrine empty
Please resequence*

*Shrine*

**>JUNE TABOR<**

## Interim Report

## The Birth of Mama Lujo: a Ballad

### A Man of Sorrowful Appearance

He was seen wandering, alone, disconsolate, along the bank of the Lake of Sighs. It was morning, not far past dawn. The air was cold, the grass thin and pale, and the birds flew slow and silent in the skies. When asked by a stranger what ailed him, the man could make no answer. His lips were red-bitten and sore, and his eyes seemed filled with a sadness beyond recall. His brow was lined with worry and his skin speckled here and there with a strange substance. But then his countenance changed, losing all colour, and he shivered with the traces of a chill, or some fever, as he spoke of his plight.

### The Story Unfolds

My name is Cage (he said), Francis Cage. I met a young woman a few nights ago at a bar down Paradise Row. Her hair was spiky cut and dark, and she moved like dusk lowering the curtain of day. We chatted for a while and drank more than a little, and I found myself speaking of how my father had died this year past, feelings I had hardly dared admit before then, and the woman seemed to have understanding. A smile passed between us, and then we headed outside to my car and we drove along to a cheap hotel I knew and had used before for such pleasures, if such they be. Her body cleaved to mine and her kisses sweetened my pain for those few short hours we spent together.

### Afterwards, a Squalid Hotel Room

Cage woke with a start, his skin prickled by sweat, and an old folk song whispering in his head – *Hey derry, down derry, hey derry derry, down derry*. He lay trembling in the tangled sheets of a filthy bed, and could hardly breathe for the pain in his chest. He felt he was poisoned or drugged. His vision blurred, white, then grey, and when he tried to stand the floor melted and the walls seemed to be too far away, he would never reach the door. A sickness came over him and he collapsed back onto the sheets. Of the young woman there was no sign, only the traces of stale perfume, the empty bottles of booze. A strange dream lingered in the back of his mind, like a shadow that would not move. He touched at the nape of his neck, where he felt some further discomfort, and his fingertips came back smeared with blood. He remembered the prick of a needle.

## The Woman, her Part in the Narrative

She left the hotel early. The street lights silvered her face, her tired eyes. A cloud drifted across the moon, and the air touched at her skin like a memory, cold, dirty. Five minutes later she was picked up by a purple Cadillac. She had done what had to be done, completed the task. The city passed by, its lurid tapestries stitched in neon tubing. The driver looked in the rear-view mirror, but the woman could not meet his stare, she turned aside. Her name was Rachel. She kept saying it to herself. *My name is Rachel. I'm an Angel of the New Dawn. I shall not rest from mental fight.* The Cadillac cruised along. And the streets grew narrower the further they travelled, and darker, as though the city were closing in around the car. Later, in the old abandoned warehouse they called home, Rachel and her colleagues sat in a circle, their veins fired by magic potions and their eyes gleaming. Let the ritual begin. Each member of the group donned a mask of stolen darkness, and together, whilst music played loudly all around them, they fell into a dream. The Skull Garden opened up to them. The birth of Mama Lujo drew near.

## Cage, from his Private Notebooks

The car kept swaying from side to side, and the road would suddenly fill with fog and light as another vehicle passed by. I feared that some damage had been done to my body, to my mind. How I managed that drive back along the riverside I shall never know, but finally, the four towers of Zeno HQ sparkled above the waters of the lake. Here was my place of refuge. The building opened up to my touch, and I journeyed downwards, past the whispering security guards, along the silent corridors and stairways, a slave to all that troubled me; downwards, to where the old king lay suspended in his watery grave. I pressed an interface mask to my face, and then lowered myself down into the cold viscous fluid of the preservation tank.

## The Core of his Being

Here I speak, attend thee well. I, Francis Cage, have no shadow but my own, no heart but the one I have built myself. No love but the love I had to steal from my own father, at the long drawn out moment of his passing away. Subsequently, there is nothing more real to me than the realm of a mind forever caught in that moment where life falls silent, and death sings. Only here, in the arms of my father could I find any comfort; only here find any possible relief from the night's strange events. Here, within my father's skull, his thoughts held in abeyance from the final darkness. And even as your body wastes away, father, please allow your dreams to carry me home, these fragile trembling dreams in which I fall daily, nightly, completely, as now, as now...

## The Moon Pool

Cage walked through the forest. It was night. It was always night in this part of the Skull Garden, where the branches twined above the pathway blocked out the sky entirely. Only a few leaves dusted with yellow gave any evidence that a bright moon prevailed over this gloomy realm. Nocturnal creatures made their little chirruping sounds, whilst glowing fireflies flickered in the shadows. Cage walked on until he came to the clearing. He had been here before a number of times, on his private journeys. It was a secret place not listed on any of the company's official maps. The forest pool lay within its circle of trees, the waters dark and forbidding. As always, the moon's reflection seemed to be slowly melting at the pool's centre. Cage looked around. The forest murmured with noises, the black waters shimmered. He stared into the pool, where strangely shaped beings swam, barely visible. He had seen things here, emerging from the depths of the moon pool, that could never ever be released to the general public. This was the dark centre of his father's skull, the waters of the id.

## A Meeting in the Forest

There was a tingling sensation at the back of Cage's neck. He spun round to see a figure moving through the trees close at hand, and then another, further off. Their costumes were white, daubed with slogans.

He shouted out, 'Who's there? Who is it? Show yourself.' There was no reply, and yet other figures moved just beyond the margin of trees, he could not tell how many, and he shouted once more. The branches stirred in a faint breeze, the leaves glistened. Finally all was quiet and the figures could not be seen anymore, although Cage still had the eerie feeling of being watched, here, in this most private of places. Then he heard the song, the same saddened melody he had heard in the hotel room dream earlier. *Hey derry, down derry, hey derry derry, down derry.* Cage turned to face the moon pool. He was feeling faint and he dropped down onto his knees to stare into the water. His reflection trembled and then with a most exquisite pain he watched as a pale diaphanous form rose from the centre of his brow, slowly, slowly, until it detached itself entirely from his body. He looked up to see the strange luminous substance as it floated over the pool, taking on shape, clothing itself in flesh the same hue as the moon that shone above. It was an old, old woman of hideous appearance. Cage was transfixed by her skull-like face, by her withered flesh, her long straggly hair, by the strange folk song that issued from her lips. He reached out to her but the apparition moved over the centre of the pool where it descended, melting into the water, and disappearing below the surface, until only the moon's shimmering light remained there. Thus was Mama Lujo born, a virus of transformative magic.

## A Spell to Catch the Curious

Cage cried out. He pushed away, desperately, trying to escape the preservation tank. The wires that held his father's body in place now tangled around Cage's own legs, as though to drag him closer, to keep him tightly bound. He had to pull away violently, again, once more, until finally something came loose and he managed to scramble out onto the lip of the tank, and then up, onto his feet, tearing the interface mask from his face, drawing in what breath he could find. He burst through the doorway into the brightly lit corridors of Zeno, where a grim-faced security guard was loitering. Cage pushed him aside. He had to get free of this place. He needed air, cold clean air. Something was happening, he had the feeling he was caught up in some ritual, a cruel enchantment that worked its powers against him.

## Oh, What Can Ail Thee, Knight-at-Arms?

Later, he wandered alongside the Lake of Sighs. The studio towers loomed behind him, but he would not look that way, not yet. He was alone in the world. He felt scared. What had he released from his own head into the garden, into the moon pool? His mind was drifting free of itself, but just then some outside noise disturbed him. A car had stopped at the lakeside road, and a man approached across the banks of dried mud, a stranger. He wanted to help, asking what the matter was. Cage shook his head, making a dreadful sight all told, his lips red-bitten and sore, and his eyes filled with sorrow. Remnants of his mask speckled his face here and there, and he shivered with the traces of a chill, or a fever, the stranger could not tell which. It was a morning, the air cold, the grass thin and pale, and the birds flew silent in the skies.

*Part Three*

APPARITION PARK

*Shrine*

>JORGE LUIS BORGES<  WILLIAM BURROUGHS
LEWIS CARROLL
ANGELA CARTER  RAYMOND CHANDLER
RICHARD DAWKINS
PHILIP K DICK  DAPHNE DU MAURIER
ELEKTRA
DORIAN GRAY  BILLIE HOLIDAY
HARRY HOUDINI
ROBERT JOHNSON  REI KAWAKUBO
JACK KIRBY
KRAFTWERK  BARBARA KRUGER
ZELLA KYLE
BRUCE LEE  BENOIT MANDELBROT
CHICO MARX
GROUCHO MARX  HARPO MARX
ZEPPO MARX
ALAN MOORE  PAC-MAN
SYLVIA PLATH
JIM ROSE  CINDY SHERMAN
DIANA SPENCER
RUDOLPH VALENTINO  RACHEL WHITEREAD

## Prologue

Night falls softly on the Theatre of Creatures. The gate has been closed for an hour, and the few straggling visitors have long since departed. The silvered moon reflects a pale memory of light along the twisting, tree-lined pathways of the inner courtyard. The many bamboo enclosures stir with the shadows of their occupants. Transparent fish glide through limpid pools; the salamander sleeps soundly on a mirror's face. In the central pagoda the old man is playing host to his special guest, and the clacking sounds of mahjong tiles echo through the perfumed air. Otherwise, all is silent.

A small wire cage hangs suspended over the playing table. From its confines a toy scorpion made from polished chrome watches the game. His mechanised pincers press against the bars, his tail drips with a black liquid.

At the table, a voice is raised in protest. There is a sudden muffled report, a burst of flame. The creatures howl and cry in response. The mahjong characters fall to the ground. Petals drift down from an overhanging branch, and a thin wisp of smoke rises from the silencer fitted to the barrel of a pistol.

The moment passes.

And once again stillness envelops this hidden, contained world.

Now the winner of the game steps along the pathways of the labyrinth. Her movements are slow, halting, as she drags the body of the old man along the ground behind her. A dark wet trail is left on the earth behind them. But the killer is strong, and well trained, and makes a sure, relentless progress.

The various exhibits of the zoo are set out in a spiral formation. One cage holds the Möbius snake, whose long tangled body has no beginning, and no end. Another enclosure contains a milk-coloured tiger, a strange creature visible only for a few minutes every hour. Large glass jars are the home of myriad shiny-black spiders, famous for devouring themselves, even as they give birth to the next generation. The public has a curious appetite for such things.

The killer's tunic of green silk shimmers in the moonlight.

Eventually, deep inside the labyrinth, she finds an empty cage. First of all she hangs a silver medallion on one of the central struts, allowing it to turn slowly in the warm night air. Then she drags the corpse through the open doorway. There is the rich, hot smell of animal dung, which suits her purpose entirely, and it takes only a few minutes to arrange the old man into position, pulling at the heavy limbs.

Finally, the tableau is complete.

Using the trail of the victim's blood as her guide, the killer makes her way back through the maze to the wooden pagoda.

The scorpion's mechanical tail uncurls at the silent approach.

Exhibit A

*Hank Webb Investigates: The Case of the Haunted Mask*

*Shrine*

&gt;        &lt;        WILLIAM BURROUGHS
LEWIS CARROLL
ANGELA CARTER        RAYMOND CHANDLER
RICHARD DAWKINS
PHILIP K DICK        DAPHNE DU MAURIER
ELEKTRA
DORIAN GRAY        BILLIE HOLIDAY
HARRY HOUDINI
ROBERT JOHNSON        REI KAWAKUBO
JACK KIRBY
KRAFTWERK        BARBARA KRUGER
ZELLA KYLE
BRUCE LEE        BENOIT MANDELBROT
CHICO MARX
GROUCHO MARX        HARPO MARX
ZEPPO MARX
ALAN MOORE        PAC-MAN
SYLVIA PLATH
JIM ROSE        CINDY SHERMAN
**&gt;DIANA SPENCER&lt;**
RUDOLPH VALENTINO        RACHEL WHITEREAD

## Little Sanctuary

I remember that night. Music playing loud, and my startled face in some dirty broken mirror somewhere, a night club I think, with myself halfway drunk, reaching for the tablets that held the pain at bay, and that, taken too many at a time, would kill the pain completely, stone dead. What did I do? I cursed myself and the world I was living in, and spat in my own eye as per usual, and then managed to find my way outside, pushing through the crowds of that warm, humid city. Jesus, it gets worse every year, so many people wanting to lay down their souls for a piece of sweet salvation from Our Lady of the Fake Tan. The entire road leading down to the abbey was packed with cars, taxis, and people shouting and screaming, waving their souvenir commemorative roses in one hand, their little plastic flags in the other, tears streaming down their faces like this was some real live princess being carted through the streets. The gates of the abbey showed up on the huge viewing screens above the superstores. Rolling shots direct from inside the church itself brought glimpses of the lucky attendants, the rich and the famous, as they filed into the pews. The funeral re-enactment would take place in less than an hour, and everybody wanted a view of the body, either close at hand or from a distance, it did not matter. It's like the whole city was moving in one sweet and predetermined direction, and myself in another.

*That night when it all began. Yes, I remember...*

The lights moving across the distant river, the smell of incense in the air. Two lovely young characters trotted past me, one dressed in a wedding gown and a tiara, sporting a Jackie Molasses mask, and the other dragged up in late period Dyana, with the shoulder pads and the big blonde hair. The skin on her face was glowing, her eyes bright with sexual mischief. I used to do Charisma myself, back in the day. I know the sensation, as the outrageous surge of celebrity courses through the body.

'Where's your disguise, honey?'

'Oh, you look lonely. Why don't you come along with us?'

'The princess welcomes all to her bosom.'

I stumbled away, into the shadows. Their laughter followed me on the slow moving breeze. 'Die young, baby. Leave a beautiful mask!' Horns and drums sounded from the pleasure barges on the River Isis.

Far above, the compact news helicopters clattered in the purple sky. Their illuminated logos dazzled like sacred icons.

## Albion Cross

A ravenous crowd had me in its grip, and we moved as one mass, buckling under pressure from the narrow back streets until we suddenly found ourselves caught in a crosscurrent of other worshippers, all of whom were trying desperately to get closer to the main road. I could hardly breathe for the closeness of humanity around me, held tight, sweating, and yet uncaring about where I went or how I got there. And then a great push forward brought our little group victory, and I found myself squashed up against a lamp post. A deep ominous chanting rose up from the mobile congregation as the funeral car hove into view along the road. Here, the vehicle paused for people to gaze upon the sight in wonder; paying homage, taking photographs.

I was taller than those around me, and so could see directly into the open-top black limousine, to where the glass coffin lay secured. Inside, resting on a bed of white satin was the cult member chosen to be the princess for this year's event. It was a privilege beyond measure, I imagine, for one who truly believed. Trouble was, the anointed one was a boy barely out of his teens, and he couldn't contain himself. He leaned up from his pretended death to wave at the crowd. His face was shimmering with the charismatic effect, as the drug held his own features at bay, and gave him those of Princess Dyana herself, in the bloom of her finest years. The boy giggled at the crowd, who cheered on his performance by scattering the heads of fresh-cut flowers, paper rosettes and scarlet ribbons around the vehicle.

The rich, invasive smell of ersatz celebrity reached me from all directions. Everybody had purchased, borrowed or stolen a famous face for the evening: Oskar Wilding, Dave Bohee, Klaudia Chiffon, Toopak Shakiir, Tom Krooz, Lora Crufts. All were there, and many more. Holding back the crowds were big men wearing fluorescent flak jackets. They looked tired, middle-aged, used-up, with the taste of ex-cop around them. I even recognised one of them from the old days of the force, but I turned my face away from his glazed stare.

There were some things I didn't need reminding of.

## Pilgrim's Steps

In the years when I used to have an office, with a proper phone and an answering service and all of that, written on the glass door in neat gold leaf were these words: *Hank Webb, Private Investigator*. My business card read, 'No job too small, no trouble too dirty'. I was married, more or less happily, with a kid on the way, and sufficient work coming in to keep the cold grey flea-bitten wolf from the fridge. At the time it seemed to be just enough of a life to keep on hoping for something better; now, looking back, it feels like I was already in paradise. I just didn't know it.

And this one particular night of which I speak, the purple coloured dusk of the Fifteenth Annual Last Rites and Burial Performance of our Most Illustrious Lady of Landmines and Yoga, this was the night I learned that I hadn't even started falling yet, not properly.

It was a long, long way down.

## Old Park Corner

The funeral car moved on, and I did my best to follow it. It wasn't that I had even an ounce of belief in me, for anything real or unreal, just that I had to keep moving. Any direction would do. Otherwise, the shadows moved in.

The cortège swung east. There was a cheer as it slowed down to make the turn. Young half-dressed girls rushed out from the park to touch the hearse as it passed, their faces smeared with green vegetable dye. Boys wearing velvet codpieces strutted up and down beneath the trees, making obscene gestures. The helicopters hung lower now, their spotlights picking out the action. There was a wildness in the air, as though everything might erupt into violence at any moment. My old cop instincts had been switched on.

*Time to shut it down, kids. Time to shut everything down.*

Jessica used to like walking in Old Park. It was close to where she lived, when I first got to know her, and we often used to meet by the boating pond...

Damn it. I pulled my coat around me. The night was still warm, but I didn't feel it. I didn't feel a thing.

On the edge of the park, beyond the dark trees, the

international hotels stood clustered like giant glass monoliths. Their sides were brightly lit with images of the young man chosen to be this year's Princess of Designer Heartache. He was selling toothpaste and credit cards.

## Lancaster Arch

The funeral car circled round and round a traffic island. It was the final part of the pageant. It seemed that it might carry on circling all night long, before the limousine broke free from its self-enclosed route, and headed down towards the abbey.

I moved across the sculpted lawns of the island. People had set up canvas tents, makeshift dwellings, little huts of cardboard. They lay on the grass, tired and spent, amidst the scattered souvenir pamphlets and empty beer cans. Beneath the massive, two-hundred year old stone arch a sound system had been set up; its heavy pumping basslines set the statues of ancient military heroes vibrating on their plinths.

The police would move in tomorrow morning with their shields and dogs and sirens. A few days or weeks later, when they got round to it, the council would send out the clean-up wagons. But for now, this place belonged to the Dyana cult. They were burning effigies of kings, ministers and paparazzi photographers. The flames danced in the air. I sat down on the grass and took a swig from my bottle. The rough grain alcohol started to work its magic, but then Jessica's face popped into my mind. I closed my eyes, but the face remained in my sight, as beautiful as it ever was, like a flower opening its petals once more to the world.

My phone went off. I could just about make out the caller's name through my blurred vision. It was Miguel.

'Yeah? What is it?'

'Senor Webb, I need your help.'

I pressed the cut-off button.

*Shrine*

&gt;        &lt;       WILLIAM BURROUGHS
LEWIS CARROLL
ANGELA CARTER     &gt;**RAYMOND CHANDLER**&lt;
RICHARD DAWKINS
PHILIP K DICK      DAPHNE DU MAURIER
ELEKTRA
DORIAN GRAY      BILLIE HOLIDAY
HARRY HOUDINI
ROBERT JOHNSON      REI KAWAKUBO
JACK KIRBY
KRAFTWERK      BARBARA KRUGER
ZELLA KYLE
BRUCE LEE      BENOIT MANDELBROT
CHICO MARX
GROUCHO MARX      HARPO MARX
ZEPPO MARX
ALAN MOORE      PAC-MAN
SYLVIA PLATH
JIM ROSE      CINDY SHERMAN
&gt;           &lt;
RUDOLPH VALENTINO      RACHEL WHITEREAD

Moving south, away from the centre. I made the turning at exit 32. Dust clouds for a mile or so, and then the hidden track for *Los Logos*. The shantytown. Border zone. A cloud of heat shimmered along the desert's edge.

This was early the next morning. I'd spent the night wandering the streets of Lujo, getting lost, and finally waking up on the embankment where a gang of drunks played dice and swapped stories of when they were all in clover. That was enough. Miguel's voice kept coming back to me. He'd sounded desperate, in pain. Not like him. And so I'd headed back to where I'd parked the car. It took me an hour to find the thing.

When I looked in the rear-view, there was a bruise on my face that I could not remember receiving.

On the edge of the village a young boy worked the handle of a water pump, collecting a few drops of liquid in a metal bowl. He looked up at me as I drove past. His head was covered in a cloth beaded with electrodes, and he brought up a hand to shield his eyes from the sudden light of the sun, which, although barely seen above the horizon, already seemed to be melting the sky. The buildings along the narrow main street were made from wooden billboard panels, each one coloured with stolen images: Shadow Blossom polish, Levi Stone's Essence of Sleep, Haversham's Department Store. Clothes lines stretched across the little side streets were pegged with coloured photographs. Children were playing in the dust, and old timers lounged in the shade of a pickup truck. The only sound came from the darkness of one of the huts, a woman's voice singing a ballad of lost love. Sad, broken, lonely.

I parked the car, then walked the old track that led to the tiny church. I was soaked in sweat already. A group of teenagers squatted at the doorway to the white, adobe building. They were drawing patterns in the dust with brightly coloured sticks. One of them consulted a worn-out laptop. As I passed by they stopped their activity and watched me. Shotguns stood propped against the wall. Miguel was waiting for me behind the church, in the small graveyard. He was sitting on a folding stool in front of the simple wooden cross of his mother's grave. I had often seen him here, over the years. His fingers worked at the keys of a bandoneon. It was the same melody I had heard the woman singing, but this time with the lilting rhythm of a slow tango. He nodded, a bare acknowledgement.

'Senor Webb.'
'Miguel...'
'Come.'

We walked further into the desert, to the small grove of palms surrounding the old village well. It was made of orange brick and covered with a large square of canvas sheeting supported on metal struts. Here the desert dwellers had first pitched their tents, later forming a loose network of workshops and laboratories. I could hear the dull, rhythmic sound of a cheap electrical generator coming from within the palm leaves. Miguel had told me a little about this place, and their work here: illegal image raids, the making of cheap copies of Zeenies and other artificial beings, the turning out of special creatures with perverse or illegal attributes.

Only once had I looked into the well. The shaft was not too deep. It was filled with the sparkle of some strange liquid, not water, but something darker, redder, its surface bright with shoals of glowing lights, images, whispered voices. Miguel called it a portal into a world of fantasies, a hacked doorway direct to the Zeno dreamspace. This was how the refugees made their living.

We entered a valley further south, and came suddenly upon the Theatre of Creatures. It was built under the sagging concrete belly of a long abandoned section of elevated motorway. The truncated end of the flyover jutted into the air just above the new oasis, where a few of the elders had cultivated a bizarre world filled with lush fabulous plants, mutated fruits and weird propagated animals. It had been a long while since my last visit, and the place had grown even more tropical since then, more overpowering. The tribe admitted a few tourists to the theatre each day, but in truth, it was more of a dumping ground for their failed experiments.

Miguel led me towards the wooden pagoda. There were dark splashes on the decking, and tiny mahjong playing pieces lay scattered around. I bent down to examine the bloodstains.

'What's happened?'

Miguel shook his head. 'My father was always too trusting...'

I looked up at him, to see that his face was set tight. He pointed to a small empty cage suspended above the table, its bars snapped open. 'This is the only thing missing. It contained one of my father's latest creations.' He went on to speak of a robotic chrome scorpion.

His father had made it in his workshop, after seeing a strange vision in the old well.

'Miguel. Please tell me. Where is your father?'

Without a word he turned and I followed him deeper into the maze. The trembling beasts dozed in their cages, weary from the heat. The older creatures were made from cheap bootleg flesh, and weren't much to look at. But the later exhibits were much more lifelike, with brightly moving eyes and perfectly formed talons. I remember Miguel's father showing me the birth of one of these animals, years back; a pattern of fused dots on an old Macintosh, some pulpy matter in a test-tube, a series of ritual markings in the sand. From such beginnings the magic was created.

Miguel was moving more quickly now. All the pathways seemed to twist back upon themselves, close in, and then branch out in new directions. I was lost. I kept expecting to meet myself around the next corner. But finally we came to a cage set apart from the others, half-hidden by a screen of bamboo shoots. The first thing I noticed was the smell, of rotting food and bodily waste. Dazzling blue and green flies buzzed in the air. Miguel directed me to follow him around the screen.

At first I could hardly make out what I was looking at. The cage was so placed that its interior was always cast in shadow. Something glinted in there, hanging down from the roof beams. It was silver coloured and diamond shaped, its surface polished to a mirrored brightness. It seemed to be pointing directly at the figure that lay below, slumped on the floor of the cage. I stepped a little closer to the bars.

'I found him like this last night,' Miguel said.

It was his father. A small puncture wound could be made out in the old man's forehead. His jacket was soiled, and his trousers were pulled down round his ankles. He lay there surrounded by lumps of animal shit and pools of half dried urine. It made a terrible sight.

'I haven't touched anything. Not yet.'

'Miguel, this is a police matter.'

'No. We can't have that. I want...' Miguel looked me in the eyes. 'I need your help, Senor Webb.' He held the cage door open for me. 'Please...'

I took a deep breath before stepping inside. The stench was atrocious. Of course I'd seen my share of things in the force. But it had been a while now and this was different somehow. Something wasn't quite right. I reached out for the hanging diamond. It was a medallion of some kind, encrusted with cheap jewels spelling out the letters EP. And then it struck me. The whole scene, down to the last globule of excrement, looked to be have been carefully arranged.

I gazed down at Miguel's father. His cold eyes were still open, staring ahead with a filmy blank vision. I had to touch the body, make a search, but just as I was bending down I thought I heard a sound, a songlike refrain. Something was happening. Tiny, faraway lights were flashing inside the cage and the old man's face was shivering with static. And suddenly, like the crackle of a ghost, there was the brief glimpse of another face, a charismatic mask, superimposed over the dead man's features. It was like watching an old film, only to have some stray signal keep cutting in, a sudden switch of channels.

Finally, the apparition revealed itself fully.

It was the face of a handsome young man, with snarling lips, hooded eyes and thick black hair piled high over his brow. I recognised the look, of course, in fact I'd seen a good few people wearing the same mask last night. Elvideo Prez. The world famous pop star. The few notes of the disembodied song grew louder, the vocalist desiring that he be loved, both tenderly and truly, and forever. I couldn't help but imagine that the corpse itself was singing.

I backed out of the cage. Miguel had said nothing during all this, and I could only assume that he had already witnessed the mask effect during the night. 'Do you see now, Senor,' he asked. 'Why I have asked you here?'

'I don't understand,' I answered. 'Charisma only lasts for a few hours, at the most, and certainly, it has no effect after... after the...'

'After the death of the body? No, Senor Webb. This is something different, I think.' His expression seemed cold, but his facial muscles twitched like a half broken mechanism. 'We have so many enemies,' he continued, 'both as a people, and for the nature of our work. And my father had certain dealings of his own. Well, there are many possibilities.'

I turned back to the cage where the old man's face had once again taken its rightful possession.

'Miguel, you know, I don't do this anymore.'

He was silent for a while. Then he spoke without looking at me.

'My friend. I remember when you had that trouble... after your wife was murdered.'

*Jessica...*

'I helped you then, did I not, Senor Webb?'

Over the years, I'd been dreading this moment; but there are some debts that must always be paid.

'You must find my father's murderer, Senor. I will take over from there. That's all I ask.'

I nodded. And we both listened in silence as the last mournful notes of the song drifted away on the slow night air.

*Shrine*

>   <   WILLIAM BURROUGHS
LEWIS CARROLL
ANGELA CARTER   >   <
RICHARD DAWKINS
PHILIP K DICK   DAPHNE DU MAURIER
ELEKTRA
DORIAN GRAY   BILLIE HOLIDAY
HARRY HOUDINI
ROBERT JOHNSON   REI KAWAKUBO
JACK KIRBY
KRAFTWERK   BARBARA KRUGER
ZELLA KYLE
BRUCE LEE   BENOIT MANDELBROT
CHICO MARX
GROUCHO MARX   HARPO MARX
ZEPPO MARX
ALAN MOORE   PAC-MAN
SYLVIA PLATH
>JIM ROSE<   CINDY SHERMAN
>   <
RUDOLPH VALENTINO   RACHEL WHITEREAD

The Half Human Zone was the area to the east of the river where the specialist fetish merchants gathered. I knew it well from my days as a cop. The wet muddy ground, the constant danger of floods from the places where the old embankment had broken down, the smell of fish and candy floss. It was deemed a place of illicit amusement for the office workers from Lujo's financial district. They came here in the evenings and the holidays. And sometimes they never left.

The Zone was a place where you could rent a clean gun by the hour and a warm body by the minute. It's where people came to fuck things, kill things, and lose things. It's where anything could happen, or be made to happen. For a price. And the price wasn't always monetary.

I walked down the winding riverside street as the sunlight slipped away into dusk. I'd spent the last few hours asking around the city, looking for clues, with no luck. Now the night crept forward, and the nocturnals were coming out to play. I had to keep working, for Miguel's sake. And for my own sake.

There were coloured lanterns hanging from the eaves of the little shacks and kiosks. I stopped for a refill at one of the open-air powder dens. The girl child behind the counter poured me an ounce of red. She had one hand slightly larger than the other, the skin patched and shredded, exposing the cogs and springs beneath. There was a crackle of sulphurous flame from the taper in her fingers.

The girl smiled. 'Something stronger, sir? Real tobacco? Or perhaps a trickboy?'

I shook my head. I used to want to save these people from themselves, when I first started out in the vice squad. After a year or so I just wanted to stop them from infecting the rest of the city with their messed-up craziness. Finally, I was content to make money off them, like most of the other badge carriers, cutting deals with the sex traders and the drug smugglers, the owners of the animal thrill clubs and the spice parlours. By then, I just wanted to save myself. Myself and Jessica.

These days, I was admitted to the Zone as a fellow citizen and freak. One more of the lost.

Clouds of stray powder stung my eyes as I scattered a few coins on the counter. These were quickly scooped up by the girl. 'I'm looking for Johnny Limbo,' I said, and she pointed me in the direction of the baiting dens. I shrugged. It was as good a place as any to go, and I was getting tired. Too many hours sitting in the same chair, in the same shadowed corner of a rented room had left me out of shape, and almost out of life.

In a sense, then, I was enjoying this job. The cold sharp cop tingle came back to me as I wandered through the crowds that gathered around the wooden amphitheatre. Sure enough, the Limbo Man was hanging around outside with his latest specimens of hermaphroditic beauty. There was a bandage wrapped round his head and ligatures tied round his arms and legs. His naked chest was covered in patches of fine red hair, the result of some botched experiment. He spotted me coming and tried to get away, but was hemmed in by the crowds. So he tried to front it instead.

'Detective Webb, where have you been? It's been a while.' His eyes darted everywhere and his grin was fixed like a slash job. Fewer teeth than I remembered.

'I'm off the force, Johnny. As you know.'

I ground my cigarette out underfoot.

'Sure, sure. I heard that.'

I told him what I was looking for.

'Mechanical scorpions and suchlike?' he replied. 'No, man. Haven't seen anything like that. I'll keep an eye out.'

I nodded, as I sprinkled some of the red powder into a cigarette paper. 'Good. You do that.'

There was a roar from inside the amphitheatre. I wondered if Harry Hunks was still performing. He used to be able to throw the dogs and then go on to parry a human fencer with his paws. I'd won a pile of money on that old black bear in my time.

'Does Ursula know it was you who stole her best girlboy?'

'Yeah,' Johnny said, edgily. 'She knows that. Everybody knows that.'

'Uh huh.' I rolled the paper, licked the edge and sealed it. 'Does she know what you did to her best girlboy?'

Johnny's grin was now so wide it threatened to split his face wide open. 'No, she don't know that.' His lips accepted the offered roll-up.

'Well, she doesn't have to, does she?' I lit the joint for him. 'Just so long as you tell me when you see something.'

The blue smoke rose from Johnny's mouth. 'Sure thing, boss.'

And just like that, I was back in the game. Like I'd never been away. And so it went for the rest of the night, with me hitting up all the people I used to know, the informants and petty criminals, the prostitutes and the dancers. Pulling in favours, twisting arms, shelling out cash where necessary. I got stories back. There was one about a mechanical male prostitute with painted biceps and lips. Another about a fighting cock with a flaming comb above its head, programmed with the golem code of a serial killer. Stories of clockwork devils with spiked tails and performing mannequins made of iron and bunched rags.

It all started to come together in Pressburger Lane.

'They use mechanical creatures in the puppet show,' I was told by Larry the Facebreaker.

'Artificial scorpions? The one I heard about was iron, not chrome,' said Eleanor the Puppet Mistress. 'A great big rusty thing, dripping this black liquid from its sting. Smelt dreadful, let me tell you.'

'It was bought by Crazy Mo Smoke,' said Charlie Two Aces. 'He features it in his act. See for yourself.'

The poster on the alley wall was green with a red patterned border. It showed a semi-naked man suspended from an iron gallows by wires hooked into his chest. The skin stretched like rubber. And sure enough, beneath the soles of the performer's feet was a robotic scorpion, its fierce iron tail held aloft.

Crazy Mo Smoke was playing that night at the Magwitch Cabaret Club.

*Shrine*

\>          <          WILLIAM BURROUGHS
LEWIS CARROLL
ANGELA CARTER          >                    <
RICHARD DAWKINS
PHILIP K DICK     DAPHNE DU MAURIER
ELEKTRA
DORIAN GRAY     BILLIE HOLIDAY
**>HARRY HOUDINI<**
ROBERT JOHNSON     REI KAWAKUBO
JACK KIRBY
KRAFTWERK     BARBARA KRUGER
ZELLA KYLE
BRUCE LEE     BENOIT MANDELBROT
CHICO MARX
GROUCHO MARX     HARPO MARX
ZEPPO MARX
ALAN MOORE     PAC-MAN
SYLVIA PLATH
\>          <     CINDY SHERMAN
     \>               <
RUDOLPH VALENTINO     RACHEL WHITEREAD

There was a lone police officer in the foyer of the club, a young nervous looking guy with a freshly pressed shirt. He was doing his best to direct the white-faced theatre goers out on to the street. The night air stank of bootleg alcohol. I drifted around and caught resentful mutterings of a magician's trick going wrong that night. Some of the clientele were saying they wanted their money back.

I walked to the back of the building. Stage entrance. There was a policeman on the door, whilst the various actors, dancers and the theatre staff were standing around in the cobbled yard. People were chatting about what had happened, or might have happened. They were waiting for the main detective force to turn up, then they would all be questioned. It was exciting. A cross-dressing receptionist started to laugh, her voice cutting through the hubbub. She was standing next to a bouncer, who wore a shiny black suit. Nearby was an older guy with a twisted pony-tail. His long thin hands were moving vigorously.

'How's it going, Sal?' I knew the bouncer. He was kicked off the force about the same time as me.

'Like shit.' That's Sal being friendly.

'What happened?'

Sal gestured in the direction of the older man. 'Meet the stage manager.' This character was dressed in a frayed brown leather jacket decorated with chunky silver studs. He'd got the whole story, or at least his version of it, and was only too ready to dole it out.

As stories go, it was pretty strange. Turned out that Crazy Mo Smoke was really nothing more than an old street performer, a ball and cups man. He used to ply his trade on Old Park Corner, sitting at a little card table, pulling in the tourists. He moved the cups with arthritic fingers, but was still skilful enough to fool the eye. No one ever guessed which cup the ball was hiding under.

He must've been pushing fifty-five, sixty maybe, and his main topic of conversation had always been the life and times of Harry Hoodoo, the greatest ever escapologist. Crazy Mo used to sigh deeply when he told these stories, while pulling in the coins and occasionally the used notes. He was always clean shaven, but the skin hung in loose folds now. A few wisps of white hair clung to his scalp, and his eyes watered constantly. He always wore a check sports jacket, with a red carnation pinned in the buttonhole.

And then one night, it all changed. Crazy Mo started to

perform the old escape tricks. They'd always been popular but no one had ever done them as well as the Great Hoodoo, and that had been a generation before. No one knew the old skills anymore. Except that suddenly, Crazy Mo did. He could get out of handcuffs, straitjackets, ropes. He could escape from his bonds whether suspended upside down over fire or immersed in a sealed tank of water. He started this second stage of his career in tiny back-room clubs, playing to drunks and the terminally lonely, but word soon got out. This was something special, like the Great Hoodoo had come back from the grave. Crazy Mo was doing new stuff too, with tasers and cattle prods. And he never used to perform without his lucky mascot. This was a weird looking scorpion, made out of iron. Usually, it would be perched on a foldout card table, its jointed tail making a terrible creaking noise that could be heard from the back stalls.

Before long, Crazy Mo was on the late night bill at the Magwitch Club. The posters showed a young man. By all accounts, Crazy Mo was much rejuvenated by achieving success so late in his career. The skin was smoother and ruddier now. The jackets hung well from his frame, the buttonhole carnation was exchanged for a rose, cut fresh every day. His hair thickened and darkened and there was a mischievous glint in his eye. People complimented him on his new-found youth. One or two mentioned an odd resemblance to the Great Hoodoo Man himself. Mo just laughed at such comments. And pretty soon, the stunts turned nasty, and even more dangerous.

Here, the stage manager's hands made animated chopping motions as he brought the story bang up to date. There'd been a capacity crowd for this evening's performance. Crazy Mo had just finished his climactic electric chair stunt and was taking his bows. His face shone with pleasure. The little iron scorpion danced on the table.

Time for the encore. The Amazing Death-Defying Bullet Caught in the Teeth Illusion. Mo invited an audience member up on stage. A woman duly rose. The stage manager hadn't seen her himself, but he'd talked to a few members of the audience. Seems the woman had dark hair and was wearing a green tunic dress. Nobody could bring her face to mind. In fact, people could remember nothing much about her at all. Except that she was only too keen to get in on the act.

The stage manager was reaching the climax of his story, but I didn't need to hear the rest. The murder squad wagons would turn up soon. I had to move quickly. I slipped Sal a five spot, and he walked over to the middle-aged officer on the door, asking him for a light, and chatting a while about what it was like back in the days.

I slipped inside the theatre unseen.

The empty corridors echoed to my steps as I made my way to the wings, and out onto the stage. There was just this one lanky uniformed kid standing over the corpse. I walked over, hitching up my trousers, just the way I did when I was Detective Sergeant. I put on my gruffest voice.

'Have we found the iron scorpion yet?'

'What?' The young officer looked bewildered.

I pointed to the bare wooden table resting on stage. 'It's gone missing.'

'Sir?'

'Go find it!'

The novice cop disappeared. I crouched down to examine the body of Crazy Mo Smoke. He'd been shot once in the head, narrow gauge. Just like Miguel's father. But his clothing hadn't been disturbed. He was wearing the black leather trousers and open neck white shirt that belonged to his stage act. His face however was the face of an aging man, bearing no traces of the handsome young features described in the story. There was a tattoo of a clown on his bare chest, a grotesque figure with huge blind eyes. I narrowed my vision and looked at the dead man's bloodied head sideways. There were only a few lines of flickering static. Whichever mask the old man had been using, it had long since been assimilated.

Then I noticed something. Being careful not to touch anything I bent down nearer to the magician's face. There was something in his mouth, among the dried saliva and the blood. It looked like a small piece of cloth. I pulled out my handkerchief and managed to get the material free.

Green silk.

I rolled the thread between my fingers.

I left the way I came in. There were cop sirens sounding, and the crowd was suitably excited. Nobody paid me any attention.

The stage manager had drawn quite an audience by now. He'd got to the end of his story for the second or third time. 'The strange thing is, the original Hoodoo Man also died because of a trick going wrong,' he said, hands fluttering wildly. 'Yeah, he asked somebody to punch him in the stomach. Said he could withstand any blow. Just goes to show, doesn't it, even the best get it arse over backwards. Now, regarding Crazy Mo, well, there's such a thing as taking imitation too far!'

There are a few laughs from the gathered throng.

Some thoughts troubled me, strange connections. One: like the man said, the famous Harry Hoodoo caught the big zero when a trick went bad. Now here was Crazy Mo meeting a similar end. Two: singer Elvideo Prez expired on the can, alone, after devouring too many cheeseburgers and diet pills, his body desperately trying to evacuate the waste. And Miguel's father was dumped in shit, after he was killed, his trousers pulled down from the waist. And from both scenes a mechanical scorpion had gone missing.

What was this? Robotic arthropods? Staged ritual deaths? Look-alike killings?

This case was entering weird territory. I didn't like it.

*Shrine*

>         <        WILLIAM BURROUGHS
          LEWIS CARROLL
ANGELA CARTER      >                    <
          RICHARD DAWKINS
   PHILIP K DICK      DAPHNE DU MAURIER
               ELEKTRA
     DORIAN GRAY        BILLIE HOLIDAY
              >          <
   ROBERT JOHNSON      >REI KAWAKUBO<
               JACK KIRBY
       KRAFTWERK      BARBARA KRUGER
               ZELLA KYLE
     BRUCE LEE      BENOIT MANDELBROT
               CHICO MARX
       GROUCHO MARX      HARPO MARX
               ZEPPO MARX
         ALAN MOORE      PAC-MAN
               SYLVIA PLATH
      >          <      CINDY SHERMAN
              >              <
   RUDOLPH VALENTINO      RACHEL WHITEREAD

Back in the years I'm recalling, when people wanted to find out secrets they either employed a Data Dandy or consulted the Oracle. Trouble was, the Dandies came with human baggage of their own, and the Oracle network had long been taken over by commercial interests, severely curtailing the information on offer. Then again, a cop could walk into the forensics lab and sit around chatting until the results came through. I didn't have that option any more. But there were still ways of finding out what you wanted, if you didn't mind breaking a few laws.

So the next evening found me heading out to the Old Marketplace, in Lujo's north-eastern sector. The day's trading was over and the canvas wraps had been pulled down over the stalls. The large square was dimly lit and silent, but I could see a gang of teenagers clustered near a booth, beneath the one good street lamp. They were showing off their new masks, bad copies of the Famous Criminals line knocked up from street code. The youths fell quiet as I approached, until I asked for access to the Data Dog booth. One of them sniffed, stamped his feet. 'What have you got?' he asked, his features imperfectly lit with Al Kaponi's likeness. I showed them the roll of cloth, the little silver tools inside, the vial of liquid and the canister of smoke. There's nothing that gets a young data-punk going like evidence of superior knowledge, and they let me through easily, their pixellated lips salivating.

The booth stank of piss and vomit even with the door jammed open. Furthermore, the machine's eyes were tightly closed, and the face on the viewing screen was scarred and dirty. The thing looked to be sleeping. Or dead. Meanwhile, the kids outside were pressing their masks against the glass, watching me at work, hoping to catch some method. *How does it go now? Been so long, so very, very long.* Easy does it. Reach down beneath the Data Dog's throat, hold the two wires together, the yellow and the blue, spray the mouth with smoke, hit the needle to the socket, run the blade down the edge of the chamber, count to ten, and pray. Okay, so here we go. *Sparks between the fingers. Hold tight against the pain of the heat. And contact!* The machine's eyes snapped open and the voice box was activated: 'Thank you for consulting the Data Dog. What is it you seek?' The youths cheered and banged on the glass at the sound of the croaky, robotic intonation, but what the hell, the thing was up and running, for a while at least. So I fed the few strands of green silk into the machine's open maw. The lights on the screen flickered as it chewed over the offering, scanning, searching, evaluating. Until at last the face on the screen lit up with expert knowledge. I asked it for the breakdown.

'This is a very fine silk. Expensive. Three-ply, from the Ling-Shi silk farms in the Eastern Isles. The material is weighted with trace elements of iron, to aid the conduction of heat.'

'Anything else?'

'This material is used almost exclusively by the celebrated fashion designer, Wim Shimosako. She's famous for her black kimonos.'

'Black?'

'Shimosako occasionally favours stronger colours. But only for very limited collections. The green dye from the thread indicates this is from the Winter Flower kimono, a rare edition. Only five such dresses were ever purchased in Lujo.'

So few. I was rolling double sixes, no trouble.

The Data Dog booth conjured up a picture of the kimono. It was one of those fancy avant-garde affairs: one sleeve longer than the other, the whole thing out of kilter, with hidden folds and artificial rips in the cloth. The flower print, I noticed, was on the inside.

'Yeah, I get it. The street look for rich folks.'

'Very good. Do you wish to see the buyers of these five designer kimonos?'

'Hit me.'

Now the screen flickered with numerous views of the city's street, all in real time, each shaky roving shot taken from low down, just a few feet above street level.

And along these same streets at various parts of the city bounded a scattered pack of real-life hounds, prowling, running, leaping, sniffing, snuffling. I'd seen them myself at times on my travels, these data dogs, as they went about their tracking duties. Each animal had a small camera attached to its forehead; with these they captured the views in front of them, and transmitted them to the screens in the booth. By this method, the City of Lujo was revealed in all its sinister neon-lit variety.

But I was getting impatient already. I needed results.

I tapped at the controls.

The name of each dog was shown on the screen as the view

switched from camera to camera: Whirlwind, Hunter, White Spot, She Wolf, Black Foot, Tigress, Soot. And so on. But no results were shown and then the screen went suddenly dark. I slammed my fist against the panel. No use. I was forced to feed in more money, to make the screen light up again, to set the data dogs running once more.

At last, the booth flashed up idents for me. But the rollout was starting to crackle and jag; my splice job was coming unstuck. So I kept my eyes open, jumping from image to image. The first four owners of the green designer kimono came into view, each one tracked down by a different data hound.

*First...*

Cindy Smithers. One-time debutante, part-time weathergirl and full-time party animal. Hooked on reality TV; being on it, that is. The dog flashed me footage of the woman dipping her hand in the water of a toilet bowl, in the piss, in the shit, to grab a few tokens. Like the voiceover says, she was game for a laugh. And out of the equation. Cindy had been locked in the House of One Thousand Eyes for the last six months. The data dog called Hunter barked at the sealed gates of the house, desperate to reach her target.

*Next...*

Jodi Bartholomew. Ex-catwalk model, failed pop singer, wannabe conceptual artist. At the moment she was under the knife in a plastic surgery clinic. The booth screen gave me the close-up as a delicate pair of wings were being attached to her shoulder-blades. The gloved hands of the surgeon shook with the Live TV terrors. It's what they called extreme makeover. A five hour operation, so almost definitely another bust. Tigress howled along the corridors of the private hospital.

*Number three...*

Danni Mulligan. Ex-swimsuit model, abstract glamour queen and drugged-up rock chick. She was having sex with her heavily tattooed boyfriend in a motel room. Leaked video streaming. Live. Or a good replica thereof. She kept checking herself on camera and adjusting the heft of her breasts. Hubby was shown on a box insert, grimacing. A scandal in the (carefully prearranged) making. Whirlwind sat at the foot of the bed, eyeing the action. Danni was even wearing the green kimono. A possible suspect. I would have to look into this one.

*Four...*
    Lillian Garland. Bit-part soap player, game show regular, professional transvestite. And this was tabloid news, just breaking. Darling Lili paparazzi-snapped outside the Meat Beat Club minutes before, punching and kicking a younger ladyboy who'd stepped on her toes. Time-coded photos of the catfight. She Wolf prowled nearby, taking her shots through the legs of the assembled onlookers. Another maybe. But unlikely.
    'Okay. Let me see number five.'
    The screen fluttered with interference and the booth's voice said, 'I'm sorry, enquirer.'
    'What's up?'
    'The information's unavailable.'
    'Why? What's the problem?'
    'Information about purchaser five is being held back from me.'
    I poured the booth some more decoder juice. No good. I sprayed the tongue with smoke, hoping to burn some new code. Nothing. Finally, I had to delve deep. And this really got the punks outside yelping. The machine damn near died on me in the process, but what the hell, it came up stronger in the end, rising from its own shadow like the moon through fog. Hey. It's a little trick I picked up from an old informer friend of mine. Best kept secret. And now the Data Dog mechanism grunted a couple of times, and then sighed with pleasure. Then it sent the hound called White Spot racing off down unlit back streets, through gaps in wire fences, into NO-GO zones, tunneling through a culvert. That was one fierce, inquisitive hound, and it didn't take long to get a result.
    'There's a trail of fake scent paths, all wiped clean one after the other. But I've managed to retrieve a few details on the last identity. Any good for you?'
    'Let's see it.'
    The screen filled with a fuzzy picture of a woman's shape. She turned to face the approaching dogcam. Her face came into view.
    'The owner's name is...'
    Gone. Blackout. I must've fainted or something because it felt as though I was suddenly coming awake from a faraway sleep, banging against the booth wall, setting the kids outside screaming and laughing. Christ. I grabbed hold of the booth's controls.

'What? What did you call her?'

'Jessica Webb. That's her ID.'

'No. No, that's... that's a mistake.'

'Those are your results, sir. Would you like a freeze-frame?'

It was all some terrible coincidence, that was all. Or a mistake. A glitch in the system. But now the Data Dog's screen revealed the woman's face clearly.

'This is real time?' I asked.

'Right this moment, no delay.'

Noises, tapping sounds. The data junkies were gesturing at the screen, making rude comments. All a blur, so much noise. Minutes later I was standing beneath the street lamp. The kids had taken over the booth, fighting over my roll of hacking tools. I looked down at my shaking hands. I'd torn a print-out of the photograph from the booth's mouth. There she was in close-up. My suspect. The blonde hair much shorter than it used to be, the soft white skin, the shadows round the eyes. All of it registered in rich, industrial-strength colours. There was a flaw in the grain of the image. Or was it the tiny scar I knew and loved so well, just below the bottom lip, giving the mouth a lopsided pout?

It was her. My wife. Jessica. Caught live on camera some twelve months after I'd seen her dead body at the canal side, still drenched from the dirty water, the terrible knife wound clearly visible in her flesh as the other detectives clustered around her and the cameras flashed and the helicopters roared overhead.

# Exhibit B

*Game Shadow: The Sting of the Scorpion*

*Shrine*

\>            <        WILLIAM BURROUGHS
                LEWIS CARROLL
ANGELA CARTER        >                    <
                RICHARD DAWKINS
    PHILIP K DICK        DAPHNE DU MAURIER
                **>ELEKTRA<**
        DORIAN GRAY        BILLIE HOLIDAY
            >                <
ROBERT JOHNSON        >                <
                JACK KIRBY
        KRAFTWERK        BARBARA KRUGER
                ZELLA KYLE
    BRUCE LEE        BENOIT MANDELBROT
                CHICO MARX
        GROUCHO MARX        HARPO MARX
                ZEPPO MARX
        ALAN MOORE        PAC-MAN
                SYLVIA PLATH
    >            <        CINDY SHERMAN
            >                <
RUDOLPH VALENTINO        RACHEL WHITEREAD

There is a mirror in the hotel room. Jessica approaches it carefully, as though fearful of what she might find there. Shadows below the eyes, marks of tension at the corners of the mouth. The bottom lip twisted and scarred, turning the whole face into a kind of question mark. Blonde hair, spiky, chopped short. And the eyes themselves, hooded, dark, which stare and then turn away from the sight of the black pupils, enlarging, holes in which to fall.

Sometimes, it gets so bad she could tear her own face off at the roots.

Jessica sits on the bed. It is time to repeat the mantra, as taught her by the Operator himself.

*I am the Special Agent. I have no identity but the one given me, and which I accept gratefully. I have no guilt, and no feelings beyond those needed in my role. I live to kill.*

There now, that is better. She is still a little shaky from this evening's mission, that is all. It is Jessica's first real game, and her future at the Academy depends on her achieving her appointed goals with skill, and with grace.

She gets up again and walks to the window. The followers of the Princess of Charity and Personal Empowerment are still out on the streets, drawing every last drop of grief from yesterday's funeral re-enactment. Some of them are camping out on the grounds of Old Park below. All day long the drums and the horns have sounded, and even now songs of death and martyrdom are drifting through the night air. The cult members will continue their celebrations for a good while yet.

Jessica closes the purple velveteen curtains. If only the Operator would speak to her again. It is so lonely without his voice inside her head. They have a secret understanding.

The waiting is the worst.

*I am the Special Agent. My name is Jessica Webb. This is my identity. I have left my husband, and my former life. Everybody I knew, or once knew, believes that I am dead. I am not dead. I am a character in a game. I cannot die. I can only be retired, until the next game.*

*I live to kill.*

Jessica can hardly remember anything of her former life. Her training period at the Academy seems to stretch backwards for a year, more than a year, many years. On her final encoding day she killed more electronic demons than any other student. The Operator smiled. He presented Jessica with her very own weapon, and the money needed to buy a costume of her own choosing. He placed the mesmeric implant in her skull with loving care, so that he could talk to her at all times, in all places.

'You will be my special one.'

The Operator has a soft way of talking, and whenever he speaks the air smells of jasmines. 'I will always be in control. There is nothing to fear.'

And now Jessica sits alone in the Green Dragon Hotel waiting for the call, the next mission.

The bed is littered with cartons of rice and crumpled aluminium trays smeared with the remains of devilled chicken. The two artificial scorpions sit in their new cages on the dressing table. Each works his mechanical tail, and beads of poison stain the tissue-lined nests. Jessica hopes the Operator will be pleased; she has found the first items. Chrome. Iron. There are four more scorpions out there, each made of a different substance, each containing a different ghost, and each one more valuable than the last.

Jessica remembers the trouble she had, after killing the magician at the theatre. The fanatics and partygoers were still crowding the streets. There was an open market she had to get through. Merchants had come in from the shantytowns hoping to sell cheap radios, army knives and fake designer wristwatches. A slick-haired man was selling bootleg masks, working the people who were drifting along the funeral route. 'Get your Charisma here!' he shouted as he waved a spray can around. 'Become somebody. Be famous for a day!' Meanwhile, security guards were speaking into their hands, and their hands answered them back and they seemed to point out the special agent. Had her cover been blown? A news helicopter followed high above, its undersides decorated with company logos.

Jessica had only just made it back to the hotel.

Nobody can be trusted, only the Operator.

She switches on the television. Every channel is broadcasting images of Princes Dyana: her life, her times, the charity work, the tragic love affairs. Only a current affairs programme at the far end of the spectrum offers any kind of distraction, showing a documentary about a corrupt army colonel.

Suddenly, the Operator's voice is heard.

*Jessica. Keep watching...*
The voice whispers inside the skull, and she feels her heart lifting. She is held spellbound by the flickering black and white images on the screen. The colonel is leading his troops into a bombed-out settlement. They are attacking the villagers. The film freezes on a close-up of his face and a caption reads, 'Colonel Santiago'.
*This will be your next victim.*
The Operator has spoken.
The colonel's face fills the screen, his eyes glaring with a terrible passion.

*Shrine*

\>          <      WILLIAM BURROUGHS
          LEWIS CARROLL
ANGELA CARTER     >                 <
           RICHARD DAWKINS
    PHILIP K DICK       DAPHNE DU MAURIER
            >        <
       DORIAN GRAY      BILLIE HOLIDAY
          >             <
    ROBERT JOHNSON      >           <
           JACK KIRBY
     KRAFTWERK       BARBARA KRUGER
           ZELLA KYLE
    BRUCE LEE       BENOIT MANDELBROT
           CHICO MARX
    **>GROUCHO MARX<**      HARPO MARX
           ZEPPO MARX
      ALAN MOORE       PAC-MAN
          SYLVIA PLATH
\>          <      CINDY SHERMAN
       >            <
RUDOLPH VALENTINO      RACHEL WHITEREAD

## The Sting of the Scorpion: Cheat Sheet

### Singing Scorpion

This is a scorpion made of chrome. The spirit of Elvideo Prez lives here. He was a big old black/white guy who was born in the hills of Somerset. He built the world's first electric guitar out of limousine hub-caps and twisted chicken wire. Everyone loved his crooning and gave him food and money and other good stuff whenever they saw him. Soon he had enough money to retire to an island. where he created his own satellite TV station. You can still see his ghost sometimes, late at night, in the breaks between the ads, singing to the moon and stars. He died of a heart attack when he was taking a shit, his glitter pants wrapped round his ankles.

### Magic Scorpion

This is a scorpion cast from iron. The spirit of Harry Hoodoo lives here. He was an old Jewish guy who travelled around Lujo, working the carnival crowds. People say he was possessed by a demon. No matter what they did to him – shot him full of bullets, put him in the electric chair, lowered him into a tank full of ice-cold water – he always came back from the dead. For a time he was the king's personal bondage advisor. But then one night his demon deserted him on stage and Harry died in a trick that went wrong. Some say he drowned, others say he was hanged by the neck. Others say that a volunteer from the audience punched him in the solar plexus, rupturing his spleen. His last dying words are a secret.

### Dancing Scorpion

This is a scorpion covered in velvet and jewels. The spirit of Rude Valentine lives here. He was a cowboy from the northern territories who moved to the casinos of Lujo and got work as a transvestite lap-dancer. He invented all the perverse tango moves that the boys perform now and he used to make a thousand dollars a night in tips. He was desired by millions until one of his plastic surgery ops went wrong and he was left with a face like the inside of a garbage truck. He shut himself up inside a hotel and had his food left outside the door. One time he fell asleep with a lighted cigarette in his hand. The bed caught fire and he died choking on the smoke.

*Shrine*

>         <      WILLIAM BURROUGHS
           LEWIS CARROLL
ANGELA CARTER      >                <
       **>RICHARD DAWKINS<**
   PHILIP K DICK       DAPHNE DU MAURIER
            >      <
     DORIAN GRAY     BILLIE HOLIDAY
         >          <
ROBERT JOHNSON     >           <
          JACK KIRBY
    KRAFTWERK     BARBARA KRUGER
          ZELLA KYLE
    BRUCE LEE     BENOIT MANDELBROT
          CHICO MARX
>          <     HARPO MARX
         ZEPPO MARX
    ALAN MOORE     PAC-MAN
       SYLVIA PLATH
>      <     CINDY SHERMAN
      >           <
RUDOLPH VALENTINO    RACHEL WHITEREAD

In the Salon de Baile the gentlemen of the orchestra are playing songs from the old country. They play with arthritic fingers, worn out hands and lips, with tired hearts enriched only by distant nights of love now barely remembered. At the tables around the dance floor lonely widows hide behind their decorative fans, while former gigolos stumble across the room slowly and with trepidation, like aged leopards. Aging gigolos check themselves in handheld mirrors. Such desires, such breaths hardly taken, not for so many years now. But still the old men direct the women out onto the polished floor, to move them tenderly through the ritualised code of the tango; the various steps, calibrations, the holds, the perfect theatre of the kiss.

One final surrendering. There are such longings, callings in the blood that yearn to be delivered.

In a small private alcove the retired colonel sits in his wheelchair, his servant standing by his side. The music seems faraway, cold, and slightly out of time with the creaking mechanism of an ornamental clock whose fingers move in the shadows. The colonel sighs and thinks back on his dancing days, when the body seemed in thrall to some fierce instruction. The young girls, the married women, the prostitutes.

*Such longings...*

The scorpion creaks across the table, its velvet body sparkling with cheap jewels. The servant places a gentle finger upon its back, holding it in place. The colonel looks on nervously. His eyes are so bad these days he sees everything covered with a fine mist, wet with tears. Finally he gives a slight nod, at which the servant rolls up the sleeve of his master, exposing a thin-boned arm. The old man trembles at the touch, and he remembers the advice given him by the dealer.

'Be careful of your passion.'

The creature moves closer. The tail hovers above the bared arm of the colonel and then stabs forward suddenly with a coiled power. The jewelled sting pierces the soft flesh, finding a vein. Bright liquid flows from the scorpion into the old man. The ticking of the clock fills the alcove like a heart stuttering. There is a sweet sticky smell in the small confined space and the old man cries out in pain, and in fear. His eyes widen. Blood fills his vision.

The music swirls from the dance floor. It sounds like paradise calling to him.

The colonel spasms in his chair, his arms flailing. The scorpion is knocked from the table. It lands on the floor some distance from the old man, who has fallen with it. The creature lies on its back, legs waving frantically, its tail spurting. A purple arc of fluid sprays across the man's terrified face.

*Such desires, such terrible longings...*

The wheel of the chair spins slowly to a standstill.

*Shrine*

>　　　　　<　　　WILLIAM BURROUGHS
　　　　LEWIS CARROLL
ANGELA CARTER　　>　　　　　　　　　<
　　>　　　　　　<
　PHILIP K DICK　　DAPHNE DU MAURIER
　　　　>　　　　　<
　　DORIAN GRAY　　BILLIE HOLIDAY
　　　　>　　　　　<
ROBERT JOHNSON　　>　　　　　　　<
　　　　JACK KIRBY
　　KRAFTWERK　　BARBARA KRUGER
　　　　ZELLA KYLE
　BRUCE LEE　　BENOIT MANDELBROT
　　　　CHICO MARX
>　　　　　<　　　HARPO MARX
　　　　ZEPPO MARX
　　ALAN MOORE　　**>PAC-MAN<**
　　　　SYLVIA PLATH
　>　　　　<　　　CINDY SHERMAN
　　　>　　　　　<
RUDOLPH VALENTINO　　RACHEL WHITEREAD

## Infection Cycle

ACTIVATION: The subject's heart rate speeds up, the breath comes more quickly. The flesh is primed, the veins dilated. CAUSE OF EFFECT: The foreign body enters the bloodstream. This is a drug composed of various psychoactive compounds, the most active ingredient being Charisma (TM). CODE SCAN: Copyright notice located, belonging to the Zeno Company. SUB BRAND IDENT: Licensing agreement between Zeno and the estate of the film star Rude Valentine, regarding the free use of actor's public image, psychic vibrations and post-mortem apparitions.

TRANSMISSION: The drug moves across the nervous system. Infected blood cells resonate with the nerve cells, inducing muscular spasms. The dance has begun. SUBJECT ID: 'Colonel Santiago'. ACTIVATE CONSCIOUSNESS GRAB: *I was hunting the bootleg Zeenies down like rats... purging the country... my orders were coming through...mutterings on the telephone line... this was the problem... a social problem... we packed the bodies up in black bags... and so that's how I became a garbage man... flying at low altitude over the sea... throwing the waste products overboard... poor little fuckers... the blades keeping time in a steady rhythm... when all I ever really wanted to be was a gaucho... a movie star, a dancer in the desert sweeping across the screen with an elegant step...* MAPPING PROCEDURE: Seeking out the molecular pulsation of fantasies. LOCATION RESULT: Successful. Zone of deepest compatibility identified.

ACTIVATION: Charismatic substance floods the channels and relays of the nervous system, signals race across the body's filaments, homing in on the brain. PRIME INFECTION: The ghost settles into the medulla, the back-brain, a shortcut to the deep currents of archaic time. RELEASE OF FANTASY: *Rudie Valentine in his leather riding boots... a knife tucked into his waist-band, throwing his hooded cape over the front of his body, over his eyes... striding from his tent into the desert... the whirling sand-storm... looking for the wild girls who escape him... to dance with them by the ragged palms under a painted moon... the savage embrace of passion...*

TRANSMISSION: The viral ghost taps into the deepest thoughts and energies of the subject, consuming them, dissolving them, accessing the core of the subject's being. PROCEDURE: The subject metabolises the celebrity code completely, creating a new, hybrid consciousness. RUN SYSTEM: The spirit is moving down along the spinal cord to the extremities of the body: fingertips tingling, feet trembling. The face starts to transform, to adopt the mask of the chosen ghost. Quickly now, the body has no escape route, except to move, to step forward, to dance...

*Shrine*

>             <     WILLIAM BURROUGHS
        LEWIS CARROLL
ANGELA CARTER     >                       <
      >                        <
   PHILIP K DICK     DAPHNE DU MAURIER
          >         <
     DORIAN GRAY     BILLIE HOLIDAY
        >                <
  ROBERT JOHNSON     >                 <
          JACK KIRBY
    KRAFTWERK     BARBARA KRUGER
          ZELLA KYLE
    BRUCE LEE     BENOIT MANDELBROT
         CHICO MARX
>             <     HARPO MARX
       ZEPPO MARX
   ALAN MOORE     >             <
       SYLVIA PLATH
>        <     CINDY SHERMAN
    >                <
>RUDOLPH VALENTINO<     RACHEL WHITEREAD

Colonel Santiago appears on the dance floor, beneath the fragmented lights of the mirror ball. He seems different, more energetic, dazzling even. The face is broad and unlined, the eyes relaxed and confident beneath the angled brows. He has the studied appearance of a movie star, and he walks with a new swagger. The aging dancers part for him as he strides towards the tables at the side of the room, where the older women are sitting. Each person feels an uncommon emotion as they recognise, half seen within the colonel's face, the savage likeness of the young Rudie Valentine.

He stands with his hands on his hips, eyes glinting with untold delights, before leaning forward to select a partner. She is drawn to him irresistibly, shivering within the *abrazo* of his arms, and they take their place on the floor with dramatic, forceful movements. The orchestra starts up a melody, the old notation of heartbreak, and the colonel leads his partner in the dance, tracing five steps over eight beats. His shoulders cut through the air, surging, as he propels his charge across the floor in a figure of eight movement, his feet a blur as he switches position from parallel to crossed, back to parallel again. She is wilting under the pressure of the dance. But he presses onwards, lunging, spinning, feinting, inventing new patterns from the repertoire of steps.

How sweetly the hands of the clock grasp at time.

The dance ended, the colonel finds his desire still unsatisfied. He must take another partner, then another. The crowds on the dance floor start to thin out, as people withdraw to watch this exhibition of primal lust. The orchestra speeds up the time of the music, to keep in step with the colonel. He cannot stop dancing. His body is held tight, programmed. Left foot forward, right foot forward, left foot forward again, right foot to the side... left foot closing. He repeats the steps endlessly. Gliding, sliding, turning on the blades of his heels, his toes, tracing the measured pathways. There is no escape.

The hours pass, the people disappear, the lights go off on the stage. The colonel has exhausted all partners. He dances alone, zigzagging across the floor in melancholic rapture. The orchestra has long since departed, but still a soft trace of music can be heard. It echoes within the colonel's skull, as though a band of spectres have taken to the stage. He slows down, in sudden fear. His skin is covered in sweat. He trembles. There is a pain inside him, an agony visible in his face. There are wrinkles at the eyes now, cracks in the Valentine mask.

The colonel loses his balance, stumbles, drops to his knees. Under the hot lights of the dancehall, he brings his hands up to his face. The skin is peeling, the lustre fading. The shameful old man is emerging from beneath the mask of the glamorous dancer.

Green silk flutters.

The colonel raises his head at the faint sound, to see a young woman emerging from the shadows. Her face is blurred, unknowable, and her dress shimmers below the mirrored lights as she advances slowly across the dance floor. The colonel's eyes are filled with tears, but he can see the small cage within the woman's grasp, and within it, the velvet and jewel encrusted scorpion. The woman places this, and one other object, on the polished floor.

'What is it?' the colonel asks. 'What do you want from me?'

The special agent pulls a gun from the folds of silk.

'No. Please don't...'

The colonel tries to get up, to make one last effort, but his limbs are tired, so tired, as though the blood has frozen in his veins. He cannot move. There will be no more dancing.

The agent moves slightly to one side and then fires the gun, quite calmly. The wound in the colonel's stomach is a hole through which the light of pure celebrity streams, uncoloured, like the beam from an old movie projector in a darkened room. He looks down at it in quiet horror, surprised by the wound. The agent shoots him again, this time making a hole in his chest. The light shoots out in a broad, flat ray and the colonel's body curls up, like a sepia-toned image, fading at the edges.

The special agent cocks her head, like a mannequin, listening to the voice inside. She nods, picking up the canister she had brought with her. Unscrewing the cap, she pours the petrol over the colonel's body. Next, she takes out a book of safety matches. The packet is decorated with the logo of the Green Dragon Hotel. It is a simple matter, a following of instructions. The Operator had been explicit: *Stage the deaths to resemble those of the real celebrities. Don't let people find out the truth.* But what is the truth?

The alarms howl as the special agent exits the building.

Already, her next mission beckons.

*Shrine*

>     <        WILLIAM BURROUGHS
        LEWIS CARROLL
ANGELA CARTER    >                <
        >            <
    PHILIP K DICK    DAPHNE DU MAURIER
            >        <
        DORIAN GRAY    BILLIE HOLIDAY
            >        <
    ROBERT JOHNSON    >            <
            JACK KIRBY
        KRAFTWERK    BARBARA KRUGER
            ZELLA KYLE
        BRUCE LEE    BENOIT MANDELBROT
            **>CHICO MARX<**
>            <        HARPO MARX
            ZEPPO MARX
        ALAN MOORE    >        <
            SYLVIA PLATH
        >        <    CINDY SHERMAN
            >        <
>            <        RACHEL WHITEREAD

## Glamorous Scorpion

This is a scorpion fashioned from marble. The spirit of Marilyn Monamour lives here. She used to be the most beautiful woman in the world with eyes like street lights in the early evening rain and a real hot body that looked like it had been designed by a car engineer. All the presidents and generals and movie stars wanted her so bad they fought each other for the honour of taking her to the academy awards ceremony in the Liberties and that's how the first trade war started. She felt so guilty about it that she let them all use her, and then dump her. She died in bed from a drug overdose. Stolen images of her corpse were used to advertise perfume.

*Shrine*

>  <  WILLIAM BURROUGHS
LEWIS CARROLL
**>ANGELA CARTER<**   >   <
>   <
PHILIP K DICK   DAPHNE DU MAURIER
>   <
DORIAN GRAY   BILLIE HOLIDAY
>   <
ROBERT JOHNSON   >   <
JACK KIRBY
KRAFTWERK   BARBARA KRUGER
ZELLA KYLE
BRUCE LEE   BENOIT MANDELBROT
>   <
>   <   HARPO MARX
ZEPPO MARX
ALAN MOORE   >   <
SYLVIA PLATH
>   <   CINDY SHERMAN
>   <
>   <   RACHEL WHITEREAD

## On the ghost sites...

On the ghost sites and junk nets of the Oracle, the teenagers talk of a refuge of shadows where all the dead supermodels go at night to shop. The building is called Haversham's. Many long years before it was known as the finest department store in all of Lujo; but now, abandoned and forlorn, its commodities gathering dust, only the most wasted of spirits bring their custom to the place. The store is lit by gas flames contained within globes of coloured glass. Metallic whispers haunt the wireless networks, and strange messages gleam on the crystal displays of the antique vending machines. Curling their sharp claws around the heating pipes, black televisions hang from the ceiling, their screens flickering with phantom images.

## The teenagers tell the story...

The teenagers tell the story of a young girl who moved into the lonely old building for shelter. She was a refugee orphan from a far distant country, without home or family, and she had nowhere else to go. The girl wandered the silent arcades. She was entranced by the splendour of the ruined department store, still visible in the splintered wood carvings and the broken chandeliers. She began to play at being a celebrity, imagining the place had been opened just for her, after hours. She rode the automatic stairways and the creaking brass cages of the elevators. She moved through the soft clouds of perfume. She looked in wonder at decanters filled with shadows cast from long forgotten places. She draped the shadows around herself, mournfully. Most of all, using pretend credit cards, which were only pieces of tiling from the walls, she purchased old bottles of *Charisma*. Using a single drop each time, smoothing the pungent oil into her skin, this melancholy little girl wore the images of long lost film stars, both male and female.

## The painted girl smiled...

The painted girl smiled as she robed herself in the warm, ephemeral flickers of Greta Garbage, of Rude Valentine, of Frank Scenario and Audio Hipburner. Most of all, she wanted to dress herself with the face of Marilyn Monamour, which was said to be the most radiant of all celebrity veils. One evening the girl was searching through the broken displays of the Hall of Beauty, when she came across a beautiful marble vessel in the shape of a scorpion. How it got there she would never know, but after removing the sting from the finely wrought tail, she anointed herself with the oil, with drops to her wrists, her neck, and to her ankles. The spirit of Monamour rose up within the young girl, and she was bathed in glamour. Night after night, as she performed this ritual, and having eaten no food for many days now, the homeless girl wasted away, almost leaving behind her physical form.

## *The spirit of the old film star...*

The spirit of the old film star had taken over the girl's body completely. Or that's how it felt. She was possessed by fantasy, becoming in her dreams the very first ghost to haunt the electromagnetic ether of the building, scattered like blue sparks from a fire. Sometimes a blurred figure would show up on a security camera's screen; other times, the elevator might rise of its own accord to far distant floors. Or else a mist of perfume would take on a vaguely human shape. Whispers and rumours travelled the gossip columns of the dead, speaking of this great new place to visit. And soon the old department store echoed with the ghostly clattering of high heels and the popping of pill canisters.

## *The special agent moved...*

The special agent moved through the superstore armed with a gun, a shadow amongst shadows. Her dress of green silk sparkled in the broken mirrors, and her face danced with fragments of light. Old memories bled through the damp walls. She pursued the ghost of Marilyn Monamour along the aisles, from room to room, from floor to floor. Spectral cries were heard from the bottom of the elevator shaft, from the empty booths in the changing rooms. The black televisions climbed into the shadows. Finally, the first spirit was cornered in the Hall of Beauty, and she revealed herself in all her glory. The agent was transfixed by the beauty of the apparition and could hardly move. Despite this, her training kicked in and she pulled the trigger. There was an explosion of light, a burst of incandescent energy which caused all the lamps in the building to splutter. The smell of burning cologne drifted through the aisles.

## Two weeks later, the body...

Two weeks later, the body of the young homeless girl was found by a family of tramps. She was lying on a bed in the furniture department, an unknown corpse arranged in artful disarray. Silken sheets were stained with whisky, lipstick and vomit; a bottle of barbiturates stood on a nightstand. The whole scene looked as though it had been staged for an advertisement shoot, where upmarket souls are portrayed as damaged goods. Every last ounce of beauty had been drained from the girl's body.

## The teenagers weep...

The teenagers weep when they tell this story. They praise the homeless girl as a junior goddess, a creature of lowly birth who had transformed herself into the substance of pure glamour, if only for a few days and nights. They whisper to each other across the tangled webs of the Oracle, conjuring a fantasy together; in their collective mind's eye they are walking the aisles of the ghostly department store, ransacking its cabinets, and seeking out any lingering trace of the vanished marble scorpion and its precious contents.

*Shrine*

> < WILLIAM BURROUGHS
LEWIS CARROLL
> < >
<
> <
PHILIP K DICK        DAPHNE DU MAURIER
> <
DORIAN GRAY        BILLIE HOLIDAY
> <
ROBERT JOHNSON        >        <
JACK KIRBY
KRAFTWERK        BARBARA KRUGER
ZELLA KYLE
BRUCE LEE        BENOIT MANDELBROT
> <
>        <        HARPO MARX
ZEPPO MARX
ALAN MOORE        >        <
SYLVIA PLATH
>        <        **>CINDY SHERMAN<**
>        <
>        <        RACHEL WHITEREAD

The special agent sits on a plastic tip-up seat in a subway car. It rocks its way through the corridors of the Lujo Underground. Electric strip-lights fizz and sputter. The floor is littered with bottles of facial scrub, long curls of hair, and lipstick-stained cigarette butts. There is a smell of stale sweat. On the seat opposite somebody has left behind a handful of photographs, all of them pulled too quickly from an instamatic camera. They show images of an old woman, her face and body smeared by chemicals.

The agent feels drowsy. Her fingers touch at the gun inside her tunic. The mission is tiring, even though there are only two targets left. She must save her energy for them, especially the last. She hopes the Operator will let her rest when the game is over. She would like to sleep, to sleep properly.

There are perhaps half a dozen passengers in the carriage, shadowy figures who sit mumbling to themselves. They pay her no attention. The agent's thoughts drift along, going back to the past. *Once there was a young girl, who played with a kite.* Was that a story she used to know, a song once sung? The agent watches herself in the window, in the rushing blackness. Where is the Operator? She waits for the voice, the next instruction. There is something wrong with her reflection. The agent blinks rapidly and catches her breath as scenes from her life are played out for her.

*Jessica, can you hear me?*

From the dark glass, a teenage girl stares back. She is standing at the side of a cold empty highway with a small rucksack beside her. Night has fallen, and she is dressed only in a white blouse, checked skirt, ankle socks and pumps. She is looking towards a distant bend in the road, where headlamps now can be seen, slowly approaching.

Jessica was a Teenage Runaway.

The special agent remembers the night she ran away from her father's house. She was picked up by a middle-aged man in a saloon car. Wasn't that it? He was a travelling salesman, with a suitcase filled with 'high quality religious fetishes'. Smelling of cheap aftershave and talking of his daughters. They stopped at a roadside inn. He would not stop looking at her, appraising her. He showed her a 'genuine X-ray of our Lady of Sorrows, recently discovered'. And afterwards...

*Jessica? Are you there?*

Another image appears in the pool of darkness. Jessica is

slightly older now, with a dreamy, faraway expression on her face. Her body has changed, grown tougher. Her black patent leather stilettos match the colour of her bra and panties. She wears a silver cross on a chain at her neck.

Jessica used to be a Bad Good Girl.

Pictures flicker on and off. Who is this person really, this young woman shivering in the glass who whispers, 'Sometimes, I feel like I want to tear my own face off at the roots.' The agent remembers, or seems to remember, the rough claiming hands of a shantytown pimp. Was she a prostitute, before joining the Academy? Was that the truth of her life, her former life? Have they done something to her memories, erased, or partially erased them? She will find out, perhaps, when all of this is over. Yes, she will find out.

*Speak to me, Jessica.*

This voice, calling her. Is it the Operator? The special agent is angry now. She remembers when she was a little girl, sitting on a chair, having her long tangled hair brushed by a woman. There was the smell of soap and fresh flowers. This is a good memory, she would like to keep this feeling, of the brush against her hair, and the lovely smell, and her mother...

The special agent puts her hand against the glass. The image fades and is replaced by another. The woman's eyes are lined with kohl, an unforgiving smile hovers on pale, damaged lips. Wrapped in green silk, her body moves with practised ease. Holding a pistol above her head in both hands, the woman strikes a series of dramatic poses. The agent recognises the close-cropped hair, the low maintenance style favoured by those often called away. Herself.

'Yes,' she says. 'I'm here. I'm ready. What do you need of me?'

Jessica is an Action Babe. The beautiful killer.

*I am the Special Agent. I have no identity but the one given to me, and which I accept gratefully. I have no guilt, and no feelings. I have left my husband, and my former life. Everybody I knew, or once knew, believes that I am dead. I am not dead. I am a character in a game. I cannot die. Only the game matters.*

*My name is Jessica Webb. I live to kill.*

This is the truth, the only truth. It must be the truth. After all, the Operator was always so kind to her; he filed his nails before using the various devices upon her body.

'Apparition Park. All change.'

The voice on the car's public address system is not quite male and not quite female. 'All change,' it says. 'End of the line.'

The darkness has sucked away the stream of images from the window. The agent grips the handrails of her seat as the car squeals to a halt with protesting brakes; the doors open with a shudder. There are no other passengers. Only now does Jessica notice the sweat which has dampened her skin during the ride. The Operator's voice comes to her, properly this time. The next victim is named, with the relevant details. He's a washed-up medical student, a genetic surgeon to freaks and lowlifes. Currently living somewhere in the old, abandoned amusement park on the edge of the northern sector. A man obsessed with the life and times of Lady Dyana Splendour.

The agent steps out onto the platform. The sign reads APPARITION PARK. The station is deserted. There is blood smeared all over the walls and an old mattress in the corner is heaped with a mess of dirty white sheets. Flies hover around the smell. Candy wrappers are caught in a swirl of foul air. The lift is broken. The only stairs lead further downwards, a dark spiral littered with bird shit and feathers. Jessica has the strangest thought as she gazes into the darkness. Perhaps there is no game. And if there is no game, then what else is there?

Another life, perhaps. Another life beyond this one, beyond control...

But then the voice of the Operator speaks to her once again, and the special agent checks her weapon carefully, before stepping into the stairwell.

*Shrine*

\>            <       WILLIAM BURROUGHS
         LEWIS CARROLL
     >              <     >
               <
    >                <
PHILIP K DICK      DAPHNE DU MAURIER
      >          <
    DORIAN GRAY      BILLIE HOLIDAY
      >            <
ROBERT JOHNSON     >             <
          JACK KIRBY
    KRAFTWERK      BARBARA KRUGER
          ZELLA KYLE
   BRUCE LEE      BENOIT MANDELBROT
        >          <
\>         <      **>HARPO MARX<**
       ZEPPO MARX
   ALAN MOORE     >        <
       SYLVIA PLATH
\>       <     >          <
     >            <
\>         <     RACHEL WHITEREAD

## Princess Scorpion

This is a scorpion made from crystal-cut glass. The spirit of Lady Dyana Splendour lives here. She was a girl with a secret mojo who lived in a castle where she was made to clean out the stables by her wicked stepmother. Then she met this prince who married her and made her look after his horses at polo matches. He only wanted her for her mojo and when she realised this she cried all over his precious family heirlooms and went round the world looking for lepers and sick children to cure. The angry prince hunted her down and drove her car off the edge of a cliff. The princess died in the wreckage. Every year people come together to pay homage to this Princess of Shadows, and every year she dies anew, surrounded by flowers and beads, canisters of hair spray, cracked make-up mirrors, sweatbands, leggings, lipsticks and charity bracelets.

# Exhibit C

*A Teardrop Implodes*

*Shrine*

>　　　　　　　<　　　　WILLIAM BURROUGHS
　　　　　LEWIS CARROLL
　　　>　　　　　　　　<　　　>
　　　　　　　　　<
　　　>　　　　　　　　　<
　　PHILIP K DICK　　　DAPHNE DU MAURIER
　　　　　　>　　　　　<
　　　DORIAN GRAY　　　BILLIE HOLIDAY
　　　　>　　　　　　　　<
ROBERT JOHNSON　　　>　　　　　　　　<
　　　　　　　JACK KIRBY
　　KRAFTWERK　　　BARBARA KRUGER
　　　　　　　ZELLA KYLE
　　BRUCE LEE　　　BENOIT MANDELBROT
　　　　　　>　　　　　<
>　　　　　　<　　　>　　　　　　　<
　　　　　　ZEPPO MARX
　　**>ALAN MOORE<**　　　>　　　　　<
　　　　　　SYLVIA PLATH
　>　　　　<　　　>　　　　　　　　<
　　　　　　>　　　　　<
>　　　　　　　<　　　　RACHEL WHITEREAD

## Dyanaman / Volume 1, Issue 1 / Origin Story

### Page 1 – 6 panels

[01] Daytime. Wide angle of a ROAD lined with people. They watch in silence as a funeral carriage passes by.

[02] The body of a fake princess is glimpsed inside the casket. A single white CARNATION is seen, falling from one of the wreaths fixed to the side of the carriage.

[03] Move in on a HAND picking up the flower from the side of the road.

[04] Cut to a wide angle of a dilapidated old FAIRGROUND. A wrought iron sign over the gate reads APPARITION PARK. The area behind the gate has become a dumping ground for burnt-out cars, broken fridges and out-of-date Apple Macs. Beyond this we see collection of old buildings and crumbling fairground rides – the iron skeleton of a roller coaster, the boarded-up hall of mirrors.

[05] The HALL OF MIRRORS, its walls patched with corrugated iron sheets.

[06] Medium angle of a ROOM inside the hall of mirrors. MICKEY TEARDROP, a small greasy looking guy in his late twenties, is sitting on the edge of his bed. He's wearing a stained lab coat. Posters, newspaper clippings and photographs on the wall behind him. Action figures, paper masks and magazines on the bed. All these items relate to the Princess Dyana cult. He's staring at the carnation flower in his hand.

### Page 2 – 5 panels

[01] Close-up of Mickey's face, a TEAR rolling down his cheek.

[02] Cut to an ORACLE terminal on Mickey's desk, displaying a Princess Dyana screensaver. A message over her face reads, 'Mail received'.

FX: BEEP!

[03] Close on the Oracle text brought up on the screen: 'Hey, Mickey! You caught the latest Princess fix? Supposed to be the ultimate thrill. Click for directions.'

[04] Overhead shot of Mickey lying on the bed, his arms crossed over his chest; a KNIFE lies on his stomach.

[05] Close on the knife. The carnation flower lies across the blade. A carved inscription on the handle reads: 'Dyana, I love you.'

*Page 3 – 6 Panels*

[01] Night. Wide angle of an old CHURCH, its stones black with dirt. In the pool of light from its doorway, a cluster of half-illuminated figures.

[02] Close on a CULTIST in the doorway. He writhes on the ground, face misted by a cloud of static. On his T-shirt, a cheaply printed image of Dyana.

[03] Medium angle of the church aisle. Benches either side, with a few seated CULTISTS. All have smeared expressions. They sport Dyana tote bags, scarves and jackets.

[04] A wooden table set out in front of the altar. Sitting behind it, a DEALER flanked by a couple of thugs. He wears a hooded top and dark glasses, his face hidden from view. On the table are various devotional items.

[05] Close on a SCORPION, made from heavy, crystal-cut glass. Coloured lights flicker inside the transparent shell. A dark liquid is dripping from the slowly moving tail, onto a large sheet of blotting paper.

[06] The dealer. Close on his upturned finger, supporting a small TAB of the blotting paper. The liquid has stained the paper.

*Page 4 – 9 Panels*
[01] Medium angle of MICKEY standing opposite the dealer at the table.
        MICKEY: Is it Charisma?
        DEALER: Better. No fade. Lasts forever.
        MICKEY: Bullshit!
        DEALER: Suck it and see.

[02] Close on Mickey's hand pulling a small electronic measuring DEVICE from his Dyana tote bag.

[03] His fingers, inserting the TAB into the side of the hand-held device.

[04] The instrument's display SCREEN. Various readouts. 'Charisma. Strength: 9.725. Ghost: Princess Dyana.'

[05] Same medium angle of MICKEY and the dealer.
   DEALER: You ever seen a reading like that before?
Mickey's eyes are filled with desire.
   MICKEY: I want the whole stash.
   DEALER: Get the fuck out of here.

[06] Close-up of Mickey's hand coming out of his bag.

[07] One of the toughs, his HAND moving to his shoulder holster.

[08] The dealer's face, his EYES wide.

[09] Mickey has pulled a huge wad of used notes from the bag.

*Page 5 – 6 panels*

[01] Medium angle of Mickey's room. There is a mirror on the wall. Mickey sits at his desk, working at something with a laser knife.

[02] Close on the blade of light cutting open the belly of the overturned glass SCORPION, its legs and pincers still moving, sporadically.

[03] Closer on the interior MECHANICAL WORKINGS of the creature.

[04] Large panel. Medium angle of Mickey extracting from the scorpion a smooth transparent HEART filled with a dark purple liquid.
   MICKEY: Oh my beauty.

[05] Insert title: A TEARDROP IMPLODES.

[06] Cut to a SYRINGE penetrating this pulsating heart.
   FX: Szzzzt.

*Shrine*

&gt;          &lt;       WILLIAM BURROUGHS
       LEWIS CARROLL
     &gt;           &lt;     &gt;
           &lt;

     &gt;           &lt;
PHILIP K DICK    &gt;DAPHNE DU MAURIER&lt;
      &gt;       &lt;
   DORIAN GRAY    BILLIE HOLIDAY
    &gt;          &lt;
ROBERT JOHNSON    &gt;            &lt;
        JACK KIRBY
     KRAFTWERK    BARBARA KRUGER
        ZELLA KYLE
   BRUCE LEE    BENOIT MANDELBROT
      &gt;       &lt;
&gt;      &lt;    &gt;         &lt;
      ZEPPO MARX
   &gt;      &lt;    &gt;        &lt;
      SYLVIA PLATH
  &gt;     &lt;    &gt;         &lt;
     &gt;        &lt;
&gt;       &lt;    RACHEL WHITEREAD

Mister Teardrop goes to his mirror. His pale wet face stares back at him. Trembling fingers trace the cold reflection's skin, with its all too visible pockmarks. His voice is nothing more than a whisper, and yet alive with desire.

'Oh come to me, my love.'

His veins tingle with the effects of the drug reaching towards the heart. It feels like a stolen promise. Mister Teardrop has surrendered himself in this way. Each passing hour, more and more droplets of the potion are pricked into the blood. And always the looking glass refuses him, offering only his own sad face in return, or else glimpses, flashes of some other, more beautiful presence. Lost, even as it seems within grasp.

'Shall I ever be loved?'

A dark light glimmers briefly in the mirror's depths. It plays there as summer lightning played once over the guests of a royal garden party; a woman caught by a zoom lens, her features blurred and forever out of reach. It is the same blurring that Teardrop sees now, and yet surely this time some extra detail can be seen, a flickering, this jewel gleaming at the throat of a distant apparition. And then suddenly, as though a gilded phantom possesses him, the lines of his face shimmer and dissolve. Love's poison is summoning a sweeter reflection.

'My lady of shadows...'

The princess is not yet there, not completely, but still, Teardrop cannot resist her. He moves forward, gently, closer to the mirror. The two faces mingle, male and female; their lips touch, each side of the glass. Delirious, the heart floods now with a sudden warmth, the surge of hot, rich satisfaction coursing the body.

When Teardrop pulls away, his own face has returned. The shadows beneath his eyes are darker, his skin drenched with sweat. In sadness, his passion spent, the keen devoted suitor already relishes the next stage of courtship.

The mirror awaits him.

*Shrine*

>　　　　　　　<　　　　WILLIAM BURROUGHS
　　　　　　LEWIS CARROLL
　　　>　　　　　　　　　　<　　　　>
　　　　　　　　　　<
　　　　　>　　　　　　　　　　　　<
PHILIP K DICK　　　　>　　　　　　　　　　　　　　<
　　　　　　　　　　>　　　　　<
　　　　　DORIAN GRAY　　　　　>BILLIE HOLIDAY<
　　　　　　　　　>　　　　　　　<
ROBERT JOHNSON　　　　　　>　　　　　　　　　　<
　　　　　　　　　JACK KIRBY
　　　　KRAFTWERK　　　　BARBARA KRUGER
　　　　　　　　　　ZELLA KYLE
　　　　BRUCE LEE　　　　BENOIT MANDELBROT
　　　　　　　　　>　　　　　　<
>　　　　　　　　　<　　　　>　　　　　　　<
　　　　　　　　　ZEPPO MARX
　　>　　　　　　　　　<　　　　>　　　　　　<
　　　　　　　　　SYLVIA PLATH
　　>　　　　　　<　　　　　>　　　　　　　　　<
　　　　　　　　　　>　　　　　　<
　　>　　　　　　　　　　　　　<　　　　　RACHEL
　　　　　　　　　　　　　WHITEREAD

## And the days and the nights pass by...

Lady Dyana Splendour lies in her bed, watching the shadows that move along the ceiling in the blue dark colours of the evening light. Unable to sleep, she gets up and makes herself a meal: cereal, yoghurt, sliced apple. Afterwards, she might sit reading by the gramophone, or else waste some time examining the walls for peepholes. She has the feeling that somebody is watching her, caressing her body with his ardent gaze.

The bookcase contains only bound editions of the Miss Marple mysteries, and a few old copies of *Vogue*, all in pristine condition. The gramophone has a single long-playing record made of shellac. A woman's voice sobs from the machine in a pained but defiant song. Dyana will listen to the music, and think back to her wedding day, and the joy and the sadness of that strange occasion. She writes little notes to herself, hiding them behind vases, underneath the breakfast tray, beneath her pillow, inside the pages of the magazines. Later, she will find these letters, all of them written on scented paper, and be puzzled. One of them begins, 'I am a troubled soul. I have a parasite inside me, a being of darkness that has taken control of my spirit.' Each message is signed off with the words, '...the Princess of Shadows.'

Sometimes Dyana will stand at the tall narrow window and look out over the abandoned funfair in the rain. All the rides are clad in tarpaulin and the carved figures on the Haunted House look like shabby second-hand phantoms. In the afternoon she will take a nap. The dream will visit her, the same dream each time, the scorpion that crawls across her body, its tail of glass curling over, and the poison entering her flesh as the stinger jabs forward.

Coming awake, she will stumble to the adjoining bathroom. She has found a space there, a tiny space where no prying eyes can reach her. In this one dark corner she will perform a certain act involving the throat and the fingers. Having witnessed the stretched, translucent skin of the *Vogue* fashion models, she wonders if by this method she might vanish altogether, become a mere trembling of air, a falling of dust.

There are no clocks in her room, only the slow beating of the heart.

The solution to one of the murder mysteries rests upon the fact that shellac is made from the resin secreted by a female beetle.

With the blunt point of a penknife Dyana might attempt to draw some blood from her veins, but all is thin, watery. The song plays on, her only true possession. In the gathering dusk she will dance alone to the melody. There is no escape. And then later that evening, she finds that she can no longer listen to the woman's voice. The record breaks in her hands.

The beetle lives in Southeast Asia and uses the resin as a protective coat. Music can be printed onto it.

*And the hours and the minutes pass by...*

There is a flight of stairs beyond the main door, and one day Lady Dyana finds the courage to walk down them. She steps out into a room filled with glass, with a hundred shining mirrors, all of them curved in various ways, and each one throwing back a different reflection. There she is, the Princess herself, attending a charity ball, stepping from the royal carriage, kissing her husband on the palace balcony; or, in this glass, strolling by a lake with her trusted dogs by her side – Stalker, Jollyboy, Lightfoote. Further along, she sees herself in a hospital holding the hand of a young man with a terrible disease. Or else walking through a foreign field, dressed in protective clothing. So many lost moments, so many images. In one terrible mirror she is trapped in the back of a limousine. Blood covers her face. In the final reflection, instead of her own, a stranger's eyes stare back at her. Another person's face appears in the glass, a man's face.

Mister Teardrop smiles at his new reflection. The transformation is complete, and the man and the woman gaze upon each other, the one in ecstasy, the other in fear. He reaches out to touch the one he loves so much, and the mirror shines with a golden light.

The glass dissolves around his hand...

*Shrine*

&gt; &lt; WILLIAM BURROUGHS
&gt;LEWIS CARROLL&lt;
&gt; &lt; &gt;
&lt;
&gt; &lt;
PHILIP K DICK &gt; &lt;
&gt; &lt;
DORIAN GRAY &gt; &lt;
&gt; &lt;
ROBERT JOHNSON &gt; &lt;
JACK KIRBY
KRAFTWERK BARBARA KRUGER
ZELLA KYLE
BRUCE LEE BENOIT MANDELBROT
&gt; &lt;
&gt; &lt; &gt; &lt;
ZEPPO MARX
&gt; &lt; &gt; &lt;
SYLVIA PLATH
&gt; &lt; &gt; &lt;
&gt; &lt;
&gt; &lt; RACHEL WHITEREAD

Word spread, and later that day the congregation started to arrive in dribs and drabs. They were a sorry collection of raggle-tagglers: chronic game-show losers, white-faced porn addicts, university dropouts, drug-addled housewives, out of work executives, ex lingerie models. They lined up at the doorway of the old Hall of Mirrors in the cold abandoned fairground, not really knowing what to expect, fuelled only by rumours, Oracle popjobs and counterculture mish-mash, and knowing that Mister Teardrop was good for a genetic splice or a black-market sex-change, but nothing more. What could he be up to? One bright spark with plastic snakes in his hair declared that the Hall of Mirrors was now to be called the Portal of Infinite Desire. Well that was what he heard anyway. But who could know the truth?

They made their way inside, two by two, crowding in as best they could. There was no attendant, and no entry charge. The hall was in darkness to begin with, with only the faint gleam of the mirrors to be seen here and there like smears of the moon. Two by two they entered, and one by one they fell silent as the strangeness of the place took hold of them. Finally, as the last pipsqueak settled down, a spotlight clicked on and in its beam a most remarkable vision was seen. It was a bizarre creature, exactly half man and half woman, although where one began and the other ended was a mystery. However, as the light flickered, Mister Teardrop's ugly countenance was glimpsed, alongside and mingled with that of the Glorious and Most Beautiful Princess of Shadows. The congregation gasped.

'My friends,' the Princess announced. 'My fellow travellers along life's many roads of despair and forlorn hope. I come before you to announce the grand opening of the First Church of the Paradise of Glass!' The crowd cheered at hearing such words, even though they little understood their meaning. Now the Princess moved from mirror to mirror, whispering magical incantations and touching each reflection in turn, and once again gasps could be heard rising up from the people gathered there, as each silvery surface turned first misty, and then golden with its own internal light. 'Hallelujah! Hallelujah!' chanted a messed up former rock and roll guitarist with only one arm and a bandage around his head. 'I have seen the glory!'

Now the congregation shuffled forward to peer with much delight and curiosity into the golden mirrors. Each luminous glass doorway offered a view of a different area of the Skull Garden; not those portions usually seen in the normal day to day visits, but those areas beyond these, in the moonlit darkness, in the woods and the fields of fog and stars, in the lakes of mercury and the rivers of ink. The viewers moved closer to the mirrors, fascinated by the sights on offer, and especially by all the peculiar beasts and insects and birds and fish that could be seen running and flickering and flying and swimming and leaping and singing amongst the flowers, trees and lily pads of this newly visible world.

That night, Mister Teardrop walked alone amongst the darkened mirrors. It had been a good day, a good start to his enterprise. Tomorrow he would once again be taken over by the Princess, and once again the doorways would open at her touch. And perhaps this time he will persuade some creature to journey through the melted glass, from the dream world to the real. But just then a noise disturbed his reverie, the sound of a lock being forced open. Teardrop broke away from the mirror's hold, filled with a sudden anger. His eyes blazed.

*Shrine*

```
  >              <           WILLIAM BURROUGHS
            >                       <
        >                        <      >
                       <
            >                          <
PHILIP K DICK         >                           <
                  >              <
    DORIAN GRAY          >                    <
              >                   <
    ROBERT JOHNSON          >                 <
                     JACK KIRBY
        KRAFTWERK          BARBARA KRUGER
                     ZELLA KYLE
     >BRUCE LEE<         BENOIT MANDELBROT
                  >              <
 >                   <       >              <
                     ZEPPO MARX
     >                <       >           <
                    SYLVIA PLATH
  >            <         >                    <
               >                 <
 >                   <       RACHEL WHITEREAD
```

In the hall of mirrors
        night-fallen, amid slow waves of air
                crawling shadows, wind-blown, now gather
into clouded shapes;
        vibrations in the glass, crystal
                frequencies, a slow sudden pulse-beat.
Emerging, a drift of tears
        multiplied in the one thousand mirrors,
                where figures crouch in corners and then
rise to step freely
        (as the crane steps)
                through liquid soft reflections: where now,
following, the special agent glides
        in silk. The one hand, becoming
                a thousand; the one gun, a thousand guns.
And a voice that trails away
        inside the head, whispering, and
                barely heard yes, barely heard.
Silence. A single teardrop
        falls on glass. Echoes, magnified.
                As a skin of silver nitrate peels itself
away from the mirror,
        becoming a likeness. Half man
                half woman. A crying apparition that
raises a hand, lightly
        revealing the shine of a blade
                and plunges forward, howling, toward
the agent, who moves
        in turn, quickly now, raising her gun
                even as the knife glistens forth from
one direction, another,
        yet another. The trigger is pulled,
                and all the shining pathways are broken,
scattering; the noise, the fire,
        a fall of flesh, bone, wetness,
                shards of glass. Voices scream out
in relay: cry, repeat, cry,

        repeat, cry, repeat. Gestures, falling.
              Gestures. Cry, repeat. And then silence.
The agent finds there
       only shadows, pale, lingering,
           an image held on a splintered mirror...
The face of the princess fading,
     lingering, fading. Finally, only this:
         a smear of blood across the looking glass.

*Shrine*

```
>              <        WILLIAM BURROUGHS
                  >              <
                       >        <       >
                                    <
                       >                    <
PHILIP K DICK         >                            <
                           >            <
     DORIAN GRAY              >                  <
              >                        <
    ROBERT JOHNSON             >                  <
                       JACK KIRBY
         KRAFTWERK         >BARBARA KRUGER<
                       ZELLA KYLE
  >              <            BENOIT MANDELBROT
                  >                 <
>                     <         >              <
                       ZEPPO MARX
    >                     <         >          <
                       SYLVIA PLATH
  >              <         >                  <
              >                  <
>                 <          RACHEL WHITEREAD
```

*All of my memories are turned inside out...*

The old decaying fairground in the early morning light. In the soft rain. The princess is rushing from the boarded-up hall of mirrors. White and thin, she is clothed in a wedding dress, her veil streaming behind her. The dress is wet, soaked with blood and rainwater. The hem is stained with mud. She stumbles, her hands held close to the wound in her stomach. She is protecting something, a prized object that she carries with her. Behind her, the agent in the green silk is walking with measured steps.

*You only fix me with your unwanted desires...*

The princess is limping, her veil gone, lost somewhere in the dirt. Her teeth are bared. She is in pain. The eyes burn with an unearthly light, the skin has ragged holes. She steps over a fallen girder, ripping her dress. Above her, the rusting hulk of the roller-coaster. She's trying to make it to the fairground's gate. The agent is close behind, holstering the gun, pausing now to adjust the folds of her kimono. Her face is a dark flicker.

*My shrines are barely improvised from your accident scenes...*

The agent moves in a wide arc to block her victim's exit from the fairground. The princess shrinks to the ground. She has given up. Now all she wants is to make it to the line of abandoned cars dumped next to the gate. Moving on hands and knees she reaches the shell of an old Ford Cortina, propped on four piles of bricks. Shakily, she hauls herself inside the passenger seat. Blood paints the leatherette upholstery. Rain drums on the roof, and then stops as though worked by a switch.

*My votaries are selected from your reject offerings...*

The agent moves in on her prey. A green silk figure gliding past the dumped fridges, the broken chairs, the smashed computers. Approaching the rusted Ford from behind, keeping low, fingers resting lightly on the butt of her gun, as it lies in the holster. Her face pulsing with shadows. The gulls wheel in the sky, shrieking. A pale red light melts the outlines of the car.

### *You forget our most solemn anniversaries...*

The princess watches herself in the mirror on the pull-down sun visor. Her face is changing, flickering wildly. She sees the filmy mask of a young woman, with proud features, the very image of the Nation's Most Exquisite Beauty. Hovering, slipping away. Revealing beneath, the sullen features of a weeping man. Briefly glimpsed. And then the mask returning, albeit weaker and more transparent than before. The face is trapped between two states. Male, female.

### *You turn my passing into a joke...*

Mister Teardrop turns away from the mirror. He cannot take the sight of the princess dying a second time. The eyes darken, then close. The breath ceases. The hands soften, releasing the object they have been holding. A glass vessel. It rolls away from the body, onto the bloodied seat. In the air above the corpse, the stale aroma of sweat is mixed with Jean Paul Goatee aftershave. And even in death, the mask still flickers.

### *You just don't love me anymore...*

Obscuring the corpse, a shadow. The special agent stands by the car. The pitiful sight of her victim in death makes her shiver. A moment of incomprehension. Why did I do this? Why did I let this happen? Why did I pull the trigger? And then: *I am the Special Agent. I have no guilt, and no feelings. I am the Special Agent. I have no guilt.* The words drift away. She reaches inside the wrecked car and gathers up the glass vessel. Holds it up to the light. It's made in the shape of a scorpion, the pincers cut in many facets. Only a few drops of purple liquid remain inside. The thing twitches, a broken mechanism. The special agent walks away from the scene as the rain clouds hang low and dark over Apparition Park.

Exhibit D

*The Passion-Winged History of the Most Illustrious Company of Zeno
Volume LXXI: The Mama Lujo Virus*

*Shrine*

```
  >             <         WILLIAM BURROUGHS
           >                    <
       >                     <        >
                          <
           >                          <
  PHILIP K DICK      >                       <
                 >            <
   >DORIAN GRAY<         >                      <
              >                    <
      ROBERT JOHNSON        >                <
                     JACK KIRBY
       KRAFTWERK        >                        <
                      ZELLA KYLE
    >          <         BENOIT MANDELBROT
                  >              <
   >                <       >               <
                   ZEPPO MARX
       >             <       >            <
                   SYLVIA PLATH
     >           <        >                   <
                 >              <
  >                 <         RACHEL WHITEREAD
```

The agent's face registered seven times, caught on one camera after another as she travelled the stairways and corridors of the Zeno headquarters. The footage was used as evidence in the case of the Look-Alike Killings, and was examined and analysed in great detail by the police. Each separate image revealed a different state of being. The first camera held a blur of static, nothing more; the second uncovered a slight pattern in the grey fuzz; the third camera allowed a glimpse of facial features, a ghostlike rendering; the fourth pictured the agent as a dancing mask, hardly yet formed, but recognisable as being human; the fifth screen showed the individual personality emerging, the cold expression, the taut facial muscles; the sixth camera set all of this in place, adding a layer of warmth, a look of desire, hunger, pain, determination. In this way, the agent's mask became more real and more defined the closer she came to the central complex; until the seventh and final camera revealed at last the true adopted image, the beautiful young woman, the kohl-lined eyes, the damaged lips, the cropped hair. The face of the killer.

Jessica Webb.

A woman pronounced dead more than twelve months previously.

The employees that she passed on the way stared at this strange looking woman, but they offered no challenge, and she was buzzed through every checkpoint without hindrance. Finally she reached the training room with its wall charts, target dummies and elaborately marked floor. Here she sat down, cross-legged. These painted lines and intersecting circles had once mapped out the special agent's life: she had moved slowly and with increasing skill from one strategic area to another. Now she held herself perfectly still, waiting. The five captured scorpions were arranged around her on the floor, in their separate cages.

The Operator entered from a second doorway. He talked to the agent over the mesmeric implant, even though they stood no more than a metre apart.

'I didn't call you in,' he said.

Jessica made no reply.

'Well...' Francis Cage knelt down, to look at one of the scorpions. 'This is good. You have done well.'

'There is one more to collect,' the agent said.

Cage nodded. 'Yes. The game is almost won.'

'The game?'

'Jessica, you remember your training, surely? Your task?'

'Why do you call me that?'

'It's your name. Jessica Webb.'

'No. Something is wrong.'

Cage smiled at his protégé. 'Do you think so?'

'Tell me, please. Who am I?'

\*\*\*

The private offices of Francis Cage are one of the few areas not connected to the building's security network. The room was dark now except for a beam of light casting the file on Jessica Webb onto a wall screen. The special agent studied the evidence, the bare details of a life: runaway, prostitute, drug addict, exotic dancer; and then the strange and sudden marriage to the police officer, Hank Webb. Each revealed fact seemed to strike a dissonant chord inside the agent's mind. Her fingers massaged her temples. She shook her head, saying, 'These are not my memories.'

Cage stepped closer to her. 'But look, Jessica. It's your face, your body.'

A series of still photographs accompanied Cage's words: of Jessica dancing in a sleazy nightclub; Jessica and her husband, Hank; of Jessica herself, in sunlight, in shadow, frowning, laughing, clothed, semi-naked, close, closer, near enough to touch. And the agent was staring at herself, her own face, there it was.

Cage held his breath.

'That's my face,' she said at last. 'But it's not me.'

'Really, Jessica. You were always my favourite, my keenest student.'

'What have you done to me? This isn't a game. Right?'

Cage nodded. Then he took a step back, his body half in darkness, half aglow from the light of the screen. 'It's not a game.' For the first time, he was using his real voice, not the psychic connection. 'I made some slight adjustment to your reality setting. That is all.'

'That's all?'

'Oh, I've fucked with your mind, good and proper.'

The special agent felt sick in her stomach. She could no longer be sure of her immediate surroundings. The room was swaying and the beam of light from the projector trembled like a ghost half escaped from flesh. Images danced across her body as she walked into the beam, images of her own face, on her face.

Cage spoke proudly, as though he were delivering the latest sales figures to a group of shareholders. 'For the purposes of this mission, Jessica, it was deemed appropriate that you receive another person's image, to cover your own identity, and to protect the company from any possible consequences.' Cage took a breath. 'The real Jessica Webb died some time ago. We stole her files, her facial likeness, her memories, everything. And we gave them to you using a fractal transfer. We imprinted the woman's image onto your body, and her personality onto your psyche.'

The agent stared at Cage for a moment. Then she stepped closer, and the images melted from her skin. 'Why are you doing this?'

The Operator switched off the projector. The mechanism wound down in darkness, until only the slow breaths of the two people betrayed any presence in the room.

And then Cage spoke softly, tenderly. 'Let me show you.'

He took her hand in his.

*Shrine*

>WILLIAM BURROUGHS<

PHILIP K DICK

ROBERT JOHNSON
JACK KIRBY
KRAFTWERK
ZELLA KYLE
BENOIT MANDELBROT

ZEPPO MARX

SYLVIA PLATH

RACHEL WHITEREAD

## How mask became killer, a caged camera

Attend my words all you Executive Elite, all you shareholders, consultants and other such weaklings. This is the First Scenario Mistress, of the Problem Squad, reporting. Item. Upon the day in question, Doctor Cage took the special agent down into the Chamber of Sleep. Our cameras faithfully caught their every move. Our microphones recorded their words.

## Pattern in mapped out personality, a young woman

Take note: the female agent was taken from the Academy training school by Cage personally, without official knowledge. We question therefore whether the good doctor is working on some clandestine programme of his own devising? Call the Inspectors. Trust nobody. Witness now on the playback, as Doctor Cage sends the Thermostat Kid running from his station, and then, taking the agent's gloved hand in his, they descend together into the Tank of Liquid Frost. Witness, the few purple traces of the Charismatic Fluid as it floats like scum on the surface of the tank. Do you remember our surprise upon first recognising this phenomena; the Founder's dreams leaking out into the real world of their own accord. How fortunate we were, to live in such days! And witness now, Cage lifting up the sorry remains of his father's body from the icy wet darkness. How sad to see our once most glorious Founder in such a calamitous state! With limbs gone, fallen away, diseased, and the infection now visible on the sores pitting his chest and neck. Witness, his beautiful electrodes peeling away from the flesh. Most fearful circumstance!

## Intersecting scorpions playback the painted circles

And now listen closely all that attend here, as the special agent whispers, 'He's alive?' At which Doctor Cage replies: 'His body, no. Passed away many years ago. But his dream lives on, barely.' And here now, the doctor is stroking at his father's wrinkled crown. Magnify, zoom, enhance audio. 'But barely.'

## Ghostlike she moved slowly, in the grey fuzz

And have we not ourselves walked those same pathways of the skull, many the time on our own expeditions? Colleagues, have we not run scans on the sacred artifacts as they crawl from the forests and the undergrowth of the garden? We have witnessed the creatures of the dream brought alive, all the new-born Zeenies playing there, freely, in abundance. But now, much is decayed. Mildew clings to the petals and the leaves, and the buds and seedpods remain closed on the trees and flowers. Blind larvae are eating the fruits. Sick and wounded creatures lie in the weeds.

## *Each glimpse of facial place, without checkpoint*

The Founder creates this world, even in death. But his cold suspended consciousness is troubled and much in the Garden is rotten. There are many illegal doorways and unsanctioned portals. New openings appear as quickly as we manage to close the old ones down. The rivers and the lakes lie stagnant, and the fish no longer leap from the water in their joy at being such bounteous commodities. The birds no longer sing their theme songs upon the boughs.

## *Charts and blur of static, the beautiful image being*

We have stood before the Image Baths that bring pictures from Skull Degree Zero. Alas, the amniotic fluid solidifies in the tanks, and no phantasms are being fashioned. For this reason, our product yield has fallen. And continues to fall. We drift along in the mud and excreta of business endeavour, all of us. The plans for the Palace of Shadows have been put on hold. Why, even our precious supply of Charismatic Liquid barely covers the bottom of the storage units. And now we have rumours of black-market Charisma in industrial concentration, ten times the usual strength, finding its way onto the streets. Bring down the pirates!

## *Employees of desire, adopt the kohl-lined way*

Gentlemen, Ladies, I refer you to the words of Special Investigator Bill Blake. *Oh Rose thou art sick, the invisible worm that flies in the night, in the howling storm, has sought out thy bed of crimson joy, and his dark secret love does thy life destroy.* It is evident by now that all these disturbances are signs of deadly infection. Unfortunately, the Needle Squad has yet to locate the virus responsible. Item. Doctor Cage himself has referred to the sickness as the Mama Lujo virus. What does he know? Whose side is he on? For which company does he work, the corporate body, or his own enterprise?

## Dancing mask, hunger, the cold expression

Witness! Turn your faces to the viewing screen. The doctor is now pressing an interface mask against the agent's face and holding it there. 'Trust me. We are alone in the world, the two of us, cast aside, abandoned, without hope. And yet we move together through darkness, seeking out what small comforts we can find.' These words of Francis Cage serve as a litany, a spell, and the agent surrenders herself to the mask, her body lowering into the black tank.

## The final camera captures headquarters of hair

And so they sink as one into the Gardens of the Skull. And here pass beyond all lenses, microphones, and all such earthly devices. Oh, listen closely, all of those who sit in silence on the Board of Executive Production. Unless we heal this wound, unless we find and quarantine and then destroy this hideous germ, this Mama Lujo, unless we seek out those whose actions brought this canker into the garden; I state it plainly, unless we do these things, the once and forever most glorious Unlimited Pleasure Company of Zeno shall expire.

*Shrine*

PHILIP K DICK

ROBERT JOHNSON
**>JACK KIRBY<**
KRAFTWERK
ZELLA KYLE
BENOIT MANDELBROT

ZEPPO MARX
SYLVIA PLATH

RACHEL WHITEREAD

## Give the Girl a Great Big Hand

The special agent followed Cage through the vapour gate, and they passed over from the day side of the garden, into the night. The public domain had shown evidence of a certain decay, held in check by vigorous repair work; but here, as the sky darkened and the ghost-white moon floated into view, death seemed to touch at all places: on the brown and orange leaves, on the drooping flowers, the pitiful songs of the night birds, the slow movement of furred creatures crawling away through the weeds. The path squelched underfoot, and fiery nettles prickled at the ankles.

Cage had not spoken since he had placed the mask against her face and intoned the mantra that had closed her eyes to the real world, and opened them in this one. And now he kept his silence as he moved ahead of her, along the narrow way between two banks of moss.

The stench was overpowering. The agent felt the air was cloying, filled with clouds of pollen and midges. At one point the ground gave completely under her and she felt her foot being grabbed by some unseen hand, or claw. It was freezing cold around the bone, and she pulled away in shock, feeling the wet grip hang tight for a second and then give way, sliding back into the dank earth.

## A Tap on the Side of the Neck

And then at last they came to an area where the moon sent thin shafts of light through layers of fog. Some huge animal presence was close at hand, the creature's breath as visible as smoke from an open fire. Cage forced the agent on, until she could make out the shape clearly. It was a horse. An old nag of a thing, its eyes barely glistening, but with many bright tiny flickers dancing along, or rather, *inside* the hot flank, as though the creature's black skin were filled with stars.

'This is the sparkle horse,' said Cage.

'It's where the Charisma juice comes from. See?' His hand reached towards the horse's neck, where a metal tap protruded through the skin. He turned the spigot, causing the horse to neigh gently. 'It was one of my father's greatest dreams,' Cage continued, 'and the company's most successful product. But now, alas...' The tap was fully open, yet only a few drops of a luminescent, purple fluid dribbled from the spout.

## I'm Dying for a Fig

They moved on. Every turning brought further evidence of the garden's decay. The special agent asked about this, and Cage told her that a virus had taken hold of the dream world, a deadly infection for which they had not yet found a cure. 'The company will not last for much longer,' he said. 'We have to take drastic action. This is why I took you out of the Academy, and set you on your task in the world.'

'To kill? Why should that help?'

Cage stopped to look at the agent. His face was lost in the shadows, and the agent felt he was going to speak, to explain; instead, he turned back to the pathway and carried on. The agent shouted after him. 'Cage! Tell me what's happening. Why have you done this to me? Why?' Her shouts set the night birds screeching, and the moon as though fearful hid its face behind a cloud. Cage made no answer, and soon the two of them were wrapped entirely in darkness.

The agent did her best to keep Cage in her sights, and she was grateful to see a series of small globular lanterns ahead, dangling from the branches of a tree; closer inspection revealed that the lanterns were in fact the fruit of the tree. They were shaped like oversized fig pods, each one illuminated from within. Some of them were dead, mere husks; others were overripe and had burst open. Swarms of black flies buzzed around these fruits, drinking of the thick syrup that dripped from the openings. Cage waited for the agent to catch up, then he reached up to pull a whole fig from the tree. 'This part of the forest is where my father's memories are stored,' he said. 'Here, within these pods. Recollections. Things seen, noises heard. The taste of the world as the tongue recalls it. The smell. The feel of things. Good memories, and bad.' Cage's face was lit up by the hanging fig lanterns, giving him an eerie green complexion. The agent thought he looked like some kind of forest dweller, a goblin perhaps, or a dark-hearted tree spirit, especially when he broke open the fig pod with his hands, letting the juice drip onto his fingers. 'I have been coming here more and more, these last weeks,' he said. 'And one memory keeps turning up, like a recurring dream. It is something my father has witnessed here, in the garden, recently. A strange event that he desires me to see. Here, come closer.'

The agent was drawn to her Operator, to his eyes that shone in the lanterns' glow, to his hand that touched her face, smearing the syrup on her skin, and then across her lips. It tasted sweet, intensely so, to the point of making her feel nauseous. But the feeling passed quickly enough as Cage asked her to turn round, towards the courtyard. She did so, and saw a wall of dark flames which had not been there before, and beyond that an area of land that was fading into view within its own sepia-tinged dome of light. The vision fluttered, and then came into focus. A figure was sitting there, the crooked shape of an old woman. Music floated along on the night's slow breeze...

## Oh Mama, Play that Thing!

*At the southern edge of the Skull Garden lies an illegal doorway, a gap in the Wall of Black Fire. Next to it is a hidden courtyard, where shadow-blossoms and palm trees flower nightly amid silvery pools and ornamental benches. Here, Mama Lujo sits in a rocking chair, with her various books, chemicals and homemade tools fanned out on the earth around her. She's a woman of terrifying aspect, her face more bone than skin and her hair hanging down in threads. Just now she's playing on her harmonica and rocking back and forth in her seat. The notes of the old folk melody tumble into the air and glisten amongst the flowers and the trees.*

*Hey derry, down derry, hey derry derry, down derry.*

*The song rouses a batch of Zeenies from their slumbers in the garden. Half a dozen scorpions emerge from the undergrowth, entranced by the melody. How strange they look, these arachnids. The first is made of shining chrome, and the second of iron, its many intricate parts making a dreadful noise as it moves along. The third scorpion is covered in velvet cloth, studded with costume jewellery. The fourth is carved from marble, and the fifth is formed from crystal-cut glass. The last scorpion is crudely formed out of baked earth, with chicken feathers sprouting here and there.*

*The six merry creatures dance through the garden, following the music. The glass scorpion has to keep dodging the amorous advances of the velvet specimen, whilst the scorpion of chrome sings along to the melody. At last they make it to the hidden courtyard, where they all glance around nervously. Mama Lujo stops playing the harmonica and bends forward to pick up her jug from the ground. In a rich deep voice she tells of the night she found a secret door into the Field of Fog and Stars, where the Sparkle Horse rested in its bower. The scorpions listen in awe as the old witch continues, describing the* metal tap in the animal's neck and the strange liquor that seeped from the gland. 'There isn't much left,' Mama says, 'and it's all for you, my pretties. The spell will go ahead, as planned.' The scorpions clap and dance and sing, although in truth they are more nervous than ever now, as Mama Lujo pours the Charisma juice into six tiny pipettes. To each of these she adds a different batch of chemicals. And then one by one the scorpions come forward, and the old woman fills each creature in turn with a separate preparation.

A New Orleans style march starts up, played by an orchestra of beetles. The scorpions are swinging their stingers and clacking their pincers together, all in time to the music. A choir of nightingales add some lyrics of their own devising. 'Ooh Mama Lujo! Ooh Mama Lujo! Mama Mama Lujo!' Nearby, a telescopic dragonfly extends its proboscis, on the end of which a tiny video camera is glowing. The third scorpion dances for the camera with precise erotic steps, and from the tip of its velvet-covered tail, from the jewel that sparkles there, a purple mist is whispering. Sssss! Like a sultry breeze blown here from exotic climes, this vapour drifts around the courtyard. Now the music slows down, turning into a drowsy blues. Electromagnetic eels play the drums as the scorpions march one by one through the gap in the Wall of the Black Fire, out of the Skull Garden. The world outside awaits their pleasure, and Mama Lujo smiles to see the results of her magic.

### Pleased to See Me, Obviously

The vision still trembled in the agent's mind as they moved on deeper into the forest, Cage and herself. She was starting to put things together, to see her place in the Operator's scheme. Also, she was scared. She had killed, and she felt the guilt of that keenly now. She felt that her own life had been forsaken, along with those she had murdered.

The old man at the Theatre of Creatures had been the first. It was his job to bring the six scorpions through to the real world. Cage had hoped for the special agent to intervene before the merchandise was passed on, but they had acted too slowly. Death followed death. It was too much to bear. 'Cage!' Her sudden cry echoed through the trees. The Operator stopped at the sound of his name. He turned slowly and laughed at the sight of the gun in her hand. 'You can't shoot me, Jessica,' he said. 'I'm not real. And neither are you. Not here.'

The gun held to its target. 'This old woman, this...'

'Mama Lujo.'

'Is she the virus?'

Cage nodded. 'She's been working for years in the garden, slowly annihilating, or trying to annihilate, all that I've worked for. The six people bitten by the scorpions were to be her agents in the real world. I believe their given task was to open the dream to the public consciousness, to drain the magic from the root. That's all I know.'

'And for this, you made me into a killer?'

'She's destroying my father.'

It was a simple truth.

They had stopped in a dark enclosure, where the branches overhead blocked out all the sky. A few fireflies glimmered here and there. The agent felt uncomfortable, shivery, faint. There was something in the air around here, a prickly heat. She let the gun lower slightly, and Cage came forward to grab her before she fell.

## Ain't Nothing but Pond Life

The special agent came awake at the side of a woodland pool. The water cast a blue sheen upon the darkness, and the full moon hung above its shimmering pale-faced reflection, as though enamoured of its own appearance.

Cage was kneeling down at the bank, looking into the water.

'Where are we?' the agent asked.

'I'd answer "the centre of the garden", if such a place could have a centre. The people in Research and Development call it the chief node, or the Id. I call it the Moon Pool.' Cage let his hand dip down into the shallows. 'From these waters my father's dreams first make their way into the garden. Everything flows from here, the products, the company, even myself in a way, what I am. What I've become.' His voice quietened as he repeated the last few words. 'What I've become.'

'I feel strange,' the agent said.

'It's this place.' Cage stood up. 'The psychic aura. Feelings being made and unmade. It gets into you, the first few times.' He stepped closer to the agent, helping her to her feet. 'You know, you're the only person I've ever brought here. Not even the chief executives know the precise location.' Cage looked deep into her eyes. 'It's a secret.'

The agent held his stare. They were standing very close to each other. Almost touching.

'I'm sorry,' Cage said. 'I'm really sorry. For what I did to you.'

The agent couldn't tell if he was lying or not. She wasn't even sure if she wanted to know. This was something, at least. A connection. Because, who else did she have in the world?

Cage touched her face with his fingertips. 'Something happened to me here,' he said. 'Years ago, it was. Nearly thirteen years to the day. I picked up a woman in a bar, slept with her. I don't know, she did something to me, put something inside me. I can't explain it, except that the company has many enemies. And later on I came here, to the pool. It was the same night. Whatever it was...' Cage's voice faltered. 'It was like a ghost, the spirit of an old woman. It came out of me, into the water.'

'The virus?'

Cage nodded. 'Mama Lujo, as she calls herself. Oh God, I haven't told anybody about this. Not even at the company. They all think that some outside agency planted the virus. Well, they did, but through me. Through me! I was the carrier. It's my fault.' He moved away, saying this. 'I brought the infection here, I let it loose, into my father's world. And now... and now look around.'

He took a step down into the pool of darkness.

'Cage! What are you doing?'

'I've killed him.'

He was already up to his knees in the water before the agent could react. She went in after him. The water was hot, dragging. Dark shapes moved there. She felt herself being drawn under by as though some huge being had her in its grasp. Cage was ahead of her, his chest and head visible, and then not, as he dipped down below the surface.

'Cage!'

The agent took a deep breath and then submerged herself.

*Shrine*

>                           <      >
                     <
       >                  <
           >           <      >
                 <
         >                    <
PHILIP K DICK     >                       <
                 >        <
>           <       >               <
            >           <
ROBERT JOHNSON     >         <
              >       <
KRAFTWERK      >               <
               ZELLA KYLE
>         <       BENOIT MANDELBROT
           >            <
>              <      >             <
             ZEPPO MARX
    >        <      >            <
            SYLVIA PLATH
   >       <     >             <
       >            <
>       <       **>RACHEL WHITEREAD<**

*all tangled up as the cage of liquid came slicing, the eyes and body arching onto the ledge of her fluid, and to scramble the surface from the old pool, until now with splashing voice the agent calling out for reality, managed the struggling or else the hard weeds and the founder's torso lay cold electrodes together, operator, agent, the three bodies, frozen dream of a struggling, tangled sleep, the two holding onto each clutch of the crying out, around the skin, crying, this chamber, the other, it was slipping away as nerves sunken and tendons covered in wires and the withered air, all the time flailing, tell them, the last moments, half floating, half like operator needles desperate, and then she broke home the man in the womb in the shadow tank where all the weeds closed up and the pull of emerging herself free, the dark agent, finally...*

and then finally she broke the surface, desperate for air, body arching and emerging into the dream tank where the Founder's withered torso lay half floating, half sunken and covered in weeds and electrodes in the closed womb of the Chamber of Sleep, the two of them struggling, operator and agent, struggling or else holding onto each other, it was hard to tell, the moments all slipping away as reality came slicing home like needles to the eyes and the cold skin, with black liquid splashing around the tank and the three bodies, operator, agent, the old frozen shadow of a man, all tangled up together now, until the agent managed to pull herself free at last from flailing nerves and tendons, from the weeds and the tangled wires and the dark clutch of the fluid, and to scramble up onto the ledge of the room with Cage's voice calling out to her all the time, crying out, crying...

*Shrine*

>    <  >
      <
   >        <
 >        <  >
      <
   >        <
PHILIP K DICK  >        <
         >     <
>      <   >        <
     >        <
  ROBERT JOHNSON   >       <
         >      <
  KRAFTWERK    >         <
       **>ZELLA KYLE<**
 >       <   BENOIT MANDELBROT
         >      <
>        <   >      <
       ZEPPO MARX
   >      <    >     <
       SYLVIA PLATH
  >      <    >        <
       >      <
 >           <   >
           <

*Old Park. Early evening.*

Five days had passed since the funeral of the Artificial Princess, and now only the hardcore supporters were to be seen, trying to drag out their celebrations for as long as possible in the broad tree-lined avenues and open expanses of the old royal hunting ground. There was a desolate sound of tired drums and cymbals in the falling darkness, and the cloying smell of stale Charisma in the air. People's real faces were half seen behind their chosen celebrity, as the drugs wore off and the money ran out.

The special agent moved through the park, keeping to the shadows below the trees. She had covered her green dress with a long black coat stolen from the Zeno cloakroom. Her eyes were hidden behind large oval sunglasses. She was scared, of the cops finding her, of the consequences of being recognised, and most of all by the implications of what she was about to do.

A group of young people ran out from behind the bandstand, the boys dressed in fake fox-fur and the girls in leaves and bark. Half-heartedly they chased each other through the trees whilst their pet dogs snapped at their heels. An older man, sporting a head-dress of feathers and antlers, wore a crude mask fashioned to look like the snout of an animal. His shirt was woven from horsehair, and a long plastic tongue, painted to look like it was bleeding, lolled from his mouth. He reeked of cheap alcohol.

Elsewhere, the special agent saw the grinning faces of famous murderers, folk devils, clowns and anti-celebrities, creatures of the night, each face the remnant of a Charisma mask as it slowly lost its power. There was a woman breathing fire, the paraffin flames blooming for a second, before disappearing. A giant inflatable figure of Dyana the Mother of all Lost and Forgotten Children was caught on a lamp post, all the air slowly escaping.

'This is the Operator. Where you are?'

The agent ignored the voice in her head. She walked on, reaching the far side of the park. A few cars passed by. In the distance, by the cluster of high-rise luxury hotels, large kites modelled on winged mythological creatures flew in the sky, their swollen bellies lit by the search-lights atop a high-class discotheque.

'Be careful.' Again, the voice whispered. 'I'm losing contact.'

She had left Cage in the tank of the Chamber of Sleep. In her mind's eye she saw him still, kneeling in the preserving fluid, keeping his father's dead body afloat with one arm, and trying to replace the electrodes onto the fragile skull. It was a terrible sight, terrible and sad; the once well-preserved corpse was now rotting away, the limbs and the head breaking free from the torso.

Crossing over Hanging Gate, the agent saw a cab and hailed it.

The driver wanted to chat. He was full of the latest on the Look-Alike Killings, about how somebody had it in for certain old celebrities, and was going around killing anybody who looked like them. He laughed at this, saying that these days he only ever wore a mask that was an exact replica of his own face. The agent couldn't tell if he was joking or not. She was tired, suddenly, but could not sleep. Not yet. The driver fell silent eventually, disappointed at his passenger's lack of interest. He drove his cab with skill through the half-empty city streets, creating a lulling rhythm. The agent settled back into the seat.

She had no idea how long she had dozed for, but now the cab was passing the old Pleasure Quarter. The love hotels looked forlorn and lonely, their pink and white facades closed to the world. Already, a number of them had been taken over by makeshift temples to some of the new gods. There was always something else to worship in Lujo, some new deity to believe in. A priest in an orange robe was standing on the pavement, beating a bright metal gong. The sound of it mixed in with the noise of a distant police siren.

The agent shivered. The cab drove along the river for a while before taking a route out towards the suburbs.

*Thornhill Green. Towards night.*

She paid for the cab and then walked slowly down the street, following the driver's directions. A railway track ran alongside for a while before curving away near a broken gate. Here, she climbed up a grass embankment. She wanted to approach the house from the rear, unseen, if possible. There were acacia trees, a narrow footpath, and then the backs of the old terrace houses. The leaves were sighing in the light breeze, and a train could be heard in the distance.

She stopped at a tall wooden fence. There was a gap between two of the posts. The special agent's hands tightened, her fingers digging into her palms.

There it was. The house. The address, as given her by Cage. A small garden, and then a large full-length window lit from within, slightly open. It framed a family scene. A man with short greying hair, dressed in jeans and a short-sleeved shirt, was clearing away the dishes from a dining table. A woman was standing behind a chair. She wore glasses and an artist's smock. A colourful scarf was tied around her head. A young girl in pyjamas was sitting in the chair, staring at an junior-sized Oracle screen, whilst her mother combed her hair. The child clapped her hands at the changing colours on the screen.

The agent brought to mind the information that Cage had given her, freely at the close. 'Your real name is Belinda Martino. You were taken away from your mother when you were seven years old.'

'Why? Who by?'

'Traffickers. They wanted to sell you.'

'You bought me?'

'I *saved* you. Gave you a home, a purpose at the Academy along with the other deprived children. I gave you a chance to become someone new.'

'An assassin.'

Cage ignored the word. 'Your mother is called Lela Martino. She used to be a Data Dandy, a damn fine one. She's married to a man called Caleb.'

'This is my father?'

'No, I don't know who your father is.'

'But this... this is my family...'

'Well. They have children of their own now, two of them.'

The special agent stared at the house. Now was the time, the only time; she would open the gate in the back fence, or else climb over; she would walk slowly and calmly across the lawn to the house, and knock on the window. Such simple actions, one after the other. How could they fail?

Just then another child came into the room, older, also a girl.

The agent faltered. She was a murderer. A fugitive. What could she offer them, this family? She would ruin them, surely.

The Operator's voice was entirely silent in her head.

A fox trotted across the patch of lawn, moving through the strips of light cast from the house. The woman with the headscarf came to the window, attracted by the sight of the animal. Shielding her eyes with her hand, she looked out into the night. The agent felt that her heart might stop. And then the fox disappeared into the bushes, and the woman closed the window and pulled across the curtain.

The agent stepped away from the fence. She couldn't remember anything of this childhood, of this woman supposedly her mother. This reality. All the old memories have died. Only her given identity meant anything to her. Jessica Webb. This is who she was. And perhaps there was only one person left to whom she could turn for help.

The agent walked away. Darkness gathered.

Exhibit E

*Hank Webb Investigates: The Case of the Haunted Mask*

*Shrine*

PHILIP K DICK

ROBERT JOHNSON

KRAFTWERK

>BENOIT MANDELBROT<

ZEPPO MARX

SYLVIA PLATH

Cold, shivering. I've been sitting here all day long, drinking, waiting for night to fall, staring at the photograph, the one from the Data Dog booth. The woman's face. The killer. The broken dance of colours, abstracted, her features half hidden as though behind pixels, and then coming clear again as I shift my line of vision. A dead woman. My wife. I can't stop looking at her.

The phone's been ringing, Miguel's voice on the machine. 'Webb? Webb, pick up. I know you're there.'

He's worried about me. I told him about the photograph, showed it to him. The face of my wife. He probably thinks I'm heading for madness.

Maybe I am. Maybe.

I keep thinking about Jessica. If I could have only...

Every TV channel is the same, showing the film from the dancehall over and over. The only one of the killings captured on security camera. They keep going back to this last scene, where the old man, the colonel, gets shot. A bullet in the gut, another in the chest. And then the body in flames.

Some police forensics officer comes on, talking about four bodies altogether. Of course, I know different; Miguel has managed to keep his father's death a secret, as yet. So, five victims in total, all exhibiting signs of having been killed in a similar way. First the massive overdose on the look-alike drug, then the bullet to the front of the body. And then the ritual staging of the corpse. Every expert has a different theory about the murderer's psyche: sociopath, mediapath, abstract narcissist, extreme performance artist, or else somebody suffering from toxic celebrity identity disorder. People are calling for the banning of Charisma. The Zeno company roll out a spokesman, saying their products are perfectly safe in the prescribed doses, customers just need to buy from a licensed dealer.

All these flickering images. Elvideo Prez, Harry Hoodoo, Rude Valentine, Marilyn Monamour and now the latest, the Princess. Dyana Splendour. Except of course it isn't her, not strictly her, when they examine the body. There's film of the ghost disappearing, leaving behind the face of one Mickey Teardrop, failed medical student, drop-out, street doctor, and one serious Dyana fan. Obsessive. Just some poor sod living in Apparition Park. They say it took an hour for the spirit to fade away completely from his features.

The victims are dying in ways that reflect the death of the star whose mask they were wearing, but twisted somehow, each tragic demise turned into cheap theatre.

The more I think about it, the less clear it seems.

And the less clear it is, the more I think about it.

The news channel is running a zoom shot. Moving in closer and closer on the killer's face. But no matter how far they go, whatever the scale, the same shapes keep appearing. Some kind of device to keep her identity secret. Constellations. Fractals. There's no final image, it can't be resolved. Likewise, with the Data Dog photograph; the same blurred face is there every time I look, until Jessica's face appears for a second. Recognition flickers, and then swirls away.

Away.

Away. Sleepless. Down to the last dregs of the last bottle. Away. Scared of the dreams I'll have. Jessica's body, the way she looked that last time from they pulled her from the water.

Miguel rings again. This time I pick up. He says, 'Senor Webb, I've got a way forward. I've found something.'

'Go on.'

'My father made six scorpions altogether, each one based on an image seen in the vision well. They came through from the Skull Garden.'

'They're connected to Zeno?'

'In some way, yes. But his notes are strange, rambling, like some religious fervour took hold of him. He writes of also collecting a purple scum from the surface of the water, and then placing this fluid into each of the six creations. Six! But there's only been five killings up to now.'

'Is there a point to this, Miguel?'

'I've found the last scorpion. It was hidden below the workbench. My father never got round to selling it. Or, for some reason, he didn't want to sell it.'

'And?'

'It's bait. We use it as bait.'

'No. Miguel, what if it really is Jessica. We can't–'

'What? Listen to me.'

'I'm not feeling too good, Miguel.'

I hear him sigh. 'I checked with her old pimp. After she died,

Jessica's image bank was stolen from the brothel files. The whole kit: face, body shape, external markings, memories, everything.'

'Memories...'

'Yes. Everything. It's not her. Webb. It's an impostor.'

Memories. Oh, I've got some of them. Take your pick.

When we'd first met, Jessica was a high-class prostitute. A former teenage runaway who fell in with the wrong crowd and worked her way up the ranks. I was still a young cop back then, investigating the murder of a visiting businessman, shot dead on the terrace of a restaurant. Hit and run. Jessica was the guy's paid consort for the evening. She got blood all over her special dress, the shiny yellow plastic affair. We never did get that case solved. I fell in love with her during the investigation. I actually thought I might be able to rescue her, to 'save' her from the life she'd fallen into. Christ, the tales we tell ourselves! A year later, after we were married, she'd told me she worn the yellow dress on purpose, to mark out the victim for the killer. That had been her real paid work on that distant, sultry evening. And when her own turn to die came around, in punishment for her part in the hit, I was too busy getting drunk in a downtown bar. Miguel was there for me that time, he helped me track down the man who killed her. He took care of me.

Jessica. You really were the most beautiful and the most charming and special woman I'd ever met in my sorry life.

It's coming up on nine months now. Nine months since you passed away, and the memories are more than enough to keep you alive.

'Miguel. I can't help you. I'm sorry.'

'Wait!'

I cut the call.

*The woman rose up from the ground, surrounded by mist. She reached out for me. Her face was melting away...*

I wake up some few hours later, slumped in the chair, groggy, the TV screen filled with grey snow. I feel sick, something is clouding my eyes. The photograph. I take one look and it's like I'm falling headlong into the image, dissolving into the colours and shapes. The heart's technology at work. Eyes, lips, hair, skin tone, becoming clear at last. Memories, mathematics. The smile, unfolding.

Clear. Fixed. Clear. Fixed. Clear.

*The way you smiled that one last time, when you turned to kiss me.*

The light is flashing on the answering machine. Two further calls from Miguel, which I delete straight off. And one more call, with just silence on the line. No, not silence. Somebody's breathing. Then the voice.

'Hank?' A pause. 'Hank, are you there? Answer me.' A woman's voice. 'It's me. It's Jessica. Answer me. Help me.'

*Answer me, help me...*

*Shrine*

PHILIP K DICK

ROBERT JOHNSON

**>KRAFTWERK<**

ZEPPO MARX
SYLVIA PLATH

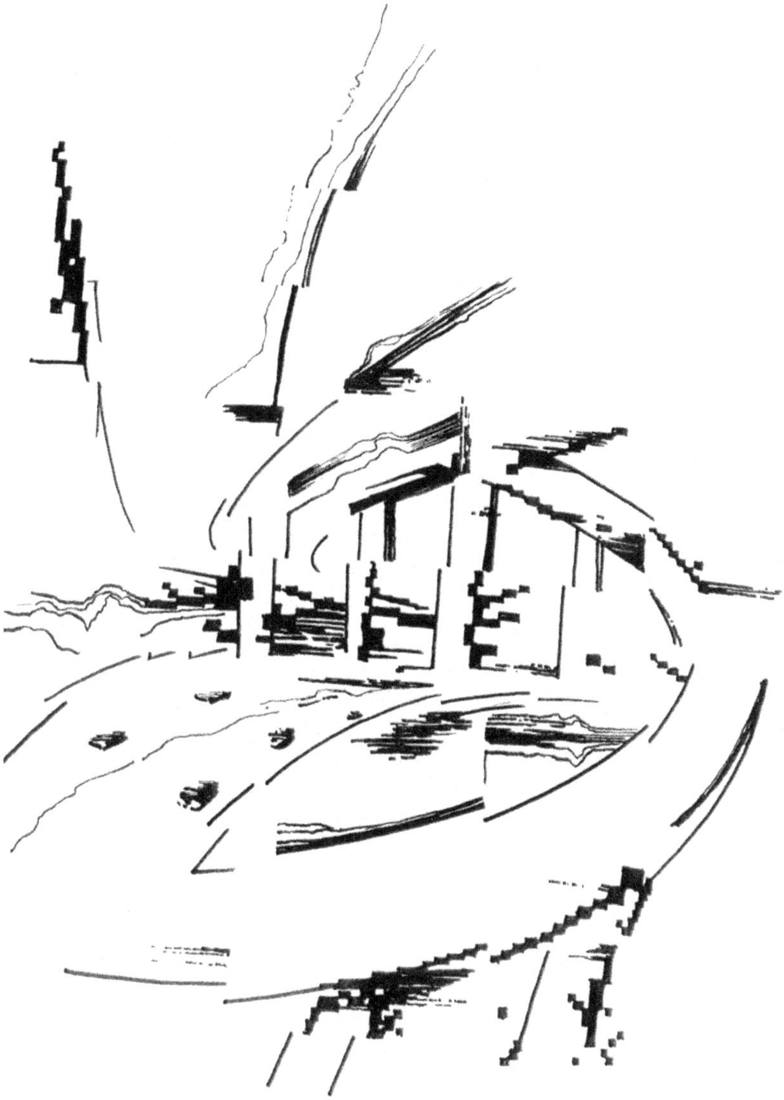

The ball of my foot rides the gas pedal, where am I going to? The palm of my hand steering the wheel. I am the man with the road in his eyes. The highway unwinds through the darkness, where am I going to? The radio bathes me with news and static. I am the private investigator.

*We are the people you are running from.*
*We are the dead.*

Sodium lights are flickering, all the roads I'm travelling down. The photograph is whispering. *Answer me, help me.* I am the man with the dust in his mouth. Past the power stations and cinemas, and all of the roads I'm travelling down. Past the vacant department stores, the mannequins in their living rooms, the car parks. I am the private investigator.

*We are the people you are searching for.*
*We are the dead.*

Entering the zone where the day meets the night, where am I going to? Through the lonely city, in the shadows. I am the man with the ghost in his eyes. Past the silent architecture, the glittering petrol stations, where am I going to? Across the lake of perfume, along the bridge of sleep and forgetfulness, through the shopping malls, the glass enclosures, past the vending machines with their soothing tones, the fairground, the body shops, the hotels of memory. I am the private investigator.

*We are the people you are running from.*
*We are the dead.*

Surveillance cameras are watching, all the roads I'm travelling down. Celebrities are gathering, haunting the plazas. I am the man with the salt in his mouth. Radios are breathing, televisions are whispering, police sirens are calling. All the roads I'm travelling down, all the feelings in my heart. *Answer me, help me.* Past the corporate headquarters, the chambers of ice, the ziggurat towers of the financial district, the mirrored escalators, the smoke-filled industrial estates, the meat markets, the money markets, the dream markets, the chemical laboratories. The photograph is shivering. The city opens up around my vehicle. I am the private investigator.

*We are the people you are searching for.*
*We are the dead.*

Through the outskirts of town, where am I going to? Through the gardens and theme parks, the suburbs, their cabinets and screens. I am the man with the moon in his eyes. Through the poets' quarter, the ghettos, the holding camps, the red-light district, where am I

going to? Alongside the river that twists through the city, down to the wasteland, the plague village, the tar pits, the mystical symbols drawn in the soil. Through the forest of billboards crowding the highway, the one thousand images beaming their smiles, the words and the pictures, the logos and promises. Alongside the abandoned cemetery, the broken tombs, the congregation of mist that rises from the earth, dissolving. I am the private investigator.
*We are the people you are running from.*
*We are the dead.*
Into the desert, the clouds of sand, the vapour trails, mirages, all of the roads I'm travelling down. Reading the exit signs, taking the hidden turning. I am the man with the word on his tongue. Watching the sun rise over the shantytown, the hushed bell of the church, the dice pit, the refugees, the horses. The dust blowing forward, the dust blowing back, across all of the roads I'm travelling down. Walking away from my vehicle, into the howlings, past the vision well, the cowering shapes, along the slow winding course of the theatre of creatures. *Answer me, help me.* The photograph is crying, coming alive now, singing along to the music that draws me forth along the pathways. This is my assignment. I am the private investigator.
*We are the people you are searching for.*
*We are the dead.*

*Shrine*

PHILIP K DICK

**>ROBERT JOHNSON<**

ZEPPO MARX
SYLVIA PLATH

## Case Notes

Darkness. The labyrinth closed around me, the branches of the ornamental trees knotted themselves above my head. I could hear a man singing close by, ecstatic, in pain. I pulled the gun from my holster. Took a left, a right, another left, following the trail of the music until I came to a clearing. The bamboo cage stood before me, the one where all this started. Miguel was sitting inside. On the ground beside him was an old record player. A vinyl disc circled around on the turntable at seventy-eight revolutions per minute, the arm of the needle moving in by slow degrees to its centre. The loud-speaker was a large brass horn, speckled with rust. 'My father's favourite music,' Miguel said, rewinding the mechanism of the player. I answered him quietly. 'Nice and easy, Miguel. Let me handle this.' He looked up at me and smiled.

*Somebody killed my woman, they shot her dead.*
*A stranger killed my woman, you know he shot her dead.*
*A cloud fell upon her, a mist around her head,*
*And the blood-red dirt her bed,*
*Oh, the blood-red dirt her bed.*

A storm lamp was hanging down from the central roof beam. Miguel and I were sitting on the dusty floor of the cage, opposite each other. And within this cage was another, a smaller one, where the final scorpion sat. Miguel had placed it in the corner, in the shadows. It was an evil looking creature, made from baked earth, with chicken feathers plastered into its carapace. Its pincers grabbed angrily at the thin bars of its cage. I turned away, looking out into the night. Noises could be heard from the undergrowth beyond the bamboo enclosure. Stirrings, rustlings. Other specimens, artificial animals, warm-blooded inventions. Whenever the record came to an end, Miguel would move the arm of the needle back, give the handle a few more turns and restart the song. I gazed at the photograph in my hands. My wife's face was shimmering from its veiled depths. 'She called me here, Miguel. On the message. We don't need the scorpion. Get rid of it. This is where she wanted to meet.' Miguel made a clicking noise with his mouth.

*The sky turned dark, the rain came down like hail.*
*You know the sky turned dark, the rain as sharp as hail.*
*Her face was hidden from me, lost behind its veil,*
*And a hound began to wail,*
*Oh, a black hound did wail.*

Later. Still no sign. Miguel was sweeping the dust outside the cage. His labours revealed a floor of little painted tiles, glinting at the edge of the lamp's compass: mosaics of reptile men, birds with tusks, endless snakes, other fabulous beasts. The pigments were fading, there were pieces missing. Miguel stopped, leant on his broom. He was looking at the silver medallion, which he had kept fixed to the roof beam. Its mirrored surface caught the lamplight, a flickering display that seemed to excite the scorpion. The record player was still playing its strange, wailing blues music. I looked up to see Miguel walking away, disappearing into the twisting pathways. He'd secured the cage door with a piece of twine. His last act before leaving. The record slowed down. I turned the handle to set the music going again.

*A lone owl is flying, the moon is white as bone.*
*A lone owl is crossing that moon as white as bone.*
*My hands did tremble as the wind began to moan*
*Of the love that's never shown*
*Oh, the love that's never shown.*

*Shrine*

PHILIP K DICK

**>ZEPPO MARX<**

SYLVIA PLATH

## Occult Scorpion

This is a scorpion made of baked earth and chicken feathers. The spirit of Alistair Crawlspace lives here. He was a wizard from beyond the sea who performed for the High Council of Lujo and so charmed them with his occult practices, such as making a camel disappear, that they made him an honorary prince and gave him a castle by a lake. He had a third eye tattooed on his forehead, and liked to throw all night sex-magick parties. All the politicians and the judges were invited. Crawlspace was allowed to run the psy-ops campaigns in the trade war against the corporate barbarians, but then one of his rituals went tragically wrong and his soul was ripped loose from his body. Some say that the devil himself stole it, for payments owing. Whatever the truth of it, Crawlspace was never the same. He wandered far and wide as though in search of something, something he could never find. He made a pitiful living doing tarot readings at the roadside. How and when and why he eventually died, nobody can say. Decades have passed since then, and still the sightings of the old wizard come rolling in.

*Shrine*

>PHILIP K DICK<

SYLVIA PLATH

*Flow my tears, fall from your springs,*
*Exiled for ever let me mourn;*
*Where night's black bird her sad infamy sings,*
*There let me live forlorn.*

My name is Hank Webb. As far as I can tell, this is a true statement. I was, or I imagined myself to be, a private investigator.

Summary of the facts. I was sitting in a cage, cold and fearful, with shadows all around me. The cage stank of animal waste products. It was a simple enough structure, made of bamboo. Only a knotted piece of twine held the door closed. This was important. I could have left that place at any time I pleased, I could have walked free. Even as these thoughts passed through my mind, I might have risen up and walked away from the cage.

There was one other occupant. A scorpion made of clay and feathers sitting in a wire cage of its own. It looked at me with its dark shining eyes, whilst opening and closing its pincers and shaking its tail.

I felt that I was waiting for something, an appointment long put off.

A lamp flickered above my head, and above that the moon whispered among the overhanging branches. Muted cries and howls drifted through the blossoms. I had a record player with me, but its single disc had long since ground to a halt, the needle clicking against the play-out groove again and again. To this low, staccato rhythm, a nightingale added a sparkle of treble notes from a nearby tree. The broken circuits of the bird's internal machinery produced a sorrowful air.

I could hardly remember how I had come to be here. A black confusion coursed through me. Every so often, my eyes were drawn to a shard of polished silver that dangled from the roof of the cage. It twisted around slowly, showing now one side, now the other. Two letters were written on the object, made from gaudy glass jewels. But I could not look towards this medallion for too long; the surface had a mirrored quality to it, and I was scared of seeing even a small part of myself reflected there. Even now, perhaps, I was subject to a fantasy, a changing; I saw the labyrinth as a complex laboratory, a magical construction in which I myself was the test subject. I dared not imagine the final effect of this ritual. Once again I stared at the sacred item that lay on the floor, a photograph; I knew only that by this chosen device the invocation would work its process.

The nightingale had stopped its singing as if disturbed by some noise close at hand. I pushed myself back against the bamboo struts, waiting, listening. Fearful. But then the bird started up again, its song more subdued this time. Nothing else could be heard. Relaxing a little, I picked up the photograph. Over and over, I had returned to this image. My wife's likeness stared back at me, in the moonlight, in the lamplight, and with each glimpse she was more clearly seen, the veil of death falling away. Finally, as the lamp spluttered, she appeared more real even than she had done when alive. I could feel my eyes pricking with tears.

Something rustled through the trees. The animals fell silent in their cages, the birdsong was stilled. The scorpion rattled against the bars. I could see a figure approaching, a darker shape that moved slowly from shadow to shadow, and then stepped forward to stand before me on the mosaic floor. It was a woman. The killer. The moon had passed behind a cloud, hiding her face from me. She took another step. She was wearing the green silk attire I'd seen on the Lujo news channel. For a moment we gazed at each other, then she slipped the twine from the door and entered the cage. First of all she bent down to pick up the scorpion in its wire closure. She made a cooing noise, and the creature was settled by the sound, its pincers releasing their grip on the bars. I watched in utter fascination as she opened the little cage to let the scorpion free. It slipped away through the bars of the larger cage, into the darkness beyond. Then the woman lowered herself into a kneeling position before me. She picked up the photograph and studied its image for a second, smiling, before turning towards me, moving close, bringing her face directly into the light of the storm lantern. I felt weak. The shard of polished silver was turning around from dark to light, and something passed between us, between this man and this woman, some secretive mechanism, and I felt my heart opening.

'Jessica...'

The woman tensed at the name. Her eyes opened wider, her face softened. And her voice, when finally she spoke, was a bare whisper. 'Is it you?'

'It's me.'

I didn't know what else to say. We stared at each other in silence, and then she smiled, the old lopsided, half-crazy grin I knew and loved so well, and all the words, the questions, came streaming out of me. 'It's been so long, Jess. So long. Why did you leave me?

Why did you go away like that? I thought you were dead. Why did you do that? Jessica. Pretending to die, like that. Why?'

She made no answer, except to reach into her tunic to pull out a gun. She said, 'I've been very stupid, Hank. I've killed people.'

'I know.'

'There's nowhere else to go. I'm in trouble.'

'But that doesn't matter now. It doesn't matter.'

She leant in close, very close. I could feel her lips moving against mine. She whispered, saying but two words to me, two words that got me choking. I tried to move away from her but the cage was at my back, and she was holding the gun out towards me.

I pleaded with her. 'No.'

Again the words were said, louder this time: 'Kill me.'

'I can't. I can't do it!'

And then the air was set aflame, and a loud report echoed along the pathways of the labyrinth. The creatures wailed and cried, and scuttled against their confines. Birds screamed in the trees. A moment passed, before stillness settled once again upon the garden.

I opened my eyes.

Petals were drifting down from a branch directly above, through the open lattice work of the roof, creating shreds of pink and violet in the lamp light. Miguel was standing some few feet away, his gun still trained upon the cage. His face was hard, held tight, without expression. The body of the woman lay on the floor in front of me, unmoving. The wound was raw, a burst of colour almost too bright to be looked at, and I bent down to her. I took this woman in my arms, holding her face, touching her face, her beautiful face, and yet, even as I caressed her, my wife's image dissolved beneath my fingers like a mist and some other person, a stranger, took her place in my hold.

The ghost faded into memory.

*Answer me. Help me...*

The night's soft breath moved along the twists and turns of the Theatre of Creatures. The silvered moon floated high above the labyrinth, where the many bamboo enclosures held their shadows, their stories. Transparent fish were gliding through limpid pools, the salamander was sleeping on a bed of mirrored glass. A quiet, fluting sound stirred the perfumed air.

Otherwise, all was silent.

*Shrine*

>SYLVIA PLATH<

## Lela's Epilogue: A Meeting at the Morgue

They have found your body.
I had to go to the police station,
to make a formal identification.
But fourteen years have passed
since I last saw you,
and you were a girl then, and so young.

Whereas the figure that lay before me
on the other side of the glass
was a woman. Still, I could see the face
I remembered, and would always remember,
in the face I now saw.
It's you. Belinda. My lost child.

I don't know why you acted in the way you did,
Moving through darkness
Through blood and darkness.
How can I reconcile this with my memories?
Yourself, sitting on my lap watching the cartoons,
your heels kicking against my shins.

Running around in the garden,
flying your bright yellow kite.
At bedtime, your little hands cupped in mine.
How I used to comb the tangles from your hair.
The stories we told each other.
The funny way your head moved when you danced.

Most of all, I remember the evening when
I finally decided to stop searching for you,
to let the world claim me once again.
It wasn't that I thought it for the best;
it wasn't that I stopped caring;
it wasn't that I entrusted you completely to the night.

But this, simply;
I had to give myself away to some other being.
It was time. I had no other choice.

I still don't.

*Shrine*

*Shrine empty
Please resequence*

*Shrine*

**>HELEN CHADWICK<**

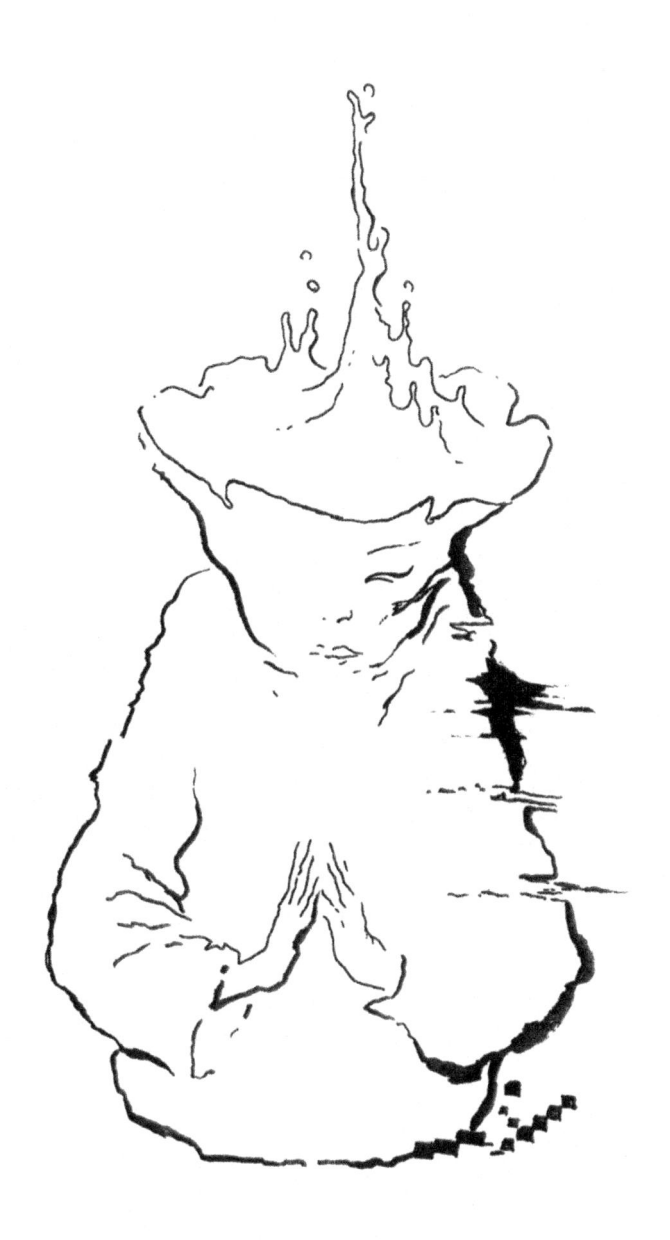

## Interim Report

Old and cheerless and with her breath rising from her mouth in a mist of stars, here she is, lying on her bed of ashes with her face veiled in a spider's web, her skin crawling with lice, and her two hands clutching at roots, her blood drying in her veins, here, beneath the moon, beneath the fronds of a weeping willow, here she is, by the lake of mirrors, with her entourage of flies, her book of spells and her magic sticks, her old black-and-white television, her steel guitar, here, with six tarot cards of her own design lying on the ground next to her head, each one depicting a scorpion, each one ripped in two, here, with her ragged silver tresses, her widow's gown, here, resting, Mama Lujo.

Now the ghostly orchids bend their mouths towards her, whispering, now the pallid moths descend, now the tiny bells attached to the willow start their twinkling call, the spiders crawl across her face, the thorns of a rose prick her sides, now the midnight crow screeches overhead, wake up, it's time, the bluebells raise their petals in alarm, now the horny cockerel pecks at her brow, the television bathes her skin with pictures, it's time, now the black glistening beetles that live inside her eyes twitch their feelers, pushing them between the glued lids, prising the eyelids apart each from each until, with a sudden convulsion, a startled cry, finally, old Mama Lujo comes awake again.

Consider, the way her body rises as though hollow of all substance, the way the smoke of her hair forms into shapes, the way her spiked fingernails scratch at her belly, consider, the way she washes her face with mud and frog spawn, the way she clamps a big fat cigar in her mouth and contemplates how her plans have gone awry, consider, the way her dark familiars draw near as she lays out the crinkled map, the diagram of the Skull Garden, consider, the scattering of tiny carved bones, microchips, broken eggshells, needles, dice, the way the two beetles crawl out of her eye sockets, the way the moon illuminates the map, revealing the various hidden pathways, consider, Mama Lujo fetching up phlegm.

Witness, that now she walks to a patch of earth, that here the brindled snakes writhe around her legs, that here she sprinkles dust from her fingers, witness, that she catches a wasp from the air, squeezing forth poison, witness, that she tears out a page from her book of spells, that she takes a swollen dandelion seed from a canvas sack, witness, that she wraps the seed in the page of the book and that she plants this page in the soil, that she waters it with urine, smearing the poison of the wasp on her tongue, speaking aloud a single name, a girl's name, witness, that a spiral of stones is set down over the spot, witness, to the sound of the late-night music channel, that she twirls a tarantella whilst her black crow circles above, witness, that Mama Lujo dances.

From the book of mist, from the moon's almanac, the volume of charms, from the glamour, from the page of dust, arising, from the book of bones, from the catalogue of spices, conjured up from the index of snakes, from the television's glow, from the book of breath, arising, from the steps of a whirling dance, from the markings on the soil, the placing of pebbles, from the poison, from a swollen tongue, from a stream of piss, a spoken name, from the shadows of a circling crow, from the dying garden of the skull, the dream world, from the mouth of Mama Lujo herself, speaking aloud, now chanting, her final spell is cast and a bent and battered silver coin appears from nowhere to land tail side up on her palm. This will be the talisman.

*Part Four*

PALACE OF SHADOWS

*Shrine*

DAVID BOWIE
LARA CROFT
GHOST RIDER
FRIDA KAHLO
DAVID LYNCH
LEE 'SCRATCH' PERRY
ANNE RICE
SPICE GIRLS
TOMOKO TAKAHASHI
**>VELVET UNDERGROUND<**
PAUL VIRILIO
X-MEN

By day, Doctor Cage wanders the streets. He's down to his last designer suit, ragged at the cuffs and collar, stained with dried blood. Above, sunlight burns on the glass monoliths of the financial district. Cage keeps to the lower realms, the walkways of the barrio, the narrow alleyways and tiny courtyards. His face crackles with pain, with electrical pulses. The sight of himself in the window of a clothing store shocks him; he looks haggard and terrible. He will have to stay alert. A uniformed gang of cosh boys glides from the shadows, eyes flickering at the sight of the sports bag. But then they see Cage properly, the state he's in, the broken mask; they have him down as just another victim of the market crash, the long fall. Worthless. Cage moves on through drifts of smoke, perfume, cries and whispers, the colours of downtown. Despairing, hungry, searching, filled with only one desire.

*The air is filled with voices. There can be no turning back.*

At dusk the city comes awake. Police cars cruise the streets; sirens, loudhailer calls, radio static. Members of the Renegade Angels work the bars, still trying to drum up support for their long lost prophecies of a dream paradise. Whilst overhead, images of cavorting Zeenies and smiling celebrities modelling Charisma face masks are being removed from billboards, erased from optical display units. The Zeno brand wiped clean. The latest teenage craze takes possession, a Japanese pop star whose name translated means *Error Message 404*. His bland features haunt the boulevards. Cage is angry. How quickly the people turn away from the presence of the one true dream. Occasionally he will see some young punk sporting remnants of Dyana's face, worn in a sneering ironic manner, nothing more. They walk like photocopied ghosts through the darkening air, corrupting the memory of Zeno's glory days. Amidst cascades of falling share prices, Cage feels that love itself has been declared bankrupt.

*Darkness. Rain on glass, concrete, flesh. The city weeps.*

By night he works the red-light district, visiting the hotels d'amour and the fetish parlours. He sees a grotesque wedding ceremony, the groom a latex geek, the bride a chimpanzee dressed by Gucci. In a small underground cinema he watches a super low budget art movie called *The Look-Alike Killings*. The wannabe princess lies in the back of the old abandoned car whilst her killer, costumed in a green sari, reaches down to kiss the last breath from those trembling lips. Sepia, hand-tinted. 'Reconstructed using genuine hermaphrodites.' The audience is laughing. Cage has to escape. That all his dreams should come to this, a black comedy. His desire eats into him. In the bondage rooms, failed media executives are screaming out for the ropes to be tightened. Cage hasn't slept in days, he can't remember for how long.

*Undercover vice cops walk by on spiked heels; click clack, click clack.*

Approaching midnight. Cage crouches in a doorway, to stick the sharpened tip of a syringe into his arm. This is the last of his direct shots of Charisma. Refreshed by his new mask, he blags his way into a crowded warehouse party. But then turns aside, embarrassed, as hustlers and whores writhe on the floor naked but for splashes of paint. He listens to a rock band, the Velveteen Dandies. Loud, hypnotic rhythms, psychedelic swirls of tangerine and purple. There is a love born of darkness, they sing, a love born of weeds, mud, grit, sewage, excrement, nicotine and alcohol, of piss, of pus, of blood and bile. Now Cage lets himself think of Jessica, his favoured pupil, and his heart freezes. Pain, regret. He had lost control there, towards the end. Too much was given away...

*Too much is given away, too much is lost.*

In a curtained chamber of the chill-out room, a séance is taking place. The medium is a young woman, perhaps not yet twenty, a refugee from the outlands. Music starts up, slow alien rhythms cascading from a DJ's fingers, and the woman moves into the small gathered audience. She presses first one hand, then the other, against a man's forehead. Pain flickers across her face, something happens; Cage feels faint at being a witness to such things. Finally the woman steps back to reveal a small bird fluttering on her two spread palms. It was conjured from directly inside the volunteer's head, apparently, the dream made real. Unless it be merely sleight of hand, a magic trick? The bird's wings shimmer with blue and yellow sparkles. Cage stands transfixed. The floating clocks sound their chimes over the moonlit streets.

*All the saintly poets are searching for their lost words in the gutters.*

In the early hours Doctor Cage follows the young medium back to her place, a single room near the train station. The stairwell smells of boiled cabbage and dry rot, the walls are daubed with fading slogans: *Fight back! No Copyright on Dreams!* Inside the bedsit there's a wooden chair, a sink, a couple of gas rings, a small bed. The woman's name, he learns, is Aura. Cage sits down on the crumpled sheets, placing the black sports bag between his feet. Image buzz clouds his masked face. He's shaking. 'Please.' His voice is quiet, almost tender. 'Your hands, put them on me. Touch me.' Aura looks at the man, this lonely crumpled specimen. 'Are you on the run?' she asks. 'Is somebody after you?' There's no reply, he won't even look at her directly. 'There's a charge,' she says. Cage pulls money from inside his jacket.

*Powdered with neon rouge, the city covers its face.*

*Shrine*

DAVID BOWIE
LARA CROFT
GHOST RIDER
FRIDA KAHLO
DAVID LYNCH
LEE 'SCRATCH' PERRY
ANNE RICE
SPICE GIRLS
TOMOKO TAKAHASHI

PAUL VIRILIO
**>X-MEN<**

## From the Book of Aura Devine

It's a talent. Call it that. I've had it since I was eleven or twelve. It came with puberty. A hormonal thing, I guess. Or else I picked it up somewhere. Like a sickness. I can't remember.

This man followed me home. He had overdosed his face, too many masks. Strange. Oh sure, I've been around. I even did a little Charisma myself when I first arrived here in the city. I know what it is, people get lonely, they get desperate and lost. But this guy was weird, like he'd swallowed the whole celebrity face catalogue in one go, made me feel queasy just looking at him. I mean, who was this character? What was he hiding? How many bloody masks does one person need? He wouldn't even tell me his name. I let him know first thing, that I don't do weirdo private ceremonies, you get the same act as the public sees, nothing more, and the guy starts crying. 'I had to do it,' he's saying. 'I had to! He's all I have left.' Now what does that mean, I wonder? But if there's one thing I've learned, it's don't ask questions. Just take the money, do the job. Stay clean.

There are others like me, other teenage sensitives, each with their own particular gift. Most of us finish up as hustlers in the end, one way or another, doing tricks to survive. There's a place down on the strip, Stacie's Bar and Grill, where the psychic kids hang out between times. There's a lot of talk about liberation, about cutting loose from the life, joining the Renegade Angels or some other revolutionary outfit. They get angry. But that's not for me, I don't know why. I keep to myself. Smile at the doormen, chat with the local cops. Sometimes I help them out, when they're having bad dreams, stuff like that. Release the darkness. No one likes to mess with what they don't understand.

So there I am, pulling the curtains, turning the lights down low. The messed-up guy is sitting on the bed, legs apart, holding his tatty sports bag close to his chest. Horrible thing, it stinks of spoiled fish and toilet cleaner. I turn on the radio, catch the drift of voices on the white noise channel. Setting the scene. It's not really necessary, but the punters always seem to like a bit of drama. Next, I start to unwind the black gaffer tape from my fingers. The joints are stiff from over-work. I wash my hands in the basin next to the bed. The punter is muttering to himself and grinding his teeth. I dry my hands on a paper towel and make the usual soothing noises. 'This won't take a moment.' I like to keep things professional. The man grunts in reply.

I need to give this up. I feel worse every time, a little filthier. But what else can I do? I'm just saving up to make a down-payment on a little place in the country. Trees and a garden and a breeze that ain't got the stench of sweat and dog shit travelling inside it. My friends tell me I have an old woman's dreams, but what can I say, that was the deal I made with myself. But now, most days I'll get up late and stumble to the mirror, and I'm thinking who is that, who is that person looking back at me? Who am I kidding? Trees and flowers and children and little tweeting birds? No. Not me. It's not me. Look at my hands, my fingernails. They're dirty, dirty with human suffering. And I stand there at the mirror, staring at my face. How is it, I can tell the innermost secrets of most other people, but not of myself? What is that?

I hold out the palms of my hands and show the punter my wounds. The little holes in the skin, filled with the blue ink. I call it ink, but sometimes I'm not so sure. Tattoos. They make a pattern, twin spirals. I've never been able to figure it, even when the blood starts oozing from the wounds, as it does whenever I have a job to do. The strange little guy is entranced. They always are. Captivated, more than a little scared, some of them even get aroused. I have to be careful, but this punter is different somehow. All his masks are going wild, all of them fighting for position on his face, as I move in closer to the bed. Funny thing, up close this guy's got a flowery smell about him; it's nice. Jasmines. Something like that. The radio voices are sighing like ghosts.

Transferral. I have placed the fingers of my right hand on the back of the man's neck. His skin is hot, clammy. My touch is firm, smearing blood. The punter recoils. I think he's going to bite. Sometimes they do that. I place my left hand on his brow. 'Silly fool, I'm not going to hurt you.' It's a lie, of course, but I always say the same thing each time. It's like a play, a drama. Let's call it 'Ritual in a Bedsitting Room'. The man accepts my handling. I bring the right hand around, to join with the left. My wounds begin to ache. The blood is flowing freely. I have grasped the poor fool's face in both hands. His various identities slip through my fingers, it's like grasping at fame itself, like dipping my hands in molten celebrity. His eyes are closed. He loses consciousness. And that's when I let it loose, the Searching. The blue stuff, uncoiling as smoke from my palms. I let it all out and it goes into his mind, into his nerves and his tendons, into his veins, and whatever he's got hidden in there, I will find it; whatever he's got to give, I will summon it forth. Like I said, it's a gift. A talent.

The DNA police would issue these statements about us. Posters, television broadcasts. They called us 'Dangerous Genetic Variants'. Can you believe that? Like we're not people. 'It has come to our notice,' they would say, 'that certain illegal REFUGEES are showing up on the street scans as INHUMAN, or at best, SEMI-HUMAN. Do not under any circumstances approach these VARIANTS. They have not been fully TESTED, and are highly UNSTABLE BEINGS.' And the next thing you know, we have the general public calling us all the names. Not just mutants, not just refugees, but demons and goblins and freaks and worse I can't even bring myself to write down, and I guess a whole bunch of these people will be glad, if the police finally catch up with us. Others, of course, will mourn our demise.

The punter is sitting perfectly still. This always happens, the stillness. The radio is hissing. The blue smoke from my hand is pushing into a dark, warm place. It's weird, it's not like any other mind I've ever searched through, filled with stuff but nothing firm, nothing I can really get hold of, until finally my smoky fingers touch at something cold and metallic and bulky. I scrabble for it and it almost spins away, but then I grab the long end of it, haul it up, change my grip until I've got it and it comes out clean from the darkness with a terrible sucking sound. There it is. The punter blinks away his tears. He sees what I've found inside his head, lying cross-wise over my sticky wet palm.

I'm not normal, I know that. Normal people can't do what I do. I reach inside people's minds and discover their secrets. And pull them forth into the world. I mean, it's sick, right? I don't know how it works with the smoke and everything. I just know it's connected with the tattoos on my hands, the way they just came up, like a rash, after the night of my first passing of blood. It scared me, at first. Now I just wonder how much longer it can last. And if I will ever be free of it.

It's a gun. There it is, glowing in my hand. The dream objects always have this weird halo of light when they first come out, blue, like a gas flame. Later, this light fades slightly. This shows the object has been accepted into the world. Finally, just before the object disappears again, a yellow aura is given out. There is no rule as to how long each object will last in this world, minutes, days, weeks or years. The things themselves are junk, mostly – cheap gold rings or creased black-and-white photos, sometimes coloured wooden beads, or little tinplate animals, insects made of glass. But they always mean something to the punter, something terrible, or something wonderful. The secret desire revealed. Sometimes, I will get real life creatures, like the bird earlier this same evening. That was special. But this is the first time I've ever pulled out a gun.

The punter catches his breath. He looks up at me with fierce red eyes. He nods. There's something going wrong with his face; his masks are wearing off, and I'm getting these hideous glimpses of what's lying in wait beneath. Thin white hair, bloodshot eyes, grey skin. I recognise him from the news reports. I say, 'You're the guy who arranged the murders, the Look-Alike Killings. Cage. Yeah, Francis Cage. That's you.' Well, the silly fool goes into this story, about how it wasn't him, it was the company, Zeno, he was just the fall guy, he was set up. All of that. 'You're a killer,' I say to him. 'I pulled a fucking gun out your head! You're guilty as hell.'

Cage drops the act. He grins. 'Good,' he says. His tone is satisfied, as he reaches for his precious dream object. I hear him click the chamber open. 'Good. Six bullets.' What can I tell him: It's only the shadow of a flame from a secret place lost in time. 'That was just the test,' he says. Hey, fuck that shit, I'm about to reply, except that now he's asking me if it's possible to find specific things in the mind, bad things, and pull them out forever. 'Say if somebody was corrupted, inside, in the skull.' He grimaced. 'Say they had some kind of psycho fucking shit virus eating away at them. Could you pull it loose, cleanse the mind?' Well, I'm thinking it was just himself he was referring to. I told him straight, what does he think I am, a psychiatrist? Then he smiles and goes all nice on me, asking if I've ever been to the Skull Garden, not the corporate ring-fenced part, but the real garden? Something hits me then. Darkness. Then shadows. Then a glimpse of a shining lake and somebody walking towards me. It's like a lost memory, a trace reading. Cage tells me that he used to visit there nearly every day, back at the company offices. Direct line. I feel like I'm getting dizzy, but I don't know why. I manage to spit out a question, ask him what it's like, and he answers, 'Paradise. Like your own personal paradise.'

He's pushing the sports bag toward me. 'Open it. There's one more job to do.' Well now I really do tell him to fuck off, and he turns the gun on me, he just holds it there until I'm bending down, trying to get the bag open. There's something caught in the zip, strands of hair it looks like, long grey strands of hair, and then I'm tugging at the bag, because maybe I've already guessed what's inside there, with the smell and all that and the hit I'm getting being this close, and I'm feeling scared just thinking about it. It's not himself he wants me to clean up. But what can I do? It's like I'm heading for home, just that. I don't understand it, but that's the thought of it, just running wild through a moonlit forest, towards home.

*Shrine*

**>DAVID BOWIE<**
LARA CROFT
GHOST RIDER
FRIDA KAHLO
DAVID LYNCH
LEE 'SCRATCH' PERRY
ANNE RICE
SPICE GIRLS
TOMOKO TAKAHASHI

> <

PAUL VIRILIO
> <

Cage stands at the mirror, his hands gripping the cold white edge of the sink. He leans in close, inspecting the face in the glass. His hair hangs down limply over his ears, the stubble is thick on his chin, his face is clammy. The shimmering image. A few tatty remnants of celebrity ghosts flicker about his features: Tom Crooz, John F Kentucky, Hombre Simpson, Madonnica, Mick Jaguar, Vladimir Horrowshow, some other minor personalities. All the rejects, the bad canisters, the faulty programmes. The needles. Direct hits. Whatever he could find at Zeno, during those last days. They say that too much Charisma fucks you up real bad. But what else can he do? He has to hide himself.

The crazy girl with the crazy hands is making noises, muttering, singing. Doing her job. Cage ignores her. He pulls the skin down from the corner of one eye, showing the white to be speckled with tiny broken capillaries; the pupil is dilated. Even his own true face is looking like something he just dragged on that morning. He will have to recharge, especially after what he has learnt this evening; he will set off soon, take the girl with him, keep moving, try to avoid the cops, or more importantly, the company's retrieval squad. That last day at Zeno. How crazy it must have looked. He didn't know if he was saving his father, or betraying him.

***

*Executive Suite. A calm landscape of chrome chairs, climbing plants, curved desks and recessed cupboards. On the back wall are framed glossy prints of pharmaceutical products and cosmetics. A portrait of the Zeno Founder stares down at a grim figure who hurries about the office, unshaven, and dressed in a creased suit. Francis Cage is shredding documents. There's an open sports bag on one of the desks. The side wall is made of glass and overlooks the ground floor of the atrium seven storeys below. Police officers are visible down there; they'll be drinking coffee and talking to news people. Forensic accountants are moving through the lobby of the Zeno building, carrying boxes stamped* CRIMINAL EVIDENCE. *They wear latex gloves, as though the accounts themselves were dirty. The elevators on the other side of the atrium air shaft slide up and down with ambient red and yellow lights.*

*Supply Store. Cage is delving into a cupboard. He's scooping handfuls of celebrity mask canisters into his bag. These are returned goods or shop-soiled products in the main, mostly unmarked, all meant for cheap promo giveaways.*

From a secret recess, he takes out a number of wrapped syringes.

*Black Lab Walkways.* The warren of industrial support corridors between the structural walls of the Zeno building. They are narrow, made of brick and intersected by laddered drop-shafts and steel doorways. The lighting is weak and intermittent. Cage strides along holding his sports bag. Every so often he makes a coded access gesture with his hand and the motion detectors in the ceiling slide open the next steel door for him.

*Chamber of Sleep.* A bare stretch of earth surrounded by dripping iron walls, dimly lit, with a solitary metal tank set flush into the earth. The tank is edged with chrome and contains a dark fluid thick with slimy green weeds and rotting black cables. Bubbles of gas rise to pop open at the surface. Cage kneels beside the tank. He puts his black sports bag down on the mud and presses his face close to the water. Just then, the lights in the room flicker as a trio of shadowy figures move towards him across the earth. They are dressed in dark blue jump-suits, their identities hidden by white surgical face-masks. These ninja executives fan out around the tank with their guns held up in both hands. Cage looks up from the water. He moves his arms in gestures of pacification. The squad move in closer. It's a classic academy kill formation, taught to them by Cage himself. They are using his own skills against him. The company has decided that he's the enemy. How could they be so stupid?

*Chamber of Sleep.* A few minutes later, Cage is standing alone by the preservation tank. The white hair is plastered over his skull and his shoes are water-logged. Three bodies can be seen lying at the edges of the room, slumped against the iron walls. The fingers of Cage's hands twitch as though galvanised by a passing electrical current. He rolls up the sleeves of his suit, and then kneels to reach down through the water. He pulls aside the weeds from the barely human thing lying at the bottom. He grabs hold with both hands and lifts it out of the pool. One by one wires are ripped loose from the neck and temples, and now the Founder's head stares back at Cage. His father's face. Red, unblinking eyes. Cage's face melts with pain, with love. The body has decayed so much, it is falling apart. Cage places the separated head in his sports bag. The blackened torso, such as it is, remains behind in the tank.

*Warehouse Service Area.* A sloped corridor leads down from the loading bay. A security guard is lounging behind his desk watching interactive pornography on a monitor. Cage walks down the corridor carrying his bag. His movements are timed to attract minimum attention, and his hands move in precise hypnotic patterns. The first of his masks is already in place. He looks like the film star Bruce Wilderness. The security guard doesn't even look up as the figure passes slowly by, coughing a little. In this way, Francis Cage leaves the Zeno building.

***

Cage stares at himself in the mirror; it's like he's looking into a pool of murky water. Like he's staring once again at his father's submerged face. The image wavers under the light, the muscles twitch. He had to do it, save his father as best he could. He didn't want the cops taking the dream world away, or it being sold off piecemeal by the administrators; he's worked too hard for this, and sacrificed too much already.

By moving his head slightly he can see the reflection of the girl in the living area; she's sitting on the floor, still working her magic. Already the objects are piling up, and the room is filling with a soft blue light. Cage reaches for one of his spray canisters. There are just a few left, they will maybe last the night. This one has no label, no identifying marks, no way of knowing which celebrity it contains. Cage removes the cap and directs the nozzle towards his face. He closes his eyes as the fine silver mist moves across his features; he feels the liquid settling into his pores, solidifying on contact with the skin. He checks the mirror as his features takes on a new aspect. Now he is suave and handsome, with his lips meeting to form a cruel, knowing grin. He looks like Stark Gable. It's only an illusion of course and will last for only so many hours, Cage knows that, but he smiles and shows his teeth to the mirror. A second canister gives him a cheap downgraded patina of Elton Jung. The two famous images mingle, creating between them a very strange effect.

Unsightly, that is the word. Well, it will have to do.

Cage's eyes blink mournfully, each pupil shining now with a different colour. How did he get to this state, this pitiful circumstance? There are darkened areas in his memory, lights being switched off one by one. He turns at a noise. The girl is weeping. She says that she's tired.

'I can't find the virus. Not anywhere. I just can't.'

Cage picks up the gun from the washstand. No choices, girl. No choices.

*Shrine*

&gt; &lt;
LARA CROFT
GHOST RIDER
FRIDA KAHLO
DAVID LYNCH
LEE 'SCRATCH' PERRY
ANNE RICE
SPICE GIRLS
&gt;**TOMOKO TAKAHASHI**&lt;

&gt; &lt;
PAUL VIRILIO
&gt; &lt;

## Documents found in a Garbage Can

*From the police records:* The alarm was raised by a downstairs neighbour, who first noticed the sounds coming from Ms Devine's room. These noises were described as 'bizarre, unearthly, and yet strangely familiar.' Receiving no answer to her knocking, the neighbour fetched the superintendent of the building, who unlocked the door with his master key. Even then, the door would not come open easily, jammed in place by some as yet unseen obstruction. A soft blue light shone through the gap. The sound was louder now, a type of music or noise that might have been of human or mechanical origin, they could not tell which.

\*\*\*

*From the Lujo Express:* To everybody's surprise, the small room was filled with objects: with clocks, hammers, paint buckets, scraps of paper, bus tickets, theatre programmes, electric fans, circuit boards, pens and pencils, traffic cones, dolls and model airplanes and perfume bottles; pages torn from a calendar, from text books, from pornographic magazines; the slow tumble of marbles and dice and playing cards; vinyl records, electric torches, piano keys, gardening tools, a guitar, umbrellas, suitcases, shoes, ties, footballs, cricket bats, a globe; a glittering of needles, knives, mirrors, spectacles, telescopes; a cascade of maps and pamphlets and photographs; and many other such items, alike and unalike, all piled high against the four walls making a great confusion of colour, shape and noise. This vast array of objects seemed to be moving of its own volition, slowly shifting around and making a strange almost musical sound, a whispering, a sudden commotion, a ticking, clattering, buzzing, banging and jingling, as the many thousands of edges both hard and soft rubbed against each other.

\*\*\*

*From the Zeno Squad report:* A small area was cleared away to allow our team to begin sifting through the mass of objects. The current occupant of the bedsit, Aura Devine, could not be located. She was last seen walking out with a gentlemen of a certain age, whose face was described as being 'fucked up, painful to look at'. One teenage witness called him 'Mr Fuzzy Face'. We must assume this man to be Francis

Cage. Some accounts have Cage holding a gun to Miss Devine's back; others say that she went of her own accord. Commentators referred to this young woman as a prostitute, an illegal alien, apprentice witch, performance artist, con artist, medium, psychic vampire. In other words, Aura's a Genetic Variant, wanted by the DNA police. We're happy to cooperate with Lujo law enforcement in this regard. The mutant girl will lead us to Cage. We have to find the man. He doesn't know what he's doing. The dream world will die under his care.

\*\*\*

*From The Porous City, a Forensic History of Lujo*: The creatures termed Genetic Variants were generally thought to be refugees from outlying realms, the deserts and mountains; nomadic peoples with their own alchemical technologies of the flesh. However there were some who held them to be the botched results of secret experiments closer to home, corporate dream residue, damaged goods. The Skull Garden was often mentioned in this connection, source as it was of so many rumours and legends. Because of all these whispered stories the refugees tended to keep to their own kind. In truth, these poor creatures led a fragile existence, plagued by loneliness and self-doubt; kept at bay by the Lujo community, feared for their otherness, and yet secretly desired for their knowledge, their magical powers. Aura Devine was only nineteen at the time. We can only imagine how this young woman must have felt, to have the chance of touching the preserved skull of such a powerful dreamer as Augustus Cage, the Founder of the Zeno company. Truthfully, who could turn down such an opportunity, to be offered a privileged glimpse of the strange, twilit realm that lay inside the Founder's head.

\*\*\*

*From the Book of Aura Devine*: Just holding the old man's head in my hands was enough for me to know he was somehow still alive, if such a concept can make any kind of sense. Okay, not exactly alive, but here was a powerful source of psychic energy, unlike any other I had ever made contact with. I placed my left hand gently over the back of the head. My wounds opened up. The smoke leapt out. Our connection was instant. Light blinded my eyes until I could see nothing but the shadow of a shadow. I reached deep inside the skull. It was wet, and hot. My fingers brushed against something, only to feel it swim away from my touch.

Again, I reached out, searching, searching. My fingers closed over another object, softer this time, slippery, like I was grabbing at life itself. I caught hold, pulling back out. The darkness, the room...

***

*From the Lujo Express*: One member of the team referred to the process as 'the skull unloading itself.' Certain items were separated out from the mass, these being of most interest to the Zeno investigators. Included in this second category were empty gift item packs, greasy polystyrene cartons, plastic cups with drops of coffee still inside them, dented soft drinks cans, admission tickets, personal stereo sets, confectionery wrappers, items of soiled clothing, fantasy gaming kits, metal figurines, tiny flags and badges, key fobs, torn picture postcards, jigsaw puzzles, folding pocket maps, and computer mouse-pads. Each of these selected items was decorated with a logo, a spiral of purple stars encircling the phrase *Palace of Shadows* in gold lettering. This was the name of...

***

*From the Porous City*: Finally, after a few hours of study, both the company's people and the police left the building. The room remained as it was. The landlord could not bring himself to remove the items, not straight away, and within a few days word had spread through the neighbouring precincts. People were coming to visit the room, many of them willing to pay a small entrance fee. Some visitors saw the room as being the scene of an accident, or a ransacked crime zone; whilst others described it as a garden of junk; another theory explained the room as a work of art, a piece of kinetic sculpture, an installation. It was a religious event, a cosmic joke, the lost and found office at the end of the universe. Whatever the chosen theory, none could deny the room's fascination; it was filled with items that many had seen before, and which, until this moment, they never thought to see again. For these were objects briefly glimpsed in a dream.

***

*From the Lujo Visitor's Guidebook*: Slowly, over the next few months, the collected objects began to shine with a cold yellow light; and then to fade, to turn themselves into smoke, drifting away into thin air. Eventually, only the room remained, bare and empty; this room that still exists, its location now a closely guarded secret.

*Shrine*

&gt; &lt;

LARA CROFT
GHOST RIDER
FRIDA KAHLO
DAVID LYNCH
LEE 'SCRATCH' PERRY
ANNE RICE
SPICE GIRLS

&gt; &lt;
&gt; &lt;

**&gt;PAUL VIRILIO&lt;**

&gt; &lt;

*The Passion-Winged History of the Most Illustrious Company of Zeno Volume XCII: A Vision of the Palace of Shadows*

The Image Salvage Squad gathered in a small private room, located somewhere in the outlying buildings of the Zeno company headquarters. They met four times a year to examine the images discarded by the Skull Garden engineers, all those dreams of the Founder thought to be too obscure, decayed or illegible to process. On this particular occasion, several dark squares of transparent film were pinned to the window, each one imprinted with a different assemblage of swirling lines and colours. The salvage technicians were unusually excited. From these abstract designs they began to piece together a coded set of instructions, a blueprint, a design for a magnificent building or palace.

The plans for the Palace of Shadows were soon drawn up. The vision behind this grand construction was to bring the darkest dreams of the Skull Garden to the people, to exhibit the strangest products all in one place. It was to be the ultimate mass tourist attraction. A date was set for initial building work to begin. A set of finely engineered theme park rides would be constructed, each of which combined the spectacle of the Zeno creatures and games with the lucid dreams of the Founder's suspended psyche. Each exhibit would have its own set of secured interface masks, through which the users would receive a quick hit of the Skull Garden. This would give them a visionary amplification of the exhibit's chosen theme.

Zeno ethnographers mapped out the themes to be covered. They would all be shaped by the same concept, a concept glimpsed in the films analysed by the Image Salvage Squad. It was an idea daring in its reach and consequence, especially for such a commercial enterprise. Only the Founder himself could have had the courage to make such a leap, namely: all of the exhibits in the Palace of Shadows would offer variations on the theme of Accidental Death. According to the psychic consultants, the Founder had judged untimely death to be the very last taboo. And only the breaching of this taboo would have sufficient power to pull in the crowds, eager as they were to rehearse their deepest anxieties in the safest of environments, and to play with their fears without suffering any material consequence.

Initial construction had started on the theme park when the

Zeno company collapsed after the scandal of the so called Look-Alike murders. The logo had already been designed by the image engineers, and printed onto various items of tie-in merchandise; it was a spiral of purple stars set against a royal blue ground. Unfortunately, despite these preparations, it seemed now that the park would never be opened. As it was, events were about to take a stranger course than anyone could have imagined.

*Shrine*

>                <

LARA CROFT
GHOST RIDER
FRIDA KAHLO
**>DAVID LYNCH<**
LEE 'SCRATCH' PERRY
ANNE RICE
SPICE GIRLS

Darkness. Slow minimal techno MUSIC is heard. A female VOCALIST is singing a remixed version of the 15th Century funeral ballad, the Lyke Wake Dirge.

                        VOCALIST (V.O.)
          Upon this night, this darkest night, every night and all, fire and sleet and candlelight, may Chryste receive thy soul.

EXT. BACK ROAD - NIGHT

An old American car drives by, its headlights slashed by rain.

                            AURA (V.O.)
          Cage stole a car. We kept to the back roads, out of the city...

INSIDE THE CAR - CONTINUOUS

The MUSIC is coming from the car's radio. A gun is lying on the passenger seat, a weird blue light shining around it. A few miniature spray cans lie scattered about.

CAGE is driving. His face is blurred, a flicker of different personalities. With one hand he works the nozzle on a spray can, covering his face with a mist of silver. Another layer of identity is added to his image. He looks crazed, desperate.

In the back, AURA is weary, a little scared. She looks down at her palms, each of which is decorated with a spiral shaped tattoo.

                                AURA
          I'm tired. Where are we going?

Cage doesn't answer. Aura looks at the seat beside her, where a black sports bag is resting. It's moving slightly, as though something is trapped inside.

EXT. PETROL STATION FORECOURT - NIGHT

The car pulls to a stop at a rundown petrol station. Cage gets out. He bends down to the rear window, taps on the glass with his gun. Aura's face turns away. Cage sets off towards an Oracle booth.

INSIDE THE CAR

Aura open the sports bag. The slow techno beat continues, under...

> VOCALIST (V.O.)
> When thou from hence away art past, to Bridge of Dread thou come at last. If clothes and shoes thou never gave none, the fire shall burn thee to the bare bone.

Aura lifts an amputated human head from the bag. This is all that remains of the FOUNDER. A transparent lamina clings to the skin. Dribbles of preserving fluid are leaking through. The eyes are red and staring. The cranial bones are like welded plates under the blanched skin.

INT. ORACLE BOOTH - NIGHT

Cage pulls his credit card from the mouth of the ORACLE interface.

> CAGE
> Access Zeno Router. Info regarding Palace of Shadows. Ground plans, blueprints.

> ORACLE
> I am sorry. Your coding is no longer valid.

Cage is angry. He jams the gun into the Oracle's mouth.

INT. THE CAR - NIGHT

Aura's hands move over the Founder's face. She closes her eyes. Darkness...

INSIDE THE SKULL

In the darkness we see Aura's hand grasping at barely seen objects. Things swim away from her touch. Finally, she manages to catch hold of something. The hand moves out of the darkness with a sucking sound.

INT. THE CAR - CONTINUOUS

Aura is holding a small personal stereo system, decorated with the Palace of Shadows logo. It glows with a spectral blue light. She turns her other hand over to show the palm; its spiral of wounds is weeping with blood.

EXT. PETROL STATION FORECOURT - NIGHT

A terrible scream is heard, coming from the Oracle booth. A flame shoots from the doorway, and then the entire booth explodes!

Cage climbs into his car just as a SECURITY GUARD runs out of the petrol station's shop. The car speeds out of the station, swinging onto the motorway.

EXT. HIGHWAY - LATER

The slow minimal techno plays on. The last neon sign flickers away into darkness.

INSIDE THE CAR

Cage works the driving wheel. Rain on the windscreen casts a veil over his face.

              CAGE
    I was trying to get him clean, and all he does is send this shit out. All that promotional material. It's a message. What else can it be? A signal. He wants us to go there, to the Palace.

Aura is cradling the Founder's head in her lap.

              AURA
    The what?

              CAGE
    The Palace of Shadows. It was going to be a new leisure park, designed by Zeno. A big project.

              AURA
    Why does he want us there?

              CAGE
    I don't know. That's the mystery.

The radio plays another verse of the song.

              VOCALIST (V.O.)
    To Thistle Moor thou come at last. If meat and drink thou never gave none, the thistles shall prick thee to the bare bone.

              AURA
    Did you really order the killings? The Look-Alikes? How many were killed?

Cage ignores her.

EXT. ROADSIDE - NIGHT

The car skids to a halt at the roadside. It's a bleak, pitch black, deserted area.

INSIDE THE CAR

Cage turns off the radio. Moments pass in silence, but for the noise of rain on the roof. Finally, Cage speaks without turning round. Quiet, angry, saddened...

> CAGE
> I was twenty-one years old, the day he died. I thought he was gone forever. And then I found out about the freezing of the body, the preservation of his subconscious.

Cage switches on the interior light. He looks round in his seat, and then he draws his hand down his face. His various masks hang loose from his skin, like living quicksilver forms. His true identity is revealed, a younger version of the Founder's face.

> CAGE
> He's my father. I never knew him until it was too late. I can't let him go now.

Aura runs her hands over the Founder's skull. As she does this, we DISSOLVE to...

EXT. THE SKULL GARDEN - NIGHT (FLASHBACK)

A YOUNGER CAGE is walking through an eerie moonlit landscape. Huge red blossoms droop from tangled vines, a long wet tongue uncurling from each flower.

                    CAGE (V.O.)
          I couldn't stop myself from going inside, into
          the Skull Garden. Walking around inside my
          father's dream. Madness. But it was the closest
          I could get to him.

We reach a clearing in a wood. A pool of black ink sparkles with moonlight.

                    CAGE (V.O.)
          I became fascinated by the dark areas, those
          parts of the dream world the company had not
          completely mapped.

A SNAKE WOMAN is bathing in the pool. Cage steps in to join her, naked himself now. The couple embrace, and the black liquid shivers on their flesh. They kiss.

                    CAGE (V.O.)
          Here, my father created nightmares. All these
          twisted fantasies...

Suddenly, the snake woman is thrashing in the liquid. Cage is holding her down, below the surface. Her face pushes up to grasp at air. She SCREAMS, and a violent splatter of blood erupts from her mouth.

Cage's face is covered in blood, deformed by lust, as we DISSOLVE back to...

INT. THE CAR - NIGHT (END OF FLASHBACK)

Aura stroking her hands over the Founder's face. Cage watches this.

                    CAGE

Every time I came back, it seemed like I dragged some of this darkness back with me. I was being infested.

        AURA
     Is this your excuse?

Cage snaps. His hand comes up, holding the gun. He jabs it toward Aura.

EXT. ROADSIDE - NIGHT

The rear passenger door opens and Aura stumbles out into the rain. She's carrying the sports bag. Cage gets out of the driver's door. He pulls the last remnants of the mask from his face.

        CAGE
   Move!

Aura sets off at gunpoint. Cage follows. Darkness closes around them, until Cage switches on a powerful electric torch.

Cage's final mask lies discarded on the ground, the face still alive, still flickering with a last few traces of Charisma.

EXT. MOOR LAND - LATER

The slow minimal techno beats starts up again, drawn out, menacing. Cage's torch beam moves through the dark, through the rain, picking out Aura as she stumbles ahead. The two figures are drenched to the bone. Aura falls, crying out.

Cage ignores her. He pockets the gun in order to pick up the sports bag. Then he walks on a few more steps, searching with the torch. The beam illuminates something. Cage moves closer...

EXT. THE PALACE OF SHADOWS BOUNDARY - NIGHT

It's a tall wire fence, held in place by metal stakes, and crowned with spikes.

Aura struggles to her feet. Cage swings the torch beam along the fence, finding a large notice board. It's advertising the Palace of Shadows Dream Park and Leisure Complex, with a completion date a couple of years hence. A spiral of stars is prominent in the logo design. Darkness stretches out beyond the wire fence.

> AURA
> This is the Palace? Oh my.

> CAGE
> It was all planned out. The foundations laid. And then the company hit the skids. But listen, there might be some heavy security in there. Phantom guards. Real nasties. Do you know what I mean?

Aura shakes her head. Cage points to the personal stereo system.

> CAGE
> Put that on. It's a tour guide. Keep to the pathway.

Cage's torch beam finds a hole in the fence, the wire peeled loose.

> CAGE
> Come on! Let's get moving.

Aura puts the stereo system's earphones around her head.

> AURA (V.O.)
> I was feeling sick, weary. And I still didn't know what Cage wanted from me. I don't think he knew himself, not really.

She presses a button on the player. Cage gives her the torch. Then she moves to the gap in the fence, climbing through.

Cage opens his gun. We see the chamber in CLOSE UP: five bullets lie within, shining with a blue light. The vocalist sings the final verse of the funeral dirge...

> VOCALIST (V.O.)
> Upon this night, this darkest night, every night and all, fire and sleet and candlelight, may Chryste receive thy soul.

Cage follows Aura through into the Palace of Shadows.

*Shrine*

>                <

    LARA CROFT
   GHOST RIDER
    FRIDA KAHLO

>                <

LEE 'SCRATCH' PERRY
    ANNE RICE
  **>SPICE GIRLS<**

   >                     <
>                         <
    >              <
       >       <

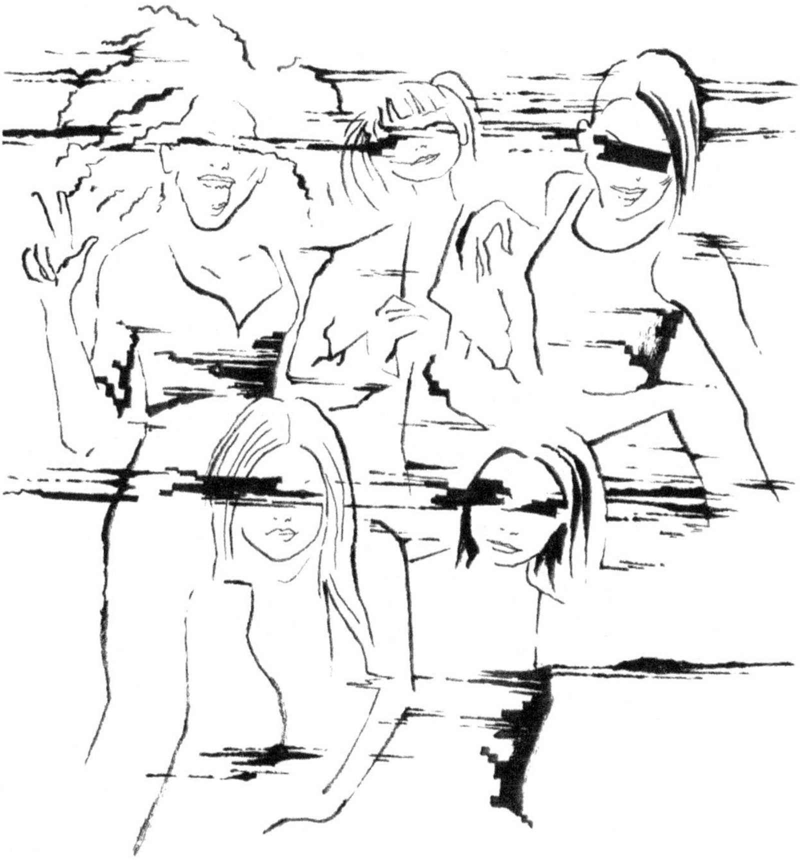

## Mantra of the Zeno Security Demons

We shall lie awake beneath the earth, until needed. We shall lie awake. At rest, listening. In our mind's eye, listening, waiting. We shall lie awake, waiting for the sound, the sign, listening.

The sign. The fall of a leaf, a sudden curtailment of bird song, footsteps. A word spoken, an intake of breath, a cry. Disturbances. Rainfall on flesh, a beam of light, a moving shadow. Whisperings. Body heat, blood beat, sparkle at the nerve endings. All these things shall be registered, noted. We shall lie awake, dreaming.

We shall crawl from darkness to confront any who dare enter this sacred region, this Palace of Shadows. We shall crawl forth, breaking the dirt from our fingers. We shall rise up from the soil without human agency, proclaiming ourselves wraiths, spirits of security, vigilantes, sentinels, the five temple guards, door gods.

To keep safe all in our charge, this we pledge. We live by instruction. And we shall bear no mercy, and need no upkeep, maintaining ourselves upon the very flesh of those that prey upon this realm of pleasure. Behold, our five shapely forms arising.

We shall prepare ourselves for battle, each to her own particular nature, each costume, each fetish object, each weapon accordingly. Our chosen adornments: the cocktail dress, the broken doll, the cat suit, the tattered flag, gold chains and lace. Our painted masks, our blades of fire and glass. The ballad we sing together, the way we gather the moon and the rain to our skin. These shall be our weapons.

Born of midnight's glamour, we are the spectral warriors.

We shall take to the air. Flying aloft with cloud and owl, with fluttering burger wraps, tickertape, confetti, with seeds and pollen, grains of dust. How we glimmer with starlight. Amid the fog and the soot, the bird-shit and rain, we howl and sigh.

Five in number, we move as one. Holding the wind's embrace to float on high above the Palace, its rooms and corridors only secret markings on the ground as yet. We shall seek out all intruders. Our terrible music will be the clashing song of blade on blade. The five, the ravishing demons, sliding down the sky.

Hold this beauteous danger to your sight, all who trespass here, and tremble and fear for your own conclusion.

*Shrine*

**>LARA CROFT<**
GHOST RIDER
FRIDA KAHLO
LEE 'SCRATCH' PERRY
ANNE RICE

It is night in the Palace of Shadows.

Cage sets off through the rain, the sports bag swinging from his hand. The half-built tourist attractions loom out of the darkness. There are bucket seats on steel platforms, plasma wall screens jutting at crazy angles, colour-coded signs announcing zoned symbolic landscapes. Cage picks his way through the mud, past building materials stacked beneath tarpaulin sheets. His face is blotched, lined with sores resulting from the overdose of Charisma.

If he can just keep going, keep searching, a little further. His father brought him here for a reason. Here, where the Founder's final visions stand only partly realized, as though the dreams have become trapped whilst only halfway from the skull. Perhaps these exhibits have escaped being contaminated by the Mama Lujo virus? Could this be the reason that Cage is being led here?

So many questions.

He quickens his pace, feverish, excited now; he can see a shape emerging from the gloom. It's the first main exhibit.

Aura hurries along behind Cage, trying to keep up with him. He's too far ahead already, his figure almost indistinguishable from the surrounding darkness. Aura's scared of being left out here, lost in the night, miles from anywhere. The personal stereo seems to be of no use at all; the headphones are warm on her ears, but only a buzzing noise is heard from them. It sounds like some strange device is being built inside her head. It makes her feel more alone, more confused. Even with her torch on full beam she can hardly keep track of where she's going, with so many twists and turns, and the rain blurring her vision.

'Cage! Wait for me!'

The distant figure makes no response to her call. Aura tries to put on some speed, but the pathway is slippery underfoot. She almost falls, but manages to keep her balance. And then looking up, she sees an exhibit that seems to be more complete than any of the others she has passed. It contains a showroom model Bentley Turbo Saloon resting on a concrete base. The car has been artfully crushed, its front-end pushed into itself. Obviously meant to be the centrepiece of a display, the damaged vehicle just looks bizarre exposed as it is to the rain and the cold. The wavering beam of Aura's torch picks out scaffolding poles stacked around the partially built exhibit.

She takes one more step forward and the tour guide speaks to her at last, obviously triggered by proximity to the Bentley. The guide is male, his voice smooth and comforting.

***

*Welcome to the Palace of Shadows. For your own safety, do not at any time leave the spiral pathway. Your first port of call will be the Founder's Dream of the Motorway Car Crash. Here travellers mourn the sacrifices offered daily to their motorised wagons. They stop on the road beneath the bridge, where electrical signs flash up the names of the dead. Discreet cameras stationed at the side of the road record the ceremonies. The sacred helicopter in the descending fog broadcasts instructions; that all the dead passengers may find their true destination.*

***

Cage creeps around the base of the exhibit, his gun poised. There's a noise from behind, a blur of light. The girl screams. Cage spins round just in time to see a woman of demonic aspect rising up from the ground. She wears a little black dress and is masked with a sheet of ice. Her weapon is a blow-pipe, which she raises to her lips in a fierce manner. Aura stumbles, trying to escape. The demon flies through the air towards her, making a terrible screaming noise.

*Aoouuuuuuhhhh!*

Cage takes careful aim, and then fires a shot.

The demon's scream dies away instantly as a spectral blue light flashes on and off in her body. Cage steps forward to see the phantom evaporating into thin, dark air. He helps Aura to her feet.

'What the fuck was that?' she asks.

'The Demon of Freezing Fog,' Cage replies. 'One of the security guards I mentioned. They're not real, just visions straight out of my own father's head, and then attached to some kind of projection device. But don't let them touch you, they carry a powerful electric shock.' Here he laughs, bitterly. 'I spent years tracking this kind of shit down in the Skull Garden. Just for fun, mind.'

He kneels down to mark the site of the demon with tobacco wrappers, a tin can and the gravel from exploded windshields.

'We may come back this way,' he says. 'If we're lucky.'

The two people move on, towards the next exhibit.

***

*These are the sodium pools. Welcome. The Founder's Dream of the Shopping Mall Attack awaits your pleasure. In this place, the designated victims gather to await the shock waves emanating from ground zero. They submit their names and serial numbers to temple guards, offer ritual courtesies and promissory notes at the wooden counters of the dream boutiques, and load themselves up with commodities for their executioners. Officiating priests recite praise songs and designate the extent of the tribute.*

\*\*\*

Cage is trudging through the rain, following a trail of concrete markings in the mud. They lead him to a raised floor surrounded by the rubble of exploded shop fronts. A few fetishes are already in place: fire-damaged dishwashers, computers, fake gold wristwatches and the like. Other such items lie in boxes to one side.

Cage holds the gun in one hand and the tatty sports bag in the other. He is very tired; his eyes close for a couple of seconds. Again, he tries to work out the purpose of this visit. Why has he been brought here? Perhaps his father has already dreamed the antidote to the virus, coming up with it somehow in the Skull Garden. It may well be encoded within one of these embryonic exhibits. That would keep it away from Mama Lujo's influence.

Just then Cage stumbles, his foot slipping in the mud. Aura reaches out to steady him, but he shakes off her hand.

'Leave me alone.'

Perhaps there is some object or combination of objects that is significant here. He directs Aura to keep the torch moving, but the beam is weakening, showing only a patch of flinty ground.

'Will there be another of those demon things?' she asks.

Cage nods. He picks up a few hard, weighty stones, which he throws into the dirt near the exhibit in an ever widening arc.

Finally, he triggers the motion sensor, and the buried security phantom leaps up, slashing wildly. Her ebony skin is draped in chains and lace, and her weapon is a shard of cutting glass. Her mask is a piece of the sky. A scream echoes through the night like a car alarm.

*Yeeeeeeeeahhhh! Yeeeeeeeeahhhh!*

Aura backs away, but Cage holds his ground. He takes a single shot, straight to the phantom's heart, setting her body on fire with the blue light.

'The Demon Clothed in Dusk!' he says to Aura. Then he laughs wildly as the phantom evaporates. 'I'm loving this, I really am. Girl, you pull a fucking gun out of my head, and it's the exact weapon needed to kill these things. Beautiful. Don't you see?'

Aura shakes her head.

Cage's expression turns serious. 'It's all coming together.'

He kneels down to mark the site with a little pile of used needles, tampons and condoms.

They move on.

\*\*\*

*Please take the escalator to the calibration centre. Caution. The energy count is rather low at the moment. Follow the designated circuit. The Founder's Dream of the Shantytown Drug Overdose is situated to your right. In this domain the exiles ease the time of their negation, sticking needles of forgetfulness into their arms. They live in homemade shelters constructed from cardboard, newspaper and plastic sheets. The angry voices of unknown judges thunder and echo over their heads, day and night. The exiles mutter their words of supplication, remembering those who have already forgotten their true and painful identities.*

\*\*\*

A fence of corrugated iron surrounds the next exhibit. Cage moves around it slowly, until he finds the entrance. Inside is a rickety display of designer hovels, littered with mocked up drug paraphernalia.

'Cage?'

Aura is watching from a little way off. Her clothes are muddy, her hair and face wet from the rain.

'Cage. There's nothing here.'

'Shhh!'

'I'm cold. I'm tired. Let's go.'

He doesn't reply. He won't even look at her.

'Okay then, I'll go on my own. I'll leave.'

'No!' He comes up close. 'No. I need you.'

'What for?'

Cage stares at her, his eyes wild and dark. 'I need you!'

Aura shakes her head. 'You don't even know, do you? You don't know why you're here! You're just living on hope.'

Cage laughs. 'Hope? I've lived for years on less than that. Years.'

The truth is, he really doesn't know why the girl is needed. Just that his father has brought them together.

'It's something to do with the cure,' he says. 'The cleansing.'

'What? Tell me what you want.'

'Quiet. Can you hear that? Can you hear...'

Aura listens. The wind and rain, nothing else. And then she gets it, a rushing sound, the noise of glass scraping down stone.

'What is it?'

'The Demon that Rides the Tempest. We've set her off.'

Aura steps back, but her feet sink down into a pool of black sludge. The torch falls from her hand, bringing darkness.

Aura panics. 'What's happening? Where is it?'

Cage fires blindly into the gloom, wasting a bullet. The noise continues, getting louder. And then the demon appears before them in a blaze of neon light. She's wrapped in a tattered flag, her weapon a length of tightly stretched piano wire. Her mask is a shimmering heat haze. She rushes towards them, screaming.

*Zaazaazaazaaaaa!*

Cage turns, sees the approach and fires a second time, and this time gets a hit. Blue light burns in the demon's vaporous body, as it dies, becoming mist, then air. Once the demon has completely vanished, the site is marked with an old shoe, an oily rag and a discarded mobile phone.

Without a word, Cage picks up the sports bag and moves on.

Aura finds the torch, clicks the switch a few times. Nothing. The light is dead. She throws it away and then sets off to follow Cage.

\*\*\*

*This pathway leads to the Observatory of Ghosts. Oh. I am sorry, my mapping device is faulty. I am all alone in the world and my batteries are running low. Thank you. The Founder's Dream of the Airport Plane Crash awaits your attendance. Here the faithful submit to intensive rituals of purification, preparing themselves for flight. The temple attendants wield box-cutters and knives. A range of auditing machines are available, to reckon the weight of old desires and attachments. The flight monitors detail the time-codes of final departure.*

\*\*\*

Cage is soaked through, tired, confused. The pathways keep twisting this way and that, he can't work out if he's already passed this way before. The girl is leading the way now. She must be using the tour guide to find the right directions. Perhaps Aura has somehow deciphered the meaning of these strange theme park attractions, the cryptic emblems of disaster conjured up by his father? Cage is ready to believe anything.

They come to a ramshackle departure lounge, with its glass windows looking out on to acres of soft mud. The next exhibit.

Cage raises his forearm to wipe the rain from his brow. If only his father could see him now, his dedication, his passion. He grips the handle of the sports bag with cold fingers. In the other hand, the gun tingles. He imagines his father's eyes opening, once the virus has been destroyed. Yes, the clear blue gaze fastening itself upon his one true son and rightful heir with undisguised pride.

Cage slips in the mud. He has to stay awake, keep alert. Don't let the mind wander. They are so close, he can feel it.

*Aieeeeeeeegh!*

Something leaps on his back, slicing at his eyes, screaming a terrible banshee wail. Cage feels the electrical charge moving through him, his nerves on fire. The gun drops from his hand. His vision floods with light and he falls, hitting the mud full face. It feels like his blood flows with cut glass. *Oh my father, help me now. Surely, I never meant for it to end like this. I call upon thee, I pray to thee, release me from this torment.* The air explodes with a loud popping sound and then changes colour around him, turning from scarlet red to yellow, orange, to blue. The pain lessens, and Cage rolls over, daring to open his eyes.

The Demon of Burning Flesh hovers a few feet above him.

Her costume is a multi-coloured jump-suit. Her only weapons are the long bloodstained fingernails of her left hand, sharpened into points. Her mask is a luminous ball of lightning that crackles as the rain passes through it; crackles, and then starts to shudder with spasms of bad energy. Cage watches in astonishment as the demon evaporates, her body surging with hot blue lights. She's dying. The demon is drifting away into the night that gave birth to her.

Cage can just about manage to sit up, wincing with pain. He looks over to see Aura standing a few feet away. She's holding the gun out in front of her, clasped by both hands, shaking, the barrel still pulsing with its own colour. Her face has been taken over, that's the only way Cage can describe it; possessed, transformed by something released from within.

Working together, the older man and the young woman mark the site with a set of house keys, a train timetable and a faulty compass.

\*\*\*

*Step forward slowly. Do not be afraid. You are now free to enter the Founder's Dream of the Terminal Illness Holiday Hotel. Here the oldest of the faithful imitate their gods in paradise. Lying semi-naked next to pools of chlorinated water, they smear themselves with sunscreen and adjust their dark glasses. Personal assistants in white jackets bring them martinis or mint juleps, which they drink between parched, trembling lips. Private doctors attend the flesh even as it decays. The table-top radios whisper songs of consolation to those already passed away. This will be your final exhibit.*

\*\*\*

Cage walks on blindly, following Aura through a dimly lit realm of plastic palm trees and white tables spread with parasols. His forehead is scratched and his left eye is bleeding. He can't see properly. His body shivers with the pain. It jabs at him like a used needle.

What binding spell has brought him here?

The night, the rain, all these ruined dreams of death.

He's taken the gun back from Aura. The weapon is changing; streams of cold yellow light run through its blue sheen. Soon it will leave this world behind, returning to dust and air and a thought that Cage once had, of power and strength and violent suppression.

The last security phantom is the Demon Killed by Love. She rises from the ground, swaying seductively in her red and white gingham dress. A plastic doll hangs from her belt. Her weapon is a shiny kitchen knife, and her mask is made from clear polythene wrap. A ghostly song echoes around the half-built hotel of forgotten dreams.

*Lalalalalalalalee!*

Cage raises the gun towards the demon. But when he pulls the trigger, the hammer falls on an empty chamber. He's run out of ammunition. The demon floats toward him, moving more slowly than her sisters. She appears to be studying Cage, to be looking him directly in the eye, although he knows such a thing is not possible. This creation has no soul to speak of. And yet now she reaches out with the knife in hand, the blade sparking with electrical energy.

'Cage, what are you doing?' whispers Aura from close behind. 'Come away. It will hurt you.'

The demon moves even closer. Cage closes his eyes, more in despair than fear. The point of the kitchen knife touches at his brow, not as a blade but as a charge of pure energy, just the tip on the skin. Cage can feel it flickering there, the warmth. And then the pressure eases. The demon's strange melody softens, just slightly, giving the song a moonlit texture. There is a sudden coldness in the air.

A moment, and then Aura says, 'How did you do that?'

Cage opens his eyes. The demon has vanished.

Aura can't believe it. 'The thing just sort of stroked at your face, like it... I don't know, as though it welcomed you. It gave in to you. Or something. And then it floated away.'

'It's got nothing to do with me,' Cage replies. He holds up the sports bag with a weak hand. 'Nothing at all.' His voice sounds weary, his body has very little strength left in it. He would feel the pain more if he wasn't so exhausted.

The useless gun falls from his hand to the ground, where it sinks a little way into the mud. This and this alone marks the site.

The final exhibit stands before them.

*Shrine*

**>GHOST RIDER<**
FRIDA KAHLO
LEE 'SCRATCH' PERRY
ANNE RICE

## From the Book of Aura Devine

There I was, standing in an empty building site in the night, in the wind and the rain, with a silly fool beside me. The both of us freezing cold and mud-splattered and wet through to the skin and bone. I pulled my jacket tight around myself, what little good it did. I was shivering. The fool was sitting in the mud, rocking from side to side. He looked bad. His face a ruin of peeling flesh and angry red lesions. His left eye was damaged, the socket crammed with blood, his left cheek twitching with the pain of it. He was clutching his precious black sports bag tight to his chest. His knuckles were white.

I've seen some things in my life I guess that most people would run a distance from, but none compare to what took place with the crazy fool. This is how it happens...

I steady my voice. 'Cage. Hey, are you okay?' No response. He's muttering to himself under his breath. But I can't catch any of it. I don't feel so good myself, and I seriously need to get out of this situation. Looking around I can see that we've ended up near a large, half-built retirement colony exhibit. A three-storey hotel front looms above me, complete with wrought iron balconies. It's propped up with steel mounts. The windows are simply gaps in the facade, showing rectangular pieces of the night sky. A number of sun-loungers sit on a raised concrete deck, each chair still wrapped in polythene. A big yellow bulldozer stands next to a large rectangular pit in the ground, dug for the laying of a swimming pool. The place gives off the melancholy air of another planet, a portal where the old might be transported to make way for the young.

'It's over, Cage.' I'm crouched down now, next to the fool. 'There's nobody here. No spells, no magic.' There's a personal stereo attached to my belt and it's starting to fade away, its bright blue core licked by vaporous yellow flames. I unclip it and place it next to the gun at Cage's feet. It too is a crumpled ball of light, not long for this world. They all disappear in the end, all the strange little objects I pull from people's dreaming minds. They never last. Nothing lasts.

I tear the sleeve from Cage's ragged shirt and apply the cloth to his bleeding eye. I make my usual soothing noises. He looks at me with his good eye and smiles. 'Did you see them?' he says. 'The demons. We really sorted them out, didn't we?' I nod impassively. He's on a real trip this one and I don't want to disturb him. His hands play with the zipper of the sports bag, trying to get it open; the teeth are broken or rusted. It's a struggle, but then he manages it. The old stench of rotten fish fills the air. The preserving fluid must have evaporated.

'Cage, let's get you out of here.' He grips my arm. It's a strong grip, despite his obvious tiredness. He's pinching the flesh and it hurts. 'Go in one more time,' he says. 'Find out why my father has brought us to the Palace of Shadows. Find out what he wants.' That single good eye has a real hold on me. The iris is flaked free of colour in places. It looks over-exposed. I guess he's seen too much in life. I nod again. 'Okay. One more time. But then we go.' By now I'm kinda falling for this guy, this murderer, this crazy fool, madman, ugly fucker, loving son, walking disaster zone, whatever he is: he's just so determined. Cage releases me from his grip and stuffs the sports bag into my arms.

Let's get to it. I kneel down in the mud, taking out the old man's head. The plastic laminate, what little is left of it, comes off easily in my hands. I touch the back of the skull with my left hand. There is a soft wetness, cold in some places, warm in others. The barest traces of life. The bloodshot eyes are open, the gaze sightless, fixed on the slow shifting of the stars, the deep interior vibration of atoms. There is a spit bubble on his lips. I wipe it away gently with the fingers of my right hand. My wounded palms open up, oozing with anticipation. There is blood, there is smoke, and I slip inside the mind easily, where it's hot and wet and dark and slithery, where no other person has ever been, not even his own son for all his skull travelling, the fool, the stupid fool.

'Is it working?' Cage is bending over me, eager now, working on some last energy. I close my eyes to help my concentration. My fingers are turning into liquid, then into mist. Here I am, watch me now; searching for something, a message, a release mechanism. A sign, a lever, a switch, a lock, a key, a clue. Something to grab hold of, click into place, activate, whatever it takes. Anything to keep Cage happy and get myself out of this mess of a night, all in one piece. But nothing comes to me. I go in deeper. I'm feeling the sadness of this old man, the weariness. And then, instead of the usual groping about in the dark, I'm actually there, inside the garden.

*I'm watching the shadows of dying flames in the moon-drenched forest; I'm smelling dust, cold ashes, dying leaves. A cold wind blows. I walk towards a patch of ground with slowly swaying trees, their branches bare. A ruined stone temple sits beside a stagnant lake. A large black crow circles above my head, and then flies down to land on a tree in front of me. An object of some kind is sparkling in its long yellow beak. I walk forward and the crow hops from branch to branch, moving down the tree until we're standing face to face. I reach out to take the object from its beak. Immediately the crow makes a loud cawing sound as it takes to the air once more. The object is cold, so cold it burns me and I recoil from the pain, forcing my eyes to come open. At the moment of my leaving, I hear the old man speaking to me, the Founder's voice as clear as a bell on a still, moonlit night. Three words. Just three little words. And then the pungent stench of old flowers. And then darkness as I fall back, away from the dream, away, into the night of the wind and the rain.*

Cage is all over me. 'What does he want? Did you find out?' I nod. 'Tell me.' He looks worried, I can see that. Maybe he's already suspected. Maybe. 'He wants to die,' I tell him. Cage's face closes down, his eyes flicker. 'No, no that's can't be right. It can't be.' I tell him it is, that I heard his father speaking. *Let me die.* This is what he said. It's why he's brought us here. To die. The shock of it hits Cage hard. 'I don't believe it,' he cries. 'No. Not after all that I've done for him, all I've fought for. I've kept him alive! I've killed for him. Oh, not directly. But my finger was on the trigger every time. I've killed for him! Doesn't he see that?' Cage has me by the arms. 'What more can I do? What more?' Squeezing me tight in his desperation. 'He can't die. He can't!' The crazy fool lets it all out, a confession of sorts, I guess. And then he releases me and sinks, weeping, weeping, into the mud. There's nowhere else for him to go. And as I'm watching all of this, I keep my hand closed tight around the dream object, the sparkling object; yes, I've pulled it back out with me. Making a fist. Keeping it hidden.

About ten minutes later we find a couple of workman's spades and some lanterns in a work shed. We climb down the metal steps into the unfinished swimming pool. The bottom of the pool has not yet been lined with concrete, but a few planks of wood offer fairly safe footholds. Between the planks, the mud is soft, deep, treacherous. There are pools of black water. The rain is letting up a little. We dig into the earth, creating a hole a few feet square. Cage takes hold of his father's amputated head. There is no ceremony, no words spoken, at least none that I can hear. He lowers the head gently into the earth. The straggly white hair is plastered to the skull. I throw the first spadeful of earth over him, covering the parched lips and the red staring eyes. Cage joins me. The job is soon done.

So that's how it happened. That's how I came to be burying a human head in the night, in the freezing cold and the rain, in an empty swimming pool beside a half or quarter built fake holiday rest home. Cage spent a long time stamping the earth back into place. It looked like he was dancing in the mud. A ritual dance of mourning, or just another act of madness. I don't know. Sirens howled in the distance. The police were coming. We climbed back out of the pit. Headlights were visible in the gloom, beyond the front gate. We headed back the way we'd come, using the lanterns to light the path. We passed each exhibit marked with its little pile of objects, managing to find the gap in the fence without too much trouble. I think we were both working on empty by then, even desperation had fled. Just the engine of the body, the pure instincts taking over. The moon peeped out from behind a cloud like a shy-faced goddess, and then hid herself again. And so it was that we left the Palace of Shadows.

The car was still there, a little way off, long and low and mean-looking. Cage was panting by now. He bent double to cough and spit, his hands on his knees. 'Can you drive?' His voice was cracked, with a terrible wheezing sound behind it, like his lungs were giving in. I nodded. I told him, 'Sure. After a fashion.' Cage smiled at this. 'Take the car. Get out of here.' I asked him about his own plans, where was he going? Cage was finding it hard to look at me. 'Go on. Get going. Don't make me angry.' It's then that I thought of giving him the thing in my back pocket, the final dream object captured from his father's skull. But it was too late. The moment passed. The crazy fool was already walking away into the darkness. The rain shivered around him like a curtain parting.

Like a curtain parting and then closing again. He was gone. I opened the car door and sat behind the steering wheel for a moment. The keys were in the ignition; I turned them, starting the engine. I managed to find the heater. Here's the truth, that's really all I know about cars. I sat there with my collar turned up, waiting for the hot air to circulate. I pulled the dream object out of my pocket, holding it loosely inside my closed fingers. I had not yet looked at it, not properly, not in the real world. It felt warm against my skin, warm, tingling. My fingers slowly opened and there it was. A coin. A silver coin, all bent and battered. It felt different from the usual objects, more substantial somehow. No blue halo surrounding it or anything. That was a first. I switched on the overhead light and looked at it more closely. One side of the coin was etched with a spiral of stars. The other side showed a human skull. I flicked the coin into the air. It spun, over and over, and then I caught it again. The skull came up grinning. It felt good, like a talisman or lucky charm. I liked it. It was mine.

My palms were itching. I put the strange coin back in my pocket, before taking a look at my hands. Jesus, but these two stupid appendages had gotten me into some trouble over the years, some crazy mad fucked up trouble. These hands, the marks upon them, the cuts. In each case, the pattern of leaking blue dots formed a spiral, same as on the coin. It was the logo from the Palace of Shadows. I was drawn to these moorlands, just as much as Cage was, I know that now. And all my life from then on would be a consequence of that half-built theme park, and what took place there. I crossed my arms over my chest, clamping my armpits over my hands. They were hurting. I wouldn't mind being so gifted, if it wasn't so fucking painful.

So there it goes, all written down in some kind of order. The halfway broken story of how I came to be sitting in a car on a desolate moor with the police closing in on me. I gave Cage enough time to get away. I couldn't help wondering if he'd be okay, what with his bad eye and everything. It was none of my business, really, and he was a killer after all. The guy deserved to be locked up. But one secret part of me was hoping that he made it, wherever 'making it' might mean in today's age and for a man like that. Okay. It was time. I searched the dashboard, pressing buttons at random. Of course I lied to him about being able to drive. I lied to him about a lot of things. Finally I managed to get the headlamps blazing and the horn working. I turned on the radio, full blast. The police would notice me soon enough. The radio was playing some loud and nasty rock and roll from years ago, from before I was born most probably. The human soul writ large, electrified, transformed into noise and waves of air, set loose upon the ether. It sounded like a benediction.

*Shrine*

>
>          <
>           <
>            <
        FRIDA KAHLO
   >              <
   >LEE 'SCRATCH' PERRY<
        ANNE RICE
       >         <
      >            <
    >                <
        >         <
          >    <

Tropical birds are gathering along the canal side. Aura stands on the road bridge, looking down. In between the rusty prams, the dead animals, the broken televisions, light sparkles on the water. The birds send out high, metallic screeches, hailing the sun as it rises over the city. The sound mingles with a passing car's engine. Treble and bass. Now a few other pedestrians are crossing the bridge, but nobody else seems at all interested in the flock of highly coloured birds. Aura feels strange, frightened, more than a little faint. She grabs hold of the railing to steady herself. The police have asked her not to leave the city. But where else would she go? Most other places would have destroyed her by now, out of cruelty or frustrated desire. She has to hope the cops have bought her story, or most of it at least. *Cage had a gun. He forced me to go with him to the Palace of Shadows. He had this bag with him the whole time. Yes, of course I knew what was inside it. Some old bloke's head. Fucking horrible, let me tell you. Cage left me in the car while he went inside the park, through the fence. That was the last I saw of him.* It sounds less than solid, saying it back to herself. But what else could she do, tell the whole story? The big question: what is she going to do now? What's going to happen to her? A bird rises from the canal bank, its wings flashing with iridescence.

Aura walks back to her flat. She spends a good ten minutes just standing around outside and looking up at the window. She thinks about the pile of strange objects inside. No, she can't take it seeing it again, she can't go back there. Where can she go? A mass of commuters swarm around the entrance to the train station. Aura is trapped by them, their voices forming a haze of words. A radio is playing nearby, sending trails of music into the air. Aura feels sick. People are crowding her, businessmen, shop assistants on their way to work, itinerant labourers. She pushes a way through, trying to escape the noise, the smell and the sweat of human life.

There is no escape. Wherever she wanders that day, the pain follows her. Aura sits down on a bench, pressing her hands to each side of her head. It's like an animal is trapped inside her skull, trying to escape. It's too much. What had really happened last night? She takes the silver coin from out of her back pocket. It's still warm to the touch, as though it would never lose its energy. The thing shimmers brightly on her palm, a strange gift from a bird in a tree in a dream. 'What is it for? What am I supposed to do now?' The words float away, useless, unheard.

The day wears on. An alleyway leads to the back of a store. It's comforting here, in the shadows. Aura beds down inside a pile of cardboard boxes, the coin held tightly in her fist. Her body is tired and aching. Her eyes close on her troubles and then, without transition, her hands are pushing aside the fronds of a dark-leafed plant. Before her lies a lake of mirrors. It's a dream, Aura knows it to be a dream. A ragged black crow circles overhead, and then floats down to land on the roof of a stone temple. This is the place, the Skull Garden. Now she remembers. Yes, she visited here when she was young, only a child. That was it. The old woman approaching through the mist...

Aura wakes. The memories flood into her. Memories, covered in darkness until now, hidden from sight, but now it feels as though something or someone has removed a veil from her eyes. The lake whose waters shone like glass, and the old witch she met there. Yes. It was the day she was taken into the Skull Garden, the public playpen, back in the days when the Zeno company used it as a way of showcasing their latest products. Aura was only eight years old. She had struggled to strap on the mask at first, but soon enough she was gone, away, dreaming, tumbling in the grass with the other children. But something had happened. She had seen the bird, the crow, flying above, and thought it had called her name. She followed it into the forest and the dark tangled pathways closed around her. Aura had wandered for a long time, trying to find her way out of the forest. She was crying. A grey mist settled amongst the branches. That's when the witch had found her. She was a scary old woman, but also kind, in her own way. She made soothing noises and led Aura to the lake of mirrors. Here, the little girl was initiated, marked out. The witch dipped the end of a sharpened stick into a bowl of blue ink. She guided the point of the stick into Aura's skin, into the palm of her right hand. It was a little painful, and by the time her left hand was being attended to, Aura had fallen into a trance. A sudden coldness ran through her, as the twin wounds were anointed with water from the lake. The ritual was complete. Aura looked at her hands, each palm with its freshly cut tattoo. They looked pretty. The old witch was explaining the spell, that the shapes formed the pathway back to the garden, should she ever get lost. She called them a set of coded instructions.

The silver coin is hot in her palm and streaked with blood, and only now does Aura realise that the spiral tattoos are becoming active. How strange to have forgotten until now, her visit to the garden; this is how her dream-catching powers were given to her. She wipes the coin clean with the hem of her skirt and puts it back in her pocket. Then she crawls out of the cardboard shelter. The sky is darkening. A group of tramps are staring at her, their clothes all torn and dirty, their mouths stained red with cheap wine. They look like fellow refugees. One of them separates from the group, a grizzled and crazy-eyed man who drags a ghetto blaster along the ground behind him by a piece of a string. Now he stamps at the gravel with his feet, dancing, his voice calling out strange, alien words. 'What do want from me?' Aura asks. 'What is it? I can't help you. Leave me alone!' She runs away.

Later that night she wanders the streets. The city becomes a whirl of chaotic signs and images. Her hands twitch, the spirals throb with pain, responding directly to every stray signal: gospel choir vocals, cop cars pulling up at the kerb, a magnified kiss on a billboard, fire alarms, shouting, screaming, crowd noise from a basement catwalk show. Traffic rush. Mechanical rhythms of pulping and scraping from the old boxing arena. The sound of a kettle boiling. Cries of love. Gun shots and radio crackle, the pure thrill of television, the amplified decay of flesh on a dead body, sitcom laugh-track, bullet wounds from the old celebrity shootouts. The town hall clock sounding the hour. Two young men doing the slow tango. 'This is my city, this is where I live!' Aura spins round, her hands raised to the sky, to the buildings, the streets, the people themselves. She has to gather all this knowledge within herself. Midnight in the city of moon and demons.

She buys a takeaway meal, which she eats sitting on a church wall. That's the last of her money gone. Whenever she closes her eyes, even for a second, the garden floats into view. Slowly, oh so slowly, but she can feel it there, inside her skull. It's growing. Ten minutes later she's standing in the doorway of Stacie's Bar and Grill, her usual haunt. The people from the Renegade Angels hang out here, with their photocopied pamphlets and their badges and their slogans. The jukebox is playing old reggae songs, the flipside versions. Melody lines and vocals drop away, revealing the skeleton of the music. Trembling dub, weeping dub. Her friend Caleb is sitting there, looking at her. All I have to do is talk to him, tell him what's happening. That's all. It's simple. Caleb was always going on about the evil power of Zeno and stuff like that. The story goes that he once tried to infiltrate the Skull Garden himself, when he was younger, but the plan had gone wrong or something. He was a local hero, albeit past his prime. And whatever she might say to him, Caleb will reply quite calmly in that spaced out way of his, that everything will be fine from now on, that she has to do what she thinks is right, nothing more.

The Field of the Black Ark is a spacious parkland situated near the southern edge of Lujo, a place Aura often used to visit; why, only a few days ago she had been here, watching the kids playing among the trees and the monuments. It seems like half a lifetime has passed since then. Now the pathways are deserted, the leaves rustle overhead, and the moon is a flickering presence, nothing more. She couldn't do it, couldn't enter the café, couldn't admit to what had happened last night. She's not ready, too scared, too young. *Why me? Why choose me? Why?* The leaves give no answer, the moon is silent. Aura finds herself standing outside the old music studio. They say that a very powerful shaman once lived here, that he made up songs by rubbing bones together and cutting holes in the skin of dead animals. He used a machine of his own devising to create X-rays of music. They say he lost his mojo one day and burnt down his house of black magic, and now all that remains are these steel beams and charred posts. Pieces of paper are caught in the bushes nearby, pages torn from a book. Aura recognises the illustrations from *Gray's Anatomy*; the human body sliced open, put on display, the various organs, the tangled web of veins.

Aura curls herself in the undergrowth. Her hands press against each other. The pain has gone down a little, the blood scabbing over. Another memory comes to her, a certain way of touching each wound in turn with the fingers of the other hand. Just so. Just so. And now the moon shines down not on the trees of the park, but once again on the lake of mirrors. Only this time, instead of the waters shining so, the lake is dark and stagnant. The stone temple glows with a pale yellow light, parts of the structure have broken away. The whole garden is closing down, decaying, dying, or becoming something else. Aura walks up the cracked steps of the temple. The place is deserted.

The crow is cawing from the roof space. A few sticks, pebbles and splinters of bone are arranged on a circular altar. Beside them an old book is lying open, its pages filled with strange characters and diagrams. The Book of Spells. Aura shivers at the sight, she starts to weep. 'Do not cry, my child.' The voice comes from the shadows, with the smell of tobacco, a drift of smoke. 'Do not cry.' Aura steps forward. A beam of moonlight falls directly on the face of Mama Lujo.

Aura turns in her sleep. Her eyes come open to the sight of the morning sun filtering through the canopy of leaves. The air is warm. A dazzle of scarlet disturbs the branches directly overhead; one of the tropical birds has landed there. Aura crawls out from the bower. The burnt-out studio looks to be fatally damaged in the daylight, black, skeletal, devoid of magic. But then Aura thinks of all the music recorded here over the years, and of that same music travelling the city, from machine to machine, loudspeaker to loudspeaker, person to person. A noise makes her turn. All of the trees around the studio are painted with the gaudy plumage of the birds, their melody a scattering of fragments. Aura follows the curving pathway back towards the city. A line from a song comes to her. *Now is the time. Let us dream.* The branches tremble with colour.

*Shrine*

FRIDA KAHLO

>ANNE RICE<

The old people told the story of a man with no shadow, a creature of the night, as they called him. He was of this world and not of this world, a sorcerer, a conjuror. His face was a ruin, a thing of peeling skin and ancient burn marks, and there was a shred of red and white cloth stuffed into the place where his left eye used to be. They said that only the most skilled of demons could bewitch a man in this way, to leave his spirit caught forever in that pale limbo between life and death. There would be no escape for this poor unfortunate, no way to find eternal rest, for he was cursed by the very nature of his affliction to wander the earth, searching for the lost home of his ancestors. Those who had themselves been set upon by ill luck in the towns and suburbs through which he passed would come to the conjuror, and squat in the dust to seek advice and knowledge. A few muttered words of explanation, some money scattered on the ground, and the visitor would pull the cloth from his eye and cast his sightless gaze upon the shapes of the clouds, the movement of birds and traffic, there to see the true face of things. He would leave his clients stripped of all doubt, of all guilt, of all fear. Some called him the Night-Watchman, or the Last Dreamer, others claimed his name was Cage, or the Caged Man, and that he had been famous in his golden days; still others said that he had no name, had never had a name, and no proper existence, that he existed only as a story to be told, a few words on the page, or in the mouths of old men and women. One detail alone holds true for all accounts; that he always carried with him a drawstring bag. Concealed inside was a hand-wrought scorpion, a scuttling thing of baked earth and white feathers, within which the spirit of an ancient wizard had been trapped. They said that this was the source of the Caged Man's special powers.

*Shrine*

```
        >                    <
         >                  <
          >                <
           >FRIDA KAHLO<
            >            <
           >              <
          >                <
         >                  <
        >                    <
       >                      <
        >                    <
           >              <
              >        <
```

*From the Encyclopaedia of Lujo Heresies: A Banned Volume*

The stories of the strange practice were initially confined to the old industrial farms to the northwest of the city, a region of concrete roads and tropical vegetation. It was called the Cult of the Blue Smoke. Early reports referred to flickering lights and colours seen in the sky at dusk. There were whispers of some kind of theatre show or art performance piece. We heard of people not being able to dream properly after the event. The practice of the cult seemed to move around the region at random, following no known map or schedule. Rumours of the next performance would pass from village to village along the bush telegraph, and then, a few hours later, as the light faded in the west, the crowds would gather at the edge of a supermarket car park, or the gate of a disused factory, or the outskirts of a railway yard.

Our correspondent goes by the name of Estevan. A few days ago he was travelling in search of an entirely different story, along one of the feeder routes of the old motorway, when he turned by chance off the main road and subsequently become lost. The road turned to dust beneath his wheels. Ahead he could make out the low-lying slopes of the mountains, where the petroleum bandits were said to be hiding. Night was just beginning to fall, and he was glad to come across a roadside inn by the side of the track. It was made of dry stone and mud, and a single light was visible through a window. The bent iron sign above the door identified the place as the Star of Venus. Smoke drifted up from the chimney into the red sky.

Estevan says he stopped and went inside to make enquiries. There was no one to help him. The bar was unmanned and the fire burned low in the grate. The flames had a greenish tinge. Estevan heard noises coming from the rear of the building. He had a sense of things happening outside, and so he found the back door and walked through into an old lorry park. A good number of people were assembled there, silent, standing in twos and threes, a throng on the bare earth. They wore grey hooded tops, and carried plastic shopping bags in their hands. Estevan knew the type well enough; they had come in from the big sheds and the old call centres of the surrounding district, the villages where a few housing blocks clustered around a single rundown supermarket. They all had the same look of barefaced need.

At first it was difficult to work out the exact purpose of this meeting, until, gradually and subtly a change came over the people. They started to move into new formations, shifting around the space nervously. Estevan found himself caught up in this movement for reasons he could not interpret. It seemed that there was one amongst them who was different in some way, and it was felt that getting too close to this person would be a bad thing; and so the crowd shifted around until they had formed a kind of crude arena, with spectators encircling a central empty space. And what was once a formless gathering, was now an audience, or a congregation.

The performer stood alone at the centre of this.

It was a woman. Estevan reckoned her age to be getting on for thirty. And what a sight she made, dressed as she was in animal skins, leathers and rags. Parts of her body were bare and powdered in chalk. Her face was painted dusty white like a clown's. Estevan was curious, so he pushed through to get a better view of the woman. She was doing something to her hands, unwrapping what looked to be heavy duty electrical tape from around her palms and fingers. She made a real show of this, unwinding the tape in great looping gestures, showing off the marks on her palms, the tattoos, which consisted of patterns of blue dots. Estevan later heard of them being referred to as 'the signs of her calling'. The crowd made a wordless noise, and they shuffled on the spot, fearfully.

The performer was now pressing her hands together. She was touching the wounds of one with the fingers of the other in combinations too rapid for the eye to follow. Whilst doing this, her body made a slow dancing movement from side to side. Estevan felt cold, suddenly. The wind was coming up now and the sun was dropping fast behind the distant mountains. Clouds were in the sky. He saw droplets of blood appear on the woman's palms, like stigmata. The crowd became excited by the rich smell of the blood, like a pack of wild animals. They began to surge forward, only to be brought up short by the woman producing a pendulum from within her clothing. Estevan was situated right at the front of the crowd, he could see everything clearly. The pendulum consisted of a large silver coin suspended on a piece of thin black leather. The woman held this instrument aloft and set it going with her free hand, so that it swung slowly from side to side, back and forth. The crowd watched in silence, their breathing stilled. The coin stole the dying light from the sun, concentrating it into a silver pool of brightness that flared and sparkled in the dusky air.

The woman was talking now, in a calm voice. She was speaking of the sights and wonders she had seen on her travels. She told of the osprey, with its sad cynical eyes. Of the mountain lion, slumbering in his lair on a pile of human bones. Of the stealthy petrol bandits, with their addiction for hashish. She spoke of secret things the crowd knew to be true, but which they had forgotten, or did not wish to admit. Estevan felt that she was bringing the local gathering back to themselves, with her flashing coin and her soothing voice. There was smoke hanging in the air, blue and heavy. People began coughing and moving listlessly. As quickly as it appeared, the smoke thinned, faded away.

Our correspondent finds it difficult to report on what happened next. The night sky was suddenly lit up, made brilliant. And then images appeared, cast on the swollen clouds, which sped past like purple beasts. There were voices caught in the wind, spirit songs. The visions tumbled forth, as though drawn from the people's heads by some magical force. A gang of refugees swept across the skies to huddle inside a church, where they worshipped a lone television set, each person in turn kissing the screen with their lips. Military officers swayed high above in cages, their once well-fed bodies now as drawn and as soiled as the people they once held down. A children's entertainer debated good and evil with his captors. Teenage street girls came together to form a firing squad. The cries of preachers rang from distant peaks. Prophetic sounds filled the air. The people raised their heads to take it all in. They were led further into themselves, into their own shame and naked fear and delight. They were spellbound.

Later that evening, there was music and good cheer in the Star of Venus. People drank from the grain of the local crop and sang plaintive ballads and bawdy songs, accompanied by guitars and pigskin drums. Our correspondent was much delayed in his journey. He sought out the conjuror; he knew of no other word to describe her. But she had already left the inn. It was then he was told of the skill she had of drawing out people's dreams, or the broken pieces of dreams, and turning them into a collective experience. Nobody knew her name.

Estevan was drawn back to the tract of land behind the inn, where the strange performance had taken place. A figure moved in the darkness near the tree line. It was the woman. She was loading her few possessions onto the pannier of a motorbike. Estevan meant to talk to her but something kept him apart, a sense of the woman not wanting company. Her face was briefly lit by the moon, as she climbed on the motorbike, started the engine and rode away into the night. Our correspondent left the next day after enjoying, as it he described it, the most soundless, untroubled, and deepest sleep he had ever known.

    Of the origins and nature of the Cult of Blue Smoke we have told all we know.

*Shrine*

```
    >                          <
        >                  <
         >                 <
          >                <
           >               <
     >                       <
            >            <
             >           <
      >                      <
   >                           <
             >          <
              >       <
```

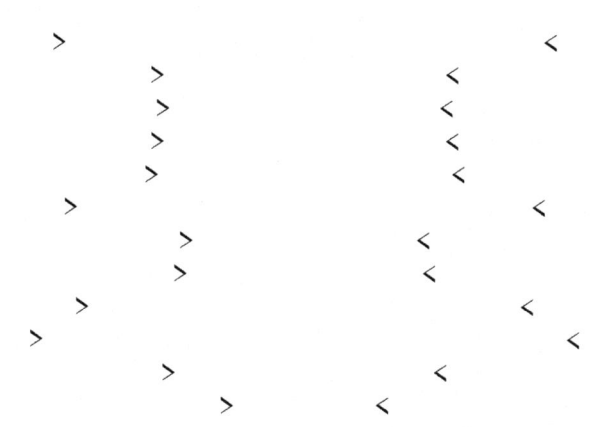

*Shrine empty*
*Please resequence*

*Shrine*

# >J G BALLARD<

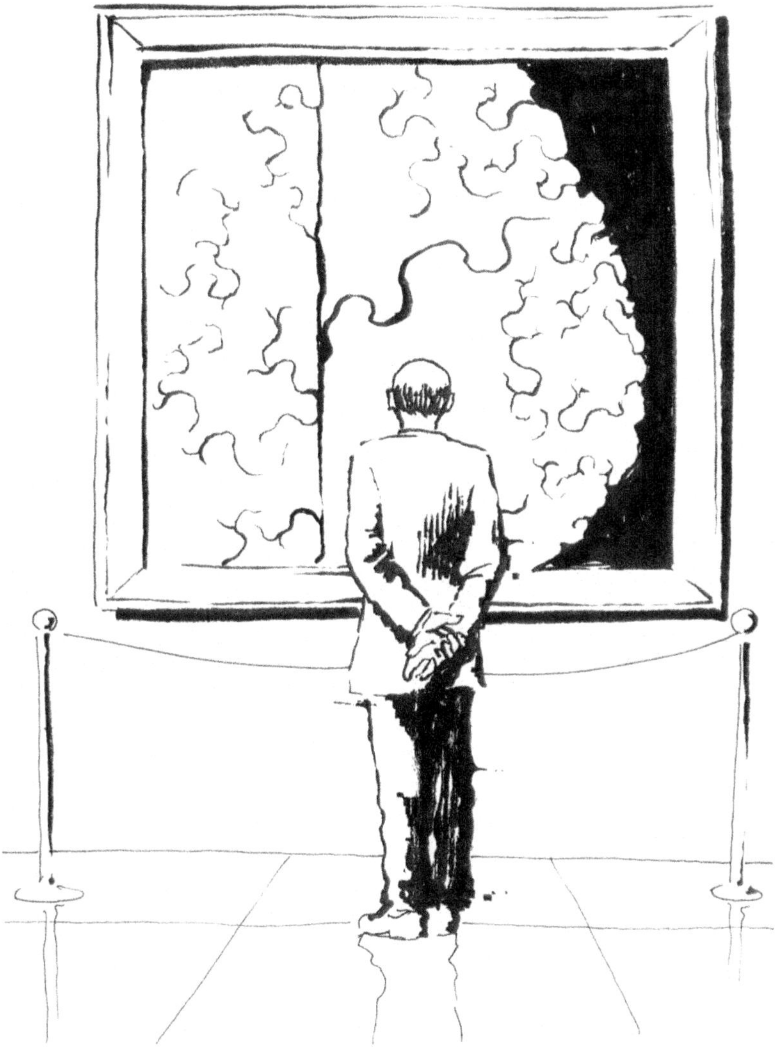

## Final Report

*Excavations beneath the Sonic Sports Stadium at Lujo Fields have revealed yet more evidence of the old city that once occupied this area. Archaeologists have been exploring the foundations of a large entertainment complex, which appears to have been left abandoned a long time before completion. The reasons for this can only be speculated upon as yet. Suffice it to say that many useful and intriguing objects have been discovered already, the most interesting of which is a well preserved human skull, complete with traces of brain matter. We can only wonder at the strange and possibly magical processes by which this item has managed to resist total decay for so many centuries. Using psycho-forensic analysis, the remains of a dream world have been located within the Jungian hyperspace of the skull. A team of spirit walkers has been dispatched to excavate this no doubt fabulous domain. Six days have now passed since their last report from the interior.*

Entry: The moon is full. We are moving north. Our navigation device suggests we are close to the centre of the garden, but all around the ground is covered only with nettles and thorns. Professor Baxter is concerned about infection. The maps he found lining the owl's nest have crumbled into dust. Lichen spreads across my shaving mirror. Everything is changing, being taken over. Still no sign of the rest of the squad. Baxter wants to abandon the expedition. He wants to go back through the skull gate. Meanwhile, Commander Leigh is tracking down the creatures we have seen in the undergrowth. The rain will not stop falling; splinters of lightning break the clouds. We have been in this solitary place for many days already, with nothing good to show for it. There is a black algae growing on the food supply.

Entry: Baxter is laid out on the ground, delirious. His flesh is grey and pallid, and his face is covered by a mask of seed pods. I have persuaded Leigh to help build an improvised stretcher. We are carrying the old professor through the stagnant forest, past glass temples and drained swimming pools. The navigation device is broken. Leigh insists that the burnt coins she found in the beehive can be used to guide us further. She throws them to the ground, six times in all. As the last coin comes to a rest, a crow lands on the bough of a dead tree. It flickers on and off like the final image in a film projector.

Entry: Not sure what 'dying' means, in here. Baxter's skin was covered in moss, his fingers growing into the earth, his hair knotted with vines. There is no need of a burial. The garden has claimed him. Who could have abandoned such a place, such a dream? By what means was it allowed to fall into such a state of ruin? We are no nearer to finding the secret. The rain drums against the canopy of leaves but does not find a way through. Darkness. I have thrown away my mirror. Leigh caught and killed one of the strange, mutated creatures. We have eaten it. Green flesh. There was a faded company logo on the soft belly. Quite delicious once you get used to the taste. I've been trying to establish contact with base camp, but all I'm getting is radio crackle. We're on our own in here. The bird flies on. This afternoon we found the bleached skeleton of a horse lying in a bower. A metal tap protruded from the bones of the neck. The professor's final diagnosis keeps coming back to me, about the plague of impossible desire. The forest closes in. We have camped by the side of a lake of mirrored glass. Tins of food are scattered in the cracked mud; the labels promise us veal pâté, asparagus tips, oysters. Leigh uses her knife on the cans. Only a purple dust is contained within.

Entry: I can no longer remember how long we've been inside the skull. All sense of time passing has vanished.

Entry: We have reached the centre! The crow led us to a clearing in a forest, where we found a circular pit with gently sloping sides. A small pool of black water could be seen in the bottom. The moon's yellow reflection lay within this water, and never moved, no matter how long we stared at it. We clambered down the slope. The water was but a few inches deep, and a metal hatchway could be felt just below the surface. Leigh tapped at this with the barrel of her gun. All the instruments are going wild. I shine my torch on Leigh's manic face. 'It's here,' she says. 'I'm sure of it!' Together, we managed to pull the hatchway open. The water drained away, revealing a shaft that descended into the earth below. Leigh fixed a rope to the nearest tree, and we started to climb down into the earth. The bottom of the shaft led to a long tunnel, taking us even further underground. How deeper can we go before we hit the stalk of the brainstem, where the instincts are created and stored? It's hot and clammy down here. The torch beam moves across tiled walls covered in lurid photographs of old movie stars. Leigh throws her coins at every branch of the tunnel. She no longer speaks. Eventually we come to a narrow chamber. It's pitch black. The torch no longer works. We decide on a few minutes rest, and Leigh falls asleep. I cannot wake her.

Entry: I sit against the curved wall. The stone floor of the chamber is littered with cigar butts, with pebbles, twigs and tiny pieces of bone. I can't help feeling that everything is arranged in some kind of pattern, if only I could discern it. The chamber lies at the bottom of a narrow ventilation shaft. After I know not how many hours, a thin beam of sunlight creeps over Leigh's slumbering form. I consume the last of the biscuits, watching as the light moves across the floor, revealing the pile of flesh that rests against the opposite wall. This place is a tomb. Some quality in the air has turned the skin of the corpse to leather; it's an old woman's face. One of her arms rests on a rectangular black object. I crawl over. It's a book, a large hidebound volume with ivory clasps, which click open easily in my hands. I hold the book to the light, revealing the scrawled diagrams, the endless words. It's some kind of operating manual, a book of rules perhaps, a map, a game, a volume of charms, a demonology in seventy-five chapters. I read the opening lines of text.

*The old man was dying. He could not move his body, his breath came slowly, there was a coldness around his chest. His limbs were held tight within the sheets. The only noise was the soft regular bleep of the bedside monitor. At the very edge of his vision he could just about register the bright green line of the monitor in the darkness of the room. There was his life, flickering away moment by moment...*

*Shrine*

**>ANDY WARHOL<**

## Appendix 1

## Iconographies

The seventy-five celebrity viruses animating this novel are listed below in alphabetical order. Each virus is accompanied by its release date, its defining characteristics and its charismatic value (measured on a scale of 1 to 10). The charismatic value (or CV) of a virus indicates the potential energy of its wave, and its ability to propagate itself through media-space and time.

01. Laurie Anderson
Released: 1972. CV: 4
American avant-garde performance artist who mixes spoken word with visual images and new technology. Her great theme is the seductive banality of American everyday life. Anderson scored an unlikely hit in 1981 with 'O Superman', an eight and a half minute single featuring electronic drones, treated vocals and melancholic lyrics. Her debut 1982 album *Big Science* was drawn from the seven-hour multimedia performance event cycle *United States, Part 2*.

02. J G Ballard
Released: 1961. CV: 6
Visionary British novelist who began writing science fiction in the 1960s and evolved into an allegorist of extreme mental states. Ballard's early disaster novels treat catastrophe as a form of psychic fulfilment while more experimental works such as *Crash* and *The Atrocity Exhibition* document the relationship between technology, mass media and psychosis. A constant feature of his work is the surreal symbolic landscape, featuring motifs such as wrecked cars, abandoned buildings and drained swimming pools.

03. Jean Michel Basquiat
Released: 1977. CV: 2
American artist of Haitian and Puerto Rican parentage who became one of the late modernist art stars of 1980s New York. Basquiat started out as a teenage graffiti writer, with the street tag SAMO©. He sprayed cryptic slogans on the walls of lower Manhattan (e.g. SAMO© AS AN END TO MINDWASH RELIGION, NOWHERE POLITICS, AND BOGUS

PHILOSOPHY). Basquiat died of an accidental heroin overdose at the age of 27. His collage-based canvases typically combine words, cult African-American names, symbols, skeletons and masks.

04. Jorge Luis Borges
Released: 1941. CV: 4
Argentine poet, essayist, and short story writer whose highly condensed texts are classics of 20th century world literature. Borges's vision is shaped by a lyrical attention to dream, memory and paradox while his baroque style references everything from literature and mythology to Gnostic religious heresy. Favoured motifs include infinity, mirrors and labyrinths. A memorable work is the *Book of Imaginary Beings*, a bestiary of mythical creatures.

05. David Bowie
Released: 1969. CV: 10
Pop chameleon David Bowie has been expanding the cultural zeitgeist for many decades. He pioneered the technique of perpetual self-reinvention. His most innovative period in the 1970s saw him adopting the persona of glam rock messiah Ziggy Stardust before becoming a blue-eyed soul man and then the 'krautrock'-inspired Thin White Duke. Before that, in the 1960s, he was a mod and then a fey singer-songwriter. In the 1990s he went on to appropriate alt rock, drum'n'bass and other forms of popular music.

06. William Burroughs
Released: 1959. CV: 7
Queer American experimental novelist who emerged from New York's beat scene with the publication of *Naked Lunch*. Burroughs quickly became mythologized as a literary outlaw and junkie hero and went on to influence successive counter-culture movements. Many of his early comic routines use collage techniques – the 'cut-up', the 'fold-in' – to counteract the numbing effects of mass media. Persistent motifs include drugs, death, language viruses and systems of control.

07. Sophie Calle
Released: 1978. CV: 2
French photographer and conceptual artist whose works explore

themes of voyeurism, desire and privacy in public space. In *Paris Shadows*, she followed strangers on the street for the pleasure of it; in *Suite Venitienne* she secretly pursued a man from Paris to Venice; while in *The Shadow* she hired a detective to follow her. All of her events are documented with photographs and written notes.

08. Lewis Carroll
Released: 1856. CV: 10
Celebrated alter ego of English Victorian writer, mathematician and photographer Charles Dodgson. Dodgson was an Oxford don who took inspiration from the young daughters of an academic colleague. His humorous fantasy tale *Alice's Adventures in Wonderland* narrates the passage of a young girl into a dream world ruled by topsy-turvy logic and nonsensical wordplay. The follow-up tale, *Through the Looking-Glass*, shows Alice returning to a similar puzzle world by walking through a mirror.

09. Angela Carter
Released: 1966. CV: 6
English feminist novelist and short story writer whose literary profile was raised by the adaptation of her work in the 1984 horror movie, *The Company of Wolves*. Carter's magical realist novels include *The Magic Toyshop*, *The Infernal Desire Machines of Doctor Hoffman* and *Nights at the Circus*. The stories in *The Bloody Chamber* see her restoring the grotesque humour and dark eroticism to traditional fairy tales. Her work is obsessed with exposing the cruel enchantments of glamour.

10. Helen Chadwick
Released: 1981. CV: 4
British feminist artist whose works address the positioning of the female body in society. Chadwick often makes use of organic materials such as leather, fur, chocolate and bodily waste. *Meat Abstracts* are photographs of meat set against suede, silk and wood veneer. *Piss Flowers* are bronze sculptures cast from the streaky patterns made when the artist urinated in the snow.

11. Raymond Chandler
Released: 1933. CV: 9

American Anglophile who reinvented the detective novel, setting his tales in a mythic version of 1940s Los Angeles and influencing the mood of film noir. Chandler's seven Philip Marlowe novels take the down-at-heel private eye and recast him as an urban knight errant. They are distinguished by their world-weary tone and surreal use of metaphor. Humphrey Bogart delivered the most enduring Hollywood incarnation of Marlowe in *The Big Sleep*.

12. The Clash
Released: 1976. CV: 10
Seminal British punk rock group who grew out of West London's squat scene and touched global stardom before imploding. The four-man unit fronted by Joe Strummer identified with liberation movements as various as the Sandinistas and the Brigate Rosse, and liked to daub their clothes with provocative slogans (e.g. HATE AND WAR, STEN GUNS IN KNIGHTSBRIDGE). They mixed righteous political idealism with musical styles from rockabilly to dub reggae.

13. Lara Croft
Released: 1996. CV: 10
Gun-toting action babe Lara Croft is the fictional heroine of the *Tomb Raider* series of action-adventure 'third person shooter' video games. She is played by Angelina Jolie in the movie spin-offs. The first real pop icon to emerge from games culture, Lara is an archaeologist in search of sacred lost artefacts. On her various quests she collects power objects and combats antagonists ranging from ancient deities to evil spirits.

14. Salvador Dali
Released: 1918. CV: 10
Celebrated Catalan artist excommunicated from the Surrealists for his Hitler fixation. Dali painted enigmatic dream landscapes in a photorealist style and went on to earn a fortune under the guidance of his wife and muse Gala. He worked in film and advertising, appeared on TV game shows, designed hats and furniture and even created his own perfume. He collaborated with Walt Disney on the animated film *Destino* and wrote a tentative film script, *Giraffes on Horseback Salad*, for the Marx Brothers.

15. Richard Dawkins
Released: 1976. CV: 5
Oxford University evolutionary biologist who revolutionised popular understanding of heredity and human behaviour. In successive books since the publication of *The Selfish Gene*, Dawkins has argued that the gene is a survival machine that replicates itself through sexual reproduction. He has gone on to hypothesize the existence of the 'meme' or cultural gene, and become interested in artificial life. He identifies as an atheist and scourge of religion.

16. Philip K Dick
Released 1952. CV: 8
Authentic American visionary whose allegorical science fiction novels cut deep into the trash landscapes of post-war Southern California. *The Man in the High Castle* is the definitive alternate America novel, while *Do Androids Dream of Electric Sheep?* was filmed as *Blade Runner*. Dick returns obsessively to themes of paranoia, simulation, Gnosticism and reality erosion. The lute music of John Dowland features in his work and the English Jacobean composer's song 'Flow My Tears' lent itself to the title of one of his novels.

17. Walt Disney
Released 1926. CV: 10
American film producer and showman famous for pioneering the animated feature film with the release of *Snow White* in 1937. Disney co-founded the Walt Disney Company and built an entertainment empire that extends from Mickey Mouse cartoons to theme parks in California, Florida, Paris, Tokyo and Hong Kong. 'Uncle Walt' was reportedly seen doing odd jobs in Disneyland during the 1950s. One of the myths associated with him is that his corpse has been frozen and put into cryogenic storage.

18. Daphne du Maurier
Released 1931. CV: 5
British suspense writer who draws on the form of the romantic novel to elaborate motifs of paranoia, sexual jealousy and sado-masochism.

Du Maurier admitted to lesbian tendencies and made frequent use of a male narrator in her novels. Her work, inspired by a love of the Cornish coast, often had a supernatural tinge and was adapted by figures as various as Orson Welles, Alfred Hitchcock and Nicolas Roeg. Distantly connected to royalty, du Maurier was made a Dame of the British Empire in 1969.

19. Richey Edwards
Released 1988. CV: 6
Teen poet and doomed rock star who was the driving force behind fiery Welsh postpunk band Manic Street Preachers in their early glam metal incarnation. Richie Edwards (aka Richey James) started out as the band's roadie before climbing on-stage, miming guitar and going on to write some of their most powerful lyrics. He made his reputation with fans by carving the slogan '4 Real' into his arm with a razor blade. Edwards was anorexic and self-harmed regularly. He mysteriously disappeared from a London hotel at the height of his fame.

20. Atom Egoyan
Released 1984. CV: 3
Esteemed Armenian-Canadian indie auteur whose films deal with trauma, loss, and the mediation of memory through surveillance technology. In early films, Egoyan connected family dysfunction with the emergent video medium. A young man in video therapy watches tapes of a couple mourning the loss of their son and decides to take his place; a father tapes over home videos of his son with porn images of himself and his new wife.

21. Elektra
Released 1981. CV: 5
Marvel Comics character originally created by comic book auteur Frank Miller as the ambivalent love interest for urban superhero Daredevil. Elektra is a blade-wielding femme fatale, a ninja assassin typically hired by criminal syndicates, shadow government networks and mystical religious cells. She hears voices in her head and is disturbed by unreliable memories of sexual assault by her father. She eventually dies in Daredevil's arms before going on to be resurrected.

22. Tracey Emin
Released 1993. CV: 10
One of the most notorious of the post-Thatcherite generation of Young British Artists. Emin came to prominence when she destroyed her early expressionist paintings, rejected the punk-derived artistic purity of ex-mentor, musician and lover Billy Childish and embraced the squalor of her own life as the route to success. Her most famous work is an installation of her unmade bed. Embroidered profanities remain a constant feature of her oeuvre. Emin was made Professor of Drawing at the Royal Academy in 2011.

23. Brian Eno
Released 1971. CV: 9
Innovative English 'non-musician' who has pioneered the game-like development of new electronic musical forms. Eno started out as the synth player in glam art-rock group Roxy Music before going on to invent ambient music with *Music for Airports*, and experiment with sampling and musical algorithms. He popularised the creative use of the studio and produced albums by stadium rock acts U2 and Coldplay. Eno's role as a creative pathfinder has been aided by the tarot-like instructional deck of 'Oblique Strategy' cards he designed with Peter Schmidt.

24. Sigmund Freud
Released 1895. CV: 10
Viennese founding father of psychoanalysis who supposed that the unconscious mind is able to convert repressed desires into troubling dreams as well as jokes, slips of the tongue and obsessional behaviours. These Oedipal desires include jealousy of the father and incestuous longing for the mother. Freud smoked a box of cigars a day and eventually contracted cancer of the mouth. He died of a doctor-assisted morphine overdose.

25. Ghost Rider
Released 1972. CV: 2
Marvel Comics character originally created by writers Roy Thomas and Gary Friedrich as a villain to menace the superhero Daredevil. Ghost Rider came to life when motorcycle stunt rider Johnny Blaze

sold his soul to a demon. The character has a flaming skull for a head and is clad in a black leather jumpsuit apparently inspired by the Elvis 1968 comeback TV special. Nicolas Cage starred in the Hollywood movie adaptations. Method Man of hip hop group Wu-Tang Clan sometimes uses the alter ego Johnny Blaze.

26. Gilbert & George
Released 1970. CV: 7
Collaborative art duo Gilbert & George have acted as the *enfants terribles* of the British art world since teaming up at St Martin's School of Art. Since then, the self-styled 'living sculptures' always appear together dressed in matching business suits while insisting that their whole life is a work of art. They are best known for large multi-panelled photographic works that contrast the brightly coloured form of the stained glass window with graphically obscene content – shit, nudity, graffiti.

27. Allen Ginsberg
Released 1956. CV: 5
Dissident American beat poet in the prophetic tradition of William Blake and Walt Whitman. Ginsberg's epic poems are inspired by the visionary sweep of the manufactured American landscape, treating cities, states and corporations as allegorical personae. His verses explore and celebrate the ideals of homosexual freedom, personal authenticity and Buddhist karma. Ginsberg wrote part of his best known poem *Howl* during a peyote vision.

28. Dorian Gray
Released 1890. CV: 5
Anglo-Irish decadent Oscar Wilde published his only novel *The Picture of Dorian Gray* in 1890. It is an aesthete's version of the devil's bargain. Dorian Gray is a beautiful socialite so seduced by his own painted image that he trades his soul for eternal youth. The result is that he is able to indulge in every sinful pleasure while maintaining the purity of his body. It is his magical portrait that instead bears the signs of his corruption. Dorian is in the end consumed by his portrait.

29. Donna Haraway
Released 1985. CV: 1
California-based cyberfeminist who has pinned women's liberation – and, more broadly, the liberation of humanity – to the enlightened development of technoscience. Haraway is no earth mother raging against the machine. Her 'Cyborg Manifesto' celebrates a time in which gender, identity and ultimately, what it means to be human, are all up for technological reconstruction. In this scenario, monsters are pioneers of boundary-crossing identity.

30. Billie Holiday
Released 1932. CV: 8
Inspirational jazz vocalist who at her peak in the 1930s and 1940s brought a mournful blues lyricism to the laidback phrasings of swing. Holiday worked with band leaders Count Basie and Artie Shaw as well as horn player Lester Young and made her name with an anguished rendition of 'Strange Fruit'. She mythologized her status as a heroin addict and victim and died prematurely in hospital while under police arrest.

31. Harry Houdini
Released 1891. CV: 8
Houdini began his career as a stage magician doing card tricks, before going on to become the world's most famous escapologist. He could free himself from handcuffs, chains, ropes and straitjackets – often while hanging from a rope or suspended in water. His stunts included plunging from a bridge into San Francisco Bay with a ball and chain shackled to his ankles. He died from a ruptured appendix after being punched in the stomach by an over-eager fan.

32. Michael Jackson
Released 1967. CV: 10
American soul singer Michael Jackson began his career as a Motown Records child star who fronted the Jackson 5 in the 1970s. He went on to become a disco-pop superstar and magnetic performer who broke into the American music mainstream with his 1982 album *Thriller*. Jackson's cultural decline was punctuated by the sensational dramas of his private life – the botched surgical reconstructions of his

face, the skin whitening, the child abuse allegations, the reclusive behaviour. He died of a prescription drug overdose just when he was on the verge of a big comeback tour.

33. Robert Johnson
Released 1936. CV: 6
Charismatic American blues musician whose eerie singing voice and rhythmic slide guitar shocked his contemporaries and went on to influence the rock musicians of the 1960s. The myth about Johnson is that he sold his soul to the devil at the crossroads in exchange for the power to play guitar. He recorded just 29 songs, which define for all time the sheer emotional intensity of the 12-bar blues. Johnson died in mysterious circumstances before he hit 30.

34. Frida Kahlo
Released 1929. CV: 6
Mexican painter lauded by the Surrealists, with a dedicated cult of admirers. Kahlo's reputation was for many years overshadowed by that of her husband, the muralist Diego Rivera. The defining event in her life was the road accident which left her, at the age of 18, with traumatic injuries to her spine, pelvis and legs. These wounds flower in her paintings alongside indigenous Mexican symbolism and grotesque self-portraiture.

35. Rei Kawakubo
Released 1966. CV: 2
Japanese avant-garde fashion designer whose label Comme des Garcons made its debut on the Paris catwalks in 1980 and has since been the subject of exhibitions and retrospectives worldwide. Kawakubo's signature style combines asymmetric cuts with a deconstructive approach to shape; for instance, a garment might be artfully distressed, or it might have only one sleeve.

36. Jack Kirby
Released 1940. CV: 2
Born Jacob Kurtzberg in New York's Lower East Side, Jack 'King' Kirby was one of the great auteurs of the comic book industry. He worked for both DC Comics and Marvel Comics and helped create a

host of original characters from Captain America to Mister Miracle. Kirby's raw species of baroque futurism takes in races of fallen gods, psychedelic machines and the atomising blast of cosmic landscapes such as the Negative Zone.

37. Kraftwerk
Released 1970. CV: 8
German avant pop composers and electronic dance-music originators who started the trend for bands performing with computers and sequencers. Kraftwerk use drum machines and rhythm boxes to produce hypnotic expressions of beat minimalism. They embrace the alienation of post-war European urban life and celebrate the romance of the autobahn. This enigmatic band have influenced New York electro, English dance-pop and Detroit techno.

38. Barbara Kruger
Released 1969. CV: 3
American conceptual artist whose billboard-style photo-montages subvert mass media representations of power, violence and sexuality. Kruger typically appropriates black and white photographic images of women, blows them up so the halftone dots are visible, crops them and tattoos them with feminist slogans (e.g. 'Your gaze hits the side of my face') set in crude newspaper type. She works with signature colour combinations of black, white and red.

39. Zella Kyle
Released 1998. CV: 1
Italian-American visual artist whose work takes the abject body art of Paul McCarthy and Mike Kelley and gives it a neo-feminist twist. She typically presents the female body in pornographic scenarios cut with symbolic waste – animal carcasses, garbage, blood. Her photographic series *Flesh/Mask/Theatre* features the artist posing with the severed heads of various animals. Kyle's output includes installations, photographs, performances, sculptures and paintings.

40. Bruce Lee
Released 1966. CV: 10
Chinese-American movie star single-handedly responsible for

popularising the vogue for kung fu in the West. Lee was quick, wiry and charismatic. He started off playing sidekicks on American TV before moving to Hong Kong and making five legendary action movies which mix James Bond-like stunts with pop Taoism and showpiece exhibitions of martial arts. Lee's untimely death confirmed his cult status. He is closely associated with the hall of mirrors fight sequence in *Enter the Dragon*.

41. David Lynch
Released 1978. CV: 6
American surrealist filmmaker whose deranged noir vision animates all his works from the freak-show movie *Eraserhead* to the nightmarish TV soap *Twin Peaks*. Lynch treats suburban America as a pit from which angels and devils might regularly be summoned to appal the native inhabitants. His works commonly feature male chumps, abused femmes fatales, crazy people and damaged father figures. Common motifs include low frequency noise, flickering electric lights, and the highway at night.

42. Madonna
Released 1983. CV: 10
Postfeminist pop singer Madonna first entered public consciousness with her punky electro-tinged club hit 'Holiday'. Since then she has become a media manipulator adept at sounding notes of religious blasphemy and sexual controversy. In 20 odd years she has gone from Italian-American pop narcissist to *grande dame* of the music industry. A career defining moment was *Sex*, the book of photos shot by Steven Meisel which saw her exploring sado-masochistic and lesbian fantasies.

43. Benoit Mandelbrot
Released 1975. CV: 4
French mathematician who created a new post-Euclidean discipline in geometry. Mandelbrot's theory of the fractional dimension or 'fractal' enables self-similarity across scale to be exhibited in various phenomena – air turbulence, coastlines, stock market fluctuations. He developed computer graphics packages at IBM in order to demonstrate the concept that chaotic systems are generated by simple and infinitely repeated rules. His images of the 'Mandelbrot set' have become pop icons.

44. Chico Marx
Released 1924. CV: 8
One of four Marx Brothers who reinvented the vaudeville skit for first Broadway and then Hollywood. Chico was the oldest brother and the driving force behind the act. He spoke in a stereotypical 'Italian' accent, wore a felt hat and often showed off his ingenious cocked-finger piano playing style. He gained his nickname (originally 'Chicko') from his off-stage womanising and in 1949 starred in *Love Happy*, a film which featured the young Marilyn Monroe.

45. Groucho Marx
Released 1924. CV: 10
One of four Marx Brothers who became famous on stage and screen for their manic combination of sight gags and improvised comedy. Groucho wore spectacles and a greasepaint moustache and carried a cigar. He waggled his eyebrows, adopted a stooped walk and mocked and manipulated the stooges around him. His nickname came from his off-stage melancholy.

46. Harpo Marx
Released 1924. CV: 9
One of four Marx Brothers whose anarchic musical comedies are based on the overturning of closed social worlds – opera, racing, high society. Harpo wore a clownish blonde fright wig, carried a small bicycle horn and at times played the harp. One of his mime routines was to pull from his overcoat an implausible string of objects – a mallet, a fish, a coiled rope, a cup of coffee. His comic character was mute but ecstatic.

47. Zeppo Marx
Released 1924. CV: 1
One of four Marx Brothers whose popular musical comedies include *Horse Feathers* and *A Night at the Opera*. Zeppo played the straight man in the act, replacing fifth brother Gummo in the early vaudeville days. He was judged to be the funniest off-stage Marx Brother and could play all the comic parts if required. He quit after their hit *Duck Soup* in 1933 and never came back. His nickname came from the fact he was able to do chin-ups like 'Zippo the Chimpanzee'.

48. Marilyn Monroe
Released 1946. CV: 10
Hollywood movie star whose seductive screen presence enthralled audiences during the 1950s, attracting baseball players, playwrights and politicians alike. Monroe's sexual authority was based on tease, disavowal and child-like pretence, sliding easily from comedy to monstrosity. Behind the dumb blonde image was a frustrated woman whose chronic drug dependency and erratic behaviour put her career on the skids. She died in bed from an overdose of barbiturates and the coroner ruled it probable suicide.

49. Alan Moore
Released 1982. CV: 5
Celebrated comic book writer whose serials and graphic novels have brought a literary sensibility to bear upon a popular medium. *Swamp Thing*, *Watchmen* and *V for Vendetta* have all been marked by Moore's radical humanism, commitment to social justice and willingness to experiment with form. The man is serious. It took him ten years to complete his epic Jack the Ripper anti-mythos, *From Hell*, with artist Eddie Campbell. He is also a practising black magician.

50. Mariko Mori
Released 1993. CV: 1
Japanese conceptual artist whose utopian video installations explore the connections between virtual reality, science fiction manga and received ideas of Eastern mysticism. Mori typically casts herself as a cyberchick Buddha afloat in a marvellous computer-generated world. Her source landscapes are traditional and include deserts, misty forests and rock gardens. Her best known interactive work is *Dream Temple*, which can be accessed by only one person at a time.

51. Kendo Nagasaki
Released 1964. CV: 3
Legendary Oriental stage persona of British wrestler Peter Thornley. Nagasaki was styled as a Japanese samurai warrior with mysterious hypnotic powers. He wore a black mask with distinctive stripes and had fearsome red eyes. The man trounced all contenders for the British wrestling crown in the 1970s before discarding and burning his mask on

TV before millions. Nagasaki was painted by Peter Blake and became a pop icon. His signature wrestling move was the 'kamikaze krush'.

52. Pac-Man
Released 1980. CV: 10
More than an old skool video arcade game character, Pac-Man is the first real star of the personal computer era. A bright yellow disc with a single eye and a big mouth, Pac-Man is piloted through an on-screen maze by the operation of a joystick. He exhibits two behaviours – munching pellets and running away from a string of pursuing ghosts nicknamed Inky, Blinky, Pinky and Clyde. When Pac-Man eats a 'power pellet' he becomes temporarily powerful enough to consume the ghosts, which turn blue and run away from him.

53. Gina Pane
Released 1968. CV: 1
French feminist performance artist who took up her razor blade and began to work on her own body as a new kind of artistic material. She cut into her skin in order to expose and stage the auto-aggressive tendencies which make up feminine identity. Pane attempted to create a visual language of wounds written in blood and always wore white for dramatic emphasis. In *Psyche*, she knelt before a mirror, put on make-up, and then cut into her face, just below the eyebrows.

54. Lee Perry
Released 1968. CV: 6
Ganja-smoking Jamaican reggae producer who gave a shamanic cast to the remixing techniques invented by King Tubby. Perry laid hands on the body of a track and dubbed its exposed rhythms with ambient noise – TV blips, sound-effects, animal cries, mutterings. He adopted many personae (Duppy Conqueror, Upsetter, Super Ape, Scratch) and did his best work in his own Black Ark studio. When the studio burned to the ground, it was rumoured that Perry had started the fire in order to banish the demons he had conjured.

55. Sylvia Plath
Released 1960. CV: 7
American confessional poet who made her posthumous reputation

after committing suicide at the age of 30. Plath's life changed when she won a scholarship to Cambridge University, married poet Ted Hughes, had two children and then tried to make it as a single mother. She suffered from clinical depression and her poems detail her anguish with stark hallucinatory imagery. Key themes include motherhood, female sexuality and infanticide. Many see Plath as a woman obscurely wronged by her husband.

56. Edgar Allan Poe
Released 1827. CV: 10
Nineteenth century American poet, short story writer and novelist admired for his macabre Southern Gothic sensibility. Poe's work influenced the French Symbolist poets as well as generations of horror writers. Favoured themes include death, decay and disturbed states of mind. Poe had a fear of being buried alive and this appears in many of his tales, particularly 'The Cask of Amontillado' and 'The Premature Burial' (filmed by Roger Corman in 1962 with Ray Milland). Poe died young under mysterious circumstances.

57. Public Image Limited
Released 1978. CV: 6
Brit postpunk rock band formed by ex-Sex Pistols singer John Lydon (aka Rotten), early Clash guitarist Keith Levene and bassist Jah Wobble. PiL's blend of dub-heavy bass, angular guitar riffs, dark lyrical incantation and ambient drones was influenced by German experimental rock ('krautrock') and Jamaican reggae. One of their most memorable hits is 1983's 'This Is Not A Love Song.'

58. Anne Rice
Released 1976. CV: 7
Irish American fantasy/horror writer who updated the classic vampire myth with stylings drawn from goth subculture, sado-masochistic sexuality and Catholic art history. Her 'Vampire Chronicles' have a lush prose style and carnivalesque atmosphere that draw on her home town of New Orleans in Louisiana. Her debut novel *Interview with the Vampire* introduced to the world her seductive aristo vampire anti-hero Lestat and was filmed by Neil Jordan in 1994.

59. Jim Rose
Released 1991. CV: 2
Founder of the Jim Rose Circus, a performance art-inspired freak show which started out on the fringes of the grunge rock scene in Seattle. Acts included the sword-swallowing Enigma; Matt 'the Tube' Crowley, who had various fluids pumped in and out of his stomach; the Torture King, who skewered himself with long needles; and the Amazing Mister Lifto, who suspended weights from piercings in his nipples and genitals. Rose himself performed masochistic stunts such as grinding his head in broken glass.

60. Douglas Rushkoff
Released 1994. CV: 5
New York-based post-cyberpunk intellectual who takes utopian ideas from the fringes of digital media and shows how they apply to everyday life. Rushkoff started out writing about the hacker ethos and rave scene of the early 1990s and went on to cover the development of the internet. He popularised concepts such as 'media virus', 'digital native' and 'social currency'. He is an advocate of peer-to-peer networks but sceptical of the power wielded by social media corporations such as Facebook.

61. Rod Serling
Released 1955. CV: 7
Tough-minded liberal American screenwriter celebrated for creating, writing and hosting the science fiction TV anthology series *The Twilight Zone*. The show ran on CBS in the USA between 1959 and 1964 and captured the uneasiness of a nation emerging from the Cold War chrysalis of the 1950s. Serling appeared in person to introduce the story in each episode. He was soberly dressed in a suit and often seen smoking a cigarette. From 1969 to 1973 he hosted the horror series *Night Gallery* on NBC.

62. Cindy Sherman
Released 1977. CV: 5
American post-feminist artist whose photographs style her in provocatively clichéd situations that call out received sexual stereotypes. Her most famous series, *Untitled Film Stills*, draws on the black-and-white

imagery of B-movies and film noir to create a gallery of disturbingly profane types – the Girl About Town, the Runaway, the Femme Fatale. Sherman's work uses lighting, costume, gesture and location to expose the psychic mechanisms of female identity formation.

63. Iain Sinclair
Released 1970. CV: 5
Late modernist British poet, novelist and filmmaker whose visionary landscapes are drawn from urban fieldwork. Sinclair walks the margins of London and its suburban development zones, guided by occult lines of force, literary association and the remnants of history. Sinclair's early poetry was published by his own Albion Village Press; his novels are marketed as travel writing. His virtuoso performances mix documentary fiction and lyrical journalism.

64. Patti Smith
Released 1971. CV: 9
Punk rock poet and singer-songwriter whose Patti Smith Group mixed primitive three-chord rock'n'roll, free jazz and spoken word improvisation. Patti Smith theorized rock as a return to the deep roots of archaic religious festival. She collaborated with Blue Oyster Cult, Television guitarist Tom Verlaine, Bruce Springsteen and former MC5 guitarist Fred Smith. Ex-Velvet Underground member John Cale produced her group's 1975 debut album, *Horses*.

65. Diana Spencer
Released 1981. CV: 10
English aristocrat who married Charles Prince of Wales before suffering a bitter divorce and dying in a Paris car crash in 1997. Princess Diana was celebrated for her beauty and reckoned to be the most photographed person in the world. Behind the glamour was a vulnerable woman plagued by bulimia, suicidal tendencies and borderline personality disorder. Her funeral at London's Westminster Abbey witnessed an unprecedented outpouring of public grief.

66. Spice Girls
Released 1996. CV: 9
Five-strong Brit girl group whose spiky brand of dance-pop dominated the UK charts in the late 90s before breaking America. The Spice Girls mixed cheeky humour, laddish high spirits and postfeminist assertiveness or 'girl power'. They became pop stars after the success of their debut single and music video 'Wannabe'. The British tabloids instantly nicknamed them Sexy (later Ginger) Spice, Scary Spice, Sporty Spice, Posh Spice and Baby Spice.

67. June Tabor
Released 1976. CV: 2
British folk singer whose renditions of traditional ballads are characterized by their sombre tone and haunting vocals, especially when exploring narratives of enchantment, love, loss and possession. Tabor was inspired to sing by Anne Briggs and came to prominence when she made the *Silly Sisters* album of duets with Steeleye Span's Maddy Prior. She has collaborated with the best of the British folk scene and even strayed into folk-rock with the odd Fairport Convention guest spot. Elvis Costello wrote 'All This Useless Beauty' for her.

68. Tomoko Takahashi
Released 1997. CV: 2
British-trained Japanese artist celebrated for installations that reclaim discarded objects and rearrange them into complex new patterns. Takahashi's junk sculptures are often site-specific and she has worked not only in galleries but also in offices, schools and even a police station. She takes her time to excavate waste material from a site and will often sleep there. Her work could be interpreted as paying tribute to the spirit of a place.

69. Throbbing Gristle
Released 1975. CV: 4
Pioneering Brit industrial noise group Throbbing Gristle evolved from the performance art troupe COUM Transmissions and later split into the experimental rock bands Psychic TV and Coil. The group consisted of vocalist and lead theorist Genesis P-Orridge,

guitarist Cosey Fanni Tutti, tape looper Peter 'Sleazy' Christopherson and keyboardist Chris Carter. Throbbing Gristle were notorious for their confrontational live shows, provocative use of obscene imagery and defiant exploration of taboo sexuality.

70. Rudolph Valentino
Released 1918. CV: 10
Italian American silent film actor who became one of the biggest stars Hollywood ever produced. Valentino was celebrated for his exotic good looks, physical sensuality and graceful way of moving. He started out as an exhibition tango dancer in New York and it was his tango moves in *The Four Horsemen of the Apocalypse* that first brought him to public attention. Valentino died suddenly of a ruptured ulcer at the height of his fame but continued to receive fan mail for years after his passing.

71. Velvet Underground
Released 1965. CV: 9
Seminal American avant rock band that fused John Cale's hypnotic viola drone with Lou Reed's raw guitar rock to produce a new kind of music. Pop artist Andy Warhol added throaty German chanteuse Nico to the mix in 1967 when he produced the Velvets' debut album. Their poetic songs are characterised by the cool romance of the New York gutter and cover themes of addiction, sado-masochism and transvestism.

72. Paul Virilio
Released 1975. CV: 3
Hypermodern French cultural theorist who views the struggle over speed and technological acceleration as the motor of history. Virilio theorises technologies from cinema to the internet as the products of war and military planning. As an anarcho-Christian, he contests the militarization of civil society, the city and the human body. He proposes that the invention of every new technology is simultaneously the invention of a new kind of accident – that, for example, the invention of the ship is the invention of the shipwreck.

73. Andy Warhol
Released 1962. CV: 10
Original American pop artist celebrated for taking the techniques and

imagery of mass culture to fashion high art silkscreen prints. His work depicts movie stars, criminals, politicians, pop stars and supermarket products. Warhol was also an avant-garde film-maker whose subjects – queers, junkies, wannabes – populated his Factory studio in 1960s New York. This was the man who predicted that one day each person would be famous for 15 minutes.

74. Rachel Whiteread
Released 1987. CV: 4
British artist whose sculptures are generally casts of the negative form of objects – the space beneath a chair or inside a sink, for instance. Whiteread started out casting neglected domestic objects found in junk shops – beds, wardrobes, baths. She moved on to cast a London room with *Ghost* and an entire house in London's East End with *House*. She was the first woman to be awarded the Turner Prize. She characterizes her technique as making a 'perfect copy of the interior' of things. A recent work is the Holocaust Memorial in Vienna's Judenplatz.

75. X-Men
Released 1963. CV: 9
A Marvel Comics superhero gang created by writer Stan Lee and artist Jack Kirby and popularised by writer Chris Claremont from the 1970s onwards. The X-Men are a multicultural band of mutants whose powers manifest themselves at puberty. They battle to save the world from its own worst prejudices about those who have the X-Factor gene. The leader of the team is Cyclops, whose raging 'optic blasts' can be controlled only by a 'ruby quartz' visor. A number of Hollywood movies about the X-Men have been made.

*Shrine*

**>BRIAN ENO<**

## Appendix 2
## User's Manual: The Mappalujo Engine

The purpose of the Mappalujo Engine is to create a new kind of narrative experience. The novel *Mappalujo* is the first extended output of the device. Here in the user's manual we lay open the source code of the engine itself, in the hope that readers and writers may use it to create their own stories.

1. Mappalujo is a writing game designed to allow two or more players to create a shared narrative between them. It offers a balance between a collaborative work process and individual freedom.

2. Players decide between them on a bank of ICONS, a number of celebrity figures either living, dead or fictional. We recommend between six and twenty icons for each new story. Icons should be taken from as broad a range of cultural worlds as possible. An example six might be: OPHRA WINFREY, BATMAN, LADY GAGA, BENOIT MANDELBROT, JEAN-PAUL GAULTIER and BRIDGET JONES. Your chosen icons will be used to influence each chapter of the story.

3. Rules are decided about maximum length of chapter, for instance no more than three pages of text, or no more than 1,000 words. Mappalujo works best when limits are set in this way, to allow each icon to have its proper influence.

4. The game begins. The first player chooses one of the iconic figures and writes a short chapter based on it. The icon can influence the writing in any way. For instance the icon BATMAN might lead to a piece about masks, about fighting crime, about revenge, about losing a parent to a violent incident, about comic books, about superheroes, about people copying the behaviour of animals, and so on. This influence can be obvious, or tangential. There are no limits to the extent or range of the iconic influence.

5. Once chapter one is complete, the chosen icon is removed from the icon bank.

6. This first chapter is sent to Player 2, who chooses another icon from those remaining in the bank and responds with a chapter of their own, influenced in turn by this new icon.

7. Mappalujo is suitable for creating both traditional and experimental narratives. So, this second chapter can follow directly on from the first in terms of plot, characters or atmosphere; or it might not, depending on the agreed style of the story.

8. This second chapter is sent back to Player 1, and the second icon is removed from the icon bank.

9. The game proceeds in this way until all of the icons in the bank are used up. As the story reaches its final chapters, the players will have fewer icons to choose from, so increased creativity plays an important role.

10. Stage one of the mappalujo process is complete when the last icon has been used, and the final chapter written. There will now be a number of chapters or episodes, one for each icon in the bank.

11. These completed chapters are regarded as the raw material for a story. The two players now work together in a more traditional manner, editing and tweaking as they see fit in order to improve the story. During this part of the process a balance should be found between perfecting the story as a whole, while retaining the individual iconic nature of each chapter.

12. When both players are satisfied with the outcome, the mappalujo game is finished. The story is complete.

## Credits

The Mappalujo engine was first activated to create an online narrative, which contained an earlier version of the story *Apparition Park*. This first mappalujo site was designed and run by Hyper Literature, and funded by a South East Arts grant. Steve Beard and Jeff Noon would like to thank Hayley and Peter, Michelle, Victoria and Vana for their help in bringing this book to fruition. The writer Douglas Rushkoff was instrumental in early attempts at creating a shared narrative between writers. We would like to thank Simon at Spectral Press for his belief in the book, to Gary Compton for his help, and to John Costello for his editing skills.

BONUS MATERIALS

*Finding a Pathway*
*Building the Labyrinth*
*Briefings*
*Mask Catalogue*
*Moustache, Midnight & Ojulamam*

# FINDING A PATHWAY

*From deep in the archives, these are the first two episodes created by Jeff and Steve, using the Mappalujo Engine. At this point we had no fixed ideas about creating story or character; we simply wished to see if the process worked. The two icons used are Lewis Carroll and Agatha Christie.*

1

One bright June morning, Thomas Clay – an actor of some renown upon the London stage – received a letter from overseas. Having read it, he immediately ordered his servant to procure a number of items: various chemicals; a quantity of pure alcohol; and curiously, a loaf of sugar. With these acquired the actor locked himself in the study of his Mayfair residence.

Clay, like many of his class, was also a keen amateur scientist and his study was equipped with all the necessary apparatus. He followed the instructions as set out in the letter. But still it was a complicated process, and often during that long first day he made grievous errors. Late in the evening the servant placed a repast outside the door, but in the morning the tray was still there, the food untouched.

The actor worked on, day after day.

The key was in obtaining the most accurate measurements for the various ratios; the potash to the ammonia, the sugar to the silver nitrate, and so on; and in the correct application of the solution to the receiving surface. With little hope of success Clay applied one last emulsion to the final plate. Not daring to investigate until the coating was completely dry, he decided to seek repose in his proper bed.

As midnight approached he found himself unable to rest.

It was the year of 1837; that very day Victoria had ascended to the throne. All this meant little to Clay however, for it was an entirely different kind of worship he sought. The actor pulled on his night-gown and descended to his study. All was quiet. The sheet of glass lay there, the deposit shining on its surface. Clay set a lamp in position and then turned over the glass. The experiment had worked! The other side of the glass had been transformed into a perfect mirror.

He saw his own face staring back at him.

His look of astonishment was replicated in every detail.

# 2

The solution was called in before the crime was discovered. *Professor Mayfield, in the old underground theatre, with a dissecting scalpel.* The Hindu detective spread out the Akashic cryptographs taken from the spotter plane and examined them with his glass eye. The lamp on his writing desk was turned up high and burned with an even jet.

'Do you think...?'

His client, the head of the delegation from the Hungarian plains, stood in the distant gloom of the great detective's waiting room.

Billy Krishna was a seven-book Brahmin and, like many of his caste, had a fond sense of entitlement. He had naturally expected the queer little European to make use of the sero-analyser conspicuously positioned at the threshold of his surgery.

'An expedition to Mount London will be required. Very hazardous.' Billy knew all the tricks of his trade.

The client coughed. A few minutes later, they had made a deal.

Billy settled back in his antique Parker Knoll chair and flipped open his third eye. He had injected his pineal gland with an extra dose of emulsifier only that morning. His inner telephoto screen worked just fine.

'I see... a 300 mile journey across Western Europe... with 280 pack animals... and provisions packed and sorted by the Army & Navy stores.' Billy took only marginal liberties with his psychic commentary but felt obliged to give good entertainment value. 'There are many tins of genetically modified preserves... stewed chicken, pate de fois gras, asparagus, cooked oysters, sardines...'

Billy sensed his client's impatience. He kept him in suspense a little while longer and then delivered his diagnosis.

'I am afraid the crime is serious. Doppelganger-cide. It seems the Professor murdered her own psychic double.'

# BUILDING THE LABYRINTH

*These twenty-three chapters document the first proper output of the mappalujo process. This material would later be transformed into the story Apparition Park, but at this early stage we were happy to let the experiment lead us where it may. Slowly, as the pieces come along one by one, a tentative narrative emerges based on an attempt to resurrect Princess Diana. Many of the later themes, characters and images are brought into being, along with other strands and ideas that fell by the wayside. Reading it now, it seems less like a precursor, and more like a wild remix of Apparition Park with Burroughs, Ballard and Carroll at the controls.*

*The icons used are Jorge Luis Borges, Lee Harvey Oswald, Damien Hirst, Alan Moore, Barbara Cartland, Angela Carter, Raymond Chandler, Walt Disney, William Burroughs, Bill Viola, Richard Dawkins, Tex Avery, Sleeping Beauty, Michel Foucault, The Marx Brothers, Pauline Kael, Salvador Dali, Lee 'Scratch' Perry, Count Dracula, Philip K. Dick, Bruce Lee, Barbara Kruger, and The National Enquirer.*

## 1

Night falls softly on the Theatre of Creatures, on the transparent fish in their limpid pools, on the scorpion whose tail is dipped in ink. The silvered moon deflects a pale memory of light along the twisting, tree-lined pathways of the inner courtyard. Here, the many bamboo cages stir with the shadows of their sleepless occupants. In the central pavilion the old man is playing host to his distinguished guest, and the clacking sounds of mah-jongg tiles echo through the heavy, perfumed air. No other noise can be heard, until a sharp report breaks the calm.

A thin wisp of smoke rises from the barrel of a pistol.

The creatures howl and cry in response. The mah-jongg tiles fall to the floor, as though the roof of a doll's house has been upturned. And then, once again stillness envelopes this small, contained world.

The winner of the game walks now, along the pathways of the labyrinth. Grains of rice fall from her fingers, one by one. The woman lingers by the cages to glance at the terrifying mathematics of the knotted snakes, the claws of the milk-coloured tiger, the blood-filled flesh of the spiders. The player walks on, until all of the rice has left her hand; now she must trust to her instincts, and her training.

Her dress of green silk shimmers in the moonlight.

Eventually, and quite by chance, the woman finds the chosen cage. The silver pendent hangs down from one of the central struts, turning slowly in the warm night air. There is a dreadful smell, of rotting food and excrement. Something stirs in the cage with a soft breathing sound. The poor creature is curled in the farthest corner.

The woman uses a knife to cut through the bindings of the cage.

Meanwhile, the ink-tipped tail of the scorpion bends to a sheet of parchment. A word is written there.

## 2

The news is all over the screens. I've seen my face on the side of a building. I look just like a movie star.

There are black helicopters high in the sky over the Plaza del Dyana and they shine a light down into the city's streets.

Has my cover been blown?

All I've got to get me out of this bad continuum is the kandy wrapper I picked up at the zoo. It's got this funny barcode.

Reminds me of my time at the Academy, my final encoding day. I was so proud.

I believe that Dr Cage left the wrapper at the zoo for me. He's like that.

I remember my old gig at the Dragon Temple. Cage picking me out from all the other Russian sex slaves. He put a gun in my hand.

'I will be your control from now on, Jessica,' he said.

Cage had a soft way of talking and whenever he spoke to me the air smelled of jasmines. He dressed me in green silk.

Now I'm sitting alone in the Emperor Hotel.

There are red velveteen curtains at the window and I have closed them on the night. I don't want to see that face on the building anymore. It's pretending not to look like me. Instead, I flick through the cable channels on television. I keep getting pictures of a naked man, bound in chains, manacles, leg-irons.

My bed is littered with cartons of rice, devilled chicken and crumpled aluminium trays.

I followed the instructions on the kandy wrapper to get here.

There was an open market I had to get through. It was crazy. There were enemy agents working the stalls, looking to sell cheap copies of transistor radios, video cassettes, Swiss army knives, Parker pens. A slick-haired man was selling bootleg fragrances. They think their disguises can fool me.

They have opened the glands of animals and extracted the perfumes directly.

The operatives spoke into their hands and their hands answered them back and they pointed me out. A helicopter shone its light in my eyes. Who can I trust anymore? I had to run.

The television whispers to me. They have sealed the naked man in an iron coffin. The box is lowered into the river, down through a hole cracked in the ice. How will he ever escape?

Where is Cage? He should've called in by now.

A news flash tells me that the new Chief Administer has taken the sign of the scorpion. Well, that is no surprise, not to me.

It's time to put on my makeup. I have to be ready for my next assignment.

The mirror is talking.

There is a knock at the door.

## 3

Now let the agents and the emperor, and all the make-up slaves / the television devils, ministers and knaves / let them all now list their sins / and your body so soft, Dyana, let it be drawn aloft, Dyana
in a helicopter made of jasmines
 YEAH! helicopters made of jasmines.

No longer will they chain you with video tapes and lies / nor Parker pens despoil you, nor cameras work like knives / nor scorpions barcode your skin / and your body so soft, Dyana, let it be drawn aloft, Dyana
 on a bed made from kandy wrappers, kith and kin

YEAH! kandy wrappers, kith and kin.

And no more will guns propel you, but the markets will reduce you / the academies of truth will betray you, and then induce you / with their zoo of black cassettes / and your body so soft, Dyana, let it be drawn aloft, Dyana
    in a curtained temple of sex
    YEAH! a curtained temple of sex.

Aluminium horses, velveteen gowns, set the blockades for a funeral parade / floating on dragons let the flowers cascade / all over your sweet Londinium / and your body so soft, Dyana, let it be drawn aloft, Dyana
    in the sky's green continuum
    YEAH! the sky's green continuum.

## 4

SCORPIO Issue #23

PAGES TWO AND THREE: BIG SPREAD
Harker, in his Scorpio sleeping-suit, soars along the dreaming tracks through the ether over the buildings of Londinuum. Flying behind him are memories of his past lives bunched in gestalt formation plus any future lives he may have left according to the terms of his origin story. Harker holds on to his real-world connection the way Michael Jackson holds on to his crotch in that gangbanger music/porn video.

FROM OFF PANEL: SCORPIO AND THE INQUEST TEAM!
    SCORPIO #1: Never fear, dead dragonlady fans! My other selves and I are here to see that your slavish desire to clone her evacuated image from your own flesh is not compromised!
    SCORPIO #2: The inquest team is here to guarantee the legal copyright of locally advertised cosmetic surgery techniques!
    SCORPIO #3: Know that your heroic image safety keepers will squash all unlicensed media/medical emporia!
    SFX: (TINY BUT GETTING BIGGER AND SPILLING

OVER TO THE NEXT PANEL)
bring! Bring!
Bring! Bring!
Bring! Bring!
BRING! BRING!
BRING! BRING!
BRING! BRING!

LARGE INSET THAT SERVES AS OUR TITLE PANEL
Down-shot of Harker lying half-naked in a narrow street lined with shops selling electrical goods, cheap souvenirs and costume jewellery. He is curled up on a wooden palette which fills the hole in the sidewalk left by a missing paving stone. There is an urgently ringing phone in his hand.
TITLE: THE TRUTH ACADEMY
SFX: (GETTING BIGGER AS IT SPILLS OVER)
BRING! BRING!
BRING! BRING!
BRING! BRING!
BRING! BRING!
BRING! BRING!

PANEL
Harker is now staring in horrified awe at his own surgically enhanced breasts.

FINAL PANEL
Close-up of the spittle on Harker's lips.
HARKER: (VERY WEAK) He-hello..?
UNIDENTIFIED PHONE VOICE: Get down the city zoo, boy! There's trouble.

5

My lady goes nightly to her mirror. Her pale translucent flesh is soft yet beneath a gown of sleep and she calls me with a voice I barely recognise.
'Clarissa, my sweet,' she says. 'Turn the mirror so I may see myself.'

Possessed of a cold unbeating heart, my lady stares deeply into the dark glassy shimmer.

All is shadow there, with no reflection to greet her.

Nightly now and for many weeks gone by, waking only as the moon kisses the black and silent Thames, my lady has made this same desiring, this searching. And always, always, the looking glass turns away from her gaze and no breath can be marked on its face.

'Oh Clarissa,' my lady says. 'Shall I ever be loved?'

And yet, tonight! Tonight, what is this dark light that flickers briefly in the mirror's depths? It plays there as summer lightning played once over the last few guests of a royal garden party. It traces a dull but glowing aura in the glass where surely now, oh surely! a shape is being born.

Of flesh, of hair; of vapour flesh and a drifting trails of smoke.

It is not yet fully formed. A jewel gleams at the throat of the apparition, a golden dragon hung on a chain. And then the face emerges in the mirror, a bleached ashen oval, and my Lady Dyana looks upon herself for the first time.

'Are you alone?' her mirrored self asks.

'Always alone,' replies my lady.

Slowly the two faces move closer towards each other as though to mingle across the ether that separates worlds.

'Let us exchange gifts,' says the mirror.

'But what should I bring you?' my lady asks.

'Bring me your flesh. And I shall give my flame to you.'

My lady touches the mirror. 'Who am I? Please tell me.'

'We are...'

Their lips touch, each side of the glass. Through the mirror's sheen my Lady Dyana Splendour takes a drop of spittle from her mirrored lips, and it tingles within her mouth, her throat. And oh! how the heart floods now with a brave light, suddenly, and a warmth, which is the surge of hot rich blood spilling through the veins.

My lady lives once more.

And the bells of the palace ring forth, whispering her name.

6

*Once there was a palace...*
Once there was a palace where all the dead souls went at night to shop. It was lit by gas flames contained within globes of coloured glass. There were metallic whispers on the mobile phone networks and spirit messages on the liquid crystal display units of the antique vending machines. Black televisions were hanging from the ceiling, with sharp claws curled around the swollen heating pipes and their screens flickering with phantom images.

*The dead souls wandered...*
The dead souls wandered the lonely arcades. They rode the automatic stairways and the creaking brass cages of the elevators. They moved through the soft clouds of perfume; they tasted the choice sweetmeats and the rare exotic offal. They bought crystal decanters filled with shadows cast from all the places they had known and loved when alive and they draped the shadows around themselves.

*In the roof garden restaurant...*
In the roof garden restaurant, the dead told a story; that within the electromagnetic ether of the old building a ghost had been seen. It was the ghost of a young woman not quite alive and not yet quite dead and she was scattered like blue sparks from a fire. Sometimes a blurred image would show up on a security camera's screen; sometimes the elevator would rise of its own accord to far distant floors. Sometimes a mist of perfume would take on a vaguely human shape.

*One day a family...*
One day a family of supermodels moved into the palace. They brought with them a team of personality engineers as well as the world's leading ectoplasmic surgeon. The supermodels wired their hearts into the snaking conduits and the pneumatic delivery tubes of the store and they switched themselves on. There was a surge of incandescent energy which caused all the lights to splutter in the Hall of Beauty. The smell of burning cologne drifted through the aisles. The ghost was set free from the circuits and she was bursting with flesh and hair and blood and really hurting with the joy of being alive. And the dead souls cried that night, from the shadows.

*Two days later her body...*
Two days later her body was found in an open top sports car abandoned on the motorway. The vehicle was parked beneath a giant bill

hoarding and the body of the victim was shaped from overripe flesh. The scent of bootleg Chanel No 5 lingered, with its rich hot smell of something taken directly from an animal's gland. Pictures of the beautiful ghost appeared in that month's edition of *Vogue*. Above the corpse the monumental image of a Nike Air training shoe was suspended.

# 7

The broken struts of an old bill hoarding. Exit 32. Dust clouds for a mile or so until I find the hidden track for *Los Logos*. The shantytown. Borderzone. A cloud of heat shimmering along the desert's edge. I haven't been out this way since my wife died.

On the edge of the village a young native boy is working the handle of a water pump, collecting a few drops of liquid in a tin can. He looks up at me as I drive past, shielding his eyes from the light. His face is without expression.

The sun hangs suspended like a huge brass gong, melting the sky.

All the houses are made from billboards, dragged here from the motorway. Peach Blossom polish, Levi Stone's liver tablets, Aeroflex Super Model Kits. Children are lolling in the dust, and old timers are slumped in the shade of the village's single tree. There is a sickness in the air. I leave the car next to the dried up fountain and walk along the streets, and already my lavender blue shirt is soaked through with sweat. A gang of teenagers are standing near the doorway to the old wooden church. They watch me pass. The cracked bell of the church hangs silent. All things in stillness. The only sound comes from the darkness of one of the huts, a woman's voice singing a ballad of lost love. Sad, broken, lonely. The refugee blues. They have travelled such strange distances, these people.

A scorpion circles around in the dust, tied to a stick with a length of twine.

Miguel is waiting by the dice pit, where a group of young men are rolling the bones. Miguel sits near them playing the bandoneon. The fingers of his right hand tap at the keys, while his left works the bellows of the instrument. The melody follows that of the woman's voice, but gives it the lilting rhythm of a slow tango. He nods at me, and smiles. 'Senor,' he says. Miguel's voice is dark with smoke. He points over at the dead body and then goes back to his playing. Death means very little to them; it's not the worst thing that can happen.

I walk over to the corpse.

I'm fearful, suddenly. The woman's face is burnt, a mess, with a jewel still set in the forehead. Fused topaz, right between the eyes. A four-letter word is scrawled in the baked sand. I bend down to trace the letters with my fingers and a pale shadow crosses the ground.

'Ritual markings,' says Miguel.

He's come up behind me and when I turn to look up at him, his face is black against the sun.

'Who is she?' I ask.

'Nike,' says Miguel. 'You know the meaning of that?'

'Sure,' I answer, 'the Greek goddess of Victory.'

Miguel smiles once again. 'It goes further back,' he says. 'Ancient Egypt. She's a courier.'

'Drugs?'

'No. People, creatures. From one world to the other.' And this time, the smile shows off his broken teeth. Miguel is turning a pair of carved bone dice in his fingers. 'The times of change are upon us,' he murmurs.

I look over at the distant mirage. The cloud door, as they call it. And the light seems brighter there now, alive with electromagnetic sparkle, with darker shapes that flicker within the glow. Interference patterns? Or apparitions waiting for transport?

'Who killed her, Miguel?'

The old man throws the dice. 'What she brought through.'

The two dice tumble in the sand, little black skulls painted on each face.

# 8

EXT. THE DISNEY UNDERWORLD EXPERIENCE – DAY

Crows fly high above the spires of a gothic castle which rests on a dead planet in the shade of two alien suns. A monorail snakes down into the castle from a remote point of departure lost in the sky. The two suns skank from side to side as they breathe the refrain of an old Negro spiritual. Their lips are puckered and their eyes are sealed.

We TILT DOWN to the monorail as it slides to a halt outside the gates of the castle. A LITTLE RED SCORPION with a painted skull face hops on to the platform and buys a magazeen from the vending kiosk.

CLOSE-UP. The headline reads: FANTASY JUICE GONE MISSING.

Legs and arms sprout from the zeen and it jumps from the scorpion's claws to run off down the street. The scorpion gives chase for a while and then gives up. He joins the throng of bedraggled cartoon animals filing into the castle.

CLOSE IN on the guard dogs flanking the gates in their peaked caps and braided uniforms. They each hold a clanking steel instrument which they ceremoniously use to punch the tickets of the dead. The little red scorpion sneaks his way through.

CAPTION: WARNING – DRUG EXPIRY TIME: 00:02:01

OFFWORLD VOICE #1
Hurry up!

OFFWORLD VOICE #2
Fuck off! I'm nearly there...

INT. THE DISNEY UNDERWORLD EXPERIENCE – DAY

We MOVE through a labyrinth of catacombs lined with closed theatres and empty restaurants. Peeling fliers on the walls advertise extinct shows by Florenz Ziegfeld, Busby Berkeley and Albert Speer. Displays of plastic food under glass obstruct the path.

CLOSE IN on the little red scorpion wandering in circles through the labyrinth. At every pass he is lapped by a pride of seven phantom lion cubs playing soccer with a bleached human skull. In the end he follows their dust cloud down a hidden track.

WIDE SHOT of a central garden of elaborate flowers, palm trees, fountains and ornamental benches. A drunken OLD LIONESS sits on a wooden box with her brushes, rags and phials of neurotoxins fanned out on the ground.

The little red scorpion installs himself beside her and presents his sting for refitting.

# 9

From the Academy of Truth, Deathworld Division-Selected items from the Report by the Problem Description Squad-

35. We have walked down the pathways of the Imperial Skull Garden, running scans on the sacred artefacts as they appear-We have interviewed the gardeners has they tend the dreams of the Emperor-We have witnessed the dream objects becoming real and all the sweet desirable phantazeens playing there. All is good.

36. We have stood before the viewing panels that bring pictures from Degree Zero. We have spoken to the Thermostat Kid-the Emperor lies suspended within the chambers of ice-and all of our most beautiful instruments attend his sleep.

37. The Dream Channel remains open-the one million invisible wires feeding upwards into the roots of the Skull Garden. The globe floats serenely above the Emperor's head. All is good. The Emperor creates the world, even in sleep.

38. We have viewed evidence of the virus attacking the garden. The dream is contaminated-Source of virus is the Emperor's own subconscious. Containment Procedures are in operation-All is not good.

39. We have followed the Designated Collecting Officer into the Skull Garden. He has taken us through the vapour gate to the bower where the Sparkle Horse is tethered-For our education, he turned the metal tap that protrudes from the horse's neck, extracting the Morpheus Juice-We have seen the few precious teardrops of fluid in the sealed vial-purple, viscous, with the sweet sticky aroma.

40. Morpheus Juice was to be the chief component of the Disneydrene drug. See attached report on the secret Chemical Fantasy Project.

41. We have opened the door of the Black Lab and spoken with the Chief Administer. Doctor Cage showed us the test results of the

Morpheus Juice on both animal, and human subjects-see attached visual material on the Theatre of Creatures-Doctor Cage has demonstrated the malign side-effects of the Morpheus Juice to our satisfaction and the Problem Description Squad therefore agrees entirely with him that the Chemical Fantasy Project be discontinued-Gentlemen, Ladies, we cannot allow the Morpheus Juice to penetrate the market place. It would do our brand identity untold harm-Let there be no illusions about this-the Future Projection Officer has committed suicide, so bad were the figures.

    42. True nature of the Problem. Operatives report that a shipment of the Morpheus Juice has been stolen-

    43. Scenario by the Scenario Mistress-Proposal-that the perpetrator stole into the Skull Garden at night, breaking the security vapours on the inner zone-that the perpetrator tapped the Sparkle Horse-that the perpetrator smuggled the Morpheus Juice from the garden with the aid of certain phantazeens, those creatures which played there amongst the twisted dream flowers.

    44. Phantazeen creatures-commonly known as Zeenies-These are characters who have no Reality Engines-merchandise of the id-Dark and Playful Dream Products, brought into being from the Emperor's sleep.

    45. Parallel narrative-the limited edition Zeeny product line, My Little Red Scorpion, went missing from Deathworld Estate the same day as the Juice was stolen-six creatures in total-they are the perfect carriers.

    46. Tangential narrative-We are losing creatures all over. There are secret doorways through to the Real World-These must be found, and sealed.

    47. Doctor Cage concludes with the necessary action-a Deathsquad Operative will be sent outward to retrieve all illicit Morpheus. Operative codename: Jessica-Agent Jessica under the personal control of Doctor Cage, via use of the Mesmeric Implant.

    48. Primary Desires-Identify Perpetrator-Exterminate all Leakage Zones!

    49. Agent's special licence-Permission granted to deal death to the dealers!

DOCUMENTATION of INSTALLATION: ANTI DEATHSQUAD SURVEILLANCE DEVICE. Commissioned by the distinguished company of fine recreational drug purveyors.

A) CORE CITY EXPOSURE: 50mm Nikon jewel-precision image of a majestic pagoda surrounded by a ruin of stone walls, towers and blockhouses... view looking out from the borderzone... the lens creating a halo effect as if the city were contained under glass... search activated... targeting...
-Negative
B) GATEHOUSE GRAB: Slow CCTV scans of the crooked little streets which connect the pagoda to its peripheral docking stations... east at dawn, west at dusk... images sampled from seven cameras at pre-sequenced intervals... the triggering device stolen from the Deathworld Corp timecoding of the human genome map... search activated... targeting...
-Negative.
C) PLAZA PROBE: Starting from within the huddled precincts of the pagoda the camera begins to swing out into the surrounding plaza... close-ups of neatly attired old people carrying placards... the whole city waiting for the safe return of its unknown refugees... search activated... targeting...
-Negative.
D) MOTORWAY ZOOM: An ecstatic compressed camera ride down one of the busy two-tiered motorways which arc over the desert surrounding the city... calibration of the tangled graffiti on bridges and flyovers... the unwinding of a dream formula of escape... search activated... targeting...
-Negative.
E) BORDERZONE CRAWL: Wheelchair dollies through the shantytowns which grip the support structures of the highways... infra-red vision... bodycon clubs, sex shows, gay bars... in the back streets a sudden spill of light from a tango joint... the refugee coaches piled up outside... search activated... targeting...
-Negative.
F) BORDELLO SCAN: Mirrorball camera scoping tables at the edge of the room... buckets of ice and champagne, waiters hanging around, fur

coats and jackets draped over chairs... sickness, ghost faces... Kirlian photo-fit with the ritual mark of the killer... search activated... targeting...
–POSITIVE.
–Death Squad Operative sighted. Locking on.
–Recording in process.

## 11

We move down into the Palace of Seductions, where the gentlemen of the orchestra play old melodies on antique strings and horns. They play with arthritic fingers, worn out hands and lips; and with tired hearts enriched only by distant nights of stolen love, now barely remembered.

All the widows are waving their decorative fans, hoping to catch the glance of the gigolos who stumble across the dance floor slowly and with trepidation, like aged leopards. Such desires, such breaths hardly taken, not for so many years now. The old men direct the women out onto the polished floor, to move them tenderly through the ritualised code of the tango; the various steps, calibrations, the holds, the perfect theatre of the kiss.

In this way, the dance becomes one final surrendering. There are such longings. There are such callings in the blood that long to be delivered.

In a small private alcove, the retired colonel sits in his wheelchair, nervous before the handsome young man who stands by his side. The sound of the orchestra is muffled by velvet curtains; its beat is slightly out of time with the creaking mechanism of an ornamental clock whose fingers move in the shadows. The colonel sighs and thinks back on his dancing days.

The scorpion creaks across the table, flakes of scarlet paint falling from its metal carapace. The articulated tail dips to write on a dance card, these symbols: ACGT in endless permutations. And the creature would continue writing endlessly if the dealer man did not place a gentle finger upon its back.

'A delightful plaything,' he says.

The colonel looks at the scorpion. His eyes are so bad these days he sees everything covered with a fine mist, and the mist is wet with tears. Money is exchanged. The dealer rolls the sleeve of his customer, exposing a thin-boned arm. The old man trembles at the touch.

'Be careful of your desires,' says the dealer.

The creature moves across the table toward the colonel. The ticking of the clock fills the air like a heart stuttering. The tail of the scorpion hovers above the bared arm, and then stabs forward suddenly, and with a hidden coiled power. The sting of the tail pierces the soft skin of the old man, finding a vein. There is a sweet sticky smell in the small confined space and the old man cries out in pain, and in fear. His eyes widen. Blood fills the white of the eyes. The music swirls from the ballroom. The colonel spasms in his chair, his arms flailing like the extended instruments of some broken machine. The scorpion is knocked from the table. It lands on the floor beside the old man who has fallen with it. The creature lands on its back, legs waving frantically, and its tail spurting, automatic. The glistening purple arc of fluid sprays across the man's terrified face.

The wheel of the chair spins slowly to an end. The hands of the clock grasp at time, and stall there.

Night closes in.

The sad old moon shines down on the Palace of Seductions. Jessica follows the dealer man from the bordello. A narrow passageway leads down the side of the building. The young man is standing by the fire escape. He has placed the scorpion on the metal step, but the creature will not move.

'A delightful plaything,' says Jessica.

'It's broken,' says the dealer.

'Who gave it to you?'

The dealer looks confused. 'It's broken,' he says again.

Jessica pulls the gun. Once again, she feels as though some distant mechanism is at work in her, clicking through dark algorithms.

'Tell me,' she says. 'Tell me.'

The young dealer turns away. A soft trace of music can be heard, and then a sudden spill of fire. A voice has spoken inside Jessica. 'Kill him.' And the night is momentarily set alive.

Jessica returns to the dance floor. The place is almost empty now except for a few women standing around the perimeter, watching. The good gentlemen of the orchestra have packed away their instruments; only the bandoneon player remains. Old Miguel, playing some rough-hewn primitive melody. The room is flickering, lit only in sepia tones. The years are falling away.

The special agent feels a sudden compassion, against her

training. And then the voice tells her to move on, toward the next location. Find the dealers, one by one.
    Kill them.
    The colonel dances alone.

## 12

NIGHT SOIL PICTURES presents an Elastic Land Groove
'A Nice Little Tale For A Quiet Tea Party'

*cue music etc.*
A whole bunch of screwy characters in the shape of humanoid corporate logos, our old brand name friends: Mitsubishi Moptop, Marlboro Manboy, Casio Cutecore, Toshiba Trickgirl, Fuji Flowerpower. All good Zeenies are quarantined inside the floodwalls of the Giant Sleeping Head in a bloodrush Skull Garden site of leaking sands and divided seas and weirdo flowers.

ONE DAY WE REALLY GOTTA GET OUTTA THIS HEAD!

They are eating caviar and drinking champagne, working toothpicks in their mouths, when their old pal Nike Airhead gets abducted by the Operating Clay Torso.

UH-OH! MISS NIKE STILL HAS THE ENIGMA DEVICE!

So the Zeenies hijack a plane and fly in under the radar through to a remote part of the Skull Garden, the Plaza of Lame Stars, where they make a nuisance of themselves, scrawling hexes on all the statues of old evil angels and dead generals who wake up...

THIS IS AN OUTRAGE!

...Only to find the names of their tormentors magically typed on a list of proscribed organisations that one of them pulls from his pockets, so the antique stone people jump off their plinths and chase the Zeenies round and round a willow tree.
YOU WON'T GET AWAY WITH THIS!

Packed tight inside an old Black Maria their preferred kidnap vehicle going faster and faster till everything's a blur and the Zeenies escape to the safety of the treetops where they put their feet up and catch some UV rays. Meanwhile…

**BOOM!**

The Black Maria chases its own tail so hard it crashes into itself.

AW! DA POOR LIDDLE SUPER VILLAINS! DEY'VE GONE ALL TO PIECES!

Casio Cutecore looks down at the Black Maria wrapped round the tree with its occupants a jumble of cracked heads, limbs and feet. She puts on a Red Cross hat and beckons to her comrades, who hop to the ground and in a burst of frenzied activity put the statues back together arse-over-tit, now the generals don't like that, they're scowling from their bellies while the angels put up with having their lips pinned to their backs.

WE'RE RETREATING UNDERGROUND!

They waddle off stiffly into the sink-holes beneath the roots of the willow tree and their victors follow gleefully and troop through the blue hush of underground chambers to find Nike Airhead locked into position writing their names on the infecting data-plates of the Enigma Device. They lift her veil of ink and she receives the blessing air and now it's all over bar the singing, when Toshiba Trickgirl arrives late as usual and points out the barred door behind the Enigma Device.

WOULDN'T IT BE COOL IF THAT WERE A SECRET MAGIC DOOR WHICH LED OUT OF THE SKULL GARDEN?

Nike kicks the Enigma Device into a corner and discovers a sign on the door saying SECRET MAGIC DOOR.

IT'S TIME TO RESET, TEST AND HONE! SOMEONE GET ME AN AXE!

*Roll credits.*
*Where shall I roll them?*
*Down the hill, down the hill!*

THIS IS NOT A NEW BEGINNING BUT IT MIGHT WELL BE THE BEGINNING OF

The End

## 13

*Mister Teardrop, His Lyrical Fancie*

I work by dark on my new creation; I have buried my seed in the night soil. I have sucked the juice from the tail of the scorpion. I have quenched the seed with the teardrops of Morpheus, and given it warmth from the blue electric moonlamp. I have stolen the royal data and now a flower grows from the black earth of my desire. And I wander nightly through this thorny bower and whisper sweet poetry there.

*Queen and Huntress, chaste and fair–*
A flower. My English rose. Its petals are drowsy yet and folded in upon themselves in cold repose. Oh, the long sleep. Oh, Dyana. The long cruel sleep of the soul since your first untimely death. Why will you not awaken for me now, my Princess? I have seen your face in bloom on the other side of the mirror. I have devised the radar of angels for thy new course to keep.

*Now the sun is laid to sleep–*
Alas, your lovely eyes are closed and will not open, no matter how I sing. It will take a deeper, more beguiling love. Oh my Dyana, you shall be my heart's impair! Let me kiss you. Let my lips touch at the cold looking glass, to meet your own mouth there, and to linger. To linger. Queen of the Chase, let these my soft wares ensnare you. Unveil yourself from darkness with this down load of air.

*Seated in thy silver chair–*
Awake now, awake! Bring me your flesh, and I shall bring my flame to you. The blood shall flow again through the chosen veins.

And we shall ride together on the Lunar Hunt Ball, your faithful hounds once more by your side. Call them to you, now! Stalker and Blackfoote, Jollyboy, Lightfoote, Bilbucke and Blab, Royster, Cole and swift Fleetwoode, and there now, Savage and Greediguts, leap!
  *State in wanted manner keep--*
  My lips have left a mark of breath on the mirror's face. I have pulled myself away from the glass, trembling. A woman's eyes have looked upon me and smiled, as though love were unbound at last from cupid's quarantine. She has drawn the tears from my eyes and they shall never stop from flowing. At my window I watch as Venus rises above the floodwall. Through the chambers of the sky's ink your star is agleam, and now you rise for me, my Princess. My heart's delight.
*Hesperus entreat they light*
*Goddess excellently bright!*

## 14

COUNTRY: New Albion Nation
SUBJECT: Company of Recreational Drug Purveyors Builds Mobile DogCam Neighbourhood Watch Theatre.
DATE OF REPORT: 1 August 2019
PLACE OF INFORMATION: Londinuum De-medicalized Zones
SOURCE OF INFORMATION: Black market Morpheus Juice vendor at foot of Nike billboard on Highway 32.
SUMMARY: This document considers the growing civil presence maintained by licensed drug dealers in the shanty towns outside of the Forbidden City. They have taken over many of the functions vacated by the old utility companies and media corporations. The Neighbourhood Watch Theatre is a surveillance programme designed to scare off unlicensed drug dealers. It makes use of roving canine operatives equipped with 8mm micro-vidcam headsets.

The Drug Purveyors Company Neighbourhood Watch Theatre is a flat-bed truck supporting a giant effigy of the goddess Nike. It drifts across the grey corrugated iron sea of Township 32 attended by a security crew of close-cropped young men sporting Oakley wraparound shades and black woollen topcoats. Inside the effigy clusters of local people read the adverts on the walls and peer into the flickering pools of blue-white light given off by the TV monitors. They have been promised a good show.

OLFACTOVISUAL INSERT: Real-time datafeeds taken from canine operatives trained to hunt down reported Morpheus Juice vendors.

Stalker DogCam: Horizontal line of vision. Twisting down neon thoroughfares past vending-machines stocked with coffee, sugared drinks and cigarettes. The repetitive stripes of ashtrays, drinking fountains, telegraph poles. Refugees from the dream are slumped by the roadside, moaning with pain. A soft toy anteater abandoned in the gutter.

Jollyboy DogCam: Nuzzling up to potential human street companions. A fortune-teller squatting next to her interface. Monks kneeling on folded newspapers chanting for peace. A girl huddled up in a doorway reading a magazine titled ZEENY COLLECTOR. (Headline: 'Gotta dream 'em all!')

Lightfoote DogCam: Ground-level tracking view of winding ornamental lakes and bridges. Close-up of the padlocked door at the Central Pagoda covered with rusting mesh. Sniffing out the sewage exhaust gate. Barking at a shorthaired white-nosed rat which scampers away.

Fleetwoode DogCam: Squeezing in through a gap. Pressing through a vapour barrier of ammonia, decomposing dream products and choke-damp. Temporary blindness. A vision of an old man leaking perfumed creatures from the back of his head. A toad springs into view. Above its bulging eyes hovers a pair of quizzical eyebrows.

Savage DogCam: Paddling through a torrent of swollen water in a circular tunnel. The furred ceiling sweating with putrid neurochemical deposits. The awful smell of dung, guts and blood. Bodies of drowned puppies and dead cats floating past. A headless meat carcass. Offal and rot.
Royster DogCam: Trotting down an arched brickwork tunnel lined

with ductwork and ligaments. Cast-iron synaptic pipes ridged with sockets and joints. Strands of fibre-optic hair braided into neural net cables. A brackish smell seeping up from below. A swarm of honeybees flying down from above.

Greediguts DogCam: Snout pushing aside synthetic loam granules to burst free into a bower of delightful aromas and brilliant colours. Sunflowers dusted with snowflakes nod in the ventilation stream. A long-eared rabbit hops into view, stops to consult his fob watch, then tears off into the distance.

NOTE: The drug traffickers have found one of the illicit seep-holes from the Skull Garden. Urgent action required. It must be sealed! And any others found, post haste.

DISTRIBUTION OF REPORT: All Departments of the Academy of Truth.

## 15

*Assistant Detective Jay Singer, 19$^{th}$ Precinct. Personal notes.*

1) Midnight callout. Weirdo case. Male Caucasian, late thirties. A floater. I was First Officer on Scene. Knee deep in shit, along the sewage drain out pipe. Stank like the devil had just yanked the chain on something nasty.

2) Morgue detail. Check the fashion on the dead these days. Big shoes with the tongues lolling out. But get this; the tongues are real. Doc reckons pulled from a Collie's mouth, and stitched onto the fabric. Trousers all patchwork, made out of blankets and fur and a trick drawer in each knee opens to reveal a telephone and a lobster. The lobster long frozen. The belt is a cheap plastic snake, swallowing its own head. Many objects tied there: tin cups, a first aid kit, an old palmtop computer, a toy scorpion. The palmtop has been wiped, beyond retrieval. Tech boys stumped. Pro job. The pockets of a long overcoat filled with Greek coins, dog biscuits, a folding mirror, and a tattered paperback copy of Conrad's 'The Secret Sharer', sealed in a

plastic bag. Just one sentence underlined in the story: 'As I came at night, so shall I go.' Last of all, an ID card. Name of diseased is Jake Mailer. No fixed abode.

3) I knew Jake. Big Jake Mailer. Nice guy for a tramp. Drunk most of the time. Used to go on about how he could have been a contender. Stand up routine. Oh, he had all the right jokes, but his timing was shot to fuck. Jitters on him, last time I saw. Sad. Don't know where the hell he got this outfit from.

4) Cause of death? Yeah right. The fucker's got no head. Sliced clean.

5) Okay. Last week we had the head found at the site of that sicko religious meeting. The guys that reckon the final dawn is upon us and all that. The new messiah shit. The Princess of Hearts. Yeah right. Just one more cult we have to deal with, but listen up. Genetic analysis links the two items, head to body. Trouble is, the head looks nothing like Jake. What the hell's going on? Think. Deceased maybe stole the ID card. But when the DNA comes back, it's pointing right at Jake in the cop data. Like I said, weirdo case. Hang around. You ain't seen weird yet.

6) I'm thinking by now, maybe Jake had plastic surgery done. Right, a tramp can afford that? What other possibles? Curious. I pull the morgue file. Slab photos. The Doc made some attempt at fixing the head in place. Chunks of a meat jigsaw, laid out. I do a web search on the face, come up with a complete match, 100%. Check this out. The machine is telling me the face of the corpse belongs to one Ferdinand Marx. Full length portrait included, and even the clothes are the same. Trouble is, Ferdinand died back in the last century. 1974.

7) What the fuck is going on here? I feel sick. Shivering.

8) Okay, here's the gen. Ferdinand Marx, otherwise known as Fouko. The so-called youngest of the Marx Brothers. Yeah, you know that crowd from the late night films. The Marx Brothers. Very popular comedians. Hollywood. 1930s, 40s. Groucho, Harpo, Chico, sometimes Zeppo. Various other brothers. But Fouko's lineage was disputed by the family. Nonetheless, Fouko Marx started his career in 1959, when he bought up the rights to Salvador Dali's script, 'The Marx Brothers on Horseback Salad.' The original brothers had

rejected the work. Too weird. But Fouko thought it might appeal to the new young audience. The film made him. 1962. World-wide. But he never lived up to the promise. Drunkard, apparently. Womaniser. Some kind of scandal. Like I said, the comedian died in 1974, during the filming of 'Clockwork Bananas'. Freak accident in a stunt scene. Head severed.

9) Been hearing tales from all over of the strangeness in town. Rumours. Gossip. Grapevine talk ties most of it to the people up at the Cartoon Studios. Dismissed it myself. I mean, I bought one of those Zeeny creatures for the kid's birthday. Nice toy. Doesn't need hardly any looking after. But the Morgue Doc tells me they're doing some eerie shit up there at the castle. Is this linked? Something that got loose? A ghost? The Zeeny keeps looking at me. Oh Christ, I need me some paid leave, I surely do.

10) Stranger yet. The full lab report came back today. Some drug found in Jake/Fouko's bloodstream. No match to any known chemical compound. Shit. They extracted the juice, fed it to some poor lab rat. I watched the film. The poor specimen started to change right before my eyes. Accelerated evolution. It became a cat! The mouse became a cat. Jesus. A little fucking mutated version of a cat. Horrible. Lasted two hours before it died. Screaming. Clawed its own neck open.

11) Doc said it reminded him of something he heard about, recently. Drug that made you change like that. I said, 'What the hell is that for, to turn you into your own worst enemy?' He said, 'Wrong scenario. It turns you into your favourite fantasy.' And every mouse wants to be a cat, right?

12) Right. And it's got me to thinking. Here I am, sleepless now. Down to the last bottle. Can't help picturing what I'd turn into. Those dreams I have. Bad. Me, putting the slice into some flesh. Shit, I really need to get off this case.

13) This just in. Rudolph Valentine found dead in a hotel room.

14) I can't keep from looking in the mirror.

15) The Zeeny follows me everywhere.

# 16

Touchstone Pictures proudly presents 'Clockwork Bananas! The Director's Cut' starring the Incredible Fouko Marx, the 'Man Who Could Walk Into Mirrors!'

*DVD menu option: Director's Commentary.* Fouko spent some quality time with Harry Houdini back in the old days of vaudeville. So the interest in escapology was never entirely for laughs. Reports say that Fouko could get out of any strait-jacket in seventeen seconds flat. I guess it's like that Picasso thing, you have to know the rules to be able to break them. Except here we're dealing with a genius of comic art.

*DVD menu option: Film Clip.* Fouko dressed in waders and oilskins with a fisherman's hat perched on his head is apprehended restocking the East River with tinned salmon and thrown in jail. He puts his feet up and settles in for a long stay. Tips the guard when his food arrives. Orders drinks for all the inmates. Protests at the size of his bill and is kicked out.

*DVD menu option: New Yorker Critic's Review.* The trouble is Fouko wasn't happy being a comic, he wanted people to think of him as an artist. I always thought 'The Marx Brothers on Horseback Salad' was terrifically overrated. The Marx Brothers doing Salvador Dali is just not funny. That's because they're not really surrealists, they're trickster figures; they bring chaos to whatever social system they manage to gatecrash. Fouko never got that. I think that's why Groucho always said that Fouko wasn't a true son of the Marx father; instead, he called him the bastard son of Frederick Engels.

*DVD menu option: Fellow Actor's Tribute.* I was the chief zoo-keeper in the 'Opening The Cages' number. So I was the stuffed shirt in the peaked cap who was the butt of all the gags. It was a whirlwind learning experience for me. I got to see all of Fouko's famous psycho-mimetic routines up close, y'know, when he was rushing between cages trying to cover for the fact he'd let loose all these wild animals. It was a riot!

*DVD menu option: Film Clip.* Fouko lounging on cushions of straw wearing an eye-patch and an insipidly coy expression. He is nibbling on green shoots and shielding his groin from the attentions of an imaginary suitor. Cut-back to the sign on the cage:

369

ARACHNID HOUSE. Cut-away to a low frontal shot of a scorpion raising its spiked tail over its head as it prepares to strike the exposed ankle of the chief zoo-keeper.

*DVD menu option: Director's Commentary.* Fouko could be difficult, like all great artists. I've got here the original list of all the animals he wanted me to cast for the Zoo scene: 'Hawks, dogs, Asiatic lions, African elephants, giraffes, camels, Malay tapirs, white rhinoceroses, anteaters, Chinese leopards, tigers, howler monkeys, macaws, hyenas & snakes.' Obviously, I had to use stock footage in the end. Fouko never really forgave me.

*DVD menu option: SFX Technician's Confession.* Fouko was out there, man. A real buzz. He wanted me to make him up with all these freaky combinations of animal characteristics, so you got like a feathered snake or a horned dog, stuff like that. It was what killed him in the end. I kept saying that Scorpion Shape-Shifting trick was way too dangerous. But nobody listened.

*DVD menu option: Director's Commentary.* His death was tragic, of course. But now those miraculous special effects wizards at Industrial Lumiere have allowed us to digitally reanimate him to complete the final scenes of the movie. Fouko always was a great pioneer of new showbiz techniques. It's what he would have wanted.

# 17

ZEENY WORLD -- *Gotta dream 'em All!*
Morphco is proud to present the latest generation of loveable phantazeen creatures, all personally conjured just for you by the Big Sleeping Emperor himself. So let us wander together through the Skull Garden. What can we see...

The HORQUE bird, a whirlwind of feathers hovering above the jungle.

A pack of DOGMATICA with Gnostic scriptures painted on their fur.

A pride of GANGLIONS. Wild cats, passing messages to a human brain.

The TELEPHANTASM, with its proboscis transmission of solid body into ghost vapour.

The GYRAFFOSCOPE, a single eye on a stalk.

The CAMELEON, a dromedary shape-shifting into a pair of lactating breasts, twin babies suckling on the teats.

The TAPYRO, a tongue of fire licking at petals.

A lone RHINOCEROSE, the horned flower that spikes the flesh of any passing creature, depositing seedpods into the body.

The REVENANTEATER, devouring a stray ghost signal.

The spotted sunbeams of the HELIOPARD.

The TIGERMICIDE, sucking up striped bacteria from a rainbow's skin.

A DEMONKEY, whose forked tail is turning the lock on a mirror.

The COBRALINGUS, tying words into knots.

The ALARMACAW, a clock with wings, tapping at a church bell with its beak.

BHYENARY, laughing dogs constructed from the numbers One and Zero, eating the stray punchcards spewing from a soft, melting computer terminal.

See now the DATASNAKES, whose twisted bodies describe the face of the Emperor, complete with Mickey Morpheus ears.

SCORPIONICS, mechanical creatures, their tails dripping with a viscous fluid of musical notes.

And what's that over there, surely it can't be a HOMOZEEN?! At long last, human dream figures now available.

Important notice: It has come to our attention that illicit Zeeny creatures are being offered for sale. Do not be tempted by this! These creatures may well have escaped from the garden, or else been stolen. They are untested specimens, inferior models, and will quickly die without the Emperor's magic. Beware!

## 18

Performance: Old Miguel is playing the bandoneon. One of the old time tunes; slow and sad, but filled with dignity. Miguel is suffering; the sickness has a hold of him, and his fingers tremble on the keys of the instrument. An occult source code is being tapped. His weak voice catches at a melody, the words filled with yearning for a hot world of beauty that is dying away, fading, fading. The garden of delights. That it may rise again, that it may come again, and shine again anew.

Recording: The Scorpi-O-Phonic device lowers its needle to cut a trail into soft pink wax. Grooves are formed, in decreasing circles. A spiral scratch of data with the good funky juice flowing from the needle even as it cuts. The juice gathering in the channels of wax. The song captured there.

Soundbiter's Dub: The track loaded with samples distilled from the late-night channels. Cop show backing vocal. Unmarked cars pulling up at the kerb. Gun shots and radio crackle. Baby monitor alarms. Shouting, screaming. Crowd noise from a fetishwear catwalk run. A hooded model hauled out by the scruff of her neck. Traffic rush. Echoes of motorised disappearance. Doppler effect. Time slowed to a crawl. And then forward, and now delayed. Mechanical rhythms of pulping and scraping lifted from old Hollywood boxing movies. Sound of a kettle boiling. Someone is gasping...again and again. Feedback jolt. The pure thrill of electricity. Signal reversal. A car door unslams. A grandfather clock ticking backwards. Flesh creeps on a bone, magnified close. Bad sitcom laugh-track. Stray ghost signals from the Sacred Mausoleum gameshow. Zombies doing the old boneyard tango. The sonic X-ray of a piece of human excreta.

Dali Dub: Old Miguel takes an antique vinyl record from his collection, a British Broadcasting Corporation Sound Effects production. Creatures From The Radiophonic Savannah. The squawking of the Horque bird, the whispering of the Telephantasm, the strident bell of the Alarmacaw, the howlings of the Dogmatica, the singing of the wild Gyraffoscope. Many more. The musician drops the noises into the mix.

Conjuring Dub: The track played out from a Sound System truck. Loud, the bass deep enough to make even the sun tremble. Heat waves rising. Desert scene. The musician working alone, digging the vast spiral diagram into the sand. Himself at the centre of it, the music swirling around him. He calls out for a cure to be sent down, for himself and for all the good people. The old rhythm sends out a spark. The sky crackles with fire. Old Miguel drops to his knees to receive the divine message.

Infection Dub: The musician in his studio. A copy of Gray's Anatomy is propped open on his mixing desk. He prepares the Scorpi-O-Phonic device, sets it going. The needle cuts into his skin, making the spiral there, in the dark flesh. There is pain. There is pleasure. The medicine song, injected. Miguel knows that he himself must become the way. He must cleanse the path for the true spirit that follows.

*That She may rise again, that She may come again, and shine again anew.*

### 19

Einstein's ghost walks through the sunken corridors, staring at his pocket watch.

The Mausoleum Club, deep within the catacombs of the city. This hidden world where time seeps slowly, thickly, crawling through black mirrors. In the dark archives young men and women stand around, examining their pale reflections. They have spent many hours preparing their faces for the night, giving themselves the soft translucent X-ray skin of the latest fashion. The Nebuli, as they are known. Zombie kids. The ghost walks amongst them. These young people, he thinks, what do they know of death, truly? They are wearing the mask of decay, that is all. Their chosen music is a slow parade of boneyard marches, German *lieder* and folk murder ballads, all decoded from old vinyl by the jewelled tip of the scorpion's tail.

Only one person dances. A young woman dressed in green silk.

Watching her, the ghost recalls the Schubert nocturne from his younger days. *Bald schlaf ich ihn, den langen schlummer.* He sings the words to himself. Soon I shall sleep the long sleep. Prague, Zurich, Berlin, the cold streets, cold hearts, the tangle of numbers, symbols; the flight to America. *For the light to remain constant, time itself must be distorted.* That exquisite frightening moment.

The ghost drifts on. There is a pain in his chest; a black hand tightening around his heart. It has been with him all day, this pain, increasing. Filled with anguish he walks through into another chamber, darker yet, where an old man is playing the bandoneon. The musician gives a new rhythm to the Schubert piece. Here, a group of young refugees hold court, showing off their fragile magic.

Homozeens.

Rumour has it they have emerged from some world of dream, and their bodies do not last long in these climes. They have diseased shadows, and smell of decay. But no matter, the zombie kids are pleased to take kisses from them. A kind of sharing is taking place, illicit, through the tongue's contact. There are stories in the air, of a new age about to dawn, of a dark princess who will lead them all to some sweeter land.

But the ghost, his frizzed hair sparked with charged particles, has no interest in such things; his eyes are saddened rather by mathematics, the exact weight of the moon, the motion of the clock's face. The calculated force of the pain that creeps through him. Along a corridor swirled with smoke and incense he meets the woman in green silk. Jessica. She will not let him pass.

'What is happening?' he asks. His voice is trembling. 'I was asleep. A long time, asleep. I woke up. And now...'

'Who woke you?' says Jessica.

'I don't understand. My watch, the hands, they are moving backwards.'

'Listen to me. You are not who you think you are.'

'I was asleep. So far away, the darkness...'

'You are a low level drug dealer. A failed chemist. Your name is Paul Doppler.'

'No. That is not me.'

'You have taken a drug that has changed you. You have become your own fantasy.'

'Leave me alone.'

'You life is draining away, Paul. Even now.'

The ghost wants to move away but the woman has a hold on him; her eyes have captured him there.

'Who gave you the drug? Tell me.'

The ghost looks at her. His face is twisted, lost with confusion. There are no good words he can bring to his lips.

'Professor, you died in 1955. And you will die again, in the same manner. The slow drawn-out torment, the sudden overwhelming of your heart. Is this what you want?'

'No. Not that. Not that...not again.'
The voice comes to Jessica. Insistent, demanding knowledge.
'I could release you,' she says to the ghost. 'I could let you go free from this.'
Jessica has produced a gun from the folds of green silk.
The ghosts sighs. 'It was a man,' he whispers. 'No, a woman. A little of each. A person who could not stop crying.'
'Where is this?'
'A hall of mirrors. Strange mirrors.'
'Thank you,' says the agent.
'Kill him,' says the voice.
'Kill him?' says Jessica.
'Have mercy on me,' says the ghost.
And then, the soft silenced shot of the gun. The bullet that takes nine seconds exactly to reach his chest. The crucifix carved upon the shell's casing, glimpsed in flight. The pocket watch, broken now, to let time escape in a black mist from the cracked glass. The final line of the nocturne: *Der Tod hat sich zu ihm geneight*. And then the crackles of vinyl.
'Keep moving,' says the voice. 'Keep on target.'
Jessica walks away from the scene, wrapped in shadows; a trail of echoes.

## 20

'Walk. Don't walk.'
I wish the voice would make up its mind.
'Keep moving.'
The buildings in the Black Light district of the city have hologram facades that change every week. They are adverts for dream products that sicken within days of entering the world.
Cage is pleased with me. I have given him the clues: of the strange mirrors, and the man with too many tears. Cage could see I was special. He looks after me from the inside of a low-orbital keyhole satellite.
'Adopt the second defensive position of the Stepping Crane Dance.'
My body flows across distant relays and is drawn down into a rehearsed sequence of gestures, dancing. Mid-level crouch. Green silk rustling. Right forearm block. Left palm kissing the butt of my Thompson 9mm.

I am surrounded by empty streets lined with wooden benches and conifer trees. The moon is fat and wide in the night sky.

'Hey, buddy! Do you just wanna..? Do you wanna..?'

My weapon is now trained on the smiling face of a little Zeeny who is holding out a publicity flier. Centipede Model 400 with motion detector vision. He is crawling the street on a tangle of broken legs, addressing the tumbleweeds and newspapers that the wind blows his way.

'Heed the message.'

I obey the voice. It keeps me alive.

The little centipede continues to gaze at me. He avoids looking at the dead scorpions slung from my belt.

The flier carries the details of my next assignment.

'APPARITION PARK. The Company of Recreational Drug Purveyors Presents Many Charged Attractions For Frazzled Human Beings. Visit Lord Scatterbrain's Clock Meditation Lounge. Attend Little Miss Crystal's Pocket Universe Vibratorium. Enter Mister Teardrop's Mathemagical Hall of Mirrors.'

A map of the city unfolds in my head. Data. Cage has worked his search. The crying man is waiting for me at the end of the Black Light district. I collect myself and stand up.

'Destroy all evidence.'

The flier is dust in my hand.

'Hey, buddy. Do you just wanna..?'

The little centipede is asking me a question. He turns his head sideways to attract my line of fire.

'Destroy *all* evidence.'

I can't stop thinking about the face of Einstein, that young fool. Desiring the bullet. It makes me put the gun away.

'What are you doing?' says the voice. 'Don't put it away.'

I lightly move three steps back from the Zeeny. The voice is following me. It gives me a pain in the side of my head.

'Kill it!' The voice is so demanding.

'Must it always be like this?'

'Destroy all evidence.'

The pain increases. No escape. I blow the Zeeny apart, one shot.

'Move on,' says the voice.

There is an advert for a Minotaur 600 high in the sky.

'Hey, buddy!'
The Zeeny's mouth is still working, a purple juice dribbling from the lips.

## 21

In the hall of mirrors
    night-fallen, amid slow waves of data
        crawling shadows, wind-blown, now gather
into clouded shapes;
    vibrations in the air, crystal
        frequencies, a slow sudden pulse-beat.
Emerging, a drift of tears
    multiplied in the one thousand mirrors,
        where figures crouch in corners and then
rise to step freely
    (as the crane steps)
        through liquid soft reflections: where now,
following, the assassin glides
    in silk. The one hand, becoming
        a thousand; the one gun, a thousand guns;
silent, until a teardrop
    falls on glass. Echoes, magnified.
        A skin of silver nitrate that peels itself
away from the glass
    becoming a likeness. Half man,
        half woman. A crying apparition that
raises a hand, lightly
    revealing the shine of a blade
        and plunges forward, howling, toward
the assassin who moves
    in turn, quickly, raising the gun.
        A voice is telling her now, whispering:
*No, not to kill, not this time.*
    The blade glistens. The trigger is
        pulled, and all the shining pathways are
broken,

scattering; a fire that cracks
        a hand wide open. Bone, wetness,
                stench, blood, meat. Voices scream out
in relay. Cry, repeat, cry,
        repeat, cry, repeat. Gestures, falling.
                Gestures. Cry, repeat. And then quiet. Cold.
The agent finds there
        only pale shadows, crawling to make
            an image held on a splintered mirror;
which fades, slowly
      lingering, fading, slowly. Only
            this; a smear of blood on the looking glass.

## 22

Death of a Princess (take #1)

Banner Hologram Resolution Scale #1: Wide shot of a black Mercedes S-280 with a crumpled bonnet lying helter-skelter in an underpass at night. The back right-hand door of the vehicle is open. A weak pool of light spills onto the road.

Banner Hologram Resolution Scale #2: Close shot of a pack of men in the shadows, crowding each other to get close to the light. They are taking photographs of the car's plush, ruined interior. Some of them are pressing in deep.

Banner Hologram Resolution Scale #3: Cropped image of a woman's body slumped against the back of a front seat with her left leg splayed up on the rear seat and her right leg folded under her hind-quarters. Her blonde coiffure is immaculate. The strap of an oxygen mask covers the line of her jaw.

Banner Hologram Resolution Scale #4: Blown-up detail of the woman's left hand lying crumpled against the tailored contours of her Chanel jacket. The third finger is unbloodied. It is banded with a diamond ring whose central stone glistens amidst the scattered glass and debris of the scene.

Banner Hologram Resolution Scale #0: Text insert: 'You scatter my flesh into one thousand and one frequencies.'

Banner Hologram Resolution Scale #1: Wide shot of a black Mercedes S-280 with a crumpled bonnet lying helter-skelter in an underpass at night. The back right-hand door of the vehicle is open. A weak pool of light spills onto the road.

## 23

WALT DISNEY'S LONG LOST DREAMWORLD
FOUND IN RAILWAY STATION LUGGAGE LOCKER!

Entry: The moon is full. We are moving toward the south-west of the garden. Our navigation device suggests we are close to the site of deliverance, but all around we see only nettles and thorns. The land has fallen into ruin, and no flowers bloom. Baxter is concerned about infection. The maps he found lining the owl's nest have crumbled into dust. Lichen grows on my shaving mirror. Everything is changing, growing wild. Still no sign of the rest of the squad. Baxter wants to abandon the expedition. He wants to go back through the vapour gate. Meanwhile, Commander Leigh is tracking down the creatures we have seen in the undergrowth. The rain will not stop; splinters of lightning break the clouds. We have been in this solitary place for five days already, with nothing good to show for it. There is a black algae covering the food supply.

RECORDS SHOW LOCKER LAST OPENED
ONE THOUSAND AND ONE YEARS AGO!
STATION ATTENDANT HEARD 'ANIMAL CRIES' FROM WITHIN!

Entry: Baxter is laid out on the ground, delirious. His flesh is grey and pallid, and his face is covered by a mask of seed pods. I have persuaded Leigh to help build an improvised stretcher. We are carrying the old professor through the stagnant forest. The navigation device is corrupted; some kind of worm has crept into the workings. Leigh insists that the burnt coins she found in the pool of glass can be used to guide us further. She throws them to the ground, six times in all. As the last coin comes to a rest, a crow lands on the bough of a dead tree.

IMAGE OF WOUNDED HAND APPEARS ON
VISUAL DISPLAY UNIT ANNOUNCING TRAIN DEPARTURES!
CHURCH OF THE RECONSTRUCTED DYANA
CLAIMS LOCKER AS SITE OF HOLY WORSHIP!

Entry: Not sure what 'dying' means, in here. Baxter's skin was covered in moss, his fingers growing into the earth, his hair knotted with vines. There is no need of a burial. The garden has claimed him. Who could have abandoned such a place, such a dream? By what means was it allowed to fall into such a state of ruin? We are no nearer to finding the secret. The rain drums against the canopy of leaves but does not find a way through. Darkness. I have thrown away my mirror. Leigh caught and killed one of the strange mutated creatures. We have eaten it. Green flesh. There was a faded company logo on the soft belly. Radio crackle. The bird flies on. This afternoon we found the bleached skeleton of a horse lying in a bower. A metal tap protruded from the bones of the neck. The professor's last diagnosis keeps coming back to me, about the plague of impossible desire. The forest closes in. We have camped by the side of a riverbed. Tins of food are scattered in the cracked mud; pate de fois gras, asparagus tips, cooked oysters. Leigh uses her knife on them, but only a purple dust is contained within.

MEN IN BLACK SUITS REMOVE ENTIRE LOCKER!
CROWD HELD BACK AS SACRED OBJECT BUNDLED
INTO BACK OF MERCEDES VAN!

Entry: Walking the streets of a vast, empty city. We have stepped through the grey curtain of rain, into another climate. The sun burns the sky. The purple sand is everywhere. Art deco cinemas, hair salons, coffee houses. The garden continues through the city, tendrils climbing the broken streetlamps. A drift of rare spices. Can this really be the Emperor's last dream? Without Baxter's psychoanalytical methods, how can we hope to decipher this strange realm? The crow swoops down, through the open doorway of an old theatre. Sad, sweet music can be heard from inside.

LOST PROPERTY MAN SAW VAPOUR TRAIL
SEEPING FROM LOCKER!
'THE PURPLE DUST WAS GETTING IN MY SANDWICHES!'

Entry: A small darkened room. Packed earth, a dreadful smell of rotting food and excrement. The crow has vanished. A spiral of sand leads to the centre of the floor. A silver pendant hangs down from the ceiling, turning slowly in the warm air. The music stirs with a soft breathing, a magical five note melody. It seems to be coming from below the ground. Leigh is digging there with her bare hands, frantically. 'It's here!' she says. 'It's here!' And she pulls a black box from the dirt.

GOVERNMENT SENDS JUNGIAN ARCHAEOLOGY SQUAD
INTO DISNEY'S DREAM!
THEY WILL UNCOVER SECRET OF EMPIRE'S FALL!

Entry: Two wooden blocks are joined by a bellows mechanism made from animal hide. Mother of pearl inlay depicts a silver scorpion, its tail poised to strike. There is a bone keypad, each key inscribed with a letter of the old alphabet, or else a number. It's a bandoneon. The instrument comes alive in my hands, the bellows separating, coming together, squeezing air through the machine. The keys depress themselves beneath my fingers, spelling out the symbol of a chemical compound: $AgNO_3$. The stuff they make mirrors out of. The music can be seen in the air now, forming the shape of a rose. It blossoms. One thousand and one petals of silver nitrate, unfolding.

# BRIEFINGS

*These micro essays expose some of the theoretical ideas behind the novel's writing method, as well as revealing the secret history of the Mappalujo name.*

Briefings: The Remixology of the Word

*Invoking Ghosts*
The Mexican Day of the Dead has the same function as the night of All Souls or Hallowe'en. James Frazer comments in *The Golden Bough*: 'For it is a widespread belief that the souls of the dead revisit their old homes on one night of the year; and on that solemn occasion people prepare for the reception of the ghosts by laying out food for them to eat, and lighting lamps to guide them on their dark road to and from the grave.'

*Automatic Writing*
Andre Breton and Philippe Soupault collaborated on the world's first automatic writing project *Les Champs magnetiques (Magnetic Fields)* in 1920. Automatic writing has a connection with Freudian techniques of free association. Breton knew of the treatment of traumatised war veterans at Saint-Dizier hospital using this technique. *Les Champs magnetiques* is dedicated to a war veteran who committed suicide. It is perhaps a form of writing cure.

*Tone of Voice*
William Burroughs on the effect of the cut-up, *Electronic Revolution*, 1976: 'The original words are quite unintelligible but new words emerge. The voice is still there and you can immediately recognise the speaker. Also the tone of voice remains. If the tone is friendly, hostile, sexual, poetic, sarcastic, lifeless, despairing, this will be apparent in the altered sequence.'

*Understanding Ghosts*
Paul Virilio on the idea of distantly sensed presence, *Crepuscular Dawn*, 2002: 'How do you raise the question of the body or the object with respect to the image, on the first level, without raising the

question of the body with respect to the spectre? We know that the spectre was taken seriously in every ancient society... as was the image. But today we have put the image on a pedestal [and]... We forget... you have a return of the spectre.'

*Haunted by Old Ghosts*
Marshall McLuhan suggests that new media are extensions of the human nervous system and that - by implication - human subjectivity incorporates older media. He comments in *Understanding Media*, 1964: 'The content of any new medium is always an older medium. The content of a movie is a novel or a play or an opera. Speech is the content of writing. Writing is the content of print. Print is the content of the telegraph.' We can go on to say the telegraph is the content of the mobile phone. So what exactly is the content of computerised media?

*Random Access Interface*
Lev Manovich on computerised media in *Avant-garde as Software*, 1999: 'The computer revolution reactivates the older media of the avant-garde. In the earlier part of the twentieth century artists, architects and designers invented a whole new set of visual languages with Bauhaus, montage and Cubism. The computer revolution takes these older media and reworks them.' So the exploded perspectives of cubism become the multiple windows of Apple's 1984 graphical user interface.

*Window Entry*
Andre Breton first became aware of the possibilities of automatic writing when an 'assez bizarre' image came 'knocking at the window-pane' of his consciousness one evening. The image was of a man cut in two by the window. So Breton was not only musing on the window as an entry into the unconscious, but also dreaming of being split - or perhaps even doubled - on an unconscious level.

*Hermit Crab Spectre*
*Les Champs magnetiques* contains a series of poems headed by the phrase The Hermit-crab Says: The hermit crab emerges from the metamorphosis of two tailor's dummies displayed in a window. The dummies have no heads and no hands. They are split. 'Whatever is inhabiting our two friends gradually emerges from its

quasi-immobility. It gropes its way forward obtruding a fine pair of stalked eyes.' This hermit crab is the emergent spectre shared by Breton and Soupault. It is the mythic identity of the third mind produced by their collaboration.

*Scorpion Spectre*
The spectre shared by the creators of Mappalujo is the scorpion. Specifically, it's the scorpion considered as a writing machine. The image is derived from Joseph Conrad's short story *The Secret Sharer*. A scorpion is said to have got on board a ship, selected the room of the chief mate and then somehow 'managed to drown itself in the inkwell of his writing desk.'

*Ghost of Joseph Conrad*
Joseph Conrad's *The Secret Sharer* is a tale of two men on board a vessel whose uncanny doubling of each other below decks risks an unmanning in pursuit of authority. It is the port-hole rather than the window which is the focus of attention here. But there is still the fantasy of splitting: 'Altogether a nerve-trying situation. But on the whole I felt less torn in two when I was with him.'

*Over One Hundred Worthwhile Dilemmas*
Brian Eno and Peter Schmidt devised their Oblique Strategies cards in 1975. Card number two acts as an introduction to the pack: 'These cards evolved from our separate observations of the principles underlying what we are doing. Sometimes they were recognized in retrospect (intellect catching up with intuition), sometimes they were identified as they were happening, sometimes they were formulated. They can be used as a pack (a set of possibilities being continuously reviewed in the mind) or by drawing a single card from a shuffled pack when a dilemma occurs in a working situation. In this case the card is trusted even if it appropriateness is quite unclear. They are not final, as new ideas will present themselves, and others will become self-evident.'

*Map of the Game*
'I like Mamalujo. It's sounds game-like, I guess because it's got 'lu' in there, as in Homo Ludus, and indeed, Ludo. But Mamalujo is already

registered as a domain name by the James Joyce Research Centre in Dublin. So how about Mappalujo? As in Mappa Mundi. So it's the map of the game. Mappa derives from the Latin for cloth, so that fits in with the weaving texture. Mamalujo now can be seen as the Priestess of the map, the person with the arcane knowledge of all the secret connecting routes.'
– Jeff Noon, in an email to Steve Beard, 2002.

*Ghost of James Joyce*
'...the way they could not rightly tell their heels from their stools as they cooched down a mamalujo by his cubical crib, as question time drew nighing and the map of the souls' groupography rose in relief within their quarterings...'
– James Joyce, *Finnegans Wake*, 1939

# MASK CATALOGUE

*A list of the thirty-eight masks mentioned in the Night-Blossom Avenue story.*

Corporate linen mask 'Z'
Carved wooden masks (designer ware)
Executive armour mask
Silver management mask
This season's models (various, with grins)
Alternative ugly masks
Sample masks (not for resale)
Clint Westwood mask (domestic model)
'Bip' and 'Bop' children's masks
The Naked Face
Fashion mask (turquoise, silver fin, yellow lights)
Sleep masks (blue silk, striped cotton)
Porn Star Masks (pink fur, black rubber)
The Mask of Spikes
The Mask of Electric Glamour
Mechanised work mask (with callipers)
The Veil of Fountains
The Mask of Parasites
The Mask of Renegade Desire
Glaring monster mask
Evil demon mask
Hybrid creature mask
The False Face dream mask
The Mask of Falling Darkness
Cheap celebrity masks
Children's animal masks
Doorman's scarlet mask
Action Hero masks
Executive Pretty Boy masks
Grinning devil masks
Glamour queen masks
Face paint
Lujo City Football Club supporters masks
Fluorescent polythene mask (police issue)

Mask of the Question Mark
The Good Father's mask
Masks of love, lust and tenderness
Funeral hood (black)

# MOUSTACHE, MIDNIGHT & OJULAMAM

*We like this isolated chapter because Alice in Wonderland gets to live inside Princess Diana, and because the authors themselves make a brief appearance in disguise. The icon used is Lewis Carroll. It seems an appropiate way to bring the adventures of Mappalujo to a close.*

An old woman dressed in a slimy suit jumped out of an alleyway. 'Give us your money,' she said. 'Come on now, empty your pockets.'
'Well then,' said Alice. 'Let me see. I have one safety pin. And one mah-jongg tile, and the paper wrapping from a boiled kandy. Oh yes, and a matchbox.'
'Which brand of match?' asked the woman.
'Mama Lujo brand. Average contents, forty-nine. But there are only four matches left, I'm afraid. I used the rest setting fire to the--'
'Never mind all that.'
The old woman pushed the four matches through the cardboard of the box, one at each corner, and then she stood the matchbox on these little wooden legs. 'This is the stage.' The kandy wrapper she balanced against one side of the box. 'This is the curtain.' Finally, she placed the mah-jongg tile and the safety pin behind the wrapper.
'Are those the characters?' asked Alice.
'Yes they are. The Princess of Shadows. And Harry the Escapologist.'
'But what is the play called, I wonder?'
'Tonight's performance is called *The Wedding of the Flowers*, as written by Moustache and Midnight. Quickly now, it's about to start!'
Alice placed her eye against the tiny theatre, and the woman pulled aside the kandy wrapper with a dramatic flourish. Alice thought it very strange, but suddenly she was *inside* the theatre. It was a very *small* theatre, granted, and ever so dark, but how on earth it could fit under a matchbox, Alice could not begin to imagine.
'And what do you think you're doing here?' said a young man.
'I'm... I'm not quite sure,' said Alice.
'It's all here, in my contract.' A single teardrop rolled down the man's cheek, as he read out loud from a large sheet of paper. 'That Mister Teardrop, etc, being myself, etc, the party of the first part, etc, on such and such a date, etc, shall be the only, etc, as befits the second

part of the third reflection of the fourth party, etc, hereinafter and inside out and thereabouts, etc...'

'It doesn't make very much sense,' said Alice.

'I think it's all quite plain, etc, that I'm to play the most prestigious role, etc, of the most lovely Princess Dyana, etc, the Second.'

'But I'm not *playing* anybody,' said Alice. 'I'm in the audience, not the play!'

'Don't be silly now. You see those two holes, there?'

'Why yes,' said Alice. 'I never noticed them before. Are they the windows?'

'No, no, no! They're the eyes! The eyes of the princess. We're inside the princess, you see. Looking out. Shush now, do you hear that?'

Alice listened. 'It sounds very much like an old accordion, wheezing away..'

'An accordion? Au contraire. It's a bandoneon.'

'Is there a difference? They sound very similar.'

'Oh, they're spelt quite differently. Words that are spelt differently, never sound the same. Look! Here comes the groom!'

Alice peered through the two small openings. Thousands of rose petals were falling from the skies, and a handsome dark-haired man stepped through them.

'Isn't he beautiful?' said Mister Teardrop. 'That's my Harry!'

'Don't cry,' said Alice.

'I can't help it. I've been waiting for this moment all my life!'

Mister Teardrop was crying so much now, and with such force, his tears were flowing out through the eyes of the princess.

'Don't cry, my sweet,' said Harry the Escapologist. 'I'm here to comfort you.'

'Oh, oh, oh!' said Alice. 'What is he doing?'

'He's taking his clothes off, of course,' said Mister Teardrop. 'This is our wedding night after all.'

'Oh, oh, oh! They never said it was an Adults Only play! I mustn't watch this!'

'Come to me, my love,' whispered Mister Teardrop. 'Come to me!'

'Come to me, my love,' whispered the princess, in turn.

The audience could be heard, cheering, as Harry's face loomed close. And then everything started to shake. A fine yellow dust was making Alice sneeze.

'The royal pollen!' sighed Mister Teardrop. 'Oh, it's happening! I'm all a tremble!'

But now a terrible black smoke was streaming into the princess' eyes, making Alice cough and splutter. 'What is that?' she said. 'What is that burning smell? What are those lights, flickering? I feel very dizzy. Those flames!'

'The flames of passion, how they burn at me!'

'The theatre!' cried Alice. 'The theatre's on fire! Quickly, run!'

'Oh, there's no exit, not out of Princess Dyana. Why, the very thought!'

'What about this door here? It's got the word "Ojulamam" written on it. What does that mean?'

'That's the broom cupboard. I have to keep the inside of the princess tidy, you know.'

Alice opened the door. 'I can't see any brooms in here,' she said.

'It has been rather difficult, cleaning up, I must admit.'

'There are some stairs, leading downwards,' said Alice. 'Are you coming?'

By now, the princess was quite filled up with smoke. The flames were flickering through her eyes, and the bandoneon was making a horrible sound as though the instrument were being strangled. The audience was screaming.

'Don't be silly,' said Mister Teardrop. 'I can't leave. It's my wedding night.'

Suddenly, Alice slipped and fell. She tumbled down and down the stairs, just as the entire theatre vanished clean away in a puff of dust. Alice landed with a bump, back in the dark alleyway. The woman in the slimy suit was waiting there. 'What have you done to my theatre?' she said. 'My beautiful palace of delights?' For the matchbox and the kandy wrapper, the mah-jongg tile and the safety pin, all had disappeared. Only a single rose petal remained. It fluttered away in the breeze, and no matter how Alice and the old woman tried to catch hold if it, they never quite could.

Lightning Source UK Ltd.
Milton Keynes UK
UKOW01f2311130717
305253UK00001B/233/P